Praise for
In the King's Service

"Kurtz is one of the best of those fantasy writers who use medieval-like settings for their novels, and this is one of her better books."
—*Chronicle*

"Kurtz's fidelity to the customs and mores of medieval Europe gives a richness of detail to her alternate medieval world."
—*Library Journal*

"Exquisitely detailed . . . the scenes of daily life at court, plus the usual church versus magic conflict, will keep fans turning the pages."
—*Publishers Weekly*

"The novel sparkles with Kurtz's attention to detail . . . can be enjoyed by fans and newcomers alike."
—*RT Bookclub* (Top Pick)

for
n's Bride

"Katherine Kurtz's triumphant return to the magical medieval realm of Gwynedd . . . Exciting and intriguing."
—*SF Site*

"Kurtz's strengths lie in her patient accumulation of telling detail, well-articulated plots, and believable magics. Should bring the fans flocking, and attract newcomers, too."
—*Kirkus Reviews*

continued . . .

"The author remains just as polished and expert as ever . . . Kurtz, one of the founders of modern historical fantasy, after nearly thirty years continues to be one of its most accomplished practitioners." —*Publishers Weekly*

"Ms. Kurtz creates compelling characters, a byzantine plot, and magical wonder for a beguiling reading experience."
—*Romantic Times*

"A good choice for most fantasy collections."
—*Library Journal*

"This Deryni yarn should satisfy all the fans the series has accumulated during its thirty-year run." —*Booklist*

"One of the happiest . . . books in this series." —*Locus*

Praise for Katherine Kurtz's

Deryni novels

"An incredible historical tapestry of a world that never was and of immensely vital people who ought to be."

—Anne McCaffrey

"A rich feast of medieval chivalry, romance, and magic—the book that all Katherine Kurtz's fans have been awaiting."

—Marion Zimmer Bradley

"At her best Kurtz's love of history lets her do things with her characters and their world that no nonhistorian could hope to do."

—*Chicago Sun-Times*

"Kurtz has created a fascinating idealization of the Middle Ages and infused it with a kind of magic one can truly believe in."

—*Fantasy Review*

In the King's Service

KATHERINE KURTZ

ACE BOOKS, NEW YORK

THE BERKLEY PUBLISHING GROUP
Published by the Penguin Group
Penguin Group (USA) Inc.
375 Hudson Street, New York, New York 10014, USA
Penguin Group (Canada), 10 Alcorn Avenue, Toronto, Ontario M4V 3B2, Canada
(a division of Pearson Penguin Canada Inc.)
Penguin Books Ltd., 80 Strand, London WC2R 0RL, England
Penguin Group Ireland, 25 St. Stephen's Green, Dublin 2, Ireland (a division of Penguin Books Ltd.)
Penguin Group (Australia), 250 Camberwell Road, Camberwell, Victoria 3124, Australia
(a division of Pearson Australia Group Pty. Ltd.)
Penguin Books India Pvt. Ltd., 11 Community Centre, Panchsheel Park, New Delhi—110 017, India
Penguin Group (NZ), Cnr. Airborne and Rosedale Roads, Albany, Auckland 1310, New Zealand
(a division of Pearson New Zealand Ltd.)
Penguin Books (South Africa) (Pty.) Ltd., 24 Sturdee Avenue, Rosebank, Johannesburg 2196, South Africa

Penguin Books Ltd., Registered Offices: 80 Strand, London WC2R 0RL, England

IN THE KING'S SERVICE

An Ace Book / published by arrangement with the author

PRINTING HISTORY
Ace hardcover edition / November 2003
Ace mass market edition / January 2005

Graphic design by Daniel M. Davis, Ann Dupuis, James A. Fox-Davis, and Martine Lynch.
Cover art by Matt Stawicki.
Cover design by Pyrographx.
Interior text design by Kristin del Rosario.

For information address: The Berkley Publishing Group,
a division of Penguin Group (USA) Inc.,
375 Hudson Street, New York, New York 10014.

ISBN: 0-441-01209-4

ACE
Ace Books are published by The Berkley Publishing Group,
a division of Penguin Group (USA) Inc.,
375 Hudson Street, New York, New York 10014.

PRINTED IN THE UNITED STATES OF AMERICA

10 9 8 7 6 5 4 3 2 1

With Love and Thanks to
Andre Norton,
Great Lady of Many Wondrous Tales

The Eleven Kingdoms

Atalantic Ocean
Northern Sea
Gulf of Northarch
Claibourne
Slavenham
Kheldish Mts
Kheldish Riding
(Old Kheldour)
Marley
Rhendall
Rhendall Mts
Cassan
Gulf of Kheldour
Kilshane
Kilarden
Bay of Kilarden
Kierney
Transha
Meara
Ratharkin
Rathark Mts
Culdi
Culdi Highlands
Laas Bay
Lough Cloome
Cloome Mts
Cuilteine
The Purple March
Gwynedd
Carmone
Valoret
Rhemuth
Eirian R.
Carcashale
Iomaire Plain
Eastmarch
Lynoruth Plain
Lynoruth Meadows
Rheljan Mts
Coamer Mountains
Tolán
Tigre
Truvorsk
Kulnan
Torenth
Beldour R.
Sasovna
The Fertile Crescent

Connait
Cashien
Jenas
Rhemuth
Molling R.
Eirian R.
Desse
Danoc
Concaradine
Haldane
Lendour
Lendour Mts
Dhassa
Rhengarth R.
Sostra
Western R.
Csorna
Beldour
Beldour R.
Corwyn
Twin Rivers
Coroth
Howicce
Llannedd
Nyford
Lendour R.
(Old Mooryn)
Orsalia
Orsalis
Ile d'Orsal
Trebaceaux
Thuria R.
Tralia
Carthmoor
Seerhowy
Pwyllheli
Joux
Vezaire
Kronburg
Brecault
Thuria
Point Kentar
Southern Sea
The Forcinn
Logreine
Lognac
Nur Hallaj
Khasifa
Atalantic Ocean
Fianna
Djellarda
Truyère
Fallon
Sabakh
Andelon
Rhanème
R'Kassi
Bremagne
Jaca
Remigny
Autun Mts.
Key
0 25 50 75 100
miles
N
W
E
Anvil of the Lord
Autun
Autun R.
Eleven Kingdoms Map Copyright ©2004 by Grey Ghost Press, Inc., www.derynirealms.com. Graphic Design by Daniel M. Davis, Ann Dupuis, James A. Fox-Davis, and Marline Lynch

Prologue

"Set not thy heart upon goods unjustly gotten;
for they shall not profit thee in the day of calamity."
—ECCLESIASTICUS 5:8

"I HEAR that you have a son at last," Dominy de Laney said to Sir Sief MacAthan, as she settled beside him at the heavy, eight-sided table in the Camberian Council's secret meeting chamber. "Congratulations are surely in order."

Across the table from them, Vivienne de Jordanet was absently twirling a dark ringlet around one forefinger as she read over the shoulder of the man to her right: Lord Seisyll Arilan, one of the Council's two coadjutors. Both of them looked up at the other woman's comment, and Vivienne gave the new father an indulgent smile.

"Well done, Sief."

Sief's face brightened, a boyish grin creasing his still handsome features as he basked in this affirmation of his male potency. After nearly thirty years of indifferent marriage, four living daughters, and a sad succession of stillborn or short-lived sons, he had all but given up hope of a male heir. This birthing had been difficult, for the child was large and his wife was no longer young, but the new babe was hale and lusty, if disappointingly unlike Sief in appearance. Of course, most infants were inclined to look like wizened little old men so soon after birth. Hopefully, the pale eyes would darken—and as yet, the babe had too little hair to tell what color it would be.

"I must confess that I am pleased," Sief allowed. "I've decided to call him Krispin. There was a Krispin MacAthan a few generations back. His sisters adore him already. I suppose it is a natural reaction of young girls, anticipating children of their own."

Dominy de Laney smiled and patted his hand, kindly mirth in the sea-green eyes. "Young boys, as well, Sief. In truth, most children seem to like babies. My own are constantly begging for another sister or brother. And well do I remember when Barrett was born. I've always wondered whether our poor parents had him to achieve some respite from me and my sisters. Especially after Cassianus died, we were determined that there should be another boy for us to pamper later."

The comment elicited a chuckle from Vivienne, who sat back in her chair just as the great doors to the chamber parted to admit the scarlet-clad subject of Dominy's comment, one of his graceful hands resting on the arm of Michon de Courcy for guidance. Barrett de Laney's hooded robes were those of a scholar at the great university of Nur Sayyid, but his emerald eyes gazed into eternity, sightless—not through any infirmity of age, for he was only two-and-thirty, but through blindness, incurred when he was hardly grown to manhood, willingly accepted in exchange for the freedom of several dozen children.

Those who had taken his sight had intended to take his life as well—a probability Barrett had been well aware of, when he submitted to the hot iron that bought the children's release. In memory of that day, he still wore his thinning hair sleeked back in a soldier's knot: faded red, where it was not streaked with white. He had not expected to leave that place alive, or that another would lay down his life instead, to secure his escape.

The man who guided him now, of his father's generation, had fostered him as a child of promise, helping to hone his natural talents, and had taught him to adjust to his lack of physical sight—a task made far easier by the powers they shared in common with the others in the chamber. For all of them were highly trained Deryni, members of that long-vilified race of sorcerers and wise men who must coexist with mortals not so gifted, in whom fear and perhaps even jealousy bred intolerance that often killed.

Even other Deryni did not know the composition of this elite and highly secretive body now gathering under the purple dome of the Council's meeting place, though most with any formal training had at least some inkling of its existence and the policing function it carried out for the good of all their race. A few individuals were believed by some to have the Council's ear, but none would ever confirm or deny. Only rarely did it intervene directly in the affairs of other Deryni, and even less often were its rulings challenged.

Mostly, its guidance was more subtle: the hidden hand in the glove of another's apparent action, quietly exerting pressure behind the scenes to discourage and hopefully prevent wanton use of Deryni powers. And while rigorous discipline and the mutual intent of its members gave it access, as a body, to power not generally available to any single individual, the Council's greater power lay in the speculations of other Deryni about what the Council might actually be able to do, and apprehension regarding what force it could bring to bear to enforce its rulings and to discipline those who strayed from responsible behavior.

For the Deryni in Gwynedd were few, and always had been, regarded by the much larger human population with varying measures of wary fascination, suspicion, and outright fear—which, in reaction to Deryni abuses, whether real or imagined, could shift all too swiftly to active hostility and murderous rampages. Once that occurred, sheer numbers could overwhelm even the mightiest of magical defenses—and had done so, far too many times.

It had not always been thus. Early in the previous century—and still, in many of the lands neighboring Gwynedd, especially to the east—humans and Deryni had cohabited in relative peace, mostly to the mutual benefit of both races. But there had always been those who harbored an uneasy mistrust of the Deryni and their sometimes startling abilities, and feared the possible misuse of powers not accessible to ordinary men. Some said that such powers were too near to that of gods, or at least of angels—or devils. Others were convinced that such powers could only be demonic, corrupting not only the wielders of those powers but those touched by them.

Such hostility, born of fear of what was not understood, had finally come to a head early in the previous century, triggering a period of persecution akin to a religious crusade.

Many had died as a result. A rigid and repressive code of laws now regulated the existence of those remaining, excluding known Deryni from many occupations and barring them from holding public office or even owning property above a certain value, under pain of fines, imprisonment, or worse. Most odious of all was to be discovered using one's powers, even with the most benign of intentions, for such folly was apt to trigger a killing rampage by frightened and irate humans—an act given legitimacy by human law.

With care and cunning, such laws could be circumvented, as all the members of the Camberian Council were well aware, but even those who lived beyond the borders of Gwynedd mostly maintained a low profile, for magic could make one a target as well as giving one a tool or weapon. Those resident within Gwynedd were extremely careful. Of the seven members of the Council, only Sief had managed to carve out a secure public position within Gwynedd itself, at the king's court in Rhemuth, as had his family for many generations. Seisyll, likewise, had achieved modest prominence among the king's courtiers, though he and his extended family lived outside the capital. Neither was known to be Deryni.

Michon, for his part, kept mostly to his modest holdings far to the west, though still within Gwynedd, only venturing to court when duty required: Twelfth Night, always, and usually several more times each year, when the king summoned various of his vassals to attend him. The others, through choice or circumstances, dwelt outside Gwynedd's borders, where those of their kind could live more openly, though even they were circumspect. Barrett, perhaps, had the greatest freedom, being currently in residence at one of the great Torenthi universities. The remaining member of the Council resided not far from where the Council met, but had sent apologies for non-attendance, being currently occupied with business concerns away from Portal access.

But six were more than enough to transact informal business; five of the seven would have been sufficient to uphold any serious ruling of the Council, though no capital matter was under discussion on this night. When possible, the Council met fortnightly, to brief one another on affairs in the areas where they lived. In the past three decades—longer than any member's span of service save Sief himself—there had been no truly serious demand on the Council's powers of arbitration. Though all of them were well aware how precariously still stood the plight of Deryni in Gwynedd, slow gains had been made in the past several generations, and the future was beginning to look hopeful.

"We should begin," said Seisyll Arilan, when Michon had led Barrett to his seat between them and taken his own. "Doubtless, Sief will wish to return to his new son. My congratulations," he added, inclining his head in the new father's direction. "Your lady wife is well?"

Sief gave a nod, still looking pleased. "Weakened somewhat, which is to be expected with an older mother, but I am hopeful that the child will show more of its paternal heritage than its maternal. I never forget that she is the daughter of Lewys ap Norfal."

"You did agree to marry her," Michon pointed out.

"It was that, or have her killed," Sief said lightly, though all of them were aware that he meant precisely that. "We could not have trusted Lewys's daughter to a nunnery."

"Yet you have trusted one of her daughters to a nunnery," Dominy de Laney reminded him.

"She is my daughter as well," Sief replied. "And each child is different. "But I would have smothered Jessilde at birth, had she shown the wayward potentials of her grandfather—or her mother."

Vivienne rolled her eyes heavenward, then glanced at Dominy, a mother like herself.

"Let us please have no more talk of smothering babies," she said emphatically. "Especially not Deryni babies. It's bad enough that poisonous priests like Alexander Darby continue to spread lies about us. Have any of you actually seen that scurrilous piece of tripe that he published at Grecotha last year? *De Natura Deryniorum*, indeed!"

"Scurrilous or not," Sief said, "I hear that it's to become required reading at every seminary in Gwynedd."

Barrett was nodding, fingers steepled before his sightless eyes. "It's been making the rounds at Nur Sayyid. Well written, they say, but utterly lacking in scholarly integrity."

"Lacking in scholarly integrity?" Dominy blurted. "Is that all you can say? Barrett, the man's a monster!"

"Yes, and he's a monster with a growing following," Seisyll

said sourly. "And I can understand why. I heard him preach a few months ago. A very persuasive speaker, and a very dangerous man."

"I've heard him, too," Michon said. "It's a pity that a timely accident can't be arranged. A fatal one. Actually, it could. But given the public profile he's already established, I suppose the authorities would quickly draw the right conclusion regarding who was responsible, at least in general terms—and *that* would spark the very kind of reprisal that we try to avoid."

Seisyll Arilan gave a disgusted snort. "We should have taken care of the problem long ago. Now it's too late for the more obvious solutions."

"It is never too late to stamp out pestiferous vermin," Vivienne said coldly. "I'm sure one of my brothers would be happy to oblige."

"No, we'll not risk losing one of them for the sake of the likes of him," Michon said.

"Sometimes risks are necessary," Sief pointed out. "You *are* aware, I trust, that the bishops already have an eye on him?"

"For what, chief inquisitor?" Seisyll muttered.

"Actually, for a bishop's miter," Sief replied. "I have that directly from the Archbishop of Rhemuth. Unless Darby puts a foot seriously wrong, it *will* happen, mark my words."

"But—he was only ordained last year," Dominy said, sounding scandalized.

"True enough," Seisyll said patiently. "But keep in mind that he is hardly your typical green young priest. He's something of a scholar, yes—though he draws all the wrong conclusions. But he also lived in the world before he took holy orders. He trained as a physician, and they say that he has all the arrogance that sometimes comes of both disciplines. That's a dangerous enough combination in a priest who also hates Deryni. In a bishop—"

He shook his head, heaving a sigh, and the two women exchanged troubled glances.

"He isn't a bishop yet," Michon said, in a darkling tone that suggested the matter might not be the foregone conclusion everyone else was assuming.

Sief shot him a sharp glance, but his reply was unexpectedly mild.

"No, he isn't. And it won't happen tomorrow, or even next week. But whatever happens to Alexander Darby, there must be no trail that leads back to any of us. Just keep that in mind."

Michon gave a noncommittal shrug, and Sief went on.

"In the meantime, we have more immediate matters to discuss. I gather that all of you are now acquainted with the recommendation regarding the young Duke of Corwyn?"

He jutted his chin toward the document lying between Seisyll and Vivienne, who both glanced at it with some distaste.

"He isn't the duke yet," the latter said, looking faintly disapproving. "Not until he turns twenty-five, and has proven his loyalty to Donal of Gwynedd." Her fair brow furrowed. "Are we really proposing that he be fostered to the Duc du Joux? And would the king allow him to go?"

"I believe he could be persuaded," Sief replied. "And what better haven for a known Deryni who is destined for a ducal coronet in Gwynedd?"

"It's true," Seisyll agreed. "Besides, Gwynedd has no other Deryni of high rank—and the current Duc du Joux has spent a lifetime cultivating the perception that he is the most harmless of Deryni. He would pass that survival skill to young Ahern—as he did to Morian ap Lewys," he added, with a nod to Sief. "I daresay that your wife's brother would not be where he is today, a trusted officer of the Crown of Gwynedd, if he had not learned to be circumspect regarding what he is."

"Morian also has his father's intelligence and gifts," Michon pointed out. "Say what you like about Lewys ap Norfal, but he was one of our best and brightest—alas, lacking in self-restraint."

"Are you suggesting that young Ahern de Corwyn is similarly gifted?" Sief asked.

Michon shrugged. "I do not know. Stevana de Corwyn was very much cast in the mold of her father and grandfather. Keryell went against our instructions in seizing her, in marrying her by force, but he, too, carries a strong bloodline. Once Ahern has come into his inheritance, I would hope to see him spend some time at Nur Sayyid, perhaps—or even at Rhanamé or at Djellarda with the Knights of the Anvil. But he is only eleven now. Time enough for that."

"Indeed," Barrett said. "Where is he now?"

"Back in Coroth, since Twelfth Night," Michon replied. "Keryell sent him and his sisters to the Orsal's court for several years after their mother died. You'll recall that Sobbon is cousin-kin to Keryell's mother. Among all those von Horthy children, I doubt Sobbon much noticed three extras."

"Was there not a prior marriage," Dominy said thoughtfully, "and a son by that marriage?"

"Cynfyn," Vivienne supplied promptly. "His mother was a daughter of one of the Torenthi dukes. But he died young, leaving Keryell without an heir—a riding mishap, while returning from his knighting."

"Which was what impelled Keryell to go seeking a new bride and a new heir," Michon supplied, shaking his head. "Unfortunately for us, his loss coincided with the passing of Stevana's grandfather, Duke Stiofan—and the rest, as they say, is history."

"What of the daughters?" Vivienne asked, a frown furrowing her fair brow.

Seisyll shrugged. "After Ahern, the eldest—Alyce is her name—is heiress presumptive to Corwyn—though I'm sure that Keryell has set aside dower lands for her, in her own right. Her brother will be the next duke, when he turns twenty-five."

"Unless, like Keryell's previous heir, he suffers a fatal mishap," Barrett pointed out. "These things do happen."

"Aye, of course they do," Seisyll said. "Which is why the king will have a say in whom she—and her sister, too—eventually wed. He will not gamble with the fate of a duchy so rich as Corwyn, in case Ahern should *not* inherit." He swept them with his gaze. "This means that the king must approve their eventual marriages—which eliminates any suitor from Torenth, for Donal would never consent to Corwyn lands passing into Torenthi control. One of the Forcinn states, perhaps."

"He could always pack them off to a convent," Sief murmured.

Dominy glanced at him frostily. "With your Jessilde, Sief?"

"It was her choice," Sief shot back.

"As if you gave her any other!"

"Peace!" Seisyll interjected. "We have often done things we

would rather not have done. Never forget that we serve a higher cause than our own desires."

His admonition left a tense silence in its wake, only lifting as Michon cleared his throat.

"On a more constructive note, I suggest that we return to the recommendation regarding young Ahern," he said. "His position, when he comes of age, will be of immense importance—but only if he can, indeed, convince the king that he is worthy to take up the title of his great-grandfather."

"And pray that it no more passes through the female line," Seisyll muttered. "I, for one, shall be greatly relieved when he's grown and married and has an heir. At least Stevana had a boy, God rest her, and blood *is* blood. . . ."

Chapter I

"Is it not a grief unto death,
when a companion and friend is turned to an enemy?"
—ECCLESIASTICUS 37:2

FAR from where the Camberian Council sat in secret session, crafting their careful, deliberate plans for the future of their race, the wife of one of its members lay propped amid the pillows of their curtained and canopied bed and waited for the nurse to bring her infant son for feeding. Two days after his birth, Lady Jessamy MacAthan was feeling far stronger, but both the pregnancy and the delivery of this latest bairn had taken more out of her than any of her previous children, even the stillborn ones.

Of course, she was older than when she had birthed any of the others—past forty now—and with a growing history of miscarriages and stillbirths. She had not even been certain she could conceive again, much less carry a child to term.

But this child was important, destined for a secret but very special role in the future unfolding for Gwynedd and its kings to come. It was too soon to tell precisely what young Krispin's magical potential would prove to be, but his parentage ensured that he would be no ordinary boy.

The nursery door opened, and Mistress Anjelica brought in the fretting, wiggling bundle that was her son, shushing and cooing over him as she laid him in his mother's arms.

"He's very hungry, milady," the woman said, as Jessamy put him to her breast.

"Yes, I can see that," Jessamy replied, smiling. "And

greedy, too. He's like a wee limpet. Thank heaven he hasn't any teeth! But you needn't sit with me. I know you must have things that need doing. Are the girls asleep?"

"Yes, milady."

"Good. I'll call you when we're finished."

She readjusted the child in the hollow of her arm and settled back to let him feed as the nurse retired, allowing the sweet lethargy of his suckling to drift her into idle remembrance, wondering what Sief would say, if he were ever to penetrate past her shields to learn the truth—though Jessamy would resist him to the death, were he ever to try.

She had never wanted or intended to marry Sief, who was sixteen years her senior. But her mother had died when she was but ten, and the loss of her father the following year had left her in the hands of guardians who insisted on the match: powerful Deryni, who had feared what Lewys ap Norfal's daughter might become, and had sought to minimize the danger by seeing her safely wed to one of their own. Though she had never come to regard Sief with more than resigned acceptance, she loved the children he had given her; and she had learned to live with the arrangement because she must, and to wear the façade of a dutiful wife, because outward compliance allowed her at least an illusion of freedom here at the court of Gwynedd—if only Sief knew *how* free. Her love of her children was one of the honest things about her life, as was her affection for the queens she had served here in Rhemuth for the past thirty years.

By now, memories of any other home had mostly receded to a distant blur, dangerous though it was to be Deryni in Rhemuth. Even before Rhemuth, her parents had never stayed long in one place, lest their Deryni nature be discovered—and Lewys ap Norfal had never been good at hiding what he was for long. Had they lived in Gwynedd those early years, she now thought it unlikely that Lewys would have survived long enough to sire any children. Even so, he had been notorious among his own kind, and had met his end attempting magic usually deemed impossible, even among the most accomplished of their race.

Putting an end to that nomad existence, Sief had brought her to Gwynedd's capital immediately after their hurried marriage, giving the care of his frightened child-bride into the hands of the king's daughter-in-law, the gentle and sensitive Princess Dulchesse, who had been the wife of then–Crown Prince Donal Blaine Haldane.

That pairing, at least, had prospered, for the two women had liked one another from the start. Dulchesse, but one-and-twenty herself and already six years married, had yet to give her husband an heir, but she had gladly taken the orphaned Jessamy under her wing and assumed the role of elder sister and surrogate mother, giving her the fierce protection of her royal station as the still-hopeful mother of kings. Indeed, in all but name, the princess had been functioning as Gwynedd's queen for all her married life; for Roisian of Meara, King Malcolm's queen, had withdrawn to a convent the same year Dulchesse came to court. The rift had come the previous year, after Malcolm was obliged to lead an expedition into rebellious Meara and execute several members of Roisian's family. One of them had been Roisian's twin sister.

Alas for Sief, placing his young bride in the household of the crown princess had not turned out at all as he expected; but by the time he realized that he had become the victim of feminine solidarity, it was too late to change his mind.

"You may be certain that I shall school her to a wife you may be proud of, my lord," Dulchesse had told the disbelieving Sief, on learning that he planned to allow Jessamy but a year's grace before consummating their marriage, "but you shall not touch her until her fourteenth birthday. She's but a child. Give her the chance to finish growing up."

"Your Highness, she is a woman grown," Sief had protested. "She has begun her monthly courses—"

"Yes, and if she should conceive so young, you are apt to lose both wife *and* child. You shall wait."

"Your Highness—"

"Must I ask the king to tell you this?" she retorted, stamping her little foot.

Before such fierce determination, Sief had been left with no recourse but to bow before the wishes of his future queen.

Accordingly, Jessamy had been allowed to spend those stolen days of extended girlhood as a pampered pet of the princess's household, acquiring the skills and graces expected of a knight's lady and carefully beginning to craft the façade that she hoped would protect her in the future. For Sief had warned her, on that numb journey from Coroth, that her very life would be in danger, were it to be discovered at court that she was Deryni.

"The king will guess," he had told her. "I know he has surmised what *I* am, though we have never spoken of it openly. But others will not be so tolerant, should they even suspect what we are."

"If it is so dangerous," she had replied, "then why do you abide in Rhemuth?"

"Because my work is there."

When he did not elaborate, she had dared to lift her chin to him in faint challenge.

"Did *they* order you to serve the king?"

His cold appraisal in response had caused her to drop her gaze nervously, pretending profound interest in a strand of her pony's mane.

"Jessamy, I shall say this only once," he had finally said in a very low voice. "I know that your father set certain controls in place to protect you, as I—*and others*—have also done. But to protect you fully would be to leave you helpless.

"Therefore, I must trust you in this, and trust in your good sense and the training you have received. I know it was not your wish to marry me, but I cannot think that you resent that enough to wish me dead, and yourself as well—which would very likely be the outcome, were we discovered. You *know* that I tell you only the truth. This is for your protection as well as my own."

Indeed, there could be no doubt that he did speak the truth—her powers confirmed that—and it never, ever occurred to her to betray him, little though she cared for her situation. Nor was she ever tempted to unmask any of the other Deryni who passed through the court from time to time—though, as her affection for the crown princess grew, she came to realize that she *would* act against even her own kind, should they pose any danger to the royal family.

But for better or for worse, most of the other Deryni she detected were old acquaintances of her father, a few of whom had even been present in Coroth on that fateful night. Instinctively, she gave them wide berth. The ones who came to worry her far more were the ones she could not detect.

Recognition of this deficiency in her abilities made her determined to rectify it, though she dared not go to Sief for the training she knew she needed. Fortunately, her studies with her father had been sufficiently advanced that she was able to shield her true intentions from Sief and begin formulating her own plans for the future, though she knew that she needed to know more. Unfortunately, she was still a child, albeit an exceedingly well-educated one for her age and sex. But at least Sief mostly left her alone for those next three years.

Once she had settled into the routine of the royal household, she had begun looking for ways to further her education—at least the conventional part of it. When she let it be known that she possessed a fair copy hand and read and spoke several classical languages, she soon found herself being summoned to the royal library to assist in cataloging the king's manuscript collection. There she came to the especial attention of Father Mungo, the aged chaplain to the royal household, who was taken with her learning and her willingness to learn (and most assuredly did not know that she was Deryni), and soon began giving her private tutorials.

She shortly discovered that both the king and the crown prince frequented the library on a regular basis—and thereby gained permission to spend time there whenever her duties permitted. Further honing of her esoteric talents would have to wait until she could figure out a way to gain access to teachers, or at least to texts, but in the meantime, Father Mungo's lessons and her own explorations in the royal library filled the time and gave her more tools for later on.

But she had known that her reprieve must end. On the day of her fourteenth birthday, on a sunny morning in early autumn, she was obliged to stand with Sief before the Archbishop of Rhemuth and reaffirm her marriage vows, in the presence of Malcolm and his new queen, the Lady Síle, Donal and Dulchesse, and all the royal household, for Sief was well regarded at court, and all agreed that he had shown remarkable forbearance in waiting three years for his bride. Reassured by Dulchesse, and gently briefed regarding what to expect when Sief finally came to her bed, Jessamy had endured her wedding night with reasonable grace.

She had conceived within months, shortly after the new queen was delivered of a prince christened Richard. Her own firstborn, a boy also named Sief, would have been a playmate for the new prince, but the infant died hardly a week after birth. Jessamy had not yet turned fifteen.

More pregnancies had followed at barely two-year intervals after that: a succession of mostly healthy girls, stillborn boys, and early miscarriages. The ones who did not survive were allowed burial in a corner of the royal crypt, for the childless Dulchesse began to regard them as the children she would never have. Queen Síle had also come to mourn Jessamy's losses—and Dulchesse's barrenness—and buried several children of her own, in time. The three women had visited the little graves regularly until Queen Síle's death, the same year as King Malcolm's. Dulchesse, finally queen at last, had died but two years ago. Now Jessamy laid flowers on the other women's graves as well as those of the children, sometimes in the company of the new queen, Richeldis, who had quickly borne King Donal his long-awaited heir.

For Jessamy herself, there had been only a few pregnancies after the birth of Jesiana, her nine-year-old, and only one brought to term until Krispin: yet another girl, now four, called Seffira, whom Jessamy loved dearly. Though Sief was mostly indifferent to his daughters, his desire for a son was still strong, and he continued to visit her bed on a tiresomely regular basis, despite the apparent waning of her fertility. Sometimes she wondered whether her own antipathy had kept her from quickening—especially when this latest child had been so easy to conceive. Young Krispin, however, had been greatly desired—though not in the sense that her husband supposed.

His very begetting had been profoundly different from any of the others—no resentful and resigned yielding to marital duty, but welcome fruit of a well-planned series of quick, focused couplings that were timed to the most propitious few days of her monthly cycle, accomplished quite dispassionately amid briefly lifted skirts in a shadowed upper corridor of the castle, where others rarely went—or bent over a library table, or braced against a hay bale far at the back of the royal stables, surrounded by the warm, dusty fragrance of lazing horses. Her pulse quickened at the very thought of those days, though it was the daring of what she had done rather than lust that excited her.

Within days she had known she was with child, and

thought she could pinpoint exactly when conception had occurred, though she let Sief think that it had come of their usual, more conventional conjugal encounters. The memory stirred a pleasant aching in her loins, quite apart from the soreness after birth, intensified by the sweet suckling of the babe at her breast.

A tap at the room's inner door announced the intrusion of the babe's nurse, white-coifed head ducking in apology as she eased into the light of the candles burning beside the curtained bed.

"You have a visitor, milady," the woman said. "The king has come to pay his respects. Shall I take the baby?"

"No, show him in," Jessamy replied. "Then leave us."

"Alone, milady?" Anjelica said, looking faintly scandalized.

"Anjelica, he's the king."

"Yes, milady."

The woman withdrew dutifully, unaware that her compliance had been encouraged by Jessamy's deft reinforcement. Very shortly, the king peered around the door and then entered, closing the door behind him and grinning. Jessamy smiled in return, inclining her head over the baby's in as much of a bow as could be managed from a mostly reclining position. As she looked up, she saw a flicker of pleased amusement kindle behind the clear gray eyes.

He did not look his age, though she knew that she looked hers, especially after the rigors of late pregnancy and childbirth—and she, more than a decade his junior. Now past fifty, Donal Blaine Aidan Cinhil was still the epitome of Haldane comeliness, fit and dashing in his scarlet hunting leathers. Gold embroidery of a coronet circled the crown of his scarlet hunting cap, and a white plume curled rakishly over one eye, caught in place with a jeweled brooch. While his close-clipped beard and his moustache were acquiring decided speckles of gray, hardly a trace of silver threaded his black hair—unlike her own once-dark tresses. The loosely plaited braid tumbling over one shoulder was decidedly piebald.

He took off his cap as he came farther into the room, tossing it onto a chest at the foot of the great bed with easy grace. He had been born in the halcyon years shortly following Gwynedd's costly victory at Killingford in 1025, the only surviving son of Malcolm Haldane and Roisian of Meara, whose marriage was to have cemented a lasting peace between the two lands. Instead, it had spawned a new dispute regarding the Mearan succession—and launched the first in an ongoing series of Haldane military incursions back into Meara.

The succession, even in Gwynedd, had remained precarious in the years that followed, for Donal was the only male heir Malcolm had produced by his first marriage, despite several children by assorted mistresses, the known ones legitimated shortly before his death but without dynastic rights. Donal's half-siblings had made good marriages and served him loyally, and Malcolm's second marriage to Queen Síle had produced another true-born prince in Duke Richard—Donal's heir presumptive until the birth of Prince Brion, little though Richard aspired to the crown. Though trained from birth to rule after Donal, if need be, none had rejoiced more than he when, within a year of his brother's new nuptials, Queen Richeldis had presented Donal with his long-awaited son: Prince Brion Donal Cinhil Urien Haldane, born the previous June.

"Good evening, Sire," Jessamy said to the father of that prince, as he moved closer beside the bed. "How fares the son and heir?"

"He flourishes," Donal replied, smiling. "When I put a sword in his hand, he doesn't want to let go. I expect he will be walking soon. He pulls himself up already. And how fares *your* son and heir?"

"He suckles well. He knows to reach out for what he wants. His father has reason to be proud of him."

"May I see him?" Donal asked, craning for a closer look.

"Of course."

Gathering the infant's blankets around him, and carefully supporting the tiny head, Jessamy held out the bundle to the king, who took the babe in the crook of his arm and proceeded to inspect him thoroughly.

"He appears to have the correct number of fingers and toes and other appendages," Donal declared. "And those are warrior's hands," he added, letting the infant seize one of his fingers and convey it to the tiny rosebud mouth. "He will be a fitting companion for a prince."

"One had hoped that would be the case," Jessamy agreed good-naturedly.

"Brothers—that's what they'll be," came the reply. "He's perfect. His hair will be like yours, I think," Donal went on, gently cupping the child's downy head. "But those are not your eyes, or Sief's."

"No," was all the child's mother replied.

Chuckling softly, Donal let himself sit on the edge of the bed, and was carefully giving the child back into its mother's keeping when the bedroom door opened and Sief entered.

"Ah, and here's the proud father now," Donal said, twisting around to greet the newcomer. "I'd come to congratulate you, Sief, and to inspect the new bairn. And to cheer the mother in her childbed, if the truth be known. My queen tells me that a new mother appreciates such things. Not that she speaks to me overmuch, of late. The morning sickness is a trial she would liefer have foregone for a few more months."

Sief found himself smiling dutifully in response to the king's boyish grin, though he could not say why he found it unsettling to find Donal here.

They had long been friends beyond mere courtier and prince. He had served Donal Haldane for most of his life—had been assigned by King Malcolm as the prince's first aide, when Sief was a new-made knight and Donal but a lad of ten—and been his confidant and brother-in-arms through many a campaign and court intrigue. It had taken most of a decade for the young prince to guess that Sief was Deryni. By then, Sief had come to realize that Donal possessed certain powers of his own that were somewhat similar, somehow related to his kingship. Malcolm had possessed them as well, and perhaps had also recognized Sief for what he was, though they had never spoken of it.

Sief had never spoken of it to the Council, either, though privately he had intimated to Donal that certain of his not inconsiderable powers were at the prince's service. After all, part of the reason for the Council's very existence—and for Sief's placement in the royal household—was to safeguard the Haldane line on the throne of Gwynedd; for the Haldanes knew, as other humans did not, that the Deryni, properly ruled, posed little threat to the human population.

In practice, Sief's direct service to the king as a Deryni had been limited, and extremely discreet. Those of his race were able to determine when a person was lying—a talent of undoubted use to a king. In addition, a trained Deryni could usually compel disclosures when a person attempted simply to tell part of the truth, or to withhold it. With care, the memories of a person subjected to such attentions could even be blurred to hide what had been done—though such investigations were always carried out in private. The court was only aware that Sir Sief MacAthan was an extremely skilled interrogator. More often, he merely stood at the king's side and observed, only later reporting on the veracity of what had been said.

Over the years, such attention to nuance of truth and falsehood had become second-nature when in the king's presence. Why, then, were Sief's senses suddenly all atingle? Surely it was not at the prospect that the queen was once again with child.

"Then, the palace gossip is correct," Sief said tentatively.

"Palace gossip," Donal said, standing up with fists set to hips. "Surely you don't pay any mind to *that.*"

"I do, when it may pertain to the welfare of the kingdom, Sire," Sief replied. "Prince Brion is still shy of his first birthday. It is still very early for a new pregnancy for the queen. Self-restraint, my lord," he added, trying not to sound self-righteous.

"A king needs an heir and a spare," Donal said breezily, "and good men to guard them and guide them as they grow. You know the heartache of losing sons, Sief. I must make certain that Brion has brothers."

Suddenly Sief caught just a flicker of subtle evasion: not a lie, but a truth not fully divulged. To his consternation, it sparked a dread possibility that had never come to mind before, but which might make sense of several things in the year since the prince's birth; but he put such thoughts aside as he forced an uneasy chuckle.

"Just now," Sief said, "methinks Prince Brion needs his mother more than he needs brothers. At least have a care for *her,* Sire. People would talk, were you to take a third queen."

Donal shrugged, and his next words again left Sief with the impression that all was not being said.

"People will always talk about kings. I little care, so long as the succession is secure."

"There *is* Duke Richard, if all else were to fail," Sief pointed out.

"True enough. But my brother Richard aspires to a warrior's fame—and he has the sheer ability to excel at it. He little cares for the finer diplomacies of the council chamber—or even of marriage, at least thus far," Donal added with a shrug. "Besides that, he is the fruit of my father's loins; not mine."

"Aye, but blood *is* blood, Sire," Sief said, echoing the words of the Council not an hour earlier. "Richard is as much a Haldane as you or the new prince."

He thought he saw Jessamy stiffen slightly at those words, though her gray-streaked head was bowed over the infant in her arms.

"Indeed," the king said mildly. "I trust you aren't presuming to instruct me in my duties as a husband?"

Sief raised a placating hand, hesitant to even consider pursuing the subject; but Donal's manner seemed increasingly evasive, making Sief wonder whether he had, indeed, stumbled on something he would be happier not knowing.

He ventured a cautious probe, but Donal was tight-shuttered against even a surface reading. That was hardly unusual for the king, for Sief had long ago realized that Donal had shields as good as any Deryni's—though whether they would stand up to any serious attempt to force them remained an unknown question. What alarmed him was that Jessamy likewise had retreated behind shields far stronger than he had believed her to possess.

Chilled, he turned to look at her sharply—and caught just a hint of something in her eyes. . . .

With a little sob, she turned away from him in their bed, shielding the infant Krispin behind her body. In that instant, in an almost blinding flash of insight, Sief *knew* what more she was hiding—and Donal, as well.

"You!" He whirled on the king, fury and betrayal in his dark glare. "He's *yours,* isn't he? You've made me a cuckold! Was it here, in this very bed?"

Even as he said it, his clenched fist lifted and he lashed out with his powers, fully aware that he was threatening violence against the king to whom he had sworn fealty—and not caring, in his rage. To his utter astonishment, Donal Blaine Haldane answered with like force: potent and altogether too focused for what Sief had always imagined was the limit of the king's power. Before he could pull back, power slammed against his own closing shields and reverberated to the deepest core of his being, forcing a breach and starting a tear in his defenses that gaped ever wider, the more he tried to seal it.

With that realization came fear and pain—more pain than he had ever experienced in his life or even imagined he could feel. It began in his head, exploding behind his eyes, but quickly ripped downward to center in his chest, like a giant fist closing on his heart. At the same time, he felt his limbs going numb, losing all sensation as his legs collapsed under him and his arms flailed like the arms of a marionette with its strings cut. Through blurring vision, he could just see Donal, right hand thrust between them with the fingers splayed in a warding-off gesture, and Donal's lips moving in words whose sense Sief could only barely comprehend.

"Listen to me, Sief!" Donal's urgent plea only barely penetrated the scarlet agony blurring his vision. "Don't make me kill you! I need the boy. I need *you!*"

"Lies!" Sief managed to whisper from between gritted teeth, as the child—*Donal's bastard!*—started wailing. "Faithless, forsworn whoreson! I'll mind-rip you!—kill the bastard!—kill . . . *you* . . . !"

Enraged beyond reason, Sief tried again to launch a counter-attack against this man—*his king!*—who had betrayed him, bucking upward from his slumped position and dragging himself to hands and knees, clawing a hand upward to help him focus—but to no avail. To his horror and dismay, the other's might was crushing him down, smothering the life from him—but he was too proud to yield, and too stubborn. All his life he had been so careful in how he used his powers, taken such pride in his abilities. He had always known that the Haldanes had powers that were akin to his own, but now, in extremis, he had not the strength or the abandon to turn his own powers to the wanton response that might have saved him.

He could feel his mind ripping under the onslaught of an attack he wondered if Donal even comprehended. (*Where* had he gotten such power, and the knowledge of how to use it?)

Hardly a whimper could he manage to force past his lips—nor could it have been heard, over the child's bawling!—but he could feel himself being dragged toward oblivion, all too aware that the damage only worsened as he struggled—and he couldn't *not* struggle! But somehow he had known, from that first flare of Donal's mind against his own, that there was neither any turning back nor any defense against this.

His last coherent thought, just before the darkness claimed him, was regret that he would leave no son from this life—for Krispin was *Donal's* son.

Yet still he tried to cling to that final image of the infant's puckered little face before his vision—the son that should have been his—as pain dragged him into an ever-darkening spiral downward and the last vestiges of awareness trickled into oblivion.

Chapter 2

"Remove not the ancient landmark,

which thy fathers have set."

—PROVERBS 22:28

THE king could feel the pulse pounding in his temples as he made his outstretched fist unclench, face averted from the sight of his friend sinking into death, but he knew that he had had no choice, once the deception was discovered.

He had feared it might end this way if Sief found out. He knew Sief's jealousy, and something of the chilly relationship between Sief and Jessamy; he well remembered when Jessamy had arrived at court as Sief's reluctant child-bride.

That had been over thirty years ago. It had been clear from the beginning that the two cared little for one another, though in time they appeared to have achieved a reasonable coexistence. Sief had shown a decided aptitude for diplomatic work, and had proven himself increasingly invaluable to both Donal and his father; and Jessamy, when she was not attending on a succession of Gwynedd's queens, had spent much of her time in child-bearing—though Donal knew that she had never departed from her marriage vows before Donal approached her.

Donal himself could not say the same, though he had told himself that it was different for men, and for kings, and that his first queen's failure to provide an heir justified his occasional trysts with other ladies of the court—though never, until Jessamy, with the wife of a friend. The several children that had come of such liaisons at least reassured him of his own virility, but there had been no true-born heir until the passing of Queen Dulchesse had allowed his remarriage with the Princess Richeldis, followed by the arrival of Prince Brion.

And none too soon, for Donal was no longer young. The child crown prince was thriving, and Donal was honestly enamoured of his new wife, but a king in his fifties might not live to see his heir grown to manhood—even an heir with the potential to wield the mystical powers of the Haldane royal line.

Unless, of course, that heir had a powerful protector: a Deryni protector. The very notion was dangerous—and Donal had never considered Sief himself, who might have other aspirations than merely to serve his king and, besides, was no younger than Donal. But what if a Deryni could be found who was bound to the young prince from a very early age? What if the protector himself was a Haldane, as well as carrying the powerful Deryni bloodline? It meant, of course, that such a child would require a Deryni mother. . . .

It could be done—and had been done. Donal told himself that it had been no true betrayal of Sief, for he had not taken Sief's wife out of lust or even covetous desire; it had been an affair of state, in the truest sense of the word.

But not in Sief's eyes. Whatever his original intentions in marrying Jessamy, Sief would have regarded royal poaching on his marital prerogatives as, at very least, a breach of the feudal oaths that he and the king had exchanged. Donal regretted that.

Jessamy, too, had betrayed Sief, though undoubtedly for very different reasons than Donal's. At least on some level, Donal sensed that she had seen this service to the king as one that she herself could render to the Crown of Gwynedd, beyond the reach of whatever arrangement had bound her to Sief other than her marriage vows. One day, when the shock of what he had just done was behind them, he would ask her what hold Sief had had over her. He suspected that it had something to do with both of them being Deryni, though he wasn't sure.

But from childhood, he had surmised what Sief was—though he couldn't explain just how he had known—and he had sensed Jessamy's true nature soon after she arrived at court. In neither case did he feel either frightened or apprehensive, though he also took particular care not to let anyone else know, especially not any of the priests who frequented the court. Donal's father had never been particularly forthcoming about what it was that made the Haldanes so special, that they could wield some of the powers usually only accessible to Deryni. But he *had* made it clear that this was part of the Divine Right that made the Haldanes kings of Gwynedd, and *that* justified extraordinary measures to protect said kingship. So far, Donal Haldane had committed both adultery and murder to keep it.

"Is he—dead?" came Jessamy's whispered question, putting an end to the tumble of speculation that momentarily had held the king apart from his act.

Donal let his eyes refocus and glanced quickly around him. He had sunk to one knee beside the big bed, at the foot of which Sief sprawled motionless, apparently not breathing. Jessamy was lifting her head from over the infant clutched tight to her breast, her face white and bloodless as she craned forward to see. Krispin had stopped crying.

"Donal? Is he . . . ?"

"I think so," the king said, a little sharply. He crawled on hands and knees to press his fingertips to the side of Sief's neck, just beneath the ear, but he could feel no pulse. The eyes were closed, and when Donal peeled back one eyelid, the pupil was fixed and dilated. But he had already known, in a way that had something to do with his Haldane kingship, that Sief's essence was fled beyond retrieving, the quick mind stilled forever.

"*Jesu,* I didn't mean for this to happen," Donal whispered, sinking back onto his heels. "But he'd guessed the truth. He turned on me. He was beyond reasoning."

"I know," Jessamy said softly, burying her face against the blanket wrapped around her child—*their* child.

"We shall say that it was his heart," Donal said dully, dragging himself upright against the side of the bed. "No one else need know otherwise. His heart stopped. That *is* the ultimate cause of all death, after all."

Jessamy slowly raised her head to look at him.

"You must not allow any of your nobles to inspect the body," she said.

At his questioning look, she went on.

"There are Deryni in your household whom you do not know. What you have just done—leaves certain signs that can be read by those who know how."

"There are other Deryni in my household!" Donal repeated, incredulous. "Besides yourselves. And you did not tell me?"

"I was not permitted to tell you," she replied. "I was physically incapable of telling you. I still cannot tell you certain things."

The king's face went even more ashen, if that were possible, but indignant question was already stirring in his eyes.

"They mean you no harm, Sire," she whispered, still clutching the child to her breast. "There are . . . those who have long been charged to watch over the House of Haldane, and to report back to . . . superiors. I am bound not to reveal their identities. They—have other obligations as well, an agenda of their own, which Sief served. It was they who required my marriage with him, after my father passed away."

Donal simply stared at her for a long moment, finally bestirring himself to draw a deep breath.

"Other Deryni," he murmured. "Why did it not occur to me before?"

When she said nothing, he slowly got to his feet, his gaze drifting back to Sief's body.

"Is your brother one of them?" he said quietly, after a pause.

"You know what he is, Sire," she replied. "And you know that he has always served you faithfully. More than that I may not tell you."

"How dare—" He had started to answer her sharply, but broke off and took a deep breath, glancing again at Sief.

"Jessamy," he whispered very softly, "you must help me in this. What we have done, we have done for the guarding of Gwynedd. But my guarding is incomplete, if I do not know as many of the dangers as possible. I must ask you again: What other Deryni are here at court?"

"I cannot tell you," she said, very softly. "I wish that I could—but I cannot."

She was silently weeping by the time Donal summoned help and men came running from outside Sief MacAthan's suite of rooms, in the part of the castle where the king's most trusted advisors were privileged to lodge. At that time, only the king himself was to know that the widow's tears were tears of relief, to be free at last of Sief's long tyranny.

THE Camberian Council learned of Sief's death the following day, shortly after the news began to disseminate within the court at Rhemuth, for Seisyll Arilan attended on the court nearly every morning. Seisyll had been surprised to hear it, since Sief had seemed in good health the previous evening, but he dutifully set in motion the usual mechanism by which the Council was summoned outside their normal schedule of meetings, and continued to gather what further information he could, until time came for them to meet.

"It seems to have taken everyone by surprise," Seisyll told his fellow Council members early that evening—now only five of them, for their missing member had yet to regain Portal access. "I'm informed that the king's own physician was summoned immediately, but there was nothing to be done."

"You weren't able to see the body?" Barrett asked.

Seisyll shook his head. "Not yet. There was no way I could manage it without calling attention to myself. Besides, they're saying it was his heart. He was about sixty, after all—the oldest among us."

"But not *that* old, for one of us," Michon said quietly. "You and I are hardly a decade younger, Seisyll."

Seissyl merely shrugged as Dominy de Laney cocked her head in Michon's direction.

"Surely you don't suspect foul play," she said.

"No. It's curious, though, that the king was with him. It would have been late. Did anyone hear him mention that he planned to see the king after he left us?"

The others at the table shook their heads.

"That wouldn't signify, if the king came to *him*," Barrett pointed out. "He wouldn't necessarily have known that the king would seek him out."

"Are we reaching for some connection between the king's presence and Sief's death?" Dominy asked. "Because I don't see any. What motive could there be, if there were? From all accounts, Sief had an excellent relationship with the king."

Seisyll nodded. "They had been friends for years. So had . . ."

Speculation kindled in the blue-violet eyes as his voice trailed off, echoed in the expressions that began to animate the faces of the others with him.

"I see," said Vivienne, "that I am not the only one to wonder whether we must worry again about Lewys ap Norfal's daughter."

Dominy shook her head, though the vehemence of her denial was at odds with her troubled expression. "What possible worry could there be? Surely you aren't suggesting that she had a hand in her husband's death?"

"Such things have been known to happen," Vivienne said dryly.

"Then, it appears that further investigations should be made," Seisyll replied. "And since I'm the one most regularly at court, the task obviously falls to me."

"What will you do?" Dominy asked.

"Try again, to have a closer look at the body," Seisyll replied. "The funeral will be from the cathedral tomorrow morning, so he lies tonight in a side chapel there. It is known we were friends. It would be remiss of me not to pay my respects."

"The funeral is tomorrow?" Vivienne said. "Does that seem over-hasty to anyone besides me?"

Seisyll shrugged. "All the more reason to satisfy our curiosity tonight."

"And if others interrupt your visit?" Vivienne asked. "Even if others of his friends do not come, the brothers of the cathedral chapter will keep watch through the night."

"The brothers can be induced to doze at their devotions," Seisyll said lightly. "If Michon will accompany me, we can certainly accomplish what is needful."

Michon inclined his head in agreement, his gray eyes glinting with faint amusement. "Audacious, as always; but I shall rise to the challenge."

Dominy de Laney gave a genteel snort, and Barrett raised one scant eyebrow.

"I suppose it's pointless to tell you to be careful," Vivienne said sourly.

Even Seisyll chuckled at that, for though Sief's death left him and Michon as the Council's senior members, both now past the half-century mark, the pair owned a long history of daring exploits on behalf of their race; Vivienne alone would reckon them reckless.

"Darling Vivienne," Michon said with a tiny, droll smile, "we are *always* careful."

LATER that night, as the city watch cried the midnight hour and most of Rhemuth slept, Sir Seisyll Arilan summoned a servant with a torch and made his way quietly down the winding street that led from the castle toward the cathedral. As a trusted royal courtier, he was often abroad at odd hours on the king's business, so the occasional guard he passed gave little response save to salute his rank and ensure that his passage was uneventful.

As expected, the cathedral was deserted save for a pair of monks keeping watch beside Sief's open coffin, there where it rested on its catafalque before the altar of a side chapel. Tall candles flanked the coffin, set three to either side, and the prayers of the kneeling monks whispered in the stillness, offered up in antiphon. After a glance to assess the situation, Seisyll drew his servant back into the nave and bade him kneel in the shadow of a pillar not far from the chapel entrance.

"Keep watch here, and pray for the soul of Sir Sief MacAthan," he whispered, also laying a hand on the man's wrist and applying a compulsion to do just that.

Satisfied that the man would not interfere, Seisyll made his way silently toward the door to the cathedral sacristy, which lay in the angle of the nave with the south transept. The door was locked, but it yielded quickly to his Deryni touch.

Inside, he closed the door behind him and summoned handfire to augment the light of the Presence lamp burning above the tabernacle behind the sacristy's vesting altar. By their combined light, he could easily make out the design set into the tessellated pavement covering the center of the floor. Stepping onto it, he composed his thoughts and focused his intent, visualizing his destination.

In an eye-blink, he was standing in the Portal outside the chamber where the Camberian Council met. Michon was waiting just outside, dressed all in black and looking uncharacteristically sinister.

"All's well, I take it?" Michon murmured.

Seisyll nodded, also inviting for Michon to step onto the Portal with him.

"Two monks praying in the chapel where they've put Sief's coffin," he replied. "I brought Benjamin to light the way. He's settled to keep watch outside the chapel while we do what needs to be done."

Merely grinning, Michon turned his back on Seisyll and allowed the other to set hands on his shoulders, eyes closing as he opened his mind to the other's direction. A moment's vague disorientation as the link was made—and then they were standing in the still-deserted sacristy at Rhemuth Cathedral. Quickly the pair glided to the door, scanned outside, then made their way back among the shadowed columns to where Seisyll's servant kept watch outside the mortuary chapel.

Seisyll said nothing as he set a hand on the servant's shoulder, probing briefly for an update. No one had come, and the monks had not ceased their chanting.

With a glance at Michon, Seisyll started into the chapel, making no attempt at stealth as he headed toward one of the monks, aware that Michon was advancing more silently on the other while attention was turned toward Seisyll. Within seconds, both monks nodded deeper in prayer, oblivious to their surroundings. With a glance back at Benjamin, who now would intercept anyone heading toward the chapel and give warning, the two Deryni turned their attention to the coffin where lay the mortal remains of Sief MacAthan.

He lay silent and pale in his funeral garb, a gauzy veil drawn across his face. As Michon ran the flat of one palm above the dead man's chest, Seisyll started to lift the veil for a closer look. In that instant, a forlorn sob barked across the length of the chapel from where Benjamin knelt just outside: his signal that someone was coming.

Hastily Seisyll drew back his hand and crossed himself to cover the movement, keeping his head bowed, at the same time sending instructions to the entranced monks to resume their formal prayers. Michon likewise bowed his head, withdrawing his hand. Seconds later, several more monks came into the chapel: obviously the relief for the ones still kneeling to either side of the coffin, who were blinking in surprise and a trace of guilt at having dozed at their posts.

No words were exchanged as the monks changed places, but Seisyll sensed that any attempt to remain longer would lead to questions best unasked and unanswered. After crossing himself again, he bowed to the new monks and headed out of the chapel, Michon silently following. With the first set of monks loitering in the nave to see where they would go, the pair had no choice but to leave, beckoning for Benjamin to join them. Outside, as they followed the servant's torch back toward the castle, they spoke mind to mind as they revised their battle plan.

Poor timing, Michon sent.

Aye, I would have preferred a bit more leisure.

There was time to sense a first impression, came Michon's reply. *He did not die easily.*

A rebellious heart can be a treacherous thing, Seisyll answered. *Are you hinting that it was something more?*

I don't know. I need a closer look.

Seisyll's violet gaze swept the shadows as they continued climbing the castle mount. *Difficult,* he sent after a moment. *They plan to bury him in the cathedral crypt.*

At least we'll not have to contend with pious monks, Michon retorted. *And it will take a few days or even weeks to prepare the tomb.*

Risky, still.

But needful, Michon replied. *I did not like what I sensed.*

Chapter 3

"Yet shall he be brought to the grave, and shall remain in the tomb."

—JOB 21:32

GIVEN that the deceased had been one of the king's most senior ministers, no one thought it unusual that he was accorded a funeral all but semi-state in its dignity. Indeed, as a single muffled bell tolled its summons in the cathedral tower the next morning, a sizeable segment of the court came to pay their respects to the king's good servant, Sir Sief MacAthan, cruelly betrayed by a treacherous heart while still rejoicing in the birth of his long-awaited son.

His widow led the mourners on behalf of that son, along with three of the dead man's daughters who knelt like stair-steps beside the coffin now closed and covered with a heavy funeral pall: the two little ones, Jesiana and Seffira, and an older girl christened Jessilde but now called Sister Iris Jessilde, whose rainbow-edged white veil and sky-blue robes proclaimed her a novice nun of the royal Convent of Notre Dame d'Arc-en-Ciel, just outside Rhemuth.

The fourth and eldest of Sief's surviving daughters was not present: Sieffany, who lived many days' ride to the west with her husband and young family. Contentedly wed to a son of Michon de Courcy, Sieffany might have heard the news by now—Jessamy had caught a glimpse of Michon himself, as she entered the cathedral. But even if Sieffany knew, her attendance at the funeral would have been far too dangerous even to consider; for only through Deryni auspices could she have learned of the event so quickly, and only by the use of a Portal could she have reached Rhemuth in time. In the prevailing climate regarding Deryni, it was best that humans were not reminded that such things even existed.

That had not deterred some of those now assembling. From where Jessamy sat behind her daughters, black-gowned and heavily veiled, she was able to single out several whom she recognized as being friends of her father's, all those years ago, some undoubtedly come by way of Portal—little though the rest of the mourners would realize that. She knew of several Portals in and around Rhemuth. One lay within the precincts of this very cathedral.

Strangely enough, she found that the presence of these men no longer frightened her the way it once would have done. She wondered whether she still frightened them. For her own part, she found that with Sief's death had come a lightening of many of the constraints by which he had bound her—or by which she had *felt* herself bound—and her status as a grieving widow would give her added protection that had not existed while Sief still lived. Let them think what they liked—that she was the renegade daughter of a renegade Deryni—but she would take many secrets to her grave, just as her husband was taking his secrets to his.

The muffled bell ceased its tolling, the last strike lingering on the silence. At the thud of a verger's staff on the floor in the west, the congregation rose as the king's council and then the king himself entered the cathedral, all of them in black, the black-clad queen and her ladies also in dutiful attendance. Following them came the cathedral choristers, who began the solemn chant of the introit: *"Requiem aeternam dona eis, Domine, et lux perpetua luceat eis. . . ."* Then the processional cross and torch-bearers, a thurifer, and finally the celebrants for the Requiem Mass now beginning, the archbishop himself to preside.

Jessamy waited until the king's party had reached the transept crossing before tottering to her feet. Having risen from childbed to be present, she was content to let observers think she was weaker than she was, affecting to lean on the arm of the maid who had accompanied her. She had become a consummate actress during her long years at court.

Now she played the role of grieving widow as befitted her

dead husband's rank and station, meekly kneeling with her daughters for their father's Requiem, confident that her façade of grief would not be broached by any of the other Deryni present. Indeed, the grief of her daughters was genuine, in varying degrees, and would reinforce her own illusion.

Jessilde's was well contained, already being channeled into the serenity and acceptance come of convent discipline, though her pretty face within her rainbow-edged veil was pale and drawn. Seffira, the four-year-old, was hardly old enough to understand that it was her father who lay in the coffin before them, but Jesiana, the nine-year-old, wept inconsolably, for she had been the apple of her father's eye.

When Mass was ended, both Donal and his queen accompanied the procession down into the cathedral's crypt as Sief's coffin was carried to its final resting place, destined for honored interment in a vault very near the tombs of Donal's own ancestors—for the king had made it known that he regarded Sir Sief MacAthan as a friend as well as a loyal servant of the Crown, worthy to lie near the Haldanes in death as he had served them in life. The place was also very near the final resting place of several of Sief's children—fitting enough, Jessamy supposed, but it also meant that she would have to pass his tomb every time she came to visit the little ones.

In the meantime, in the days until the stonemasons had finished their preparations, the coffined body would lie atop the table-like tomb-slab of another long-ago good servant of the Haldane Crown: Sir Ferrol Howard, slain with King Urien more than fifty years before at the Battle of Killingford. A tattered banner from that battle hung above Sir Ferrol's tomb, honoring his sacrifice, and its edge trailed over the floral tributes now laid atop the polished oak of Sief's coffin, after the pall was removed. Before leaving, Jessamy had offered lilies on behalf of her absent daughter, and a single red rose for the infant Krispin, who would never know the man whose name, but not blood, he bore.

Afterward, up in the cathedral narthex, she and her daughters lingered briefly to receive condolences from a few of those who had come to pay their last respects—though not many showed such fortitude. While mere association with Deryni no longer carried quite the stigma it once had done, most deemed it prudent not to attract unwelcome scrutiny from those less tolerant of such associations. Archbishop William was known to be one such individual, though he had chosen not to offend the king by declining to celebrate Sief's Requiem Mass; but even the power of a king might not be enough to protect those who fell into the archbishop's active disfavor.

Both king and archbishop were standing on the cathedral steps as Jessamy and her daughters emerged through the great west door, the queen and her ladies already heading down to the horses waiting in the square below. Maintaining a façade of meekness, Jessamy paid her respects to the archbishop and followed, the king trailing behind with several retainers when he, too, had taken his leave.

THAT night, while Jessamy cradled her infant son and pondered his future—and hers—and the king likewise considered what might come of what he had done, two men of whom both of them had cause to be wary were making their way back to Rhemuth Cathedral. The pair's mission required that neither of them be seen, so they came by way of the Portal in the cathedral's sacristy.

They arrived after the last of the night offices, when the monks of the cathedral chapter were likely not to be about again until Matins, several hours hence. The cathedral was deserted, as they had hoped it would be after the day's obsequies. Racks of votive candles in the various side chapels spilled wavering patches of illumination across the cavernous darkness of the nave as Seisyll Arilan and Michon de Courcy made their way silently back to the mouth of the stairwell that led to the royal crypts. There, while Michon kept watch, Seisyll used his powers to shift the tumblers in the lock that secured the gate to the stair, stilling any sound it might have made as they swung it open far enough to slip through.

Quickly they ghosted down the worn steps, their way now dimly lit by the faint violet glow of handfire that Seisyll conjured for that purpose. He kept it small, and shielded it with his hands as best he could, for brass grilles pierced the ceiling of the crypt to admit air and light from the nave above—and would also betray their presence, if anyone entered the nave and noticed light from below. But some light they must have to make their way among the tombs to where Sief's coffin lay.

Threading their way between the tombs of generations of dead Haldanes, they came at last to the side vault where Sief's coffin awaited proper interment. Here were no ceiling grilles to betray them, but the scent of the wilting floral tributes was strong, and Seisyll found himself stifling a sneeze as he and Michon eased to either side of the coffin. He was already pulling a pry bar from his belt as Michon began moving the flowers to one side. They had known the coffin was sealed, so they had come prepared.

You can put a damping spell on this, while I pry? Seisyll asked, as Michon laid his hands flat on the coffin's polished top.

Give me a moment, came Michon's reply.

The pale eyes closed. A slowly released breath triggered a working trance. Soon a faint, silvery shimmer began to crawl outward from Michon's hands, gradually covering the lid of the coffin and then spilling down the sides. After another slow-drawn breath, Michon opened his eyes, moving his hands apart but still touching the coffin lid. At his nod, eyes vaguely unfocused, Seisyll applied his pry bar and began to work the nails out of the oak.

There was no sound save Seisyll's increasingly labored breathing as he prised each nail free. Michon collected them as they were removed, dreamily laying them beside the flowers on a nearby tomb-slab, keeping the muffling spell intact until the coffin lid moved under their hands.

Together, he and Seisyll slid the lid partway toward the foot of the coffin, exposing the shrouded body nearly to the waist. The waxed linen of the cerecloth had molded itself to the dead man's profile, and retained something of its outline as Michon reverently peeled it aside. A whiff of beginning corruption joined the stink of wilting flowers and the dank tomb-scent of the vault, and Seisyll drew back a little in distaste.

You're welcome to go first, he whispered in Michon's mind.

Michon merely gazed on the dead man's face, obviously still deep in trance. In repose, Sief's features were sunken and yellowed, bearing little resemblance to his appearance in life, but Michon's touch to the dead man's forehead was gentle. Again his pale eyes closed.

For a long moment, only the gentle whisper of their breathing stirred the silence of the tomb—until a little gasp escaped Michon's lips.

"Jesu!" came his breathy exclamation, quickly stifled.

What is it?

Read with me on this, Seisyll, Michon ordered, shifting back into mindspeech. *There isn't a great deal left, but I'm not liking what little I'm seeing.*

Without comment, Seisyll put his repugnance aside and laid his fingertips beside Michon's on the dead man's forehead, extending his Deryni senses for a deep reading. His first impulse was to recoil, for Sief had been dead for several days, and physical decay had left little in the way of a matrix to hold his memories to any coherence. But he mastered his distaste and made himself delve deeper, following the pathways already broached by Michon's probe—and began touching on fragments of memory that he liked no better than Michon had done.

For images from the time of Sief's death showed disturbing glimpses of Sief's wife and her infant son—and the king's presence, as well—and harsh words exchanged between the two men, though Seisyll could not pin down the sense of them.

Far worse was to follow. Harsh words had quickly escalated beyond mere anger. The clash had never reached the point of a physical exchange, but the result was just as deadly—and unexpected. Little to Sief's credit, he had started to lash out at the king with his magic—and was answered by Donal's response in kind, summoning magical resources of a magnitude they had not dreamed him to possess.

Very quickly the king's reaction had pressed beyond any merely physical defense both to rip at Sief's mind and close a psychic hand around his heart. Nor had the king relented, even as the damage went beyond the level of any possible repair, dragging Sief through an agony that was at once physical and psychic, down into unconsciousness and then beyond, into death, until the silver thread was stretched to the breaking point—and snapped.

Seisyll was gasping as he surfaced from the probe, turning blank, unfocused eyes on Michon, reeling a little in backlash from what Sief had suffered.

"That isn't possible," he whispered, lifting shaking hands to look at them distractedly—and shifting back to mindspeech. *Donal did it? He has the ability to mind-rip one of our own number? A member of the Council?*

Apparently he does, Michon returned. *Setting aside the question of How, the further question is, Why? The presence of Jessamy, and the fact that she apparently made no effort to interfere, suggests that she condoned the attack—or at least had cause to allow it.*

Shaking his head, he drew the cerecloth back over Sief's face and began pulling the coffin lid back into place, Seisyll belatedly assisting him. The nails he drove back into place with his mind, silently, letting his anger and horror defuse with each one.

"YOU'RE certain of what you saw?" Dominy asked, stunned, when Michon had reported back to the Camberian Council later that night.

"I am certain of what I saw," Michon replied. "I am not necessarily certain of what it means."

Oisín Adair, their previously absent member, drummed calloused fingers on the ivory-inlaid table, blue eyes animated in the darkly handsome face. His eyes were a startling sapphire hue above a neatly trimmed beard and somewhat bushy moustache, the night-black hair drawn back neatly in the braided clout favored by Gwynedd's mountain folk. By his attire, clad in oxblood riding leathers and with a whiff of the stable about him, he had come but lately from the back of a horse.

"It would appear that the canny Donal Haldane has gained access to the powers anciently attributed to his Haldane forefathers," he said quietly, the soft burr of the north softening his words. "Can none of you venture a reasonable surmise as to who might have helped him?"

"The daughter of Lewys ap Norfal," Vivienne said, venom in her tone.

"We don't know that," Barrett reminded her. "There is always the possibility that it was someone else entirely, in which case, we have a far greater problem on our hands than we could have imagined—though the thought of Jessamy following in her father's footsteps is sobering enough."

"Which 'someone else' did you have in mind, dear brother?" Dominy asked. "Given that it's unlikely to have been Sief, that leaves only four other Deryni with regular access to the court of Gwynedd—and I believe we can eliminate the two sitting at this table."

"And I point out, in turn, that both of those remaining are the children of Lewys ap Norfal," Barrett said.

"Yes, and we began grooming Morian ap Lewys well before his father's death," Seisyll said sharply. "That was before some of you were out of leading strings, but I assure you that our predecessors did not take this responsibility lightly."

The grudging silence that met this declaration was broken by Michon clearing his throat.

"It appears I should remind everyone that Morian was squired to the court of Gwynedd at the age of ten, even before the death of his father. Never has he put a foot wrong, in all the years since then. I can, of course, bring him in for examination, if that is your wish, but I assure you that his loyalty has never been in question, to the crown or to his blood."

"I think that none of us question either loyalty," Oisín said. "Where is he now?"

"In Meara, on the king's business, as he has been for most of the past year," Seisyll supplied. "In truth, he has never spent much time at court—or in his sister's company. I think it highly unlikely that Morian was involved, or even knew."

"Which brings us back to his sister, who perhaps has had more access to the king than the rest of us combined," Vivienne said coldly.

"That does appear to be the case," Oisín said. "I find it disturbing that she was present when Donal killed her husband. There can be no doubt that she is of a powerful bloodline, whether or not she shares her father's aberrations. That should have given her the ability to protect Sief, even from a Haldane. Unless, of course," he added thoughtfully, "unless there was some other bond between Jessamy and the king that was stronger than her duty to her husband, the father of her . . . children. . . ."

These last words fell into a sudden, deathly silence. After a moment, it was Barrett who dared to voice the suspicion that had begun to take shape in all their minds.

"It would not be the first time that a king has sired a child on a woman not his queen," he said. "His father did it. More than once."

"So has Donal," Seisyll whispered, chilled. "I know of several others."

"You're suggesting that Krispin MacAthan is actually the king's bastard," Dominy said flatly, not wanting to believe it.

"I believe we are suggesting," said Oisín, "that the prospect certainly bears further investigation. If the child is, indeed, Donal Haldane's by-blow, and Sief found out, I think we need look no further for a motive for his killing."

"That still doesn't explain how Donal acquired the power to overcome a fully trained Deryni mage," Vivienne said.

"I think that much is clear, if the rest is true," Barrett replied. "Jessamy must have helped the king to enable his full Haldane powers—whether before or after the conception makes little difference."

"It makes a difference if she did it in the hopes that he would kill her husband for her," Vivienne pointed out. "She knew Sief's temper. She must have guessed how he would react, if he found out her child was not his. I think we can all imagine his rage when he discovered that his long-awaited 'son' was not his son at all."

"Poor Sief," Dominy murmured after a moment. "And he would have had no inkling that the king had powers to match his own."

"To *exceed* them, apparently," Barrett retorted.

"He does seem to have been taken by surprise," Michon said quietly. "And circumstances do suggest that the king was responsible—though I think it may have been a reaction of the moment, when Sief guessed the truth of his 'son's' paternity. But I saw nothing to suggest that Jessamy had any direct part in her husband's death."

Seisyll slowly nodded. "I agree. And I very much doubt that there was premeditation on the king's part. He can be a devious man—a king *must* be—but I have never known him to be a murderer."

"A passion of the moment, then, on Sief's part," Barrett ventured, "a reflex reaction to the shocking truth of the child's paternity, that escalated into a murderous attack—and self-defense to counter it."

"That would be my guess," Michon said with a nod.

"We cannot merely guess," Oisín said. "We must know. And we must know the truth about the child."

"Dear God," Vivienne whispered, "not only a grandson of Lewys ap Norfal, but a Deryni-Haldane cross. The notion doesn't bear thinking about!"

"Unfortunately, we *must* think about it," Michon pointed out.

Seisyll gave a nod. "I shall endeavor to meet privately with Jessamy," he said.

"An examination of the child might prove more useful, and more immediately possible," Dominy replied.

"I shall keep both options open," Seisyll agreed. "And I shall exercise extreme caution in the king's presence. In the meantime," he glanced around the table at all of them, "we must give immediate consideration to Sief's replacement. If the king has sired a Haldane bastard on the daughter of Lewys ap Norfal, we must be certain that we are operating at full strength."

Chapter 4

"If children live honestly, and have wherewithal, they shall cover the baseness of their parents."

—ECCLESIASTICUS 22:9

DESPITE Seisyll Arilan's intentions, he could find no immediate opportunity to speak privately with Sief MacAthan's widow or to examine her son. Within days, a border incident near Droghera caused the king to send him on an embassy to Meara, to observe and report on negotiations going on between the royal governor and increasingly militant partisans of Mearan separatism. As he set out on the road to Ratharkin, the Mearan capital, it occurred to him to wonder whether the timing was coincidental—whether Donal was, in fact, sending him from court because he feared he was under scrutiny regarding Sief's death.

Except that the Mearan situation was nothing new. Both Seisyll and Sief had been part of that last expedition into Meara with Donal's father, which had claimed the lives of several of the old queen's Mearan cousins. Perhaps Sief had even revealed or at least intimated to Donal that Seisyll was Deryni—or Jessamy had. But the balance in Meara had long been volatile; and Seisyll was one of the king's most skilled negotiators.

Accordingly, it was Michon de Courcy who contrived to be present at the christening of the widow's son, a week after Seisyll's departure. Though Michon had not actually been in residence at court when Sief died, he had explained his presence at Sief's funeral by a chance coincidence of business in the capital: a matter at law, concerning one of his properties in Ardevala. The pretext now served to justify remaining in Rhemuth while he carried out discreet investigations on behalf of the Council. Given that he was related to Jessamy by marriage, his attendance at the christening was not inappropriate. He knew, however, that it would put her on her guard.

And probably for good cause, Michon decided, when he learned that the ceremony would take place in the chapel royal of Rhemuth Castle, and that Queen Richeldis had agreed to be one of the child's godparents. That, in itself, was not unusual—that a member of the royal family should stand as baptismal sponsor to a child of a favored lord. Indeed, the child's mother was one of the queen's closest friends; and Sief had faithfully served the royal house for many years. Under the circumstances, even the venue might be regarded as a fitting tribute.

Michon did find it disturbing that the king allowed the priest, Queen Richeldis's own chaplain, to use the silver christening basin customarily brought out only for the baptism of royal princes, as the boy was christened Krispin Lewys Sief MacAthan. And afterward, the king let it be known that the widow, her younger daughters, and her infant son should have a home at court for as long as they chose.

"I shall miss both the counsel and the companionship of Sir Sief MacAthan," the king declared, when Father Angelus had finished welcoming young Krispin into the family of God. "This is the least I can do, as a mark of my continued appreciation for a family that has served me so loyally and for so long. Young Master Krispin shall be educated alongside Prince Brion and the child my lady wife now carries beneath her heart, and the Lady Jessamy shall continue in her service of the queen.

"As for these two demoiselles," he added, indicating the widow's young daughters, "you both shall have proper dowries when you are ready to wed—which will also give you the choosing of just about any of the young squires at my court, I think. Does that please you?"

To the good-natured amusement of the court around them, Jesiana gave the king a shy smile and dropped him a charming curtsy; the four-year-old Seffira merely hid her face in her mother's skirts, too young to understand the significance of this sign of the king's favor. The child's innocence elicited a pleased chuckle on the part of the king and a smile of obvious approval on the face of the queen, as Jessamy graciously inclined her head and murmured words of gratitude. Nothing rang false on the part of anyone present, but Michon still found himself wondering whether all was as it appeared.

Instinctively, he avoided approaching the king or exchanging more than the most perfunctory of courtesies with him. Though he did not think Donal suspected he was Deryni, he was reluctant to test that belief until he had sounded out Jessamy—who, if she had been the one to empower the king, might well have discovered how to over-ride the prohibitions set in place by her father and her late husband regarding the identity of the Camberian Council—and might well have warned Donal that Michon was Deryni. He already found it worrisome to have learned that the king possessed hitherto unsuspected powers, and of a magnitude sufficient to have overcome Sief, whatever the provocation.

But he had resolved to speak with Jessamy, at least, and contrived to drift into the castle gardens with the others, after the ceremony. He had hoped for a closer scrutiny of the child in her arms; but as he approached her, standing with her daughters and the queen amid half a dozen of the queen's other ladies, she handed the boy into the keeping of the queen herself, excused herself with a curtsy, and came to meet him before he could join them. Her expression was composed beneath the black wimple of recent widowhood that she wore, but he thought he detected wariness in the deep violet eyes. The marriage of her eldest daughter to his son, like her own marriage to Sief, had been arranged and required by the Camberian Council.

"My Lord Michon," she said coolly, offering him her hand. "Your presence honors this gathering. I caught a glimpse of you at my husband's funeral, but there was no opportunity to seek you out among the other mourners. How fortunate that you happened to be in Rhemuth when he passed away."

He knew she would be aware that his presence had owed little to mere fortune, then or now, but he made a courtly bow over her hand, unsurprised to find his cautious probe casually deflected and even dissipated by the odd, fuzzy shields that characterized Lewys ap Norfal's line. So far as he could tell, she did not seem to notice.

"Fortunate, indeed," he murmured. "And you have borne up bravely, through all of this. What a cruel irony, that Sief's heart should fail him when he finally had a son."

She withdrew her hand and inclined her head, faint challenge in her eyes. "Fate often does deal in ironies, doesn't it?" she replied. "Pray, what keeps you here in Rhemuth?"

"I have business interests here, as you know," he said neutrally. "They are nearly finished now." He glanced at the knot of women cooing over the infant Krispin, who had set up a wail. "Your son seems a lusty bairn. Does he resemble you, or his father?"

"I couldn't possibly say. Both of us? Neither?" The answer was truthful but ambiguous, as Michon was certain had been her intention. "When they are this age, I have always observed that one baby looks remarkably like the next."

Michon allowed himself a tiny smile. "Indeed. Well, I shall be certain to render a glowing account of his christening to his sister and her children back in Rhondevala. No doubt she will be relieved to hear of his Majesty's generous gesture, in inviting you and his other sisters to remain in the royal household."

Jessamy inclined her head with prim graciousness. "I am a poor widow now, my lord, with no means of my own, so I am grateful that I and my children shall continue to have a roof over our heads and food in our mouths. And for Krispin to be educated alongside Prince Brion is a great honor—as is the dowry the king has promised his sisters."

"You are, indeed, fortunate," he said. "Clearly, faithful service to the king is very rewarding."

A hint of what might have been uncertainty briefly flickered in her eyes, but she did not lower her gaze.

"Both Sief and I have served the House of Haldane for many years, my lord," she said carefully, "so I hope that I and mine shall always remain their Majesties' good servants." She glanced back at the women surrounding the queen and the fretting Krispin. "You must excuse me, my lord. Sometimes only a mother's arms will serve to soothe a baby's crying. I pray you to give my devotion to my daughter and grandchildren."

"My lady."

He bowed to her back as she turned and hurried back toward the queen and her ladies, reviewing their exchange and considering all possible interpretations. Later that night, he recounted their conversation to the Camberian Council.

"She was very careful, wasn't she?" Barrett said, when Michon had finished.

"Methinks that she had reason to be," Michon replied.

"Then, you believe that Donal *is* the boy's father?" Vivienne asked, looking decidedly scandalized.

Michon shrugged. "I cannot be certain without examining the child, of course—or subjecting Jessamy herself to a proper interrogation—but I would say that it's entirely likely."

"Might it be possible to bring Jessamy here for questioning?" Dominy said.

"Not of her own accord. And I doubt she could be brought against her will without it coming to someone's notice."

"What about examining the child?" asked Oisín.

"That will be very difficult. I gather that he's to live in the royal nursery, apparently to be raised alongside Prince Brion—which is also suggestive of his true paternity."

Barrett sat back in his chair with a perplexed sigh. "Then, it appears that, at least for the nonce, we cannot resolve this question."

"I would have to agree," Michon said. "But if we're dealing with a Haldane by-blow—and a grandson of Lewys ap Norfal, as well—he's still an infant, only weeks old. It will be years before he could become any kind of serious threat—plenty of time to consider our options. Meanwhile, we have a vacant seat to fill on this Council. Has anyone had a change of heart?"

When no one spoke, he gave a nod to Oisín, who rose and went to a side table, where he pulled a drape of deep violet velvet from a fist-sized amber crystal set on a simple wooden stand. Shrouding his hands with the velvet, he picked up crystal and stand and carried them back to the table, setting them before the chair of the absent Seisyll. The drape he laid across the arms of that chair before taking his own seat again, to the right of Seisyll's.

"Is it late enough to be certain that he's asleep?" Vivienne asked.

Michon, to her left, gave a knowing chuckle.

"The governor's court at Ratharkin is not known for its scintillating night life, especially in these troubled times, and the negotiations being carried out by day will have been tedious, if not exhausting. I have little doubt but that Seisyll will have retreated to his bed by now. Nor, I think, could he long ignore our summons, amplified by Oisín's wee bauble." He nodded toward the crystal and laid his open palms to either side in invitation. "Shall we get on with it?"

The smiles of the other four acknowledged Michon's observation concerning the court of Meara, and they likewise laid their open hands to either side, each turning the left palm downward to overlap the neighbor's open right hand. Those flanking the empty chair called Camber's Siege stretched slightly to bridge the gap, and those to either side of Seisyll's chair lightly set their fingertips to the crystal, completing the circle.

"Now we are met. Now we are one with the ancients," Michon murmured.

"Benedicamus, Elohim," Oisín responded.

His long-drawn breath and whisper of a sigh set the trigger for all of them to begin settling into trance. Some of them briefly closed their eyes, each centering in his or her own way . . . stilling, focusing, shifting into another mode of consciousness. As a silence that was almost palpable settled on the room, every gaze gradually turned to the giant *shiral* crystal set before Seisyll's place, each one's concentration melding with the crystal.

At length a faint spark seemed to kindle within its amber depths, flickering and then flaring to a glowing heart that throbbed with a pulse-beat like a living thing—erratic at first, but then steadying as the heartbeats of the five settled into synchronization. It was Michon who then set the call, reaching out for the mind of their absent member and willing him to respond. After a moment, a mist began to form around the pulsing flame, swirling and then coalescing into the face of Seisyll Arilan.

I am here, came Seisyll's focused declaration. *What is your wish?* The handsome face was still and tranquil, the violet eyes dreamy and unfocused.

We have agreed on a candidate, if you concur, Michon replied. *It would be useful to bring the Council back to its full strength as soon as may be accomplished. When do you anticipate returning to Rhemuth, or to some other place where you will have Portal access?*

A frown crossed Seisyll's face. *It could be weeks, perhaps even months. The Mearan situation is delicate, and requires careful handling. The king was right to send me here instead of others he could have sent, but I dare not leave until it is resolved. What candidate have you agreed?*

Focusing his intent, Michon sent their recommendation in a burst of knowledge and information. Seisyll's image immediately nodded.

I concur. But I would advise that you receive him as soon as can be arranged. Do not wait until I can be present.

I agree that such a delay would be inadvisable, Michon replied. *We shall make suitable arrangements—provided, of course, that he accepts.*

I expect that he will, at least for a limited term, the face in the crystal said. *Is there anything else?*

Naught that cannot wait until this is settled, came Michon's reply. *You should know, however, that the queen stood as godmother at the christening of Jessamy's son.*

The face in the crystal grimaced in sour disapproval. *Indeed. One might have expected that it would be the king. But then, if he is the boy's father, that would not have been canonical, would it?*

Nor is fathering a child on a woman not one's wife, Michon pointed out blandly. *Merely think on it, for now. Our brother Barrett has rightly pointed out that even a Haldane grandson of Lewys ap Norfal can pose no serious threat while he is yet an infant. We have time to consider our options.*

The best option is one most easily carried out on an infant, Seisyll returned coldly. *But I shall await your further deliberations. Please convey my fraternal greetings to our new member.*

With that, his image faded in the crystal and the spark in its heart died out. Dominy de Laney sighed and briefly closed her eyes, and Vivienne eased a crick in her neck and shook out her hands. Barrett had briefly palmed his hands over his sightless eyes, and Michon and Oisín exchanged glances.

"Exceedingly well done, all," Michon said to the room at large, and grinned as he added, "I did tell you that Seisyll would be abed at this hour."

"Disturbing, however, that more progress has not been made in Mearan matters," Barrett replied.

"Aye, but that does not surprise me," Michon replied. "There will be war in Meara before another decade is out—mark my words. It will be yet another legacy of Malcolm's marriage with the Princess Roisian: they, who had thought to settle the Mearan succession by the marriage bed rather than war, after Killingford."

The others merely looked at him, knowing that he had the most direct experience of that great battle, for though none of them had been alive for that war, Michon's father had fought there and lived to tell of it. An uncle and a cousin had not been so fortunate.

"Enough of thoughts of war," Oisín said quietly, after a moment. "Do you wish me to approach our new member-elect?"

The others immediately turned their thoughts from the Mearan question, and even the question of Sief's death, to the more immediate question of Sief's successor. Slowly Michon nodded.

"Can you bring him tomorrow night?"

"I can bring him tonight, if you wish. If he accepts, he can be sworn to the Council immediately, and we can be about our further business."

After a glance at the others, Michon slowly nodded.

"Go, then. We shall await your return."

Chapter 5

"Without counsel purposes are disappointed;
but in the multitude of counselors they are established."

—PROVERBS 15:22

IN the royal palace at Djellarda, in the princely state of Andelon, Prince Khoren Vastouni made his way back to the workroom adjoining his apartments, pleasantly fuddled with good wine and good company and well content with the course of the day.

He was a younger son whose elder brother had sons, so he had never entertained much likelihood of ever having to rule; but that had left him free to pursue interests of his own choosing, more artistic and academic than the arts of war and political intrigue, and to anticipate becoming a mentor to his nephew's children in due course. Now nearing his half-century, he was blessed with a loving wife and family of his own, and that morning had seen his young nephew, his brother's heir, happily remarried.

Which was well, because Fate had dealt the redoubtable Mikhail of Andelon a double blow in the past twelvemonth, making him Sovereign Prince the previous autumn, through the death of his father and Khoren's brother, Prince Atun, and then taking Mikhail's beloved Ysabeau in childbirth in the spring just past. At twenty-seven, having gained a throne but lost a wife, Mikhail had only daughters by his first marriage—the two-year-old Sofiana and the infant Michendra—but his new bride, the Lady Alinor, adored his children, and had professed herself eager to give him sons as well as more daughters, and as soon as possible.

"Oh, Mikhail, I do want lots and lots of babies!" she had declared, as she dandled little Michendra on her knee at the wedding feast and watched Sofiana playing with Alinor's own little brother, the two-year-old Thomas. "Mother, would you look at this sweet, chubby little thing?"

Approaching the door to his workroom, happily replete with good food and excellent wine, Khoren found himself smiling and even shaking his head a little at that sweet image of domestic anticipation. There had been several stillborn sons in the early years of Mikhail's first marriage, so Khoren hoped that the lovely and radiant Alinor would soon attain her heart's desire and that, in her embrace, his nephew would speedily find new happiness—and sons!

In all, the marriage augured well for the future. Only reluctantly had Khoren taken early leave of the continuing wedding festivities—which were very much a family affair, bursting with Vastouni and Cardiel cousins and even a smattering of younger royals from neighboring Jáca and Nur Hallaj. His wife would linger happily in that company for many more hours to come, along with several of their children and grandchildren, but Khoren could no longer ignore the call of a particularly intriguing manuscript he wished to consult again before retiring, written in a dialect that only slowly was yielding up its secrets.

For a fine point of translation had been eluding Khoren Vastouni for nearly a week—and had crystallized in an almost staggering flash of insight during the most solemn part of the nuptial Mass earlier in the day, nearly making him laugh aloud with sheer delight. His beloved Stasha had given him the most mortified look.

Still basking in the satisfaction of his moment of revelation, Khoren set his splayed hand against the lock plate on the door and keyed the spell that would release the lock. At its click, he pushed the door open and slipped inside, at the same time removing the jewel-studded cap he had worn in lieu of a coronet.

This he set jauntily atop a human skull on a stand just inside the door; the reassembled skeleton of its owner hung by wires from a hook in a corner of the room, for he was an anatomist among his many other interests. Then he shrugged off his outer robe and tossed it over a nearby stool, emerald damask spilling onto a carpet patterned with pomegranates as he headed toward his worktable and the unfurled manuscript lying open upon it, its edges weighted down with several stream-polished rocks, pleasing to hand and eye.

It was then that he noticed the faint glow emanating from around the edges of a velvet curtain screening off a corner of the room: his Portal, set in semi-trap mode. It enabled visitors to come and go at will, and even to leave messages, but no one could venture past the Portal's boundaries unless he gave them leave. Khoren had no enemies—at least none he was aware of—but even in Andelon, where Deryni were accepted as a matter of course, one could never be too careful.

"All right, who's there?" he called out, heading toward that corner of the room. "Anyone with half a brain would know that I've been at my nephew's wedding today."

A flick of his arm sent the curtain skittering to one side in a slither of fine rings against wire. The man waiting behind it was well known to Khoren: trim and comely, of somewhat middling height, casually clad in riding leathers of a rich oxblood hue. As a patient smile touched his lips, the calloused hands lifted in a gesture of guileless denial.

"In truth," the visitor said lightly, "I expected you'd be working on that manuscript I brought you; I knew how close you were to cracking the translation. I've not been here long, though—and even from here, I *have* enjoyed just taking in the peacefulness of your workroom. You should have been a monk, Khoren."

Khoren snorted and released the wards on the Portal with a wave of one capable hand, grinning as he opened his arms to the man who stepped across its boundaries.

"Oisín Adair, I might have known it would be you," he said as they embraced. "Seriously, what brings you here at this hour, when you knew what my day would be like?"

"Seriously, I've come on a mission of the utmost importance—though I'd forgotten that today was Mikhail's wedding day. Still, will you come with me for an hour or so? I mayn't tell you where."

Khoren drew back to look into the other man's eyes, feeling the rigidness in the other's shoulders that echoed the shields suddenly stiff between them.

"This sounds serious, indeed," he said quietly. "Can you give me no clue?"

Oisín's bearded face settled into stillness, regret in the blue eyes.

"Sief MacAthan is dead, my friend. It's the Council that summons you. Will you come?"

"Sief, dead? But, how—"

"That is for another place," Oisín said firmly, refusing to be drawn. "Please, ask me no more questions. All will be revealed, in due course."

Briefly closing his eyes, Khoren made himself take a deep breath and slowly exhale, doing his best to banish the heady afterglow of the wine he had drunk, regretting that he had taken any drink at all. No Deryni looked forward to a summons from the Camberian Council, though he knew that his could be for no failing on his part. The news of Sief MacAthan's death made it likely that Khoren was about to be offered a seat on the Council—not altogether unexpected, given his abilities and his spotless reputation, but it was still a prospect both intriguing and daunting. Membership in that almost mythical body was never to be taken lightly, and forever changed those who accepted its burden.

Yet some there were, willing to take on that burden, for it offered an opportunity to enforce and reinforce the ethical precepts instilled in all Deryni of good formal training. Beyond the borders of Gwynedd, in Torenth and the lands to the south, these precepts were mostly followed—and when serious breaches occurred, the Camberian Council could and often did step in; but in Gwynedd, the heartland of the original Eleven Kingdoms, backlash from the failure of Deryni to police their own ranks had all too often been the death of innocent members of their race. To serve the Council was to place oneself in a position to possibly make a difference.

"I will come, of course," Khoren murmured returning his gaze to Oisín. "You do realize, though, that I'm in no fit state for any serious working? I've just come from a wedding feast, for God's sake."

"That will not affect your interview," Oisín replied. "Come."

He set his hand on Khoren's elbow and drew him onto the Portal beside him, turning Khoren away from him to set one hand on the back of his neck. The other hand reached around to cover his eyes as he continued.

"You will understand that it is not permitted that you should sense the coordinates of the Portal where I am taking you," Oisín murmured, "and once there, your physical sight will remain sealed until I release you."

"Of course."

"Then, open to me now."

With those words, his mind surrounded Khoren's, surging in behind the shields his subject obediently let fall. As all physical sensation receded into a gray void where it was too much bother to do anything at all, Khoren vaguely felt a gentle tugging at the edges of his consciousness, then a faint lurch in the pit of his stomach—and a subtle undulation of the floor under his feet, which immediately stabilized.

"Move forward with me now," Oisín murmured.

Though the hand across Khoren's eyes was withdrawn, he kept them closed, well aware that it would be disorienting to open them and not be able to see. He also kept his shields well down, cleaving to the discipline of only what physical senses might tell him as Oisín urged him forward and to the left, one hand grasping his elbow and the other arm curved around his shoulders. He could feel grit under his boots as they moved half a dozen steps away from the Portal, and caught the faint scent of sandalwood, a freshness to the air itself. It was cooler here than in Djellarda, but he had no idea where *here* was.

"I must leave you for a few minutes," Oisín said in a low voice, as he set Khoren's hand against a wall. "Don't move. I'll return shortly."

The other's footsteps receded. Khoren thought he could hear a door opening, and he definitely felt the stir of air, perhaps of the door closing again. The stone under his hand was smooth and cool, but he resisted the temptation to seek out further clues as to the room it contained, for even Oisín's simple instruction might be a test of his obedience.

He waited. He could hear no sound save the gentle throbbing of his own heartbeat—until he felt as well as heard the whisper of the door again. Then Oisín was beside him once more, a guiding hand again set under his elbow.

"Walk with me," came the murmured instruction, as the other firmly moved him forward.

Khoren sensed a larger space as their footsteps took a more hollow tone. Very soon, he was brought up short against something that pressed along the tops of his thighs—a table, he realized, as he was made to sit in a chair of substantial proportions, with heavy arms. No sooner had he settled into it than someone pushed it and him closer to the table, containing him within the compass of the chair arms. He could feel the silence as an almost palpable presence as Oisín moved to his left side and sat, his controlling hand never leaving Khoren's shoulder. But it was not Oisín who spoke first.

"This room has been the meeting place of the Camberian Council since the time of Saint Camber himself," said a woman's voice ahead and to the left. "Before that, we believe that it served the use of the Airsid. Do you know of the Airsid, Khoren Vastouni?"

Khoren considered the question. It was not what he had been expecting.

"I do not know as much as I would like," he said candidly, for only the truth would suffice in this company. "I was taught that our high magic sprang from their teachings, at least in part. I have heard it said that the great Orin may have had Airsid teachers. Some say that they came from Caeriesse, before it sank beneath the sea," he added, a little less certainly.

An amused chuckle came from directly to his right—another woman's voice, lighter than the first.

"So some say. Would it surprise you to learn that some of the founders of this Council actually looked upon the mortal remains of Orin and Jodotha, his great disciple?"

Khoren found himself sitting forward more attentively, longing to open his eyes, for the Airsid and their teachings had long been his academic passion, and Orin and Jodotha were legendary.

"Here?" he managed to breathe.

"No, not—here," said a man's voice straight across from him, who sounded somewhat familiar. "We believe that this place, however, was built by the Airsid—or at least begun by them. It had been long abandoned by Saint Camber's time, but the Council's founders rediscovered it and adopted it as their secure meeting place—Camber's kin and other close associates. You are sitting, by the way, in the seat called 'Saint Camber's Siege.' It is one of eight, though it is usually left vacant, to remind us of our patron. For the most part, only potential new members of the Council are ever seated there—or those we call before us to answer for their actions."

The further words at last had identified at least one of his interlocutors: Michon de Courcy, who had been one of Khoren's classmates when both of them studied with the great Norfal—which would have reassured him, except that he now knew that he was sitting in Camber's Siege. Inexplicably, he found himself straightening a little under Oisín's hand, halfway convinced that the saint himself was suddenly among them.

"I think you will have guessed that we have not called you here to answer for your actions," Michon went on, in a conversational tone. "You may open your eyes now."

Khoren felt nothing save the weight of Oisín's hand lifting from his shoulder, but when he cautiously obeyed, his vision and powers were intact. His first, blinking visual images confirmed his impression of vaulted space above the table—which was ivory and octagonal—and Michon sitting directly opposite, flanked by a handsome, auburn-haired woman and another old acquaintance: Barrett de Laney, wearing his Nur Sayyid scholar's robes. Vaguely he was also aware of Oisín to his left, and another young woman on his right—and that all of them were Truth-Reading him, and had been doing so from the beginning, except that Oisín had been obscuring that awareness before.

"I trust that you will not object to being Truth-Read during this interview," said the woman to his right. "Coming directly to the point, we are minded to offer you the seat left vacant by the passing of Sief MacAthan." She gestured toward the empty chair between herself and Barrett, before which lay a slender ivory wand of office and one perfect rose, creamy white and emerald green against the more yellowed ivory of the table.

"Ordinarily, we would have secured your agreement to this appointment before seeking your counsel," she went on, "but a certain urgency attends our deliberations, because of the manner of Sief's passing. Therefore, this trial of your functioning among us. If you should choose not to accept this burden, you will be free to go, though we will require a bound oath not to reveal what you shall have seen and heard here. In the meantime, however, we would value your opinion regarding the circumstances that have left our numbers thus reduced. Incidentally, you know me somewhat, though we have never met. I am Dominy de Laney, Barrett's sister."

He had turned his gaze to her as she spoke, aware of the touch of their minds against his. With a quick glance at Barrett—who had, indeed, mentioned a sister, many years go—Khoren gave a faint nod that was both acknowledgement and assent, already turning his thoughts to what little he knew of the dead man besides a name.

"I—gather that the death of Sief MacAthan was unexpected," he said uncertainly. "Was he killed, or did he die of natural causes?"

"That was our question as well," Michon replied. "The official statement from the court of Donal Haldane of Gwynedd would have it that Sief's heart failed him shortly after the birth of his son, in the presence of his wife and the king, who could do nothing. On its face, this much is true."

"But there is more," Khoren supplied.

Michon gave a nod. "What could not have been known in Rhemuth is that Sief was present in this chamber no more than a few hours before his death. He seemed in excellent spirits, and had certainly never exhibited any sign of ill health."

Khoren's gaze flicked to Michon. "And you conclude—?"

"We do not believe that a failing heart caused Sief's death," Michon replied, "or, if it did, its failure was helped along. By magic. At the beckoning of Donal Haldane. Possibly with the connivance of Sief's wife—who, you may recall, is Jessamy ferch Lewys, the daughter of Lewys ap Norfal. We further wonder whether Jessamy's son may not be Sief's at all, but Donal's, and that it was this discovery that may have triggered a confrontation between the two men."

Khoren's jaw had dropped farther with each of Michon's disclosures, and his mind was whirling with the implications.

"But—you mentioned magic. Yet Donal Haldane—"

"The Haldane kings are capable of wielding power very like our own," said the woman seated next to Michon, "and without having to go through extensive training in order to access those powers. What they *do* require is the assistance of a Deryni—or so we have always believed."

"But, who—"

"We suspect that Jessamy may have been responsible," Barrett supplied, "but if she was *not,* we find this possibly even more alarming, because it would mean that there is another powerful Deryni at the Haldane court who is unknown to us. We aren't sure how the fathering of the child fits into this," he added, less confidently, "or even that we're right about its paternity. But Sief's body was examined, and signs of magical interference were found. From the king."

The implications of that alone, Khoren found staggering—that Donal Haldane had acquired sufficient power and knowledge to overcome a full Deryni as well trained as Sief must have been.

As to how he had acquired it—that, too, had sobering implications. The possibilities were equally frightening, if in different ways. If Jessamy had helped him, that was one thing; an unknown Deryni was another matter entirely, for it could possibly realign the entire balance of Deryni influence on a larger scale. And it occurred to Khoren to wonder whether Donal Haldane possibly could have done it on his own. . . .

Khoren shook his head, reluctant to believe any of it—though he had no reason to doubt what he was being told. Although, as a prince of Andelon, he had no direct interest in the affairs of Gwynedd, he was well aware that Gwynedd had long been a ground of contention between Deryni and the very much larger human population—legacy of a careless and often irresponsible interregnum in Gwynedd nearly two centuries before, set in place by Deryni invaders from Torenth to the east, which had triggered a vicious backlash against Deryni, once human rule was restored.

For a time, the violence had spilled over into the lands surrounding Gwynedd, so that even the more benevolent of Deryni rulers had been obliged to curtail much of their previous interaction with Gwynedd. Only recently had that begun to ease—though matters for Deryni in Gwynedd remained extremely delicate.

Given this background, and the incontrovertible fact that Sief's wife appeared to be involved in some sort of relationship with Donal of Gwynedd, Khoren decided that it was Jessamy who was the true key to this present situation. Though it would be useful to know how Donal had acquired access to his powers, the fact remained that he had them, he had used them to kill Sief MacAthan, and Jessamy had been present when he did it.

Most alarming of all was the prospect that the daughter of Lewys ap Norfal might have followed in the footsteps of her father, who had defied the Council's authority, for the Council had been a powerful check on many a would-be tyrant among ambitious Deryni. If Jessamy had, indeed, enabled Donal Haldane to best one of the finest Deryni minds known—for such Sief surely must have been, to be part of the Camberian Council—the implications were serious, indeed. And this was all apart from the possibility that she might have meddled with the succession of the ruling House of Haldane—who were human, but also something more, very like Deryni—by bearing a Haldane by-blow. . . .

Such a child would actually be a double threat, both a Haldane and a grandson of Lewys ap Norfal—and that, too, must be dealt with. He wondered whether it might be possible to steal away the child—for certainly, it would be dangerous in the extreme, to let him remain under his mother's influence, if he was, indeed, Donal Haldane's son. Indeed, if the boy *was* Donal's son . . .

"It may be necessary to kill the child," he found himself saying, somewhat to his horror. "If Donal Haldane has fathered a son on the daughter of Lewys ap Norfal, it cannot be allowed to reach maturity."

Chapter 6

"Two are better than one;

because they have a good reward for their labour."

—ECCLESIASTICUS 7:24

KHOREN'S flat statement only verbalized what the rest of them had been reluctant to voice. Though killing was not unknown to the Camberian Council, either to protect other Deryni or to thwart illicit activities by wayward exemplars of their race, it was usually in the context of defense or judicial execution, even if made to look like death by natural or accidental causes. To take the life of an innocent babe, even a potentially dangerous one, required a ruthlessness that was anathema to any civilized society. Further, it smacked of the policies of pitiless extermination that had characterized the years of Deryni persecution following the Haldane Restoration. Yet to let the child live only added to the possible danger, and made its eventual elimination all the more heart-wrenching for all concerned.

"What if the child is *not* Donal's?" Dominy murmured, looking as distressed as the rest of them felt. "And even if it is, it might not manifest potentials that would be dangerous. Surely we can afford to delay, until we know for certain."

The plea gave all of them an excuse to back down from any immediate decision, especially until the child could be examined. After further discussion, it was agreed that the matter might be tabled until Seisyll should return from Meara, since he had most ready access to the court. Michon, meanwhile, would linger in Rhemuth, on the chance that he might find opportunity to pursue the investigation.

"It only remains, then, to make a final decision about our vacant Council seat," Michon said, with a confirming glance at the others. "Khoren, as you undoubtedly have gathered, it is not our usual practice to immerse a new member in our affairs before certain oaths are sworn, but you have acquitted yourself well. May we assume that you are, indeed, willing to serve?"

Khoren flicked his gaze to each of them, in return, well aware of the extraordinary responsibility that went with agreement, then inclined his head.

"*Volo,*" he said. I am willing.

"Excellent," Michon said. "You are aware, of course, that those certain oaths will still be required of you."

"Of course."

"Tonight perhaps is not the best time," Vivienne said. "We have summoned you from a wedding feast, and the oaths by which we bind our number are best sworn . . . with a clearer head."

Khoren quirked her a grim smile.

"It's certain I've not been fasting," he said. "When would you prefer?"

Casually Oisín reached across to clasp Khoren's wrist, using the physical link to probe his degree of inebriation.

"It can be done in a few days," he said. "Meanwhile, I shall only remind you that what is discussed here goes not beyond these walls. One of us can bind you to that prohibition, but I think there is no need. You're aware what is at stake."

At Khoren's nod, both of acknowledgement and agreement, Oisín withdrew both his hand and the link.

"Perhaps a week, then, if we are all in agreement," Michon said. "You shall be given ample time to prepare."

And so it was agreed.

IN fact, several weeks passed before that task could be accomplished, though this changed nothing regarding access to Jessamy's infant son. Prince Khoren Vastouni was duly pledged to the Camberian Council at midsummer: a season that brought its own new worries for the court of Gwynedd.

At least the crises of that summer of 1082 were of a more common variety than what the Council feared. Negotiations in Meara continued to stall, and Seisyll Arilan's return along with them, but domestic matters throughout the Eleven Kingdoms gave increasing cause for more immediate concern.

Little rain had fallen for many months. As the verdant plains of Gwynedd dulled to gold and then to brown, farmers turned their energies to hay-making, which was abundant, but other crops began to suffer. And as a sultry June gave way to even fiercer heat in July, word came of the sudden illness of the queen's mother, Gwenaël, Sovereign Queen of Llannedd, beset by a canker of the breast.

Immediately Queen Richeldis made ready to depart for Llannedd, to attend on her mother during this time of crisis. Jessamy, though but lately recovered from childbed, made certain of her own inclusion in the queen's party, for the journey would provide a timely ploy to remove her from the court for a few weeks, hopefully beyond the reach of any of Sief's friends who might have suspicions about his death. Seisyll Arilan was safely removed in Meara, for the moment, and Michon de Courcy had not been seen at court since Krispin's christening, but she knew not what others might come sniffing around. It was somewhat worrisome that, if they did, Donal would be somewhat left to their mercy, should a connection somehow have been made between the king's presence and Sief's death; but after seeing him matched against Sief, she decided that Donal probably was well capable of looking after himself.

As for young Krispin, surely he could not be safer than in the royal nursery with Prince Brion. Whatever Sief's friends might think of *her*— and there was nothing whatever to link her with her husband's death, other than that she was present when it occurred—what part could a two-day-old babe have had in it? She knew that, later on, signs of his true paternity might start to emerge, to the consternation of her enemies; but not yet, and probably not for many years. No, for now it was safe enough to leave him—and infinitely safer for *her* to absent herself from closer scrutiny.

The queen's party sailed for Llannedd the day after receiving the news: Richeldis and Jessamy and four more of the queen's ladies, plus a handful of domestic servants from the royal household and a score of knights as escort, under command of Duke Richard Haldane. They went by royal barge as far as Concaradine, for it was thought that travel by water would be easier on the women than a journey overland, especially in the heat and with the queen still suffering from morning sickness.

But the weather remained sultry and hot, with nary a breath of air stirring as they made their slow progress downriver. Spirits wilted and tempers began to fray. At Concaradine, the party transferred to a royal galley, better suited for sea travel along the southern coast of Llannedd, but still with no wind to swell the sail. The men at the galley's sweeps suffered from the heat, and the river was sluggish, running low, making a navigation hazard of sandbars that ordinarily were well-covered.

Not until they were passing off Nyford did a light breeze at last rustle the galley's red canvas; even then, the heat hardly abated. But as they sailed at last into the bay below the Llanneddi capital of Pwyllheli, with Gwynedd's royal banner flying at the masthead, they could hear the muffled knell of the great cathedral bells tolling the passing of Queen Gwenaël.

Shock and grief, coupled with the heat, caused Queen Richeldis to miscarry, too soon even to determine the gender of the child. Beset with weeping, grieving over this dual loss, she lay despondent at Pwyllheli for several days, recovering physical health with the relative resilience of youth but less quick to heal in spirit.

"I should have been here for her," she told Jessamy that first night, in between disconsolate sobs. "She never even got to see little Brion, much less the child that I lost. And now Brion will never know his grandmama. She would have been so proud of him."

"Of a certainty, she would have been," Jessamy reassured her. "But remember that she is with God now, embraced in His love. And you would not have wished her suffering to continue. From all that you have told me of her, she was a good woman."

"She was," Richeldis whispered. She paused to dab at her eyes and blow her nose, then glanced uncertainly at Jessamy. "You believe that, don't you? That she is with God now."

"My faith tells me that she is," Jessamy replied. "Do you not believe it as well?"

Richeldis lowered her eyes, twisting her handkerchief in her hands. "I do," she said in a small voice. "I *must.* But you—Jessamy, you're Deryni. You *know,* don't you?"

Jessamy looked at her in some surprise, for she and the queen had never discussed what she was. She supposed that Donal must have told her.

"My lady, I—we have no special relationship with God, other than to believe that, like all His creatures, He made us and cares for us."

Richeldis glanced at her quickly, then dabbed at her eyes again. "You needn't deny it," she said. "I am not frightened of you. Well, perhaps I should be," she conceded. "The Church teaches that Deryni are evil; but I have never known you to do harm to anyone. And my husband trusts you implicitly, as he trusted your husband."

Jessamy glanced away, feeling vaguely guilty over the deceptions she and Donal had carried out, both by engendering young Krispin and for their part in Sief's death. But she told herself that both had been done in the service of Gwynedd, and therefore could involve no true betrayal of Gwynedd's queen.

"My lady, I have lived my life in service to the Crown of Gwynedd, as did my husband," she said honestly, "and I am more grateful than you can possibly know, for this expression of faith on your part. Would that others shared your tolerance and goodwill."

The queen ventured a tremulous smile, awkwardly reaching out to pat Jessamy's hand. The mother she had just lost had been but a few years older.

"Jessamy," she said in a steady voice, "sacred writ tells us that God made man a little lower than the angels. But I think that perhaps you Deryni lie somewhere in between." She glanced pointedly and a little defiantly toward the door. "If a priest were to hear me say that, I should probably be excommunicated, but that is what I believe."

"Then, you are one among few, my lady," Jessamy replied. "But bless you for saying it."

THE conversation seemed to ease the queen's grief, enough so that, two days later, she was able to face the emotional trial of her mother's funeral with a serenity beyond her seventeen years, dutifully walking with her brother and his wife as they escorted Queen Gwenaël's oak coffin into the royal vaults beneath the cathedral and laid her to rest in a tomb of porphyry, near to those that housed the remains of other sovereigns of Llannedd.

But one further duty remained to Richeldis before they might set out for home, and this she prepared to perform with a lighter heart. Her brother Illann was already king in neighboring Howicce, by right of their late father, for the two kingdoms had been separate until the marriage of Colman of Howicce and Gwenaël of Llannedd. Now Illann would take up the second crown as well, as had been his parents' intent; and being already anointed and crowned in Howicce, his accession in Llannedd would be marked by only a simple inauguration and enthronement, accompanied by the exchange of oaths of fealty with Llanneddi nobility. The presence of his sister, herself a queen, would lend added dignity to the occasion.

"Madam, it still seems to me curious, that your brother became King of Howicce when your father died," Jessamy said to Richeldis, as she and a lady-in-waiting called Megory arranged the dark coils of the queen's hair. Richeldis wore the white of royal mourning for her mother—and for the child she had lost—but the fine silk damask of her gown was sumptuous, embellished with her royal jewels, befitting the dignity of her brother's accession. "Your mother was still alive, and had been queen of both realms. If your parents' marriage was to have united the two kingdoms, I would have thought that your mother would then have ruled both kingdoms until she died—and *then* Illann would have inherited."

"So one would have thought," the queen said with a smile. She held a dark braid in place while Lady Megory pinned it. "But Howiccan law can be a little odd—or perhaps it's Llanneddi law that's odd, since it allows queens regnant. Few kingdoms do, you know. The *crowns* are now united in my brother Illann, but the kingdoms remain separate."

"That seems very strange, Madam," Lady Megory said. "What if you'd had no brothers? What would have happened to Howicce after your father died?"

"Since Howicce must be ruled by a king, I expect there

would have been a regency council, until I had a son," Richeldis replied matter-of-factly, tilting her head before the mirror to inspect her coiffure. "Actually, that son wouldn't be Prince Brion, because I probably wouldn't have been allowed to marry the king at all."

"Not married the king, Madam?" another of the ladies gasped, scandalized.

Richeldis shrugged. "Well, they couldn't have allowed Howicce to be swallowed up by another kingdom, Clarisse—and Brion *will* be King of Gwynedd some day. It wouldn't have done for him to be King of Howicce, too."

"I—suppose not," Clarisse said dazedly.

"No," Richeldis went on, "a regency council would have ruled Howicce until I'd had a male heir. Of course, my mother would have sat on that council. But instead of marrying the king, I would have been married off to some other likely prince who was not apt to become a king in his own right—and hopefully, we would have had sons. As it is, if something were to happen to my brother and all his brood, I expect that the Howiccan council would reach an agreement with the king whereby the Howiccan Crown would pass to a younger brother of Brion, once there was one, so that Howicce could have a separate king again."

"Then, that explains why you must do homage to your brother," Jessamy said, as she adjusted a gold circlet of Celtic interlace atop the queen's veil. "Because Prince Brion is the next heir after your brother and his sons," she added, for the benefit of the other ladies.

"Exactly correct," the queen agreed.

"But, Madam, what if—"

"Clarisse, don't worry," Richeldis interjected, smiling as she touched a reassuring hand to the younger woman's wrist. "It isn't likely to happen. My brother and his wife are breeding like rabbits, and God willing, Brion will have brothers. But if the male line *were* to fail, I suppose a regency council could—oh, elect a new king from among their number."

"Elect a king, Madam?" Lady Megory asked.

"Yes. Odd, isn't it? But that's Howiccan law for you."

"Odd, indeed," Jessamy agreed. "But I suppose it's all a matter of blood, in the end."

"Aye, it is."

The queen peered at her reflection once more, pinching her cheeks and twitching at a fold of her veil, then turned to smile resignedly at Jessamy and the others—all, save the two of them, gowned in the bright colors usual at court. Though Jessamy wore the black of conventional mourning, her gown was cut of rich brocade, embroidered with jet and crystal, and the narrow fillet of emeralds binding her black veil had come from the queen's own coffers.

"Goodness, would you look at us?" Richeldis said with a gentle laugh, catching up both of Jessamy's hands and glancing at the others. "We look like a pair of magpies, amid all these brightly colored songbirds! But Illann will thank us for our effort, I think." She released Jessamy's hands and made shooing motions toward the door. "Come, ladies. We must do Gwynedd proud."

Chapter 7

"Hast thou daughters? Have a care of their body, and show not thyself cheerful toward them."

—ECCLESIASTICUS 7:24

BACK in Rhemuth, during Jessamy's absence from court with the queen, the father of both their children paid regular visits to the royal nursery, where the boys were thriving. Prince Brion had reached his first birthday in June, and took his first steps shortly after the queen's party sailed for Llannedd. The baby Krispin would need a few years to catch up with his elder half-brother, but he was growing quickly. Given that the boy had lost his presumed father shortly after birth, and his mother and godmother were absent, no one thought it odd that Donal doted on Jessamy's child along with his royal heir.

Seisyll was not there to observe it, being still detained on the king's business in Meara. Nor could Michon gain ready access to the royal children, though he made several low-key appearances at court during those weeks, hoping for an opportunity—and eventually had to give it up. Had the boys been a few years older, beginning to engage in the activities of pages and the like, finding a few minutes' access would have been no very difficult matter; but the very young children of the royal nursery were rarely brought farther than the fastness of the castle's walled gardens, and then only in the company of many governesses and wet nurses. Further examination of Jessamy's son would simply have to wait until he was older, or until Jessamy herself could be persuaded to allow it, regardless of any suspicions the Council might entertain regarding this grandson of Lewys ap Norfal.

Meanwhile, the summer wore on—one of the hottest and driest in living memory. In Pwyllheli, as Queen Richeldis prepared for her brother's investiture as King of Llannedd, almost daily letters from her husband reported drought and falling river levels. In one that arrived the very day of the investiture, while the royal party was occupied at the cathedral, Donal declared his intention to move the royal household to his country estate at Nyford until the heat broke.

"Good heavens, he'll already be on his way by now," Richeldis said to Jessamy, as she read through the letter. "Listen to this.

"I bid you meet me at Carthanelle, rather than returning to Rhemuth," Donal had written, *"for the heat will be much eased, closer to the sea. I have taken this decision for the sake of Prince Brion, in particular. The royal nursery is stifling in the heat, and I cannot think that is good for small children. Nor would I subject them to the rigors of travel by horse-litter, which I must do if I wait too long and the river continues to fall. Already, the waters of the Eirian are near to impassable from Desse to Concaradine—though I have obtained several barges of very shallow draft that will still serve. You may tell the Lady Jessamy that her son will be traveling with the other children of the court, so she need not fear for his health. Both boys are well."*

The queen glanced up at Jessamy, who had bowed her head over folded hands.

"Be of good cheer, dear friend," the queen murmured, smiling as she handed the letter to Jessamy. "This means we shall be reunited with our sons all the sooner. Megory? Ladies?" she called, clapping her hands toward an open door for the rest of her women.

"Ladies, we shall be leaving as soon as can be arranged," she continued, as they began to appear. "The king summons us to Carthanelle—which will be a far more pleasant place to pass the rest of summer than Rhemuth. And he's bringing all the royal household—and the children."

This announcement elicited a flurry of happy speculation among the women, for several besides Jessamy and the queen herself had left young families behind in the capital, and now could look forward to an earlier reunion than had been thought. The prospect lent extra deftness to eager fingers, so that the royal party would have been ready to depart on the following day, except that King Illann asked his sister to stay a while longer, in the aftermath of his inauguration.

The royal galley finally departed Pwyllheli early in August, its limp sails augmented by the men at the sweeps as they skirted the Llanneddi coastline east and northward, into the sheltered waters of the Firth of Eirian. The sea was like glass, the air close and humid, but toward noon of the second day out of Pwyllheli, as they struck out across the estuary, the lookout sighted the chimneys and towers of Nyford town, slowly emerging from the heat-shimmer.

"Nyford ahead," he cried.

The ancient market town of Nyford possessed an anchorage rather than a true harbor, mostly concentrated within the further shelter where the River Lendour met the Eirian. Standing far forward on the galley's port side, Jessamy squinted up at the sun overhead, then returned her attention to the scattering of ships riding at anchor before the town. Most showed the colors of Gwynedd at masthead or bow, but some hailed from elsewhere. A few were drying sails aloft, but the air was very still. Indeed, only the faintest of breezes from the galley's own passage stirred the crimson-dyed canvas of its sail, painted with its Haldane Lion. Jessamy was lifting the edges of her black widow's veil to fan her face when the queen joined her, today gowned in the scarlet and gold of Gwynedd for her reunion with her husband.

"There are more ships here than I expected," Richeldis said.

"No doubt, because the king is here," Jessamy replied.

"Aye, that's probably true." Richeldis shaded her eyes with one hand to gaze more closely at two galleys tied next to one another. "It appears we have a visitor from the Hort of Orsal," she noted. "And can that be a Corwyn ship alongside?"

Somewhat surprised, Jessamy turned her gaze toward the two vessels, squinting against the brightness until she could, indeed, pick out the green and black of Corwyn trailing from the stern of one of the galleys—and Lendour's scarlet and white beside it, for Keryell Earl of Lendour was guardian and regent for his minor son Ahern, whose claim to the Duchy of Corwyn came through his mother. For now, however, the title of duke was a courtesy only, its authority held in abeyance until Ahern should reach the age of twenty-five, for the ducal line was Deryni, and allowed to be so, because Corwyn provided a strategic buffer between Gwynedd and Torenth to the east, and because the dukes of Corwyn, Deryni or no, had long been loyal to the kings of Gwynedd.

"I knew the mother of the young duke," Jessamy said wistfully.

"She died, didn't she?" Richeldis replied. "In childbed, wasn't it?"

"Not exactly," Jessamy said. "A pregnancy gone badly wrong, in its very early months—and she had never really recovered her health after she bore Ahern. He must be ten or twelve by now. But Keryell wanted another son. . . ."

The two fell silent at that, for both were well acquainted with the realities of dynastic duty and the cost it sometimes demanded. Just how high that cost could be was something that Jessamy hoped the young queen need never learn firsthand.

Slowly the galley glided to a halt a few cable-lengths from a cargo vessel with Bremagni markings, and the crew shipped their oars. The splash of a lowering anchor turned the women's attention toward the bow, where Duke Richard was overseeing the deployment of lines to secure the galley. Abaft, one of the junior squires was already aboard a small dinghy drawn alongside, and was fixing the queen's colors to a small flagstaff in the bow.

"It appears we shall be ready to go ashore very shortly," Richeldis said, turning back to Jessamy. "We'd best make ready. I can hardly wait to see the boys!"

A MOUNTED escort was waiting to conduct the queen's party up to the manor house in the hills above Nyford. On this August afternoon, Donal had sent the Duke of Cassan to meet them: the loyal Andrew McLain, of an age with the king, who was veteran of many a military foray in the company of king and royal duke. The duke's eldest son was one of the senior squires in the queen's party—Jared Earl of Kierney, due to be knighted at the next Twelfth Night—and he gave his father a cheerful nod as he took charge of the queen's horse, brought up by one of the men accompanying his father.

"Welcome home, your Majesty," Andrew said to the queen, as he made ready to help her mount. "I trust that my son has not disgraced his good name while in your service these past weeks."

"Indeed, he has not." Richeldis favored young Jared with an affectionate smile as she settled into the saddle. "You and Richard have trained up a noble company of squires." She gestured back toward the ships riding at anchor. "What visitors have we?"

With a lift of one eyebrow, Andrew turned his attention to adjusting one of the queen's stirrups, pointedly not looking up at Richeldis or any of the other women, and especially not Jessamy. "An envoy of the Hort of Orsal, your Majesty. And the Earl of Lendour is here, with his three children."

His tone was carefully neutral, here within Jessamy's hearing, but she could sense the wariness that it masked—and saw, by the flicker that passed across the queen's face, that Richeldis also recognized it. Unlike many at court, Andrew never allowed antipathy for the Deryni to color his courtesy, but it was also clear that his comment was meant as a guarded warning to the queen.

"I have heard that they are lovely children," Richeldis said quietly. "And Earl Keryell has ever been loyal and true to the House of Haldane."

"You know what they are, m'lady," Andrew murmured, in an even lower voice.

"Yes. Thank you, Duke Andrew." Richeldis gathered up her reins and shifted slightly in her saddle, deliberately turning her attention to Jessamy and the other women. "Come, ladies. I am eager to see my son, as I know the rest of you are eager to see yours. I am told that Prince Brion has taken his first steps, but I would wish to confirm that with my own eyes!"

WITHIN an hour they were entering the demesne of Carthanelle, the royal manor, perched on a hillside that overlooked the River Lendour and Nyford town and port, to the south. Long a summer residence for the dukes of Carthmoor, it was rarely used by the incumbent, the bachelor Richard, so King Donal and his family were wont to use it themselves. Though discreetly fortified, the house was set within walled parkland so extensive that it gave the illusion of being undefended, with fat cattle drowsing in the golden paddocks to either side of the long avenue approaching the house.

When the new arrivals had dismounted in the stable yard, one of Carthanelle's resident stewards was waiting to convey the queen and her ladies to the king. They found him relaxing with several of his gentlemen on a shaded terrace adjoining the formal gardens, tossing crusts of bread to a pair of peacocks. Beyond, dotted among the wide-spreading shade trees, a scattering of nursemaids and governesses were overseeing nearly a score of children, all of them under the age of ten.

"Over here, my dear," Donal called, standing and holding out a hand to Richeldis. "Lady Bronna, please bring Prince Brion," he added, to a neatly clad middle-aged woman not far away, who was holding both hands of a dark-haired toddler as he took a succession of wobbly legged steps.

With a glad cry, the young queen lifted the hem of her gown and ran across the lawn to sweep the toddler into a joyous hug, showering him with her kisses. At the same time, Jessamy espied her daughter Seffira and her own son's nurse, Mistress Anjelica, fussing over a large wicker basket, the four-year-old peering over her shoulder.

Allowing herself a somewhat more restrained smile than the queen's, Jessamy made her way across the lawn at a pace more appropriate to the heat and her age and slipped an arm around her daughter to kiss her, also sinking to her knees beside the nurse.

"Hello, darling, have you been a good girl while Mummy was away?"

"*Maman,* you're back!" Seffira squealed, twisting to throw both arms around her mother's neck and bestow a noisy kiss. "I've missed you terribly. And look how big Krispin has got!"

"Yes, I can see that," Jessamy replied, nodding to Anjelica, who smiled as she gathered up the infant and laid him in his mother's arms. "My goodness, you two have done a wonderful job while I've been away."

"Jesiana helped, too," Seffira admitted, "but I did a lot, didn't I, Tante Jeli?"

"Indeed, you did," Anjelica agreed. "He's a good baby, m'lady. "Sleeps through the night, and hardly ever fusses."

"I am glad to hear it," Jessamy replied.

Quickly she inspected her son, briefly probing the tiny mind, then settled on the edge of a fountain with Seffira beside her, the babe laid across her knees. Across the lawn, the queen had shifted Prince Brion onto her hip as she and Donal spoke with a tall, sandy-haired man of middle years, brightly clad in red and white, who was standing with a protective hand on the shoulder of a lad she judged to be eleven or twelve. Two retainers in the green and black of Corwyn hovered nearby, along with a matronly woman in russet and a thin, ascetic-looking man in vaguely Eastern-looking priest's robes and a flat-topped hat.

"Anjelica," Jessamy said in a low voice, beckoning the nurse back to her side, "do you know who that man is, with their Majesties?"

"The Earl of Lendour, m'lady, and his son and heir."

"I thought as much," Jessamy replied, nodding. "Do you know what brings him here?"

"Aye, m'lady. He has brought his daughters as well, to be fostered to the queen's household. I believe he intends that they should also spend a year or two at the same convent where your daughter resides."

Jessamy nodded thoughtfully. "That will be Alyce and Marie. Goodness, I've hardly seen those children since their mother died. Where are they, Anjelica?"

"There, m'lady, under the lilac tree with Lady Jesiana."

Affecting only casual interest, Jessamy turned her gaze in the direction indicated by her maid, far across the lawns, to where three young girls were chattering with a pair of handsome, somewhat older squires, all of them seated on the shady grass and with the girls' bright skirts spread like blossoms. The youngest of the girls was her own Jesiana, the nine-year-old, dark curls loosely tied back by a yellow ribbon.

The other two were clearly older, but not by much. One was fair and delicate of feature, golden hair tumbling around her shoulders and bound across the brow with a rose-pink ribbon-fillet that matched her simple gown; the other, clad in tender leaf-green, had hair more resembling bronze. Seeing them there, all full of hope and youthful innocence, Jessamy was reminded of a similar pair of girls in a similar season, that dreadful summer of her own passing into adolescence, when her father had died and everything in her life had changed.

That long-ago summer had borne Jessamy betimes into marriage and motherhood—estates that had come somewhat later to that other girl, the heiress Stevana de Corwyn: eventually abducted and married by force to the man now standing with their son and heir, young Ahern. (The boy was, in fact, a twin to young Marie—Stevana's second set, though Alyce's twin very sadly had died shortly after birth.) In the early years, when both their families were young, Jessamy had visited her friend as often as she could, and had brushed the minds of all three Corwyn children. The two women had remained friends until the day Stevana died, miscarried of yet another set of twins that would have been more boys for Corwyn's line—but sadly, not meant to be.

Jessamy had seen Stevana's surviving children but rarely in the years since then, but she was heartened to see that they appeared to be growing into handsome young adults—and now, apparently, were being prepared to enter the adult roles to which their birth entitled them.

Thoughtful, Jessamy handed young Krispin back into the care of Seffira and his nurse and rose, smoothing her skirts as she made her way toward the lilac tree. The squires, who were wearing the livery of Lendour, scrambled to their feet at her approach, as did the girls, and Jesiana darted into her mother's embrace with a glad cry.

"*Maman!* We saw your ship this morning, from the tower atop the house!"

"Yes, well, there was very little wind," Jessamy replied, kissing her daughter's cheek and nodding acknowledgment to the older girls' curtsies and the bows of the two squires. "Young sirs, should you not be about your duties?" she said mildly to the latter.

The pair took their leave with alacrity, to the obvious regret of the girls, and Jessamy opened her arms to Stevana's daughters.

"Dear Alyce, and darling Marie, come and give your Tante Jessamy a kiss," she said. "Do you not remember me? Your mother and I were of an age with you when first we met. She was like the sister I had never had."

Relieved recognition lit both young faces, and the girls crowded eagerly into her embrace.

"Of course we remember!" said the shorter of the two, the one with bronze-colored hair, as she bestowed a kiss on Jessamy's cheek.

The blonder one simply laid her head briefly against Jessamy's shoulder and breathed a sigh of contentment.

"My, but you *have* turned into quite the beauties," Jessamy said, drawing back to look at them. "Alyce, you are the image of your dear mother. And Marie . . . lovely. Simply lovely. Stevana would be so proud of you."

Alyce nodded her blond head. "Would that Papa agreed. He intends to marry again. Unfortunately, his intended bride does not like the idea of grown stepdaughters," she said bleakly.

"She's very vain," Marie chimed in, with a wrinkle of her tip-tilted nose. "We don't much like her."

"I see," Jessamy said, containing a smile of gentle amusement at Alyce's description of the two of them as "grown." But she could sympathize with the girls' recognition of their incipient stepmother's resentment. "Jesiana, why don't you go and see if your sister and Mistress Anjelica need help with Krispin?"

"Yes, *Maman*."

As the younger girl dipped her a curtsy and headed off at her mother's bidding, Jessamy drew Stevana's daughters farther under the shade of the lilac tree and sank down, patting the cool grass beside her.

"Sit down, my dears. I understand that you are to be fostered at court."

Marie's rosy lips parted in amazement.

"How did you know? You've only just got here."

"It often happens," Jessamy replied, not unkindly. "Do keep your voice down, child. Your father's new wife will wish to establish her own children in their father's affections. It is the natural wish of any mother."

"She shall not have our brother's title for her own sons, no matter *what* she does!" Alyce said in a fierce whisper.

"Of course she shall not," Jessamy agreed, patting her

hand. "Your brother shall be Duke of Corwyn by right of your dear mother. Nothing can change that. In due time, he also shall be Earl of Lendour, for that is the right of your father's eldest son. And if, by chance, dear Ahern were to form an affection for a half-brother by this new marriage of your father's, it would be his right to decline the secondary title in favor of his brother—but that would be *his* decision, and no other's.

"As for you"—she drew the two of them into her embrace again—"your father does you a great service as well, by fostering you to court, for brilliant marriages can be made for the sisters of the next Duke of Corwyn."

"Aye, to some whiskered old graybeard who only wants our dowries," Marie pouted, as Alyce made a moue. "I want to marry for love!"

Jessamy regarded them with sympathy, but it would do no good to pretend that their station did not carry duties and responsibilities.

"Of course you do," she agreed. "But being who and what you are, that may not be possible." She cast a quick glance around to be certain she could not be overheard. "Even were you merely human, your ducal bloodline would demand that you marry to a certain station—that, else take the veil—and that you may not do until and unless your brother produces an heir."

Alyce lowered her gaze, shaking her head bleakly. "It matters little. I have no call to the religious life—and Marie certainly does not."

"I did not suppose that either of you did, child," Jessamy replied. "That grace is given to few—though I am told that you are to spend some time in the convent to finish your education. Don't pout; you may find that a very rewarding time. I understand that you are to go to Notre Dame d'Arc-en-Ciel—Our Lady of the Rainbow. It is just north of Rhemuth. Did you know that one of my daughters resides there?"

Marie looked startled, and Alyce's jaw dropped.

"She does?"

"Aye, my second daughter Jessilde—or Sister Iris Jessilde, as she is now called. She has found great contentment there."

Alyce bit at her lower lip, clearly taken aback.

"If she has a true vocation, then I am glad for her," she

murmured, "though I cannot imagine it is a comfortable place for those of our kind."

"Actually," Jessamy said, with another glance over her shoulder, "the Church is quite happy for *women* of our kind to take up the religious life. Shut away in a convent, we are unlikely to reproduce more of our race." At the girls' scandalized expressions, she added, "You needn't look shocked, my dears. It does happen. Not all are able keep a vow of chastity. But such a life does have its compensations, of course. A cloister provides safety, sustenance, and ample time for study and contemplation. There are far worse fates."

After a pause, Alyce whispered, "Mother told me how you were forced to marry when you were near our age. Will the king force *us* to marry so young, do you think?"

"I shall do my best to see that he does not," Jessamy replied. "He will certainly weigh any prospect of your marriages with great care. Never forget that, as Deryni and the sisters of a future duke, your continued existence will always be, first and foremost, a matter of expedience. I cannot stress enough the narrow knife-edge upon which all those of our race are forever balanced—and any stumble could mean your deaths, or the deaths of others.

"But be of good cheer," she added, at their glum expressions. "I cannot promise regarding the demands of state, of course, but I count myself fortunate that both their Majesties regard me as a friend as well as a servant of the court."

"The queen looks a kind woman," Marie said hopefully.

"Darlings, she is hardly more than a girl like you, for all that she is already a mother," Jessamy reminded them, laughing gently. "She was not yet fifteen when she married the king, and she conceived almost at once. Come November, she will be but seventeen. But—you've not yet been presented to her, have you? Of course you have not; we've only just arrived."

The two girls shook their heads, eyes wide.

"Then, come, you must make her acquaintance," Jessamy went on, as the three of them got to their feet. "She will be glad of company closer to her own age. Most of us in the royal household served one or both of the queens before her, and are old enough to be her mother—or yours. And the young men at court will adore you."

Smiling encouragement as she moved between them, Jessamy shepherded them back toward where the queen and Prince Brion's nurse had taken over the glad occupation of leading the young prince in a few halting steps, his little hands supported from either side. The king had drawn apart with Earl Keryell and his son for earnest discussion, but kept glancing back at his son.

Brion was a sturdy, handsome child, with clear gray eyes and a shock of straight, silky black hair cut short across the forehead and all around his head in imitation of his father's. On hearing his happy chortle, Donal turned and crouched to hold out both hands, beckoning for Brion to come to him. With an exultant squeal, the boy let go of both supporting hands and toddled confidently into the arms of his sire.

"Jessamy, would you look?" the queen cried, looking up at her and the demoiselles de Corwyn. "My little man is walking! I can't believe how much he's grown while we were away. It has only been a few weeks."

Jessamy smiled. "He has, indeed, grown, Majesty. A proper prince he is."

"I see that your Krispin thrives as well," Richeldis observed, with a glance toward the baby's basket. "He's a fine, fat babe! And who are these pretty maids?" she added, jutting her chin at the girls.

"Majesty, these are Earl Keryell's daughters, Lady Alyce—and Lady Marie." The girls made grave curtsies as their names were spoken. "They tell me that their father wishes to foster them to court."

"So the king has informed me," the queen replied, leaving Brion to his nurse as she came to let the girls kiss her hand. "Ladies, you are most welcome—and you mustn't be afraid of his Majesty," she added, in a conspiratorial whisper. "If he sometimes seems gruff, it is only because he cares so much for all those under his protection. I hope you will be very happy as part of my court."

The girls curtsied again, eyes wide as saucers, and Richeldis gave a gentle laugh.

"You needn't look so serious. I'm sure we shall be good friends. Since you already know Lady Jessamy, I shall place you in her charge—if that is agreeable to you?" she added, with a glance at Jessamy.

"I shall regard them as my own daughters, Majesty," Jessamy replied. "I am certain they will prove a credit to your Majesty's household."

"I am certain they shall," the queen agreed, with a nod of dismissal to the three of them as she returned her regard to her son.

Thus did the demoiselles de Corwyn begin their life at the court of the King and Queen of Gwynedd.

Chapter 8

"The elder women as mothers;

the younger as sisters, with all purity."

—I TIMOTHY 5:2

KERYELL Earl of Lendour departed for his own lands on the day following the queen's arrival at Carthanelle, taking with him his son and household and leaving his daughters behind.

The king bade him farewell at the great hall steps, his heir in his arms and his queen at his side, and sent him on his way with the Duke of Cassan and his own brother for escort. Alyce and Marie were permitted to accompany them as far as the harbor for a final adieu, riding with their brother and the two squires, but that only made the final parting more difficult, as they kissed father and brother good-bye and watched their galley sail out of Nyford.

They were in tears for most of the ride back to Carthanelle, though both dukes tried to cajole their young charges into better spirits. Alyce had mostly contained her misery by the time they got back, but Marie was less successful. They ate little at supper, and Marie cried herself to sleep that night, seeking comfort in her elder sister's arms, but finding it only in the stuffed dog that one of the children thrust at her after supper, seeing her sadness.

The royal household remained at Carthanelle until mid-October, when the weather finally broke. Meanwhile, the heat kept tempers short and often frayed. Though both demoiselles de Corwyn were dreadfully homesick for the first few days, they tried gamely to take their minds from their misery by pitching in with the care of the children of the household, and gradually succeeded. The little girl who had given Marie the stuffed dog, a daughter of one of the queen's ladies, developed a particular affection for both girls, and often came to climb onto one of their laps and beg for a story, when she was not trying to coax a smile from them with her winsome antics.

The other children soon followed suit, particularly Prince Brion. At least with the children, both Alyce and Marie soon made themselves favorite playmates, for they were hardly more than children themselves.

They were less successful with the children's mothers, though Jessamy and her daughters did their best to make the newcomers feel welcome, as did the queen. But the other women were caught up in their own concerns, and remained mostly aloof. It was a pattern that would repeat itself often, as the two girls gradually moved farther and farther from the life they had known in their father's house.

The change of weather, when it finally came, was marked by more than a week of solid rain, when very little moved. It heralded a flurry of preparations for the journey back to Rhemuth, made more exasperating by bored children underfoot, cranky at being kept indoors, and by grown men grumbling about the rain, eager to be on their way. The king was as bad as any of them.

But finally came word that the river again was running at near-normal levels, fit for the royal barges to make their way back up the Eirian to Rhemuth. The trip northward was hardly better than being cooped up at Carthanelle, for each day still saw at least one deluge, but at least the scenery was different, and the rain was good for the land. Alyce tried to remember that, on the day they docked at Desse and switched to horses and litters to complete the journey to the capital. Rhemuth Castle proved to be damp and chill after weeks of rain, and it was growing colder as autumn began giving way to winter.

One reprieve they were granted: that their convent education should not commence until after the festivities of Christmas and Twelfth Night court, which were fast approaching. This was a mixed blessing, for the foothold they had gained while resident at Carthanelle was soon swallowed up in the expanded court that dwelt year-round in Rhemuth.

Marie coped by casting her lot with the other children, all younger than herself, letting herself be swept up in their festal preparations. Alyce, a year older, found herself caught in a curious limbo, no longer a child but not yet a woman, unable to fully embrace either state—and owing to the transitory nature of her residence at court, few made much effort to get acquainted or to help her through it. The queen herself was probably closest to Alyce in age, but her young son and her own duties occupied most of her available time and energy.

As autumn gave way to winter, the weeks of Advent seemed to stretch forever, as cheerless as the shortening winter days. But for Alyce, this time of preparation for the birth of the Christmas King also marked the necessary shift in her frame of mind. The solemnities of Christmas brought a kind of respite, as she dutifully turned her thoughts to the wondrous birth in Bethlehem, and she found herself becoming caught up in some of the excitement as Twelfth Night approached, the most important court in the cycle of the year.

It would be her first at the Haldane court, made all the more special because it would mark the knighting of two of her father's squires, sent from Lendour to receive the accolade from the king's own hand. The two honorees were friends of her childhood: Sé Trelawney and Jovett Chandos, the squires who had had been with her father's party at Carthanelle. Since the conferral of this honor had been set long before Keryell Earl of Lendour decided to take a new wife at Twelfth Night, he had delegated his elder daughter to stand witness in his stead, with her hand on the sword with that of the king, and had directed that she and her sister should perform the office of investing the two young men with the white belts of their knighthood.

"Ahern said to tell you that he would far rather have been here with us," the newly dubbed Sir Sé Trelawney told her that evening, seated beside her at the feast following the court. Marie had started out sitting on his other side, but had moved to sit with Jesiana.

Alyce rolled her eyes and gave him a sidelong glance as he passed her a platter of fine manchet bread, saying nothing as she took a thick slice and started tearing out the soft center. Both Sé and Jovett were Deryni, though not known to be so, and Sé was well aware of her feelings about the wedding festivities no doubt in progress back at Castle Cynfyn—and Ahern's feelings as well.

"She will probably be wearing our mother's jewels!" she muttered so that only Sé could hear her.

"She will be sleeping in your mother's *bed,*" he returned, in the same low tone. "But there's nothing you or I or anyone can do about that. It's what your father wants."

"I suppose." Alyce had been squeezing the wad of doughy bread into a ball, and she pressed it between her palms to form a flattened patty before tearing it into quarters. Across from Sé, the other new-made knight, Sir Jovett, was watching her curiously, and she caught his eye as she reached across Sé to hand each of them one of the pieces.

"Friends forever!" she whispered, very deliberately putting the third piece in her mouth and chewing.

"Friends forever!" they answered, doing as she had done.

"And take this last piece to my brother," she added, placing the remaining quarter in Sé's hand. "Make him the same pledge."

"I will," Sé promised, and slipped it into a pouch at his belt.

Alyce glanced toward the center dais, where the king and queen sat flanked by several of their great lords and their wives, and sighed.

"I wish Ahern could have come," she said in a low voice. "He would have liked this *much* more. Sé, you and Jovett *will* write to me, won't you? I've missed both of you so much already!"

"Of course we'll write," Sé assured her. "And better than that, I think your father intends to send someone at intervals to continue your training—probably Father Paschal. If we can, we'll try to persuade him that Jovett and I should be his escorts. Not that *we'll* get to see much of you, with you in the convent. But at least we can bring you letters in person."

Alyce smiled shyly, lowering her blue gaze. "Thank you—both of you. At least I'll have *something* to look forward to."

But the brief respite of the presence of friends from home was not to last. The orders of Keryell Earl of Lendour required the two young knights to depart the following morning, with but scant time to bid his daughters a proper farewell.

"Ahern wants us back as well," Sé told Alyce, as he and Jovett waited for the grooms to finish saddling their horses. "It won't be easy for him either, you know."

"You'll make sure he's careful, won't you?" she said to both of them, not voicing the concerns they had shared with her about the new lady of Cynfyn.

"You needn't worry, little one," Jovett said fondly. "We'll look after him."

THE drab, dreary days of winter seemed even more oppressive, once the two left. Alyce pined for several days, knowing that it was only a matter of time before she and Marie were sent away. Jessamy did her best to see that her young charges were included in appropriate activities, along with her own children, but Alyce found that the turning of the new year only marked the uncertainty of what lay ahead.

It was mid-January when the dreaded summons came from the queen. The two sisters had found an abiding affinity with young Prince Brion, and he with them, so they were inclined to spend many of their waking hours playing with him and minding Krispin, who was a mellow, contented baby. On that fateful morning, Jessamy came to fetch them from the solar, where the two of them were sprawled before the fireplace with Jesiana, Krispin in his basket between them, watching Brion tussle with a chubby hound puppy. Krispin was chewing on the ear of a stuffed toy that might once have been a cat or rabbit.

"Alyce, Marie, the queen wishes to see you," Jessamy said, as all three girls scrambled dutifully to their feet and Jesiana came to give her a hug. "Go now, please. She's in her bedchamber. I'll stay with the boys."

Both girls hurriedly adjusted their clothing and inspected one another's hair and faces, Alyce brushing at a wayward curl escaping from her sister's ribbon-fillet.

"Do you know what it's about?" she asked.

Jessamy inclined her head. "I do—though I think it will not please you overmuch. The queen informs me that you are to go this week to Arc-en-Ciel. Probably in the next day or two."

Alyce thought she had hid her dismay reasonably well, but Jessamy came to tilt her chin up slightly, also giving Marie a hug.

"You needn't look so glum," she said with a chuckle. "A convent education has much to recommend it; and Arc-en-Ciel is better than most. I would not let you be sent there, if I did not approve."

The sisters exchanged dubious glances.

"*Must* we go there, Tante Jessamy?" Alyce said in a low voice.

"I'm afraid you must," Jessamy replied. "The nuns can teach you a great deal. Their discipline is firm, but their devotion to the Blessed Lady is sound, and their confessors seem tolerant of our race—so long as one does not flaunt one's powers, of course. My daughter has found it quite satisfactory."

"Has she a true call to the religious life?" Marie asked doubtfully.

"Of course. At least she assures me that she does. This is not to say that all who take the veil have a genuine vocation; indeed, some are even forced to do so, as we all know well.

"But that will not be your case, I assure you. You will find that most of the girls in the school are gently born, come there to learn the gentle arts and skills expected of noble wives and mothers. Believe me, there are far worse fates. I was younger than you when I was married off to a man old enough to be my father. The king hopes to spare you that—as does your father."

"I think I remember Uncle Sief," Alyce said quietly, after a reflective pause. "If the choice had been yours, would you have taken the veil rather than marry him?"

Jessamy shrugged, smiling thinly. "I was *not* given the choice," she said. "But I cannot say that I regret my children—who would be very different people, if a different father had been theirs. As for my marriage—" She shrugged. "It was no better or worse than most. Sief was not a *bad* man. And I have the old queen to thank for the fact that I was spared the marriage bed for the first few years, allowed to finish my girlhood in the household of dear Queen Dulchesse.

Service to Gwynedd's queens has brought me a great deal of satisfaction."

Neither girl answered that comment, only bobbing dutiful curtsies before taking their leave.

"It won't be that bad, Mares," Alyce murmured to her sister as they walked, laying an arm around her shoulders. "Think of all we can learn. And we'll be safe for the next few years."

Marie merely bit at her lip and said nothing as the pair of them made their way to the queen's chambers.

THEY found Queen Richeldis seated before the fire in her boudoir, well-wrapped up in a fur-lined robe. Two maids were combing the tangles from her long black hair, recently washed, and her face was aglow from the warmth of the fire—and not alone from that, for she was breeding again, though she bore this pregnancy with far less discomfort than that of Brion or the ill-fated child lost in Pwyllheli.

"You sent for us, Majesty?" Alyce asked, dipping in a curtsy.

"Dear Alyce . . . Marie . . . come sit by the fire," the queen replied, indicating a place in the fur rug at her feet. "You may leave us," she added, dismissing the maids.

"Ladies, I have news for you that brings me little joy," she said, when the maids had gone. "The king has decided that it's time you took up your studies at Arc-en-Ciel. If the weather holds, you're to go tomorrow."

"So soon?" Marie blurted, falling silent at her sister's sharp glance.

"Pray, pardon my sister, Madam," Alyce said hastily, taking her sister's hand. "We know that this but fulfills our father's wishes—and we are grateful that we were permitted to stay at court until after the feasts of Christmas and the new year."

"Yes, well, you did turn many a young man's head during the festivities," Richeldis observed with a droll smile. "And not a few old men's heads as well, I am told. I suggest that you view your time at the convent as welcome respite from the marriage mart. And you needn't pack your lovely court gowns. The girls at Arc-en-Ciel wear a form of the order's habit. It's tidy and warm and saves squabbling over whose gown is prettiest. Believe me, this is useful. I spent some time in a convent school myself."

"In Llannedd, Madam?" Alyce dared to ask.

Richeldis inclined her head. "Ladies destined for noble husbands must learn reading and writing and ciphering as well as the domestic arts necessary for running a great lord's household. I hope you will make the most of your time there. Jessamy's daughter will befriend you, I'm sure."

"But, she's a *nun,*" Marie said doubtfully.

"That's true," Richeldis agreed, smiling, "but she isn't a very *old* nun; I've met her. Not so many years ago, she was a girl just like you. Do give her a chance—both of you. You will need a friend there."

The slight waver in the queen's final words reminded Alyce that Deryni like herself and Marie would, indeed, need a friend within the constricted atmosphere of convent life, and she bowed her head briefly.

"I shall miss the children," she said quietly.

"And they shall miss *you,*" Richeldis replied. "And *I* shall miss you!" She rolled her eyes in mock exasperation. "In truth, I almost envy you. Most of my other ladies are *decades* older than I. Your presence at court has taken me back to more carefree days of my own girlhood."

"It has?" Marie said, brightening.

"It has!" The queen hugged the younger girl briefly around the shoulders and smiled. "You'd best be off now. I'm sure you'll wish to take a few things with you. And it will be an early start in the morning, I'm sure. The king wastes no time, once he's made a decision."

THAT night, the two of them supped in the nursery with Jessamy and her children, after which Jessamy helped them select what to pack for the morrow. Later, when huddled beneath their sleeping furs and coverlets in the bed they shared, the sisters conferred about the future.

"What will it be like, do you think?" Marie whispered. "Will the nuns be very strict?"

"I don't know," Alyce admitted. "But Lady Megory says that Tante Jessamy's daughter likes it there."

Marie's snort managed to convey both acknowledgement and skepticism.

"I don't want to wear a habit!" she said after a short silence.

"Well, we must," Alyce replied. "Think of it as camouflage, so that we'll blend in with the other girls," she added. "But Tante Jessamy says we don't have to wear the wimple."

"Thank God for that!" Marie retorted. "What do you suppose they'll teach us?"

"Not what we'd like to learn, I'll warrant!" Alyce said with a snicker. "Father wants us to learn lady-things, like fine needlework. And I think he hopes that Tante Jessamy will teach us some of the other things we do want to learn."

"She has to be careful, though," Marie said. "Even with the king as her patron, she daren't be open about what she is."

"No, and we mustn't be, either," Alyce replied. "Promise me you'll be discreet, Mares."

"I'll certainly try," Marie agreed. "Oh, Alyce, what's to become of us?"

Alyce merely hugged her sister close, for there was no answer to that question. Come the morrow, they would know all too well, for better or for worse.

ALYCE had feared she would not sleep at all, as visions of what might be danced behind her closed eyelids, but all too soon, Mistress Anjelica was shaking her to wakefulness, a candle in her hand.

"Wake you now, little ones," she murmured. "You'll want something warm in your stomachs before you ride out into the cold. At least it looks to be a fine day dawning."

It was, indeed, a fine day, once the sun came up—bright and sunny, if very cold. The king had assigned a ginger-haired young knight called Sir Jiri Redfearn to escort them, along with half a dozen of the household guard. Jessamy had decided to bring along her nine-year-old, for a surprise visit with her sister. A maid also rode with them, for they would stay the night in the convent's guest house, and a manservant to manage the single pack horse.

Their little cavalcade was on its way not long after first light, wending its way northward along the east bank of the river, past the seminary called Arx Fidei, and then into the foothills. They rode slowly, perhaps in deference to Jessamy, for though fit enough, she was of an age to be mother of all of them save the maid and the manservant.

The short winter day was drawing to a close as their party crested a hill and came, at last, within sight of the convent's bell tower. The gold of the dying sun kissed the snow before the barred convent gates, and shone in rainbow shimmers on the mist beginning to rise as the day's warmth faded and the shadows lengthened. As they picked their way down that last slope toward the entrance, a bell was ringing out one of the afternoon offices.

"There it is, my dears," Jessamy announced. "Notre Dame d'Arc-en-Ciel, the royal convent of our Lady of the Rainbow. The order began in Bremagne, did you know?"

When both her young charges shook their heads, Jessamy continued affably.

"Well, then. Its foundation dates back several centuries, to the site of a very ancient holy well now contained within the grounds of the Mother House at Fessy, near Remigny. The well had long been a place of popular devotion, perhaps even pre-Christian, but one spring afternoon, after a very emphatic rain shower, an apparition of our Blessed Lady appeared from within a rainbow. It was witnessed by three young girls of noble family who had stopped to pray for a sign regarding whom they should wed."

"What kind of an apparition?" Marie wanted to know. "What did it look like?"

"Well, it's said that our Lady appeared as a young woman little older than yourselves," Jessamy replied, "arrayed in a sky-blue robe and veil and clasping a rainbow around her shoulders like a shining mantle. No one knows precisely what she told them, but within two or three years, they had gained the support of the Archbishop of Remigny and had persuaded the king to give them a generous endowment of land just outside the city, where they established a convent for the domestic education of young ladies of gentle birth.

"For their habit, they adopted the pale blue of the apparition's robes, with a white wimple and a band of rainbow edging to the veil. The vowed sisters wear it on a blue veil, and also on the bottom of the scapular—which is a sort of tabard or apron—and novices take a white veil with rainbow edging, but you'll wear neither—though you *will* wear the blue habit. Those who come for the school do not take binding vows, of course. Like you, they come for finishing as proper ladies, though some do stay—which you will not. But this will be a sheltered place for you to spend your next few years. I promise I shall stay in touch regularly."

They had reached the convent gate by now, whose arch displayed a rainbow picked out in mosaic tiles, and Jessamy bent to pull a tasseled rope that rang a bell within. Almost immediately, a tiny aperture opened at eye-level and a pair of hazel eyes peered out.

"Blessings upon all who come in peace," a musical voice said. "How may I assist you?"

"I am Lady Jessamy MacAthan, mother of Sister Iris Jessilde, and I bring two new students seeking refuge beneath the Rainbow," Jessamy said easily.

"Under our Lady's grace, all who seek shall find such refuge," the voice replied. "A moment, if you please."

The aperture closed, they heard the sounds of thumping, of metal against metal as a bar was withdrawn, and then a wicket gate opened in the larger door, just high enough for a single rider to enter, crouched down. Drawing aside, Jessamy nodded to her daughter, who urged her pony through the opening, then gestured for Alyce and Marie to follow. Except by special permission, men were not permitted within the walls of Arc-en-Ciel, so their escort would retire to lodgings in the nearby village for the night. Meanwhile, Jessamy and the maid followed behind Alyce, Marie, and Jesiana, and the servant with the pack horse gave its lead over to a nun who led it through the doorway.

Inside, Jesiana was already off her pony and hurtling toward a slight figure in blue robes and the rainbow-edged white veil of a novice. Three more blue-robed women were waiting a little beyond, on the bottom step leading up to the chapel door, all wearing the sky-blue veil of professed sisters. The one in the center, a handsome woman of indeterminate years, also wore a silver pectoral cross.

"Welcome back to Arc-en-Ciel, dear Jessamy," she said quietly, holding out both her hands in greeting. "And these must be the two demoiselles of whom you wrote."

"They are, Reverend Mother," Jessamy replied, dismounting. "And thank you for meeting us in person."

She went and bent to kiss the woman's hand and then embrace her. Alyce and Marie also got down from their ponies, coming shyly forward as Jessamy beckoned.

"Mother, these are Alyce and Marie de Corwyn, daughters of the Earl of Lendour," Jessamy said, with a sweep of her hand. "Girls, this is Mother Iris Judiana, in whose charge you will be for the next several years."

Dutifully Alyce and Marie came forward to dip in pretty curtsies and kiss the mother superior's hand, earning them a faint smile of apparent approval.

"I bid you welcome, dear daughters," said Iris Judiana. "Sister Iris Rose will take you to the robing room, where you may clothe yourselves in the habit of our order. We shall meet you in the chapel shortly, where you will be enrolled beneath the Rainbow. Jessamy, I believe your Jesiana has already gone with her sister to the parlor. You are welcome to join them for a few minutes, if you wish, while the girls prepare themselves. I believe you know the way."

"Yes, Mother, thank you."

With a nod to the mother superior and a wink to Alyce and Marie, Jessamy hurried off in the direction her daughter had disappeared. At the same time, the novice called Iris Rose gave the newcomers a shy smile and indicated that they should follow, conducting her charges silently into the cloister enclosure. Passage along a short stretch of corridor paved with encaustic tiles in cream and blue brought them at last to an arched door whose rounded door case had been painted like a rainbow.

"In here, please," Iris Rose murmured, finally speaking, as she opened the door and stood aside to let them enter.

The robing room was cozy and warm, near to the parlor where visitors were received, and had its own fireplace and several screens to provide for the modesty of those who used it. Several robes of pale blue wool were laid out on a table before the fire, along with a folded stack of white wool undergowns and a pair of cinctures plaited of different-colored cords of rainbow hues. Fingering the lining of a dark blue mantle draped over a corner of one of the screens, Alyce decided that the fur was rabbit, or possibly squirrel. Not so sumptuous as the fox-lined cloaks she and Marie wore at present, but clearly the sisters of the rainbow did not intend their votaries to freeze to death.

"May I assist you with those?" Iris Rose asked, lifting tentative hands toward the cloak Alyce had started to unfasten at the throat. "Oh,'tis heavy as well!"

She hugged the cloak against her body as she gathered up its folds, letting out a faint sigh as her appreciative gaze took in the fine gown of forest green wool beneath, and the deep blue one that Marie wore.

"Ah, me, I fear our habits are not nearly so elegant as the gowns to which you must be accustomed," she sighed. "But we believe they are pleasing to our Lady," she added, lifting her chin in faint challenge for Alyce to say otherwise.

"No, I'm sure the habits are quite suitable," Alyce said diplomatically, as she picked up one of the blue gowns and held it against herself to measure its length.

"You'll find several different lengths and sizes to choose from," Iris Rose said helpfully. "We never know what our new postulants will look like."

"We aren't postulants," Marie said briskly, shaking out one of the under-gowns. "We've come as students."

"Oh, of course you have," Iris Rose said lightly. "Please forgive me. I didn't mean to imply that you're expected to make vows. I suppose it's the habit of the habit." She essayed a tentative grin.

"You *will* be asked to promise that you'll abide by the rules governing the school, that you'll be obedient to the direction of Mother Superior and the sisters in charge of you, but that doesn't bind you from leaving, when your guardians determine that it's time for you to go. Surely someone told you that?"

Alyce made herself relax a little and began removing her outer garments, deciding that she liked Iris Rose. Though the other girl appeared to be a few years older than she and Marie, her carriage suggested gentle breeding—though perhaps that came of the convent education. With care, Alyce thought she might be able to find out more about what would be expected of her here; and it was always good to have a friend.

"Oh, of course we were told," she said, touching the other

girl's hand in reassurance, though she did not yet dare to try establishing any kind of Deryni link. "My sister has heard too many horror tales of girls locked up in convents against their will. Tante Jessamy assured us that this is not the case at Arc-en-Ciel. In fact, she told us that her daughter has been quite happy here—though I must confess, we've not met her. I assume that you know Sister Iris Jessilde. . . ."

"Oh, we all know Iris Jessilde." Iris Rose grinned, her brown eyes taking on a new animation. "She can be *so* funny—and she's quite the accomplished embroideress. Very pious, too. But—how can it be that you've not met her? Is she not your cousin, if Lady Jessamy is your aunt?"

"Well, I suppose she *would* be our cousin," Marie said, from within the folds of outer gown she was pulling off over her head. "But Tante Jessamy isn't really our aunt. She and our mother were like sisters, so we've always *called* her Tante Jessamy—"

"We only came to Rhemuth in the autumn, so we don't even know Tante Jessamy very well," Alyce said, picking up one of the white wool under-gowns. "Before last summer, we hadn't seen her for years."

"Oh," said Iris Rose. "Well, I know that Jessilde went home last spring for her father's funeral, but obviously you weren't there yet. So, where *did* you come from? You don't sound local."

Flashing Iris Rose a smile, Alyce stepped behind one of the screens nearer the fire and continued to undress.

"We're not at all local," she replied. "We were raised with our brother at Castle Cynfyn, in Lendour. But our mother died when we were very small, and our father has finally decided to remarry. Unfortunately, our new stepmother—"

"—didn't want rivals around for his affections," Iris Rose finished for her. "So he's packed you off to the convent for finishing."

"Well, we *will* need to manage large estates someday," Alyce replied, pulling on the new under-gown. "Our father is an earl, and our brother will be a duke when he comes of age—through our mother's inheritance," she added, at Iris Rose's sound of inquiry.

"I'd heard who your parents are," Iris Rose said neutrally. "Not that it matters to me—that you're . . . well, you know."

Alyce stepped from behind the screen to look at Iris Rose's back, ramrod straight in its pale blue habit, topped by the white wimple and novice veil. For her own part, Alyce's own image could not have been more innocent, with her golden hair tumbled onto the shoulders of her white under-gown. Still behind the screen, Marie had frozen, listening.

"Do you mean that?" Alyce asked quietly.

Iris Rose turned slowly to face her, brown eyes looking fearlessly into Alyce's blue ones.

"I do," she said. "In the years I have been here, I have come to know and love Sister Iris Jessilde. I cannot believe that it is evil to be—what she is. Or what *you* are."

Alyce simply stared at her for a few seconds in shock, uncertain whether to take this bald statement as a declaration of trust or a test. But by Truth-Reading Iris Rose, Alyce could see that she believed what she had just said. As she started to reach for one of the blue over-robes, Iris Rose bustled forward and scooped it up instead, briskly rearranging its folds so that she could ease it over Alyce's head.

"You're very brave," Alyce murmured, from within the folds of pale blue wool.

"Bravery isn't nearly as important as vigilance," the other girl replied in a low voice, as Alyce's head popped free. "You should know that there's a new chaplain recently come here who does not like . . . well, women with minds of their own." She gave Alyce a meaningful look as folds of pale blue wool fell to ankle-length around her, including Marie in her comments as the younger girl stepped into view once more. "Sister Iris Jessilde would have warned you, but I got to you first. Just be very careful."

Alyce inclined her head slightly as she settled the skirts of the blue robe. "Thank you, I'll keep that in mind. But surely *you* have nothing to fear from him."

Iris Rose glanced sidelong at the door as she handed one of the multi-colored cinctures to Alyce, then to Marie. "Lady Alyce, I may not be—what you are," she said in a low voice, "but I do have a mind of my own—and perhaps tend to speak it more often than I should. He believes that women should be silent. He assigns very harsh penances when we're not."

"I see," Alyce replied. "And does this paragon have a name?"

"Father Septimus. He's young and handsome, and can be very charming, but don't let that fool you. Mother Judiana knows him for what he is. We're all hoping and praying that he won't be around very long."

Astonished, Marie glanced between Iris Rose and her sister. "But—if he's that unpleasant, how did he get here in the first place?"

Iris Rose rolled her eyes. "His brother is a bishop down in Carthane: Oliver de Nore. Mind you, he's only an itinerant one, but he still has a great deal of influence. Any bishop does."

A clatter at the door latch announced the bustling arrival of a much older woman in the habit and blue veil of a vowed sister.

"Are we ready yet?" she asked, mouth primping in an expression of disappointment as she noted the two girls' somewhat disheveled locks. "Good heavens, you can't go to Mother looking like that! Iris Rose, you haven't done their hair yet. Let me lend a hand. I'm Iris Mary," she added, as she came to lift a handful of Alyce's curls. "Dear me, this mane badly needs closer acquaintance with a comb—but you'll wear it in a plait while you're here among us," she said, as she began dividing it into sections to do just that. "Now, which one are you, Alyce or Marie?"

"She's Alyce," said Iris Rose, smiling as she began a similar service of Marie's ruddier locks. "And this is Marie. And you mustn't worry, girls. Sister Iris Mary isn't nearly as ferocious as she pretends to be."

"Goodness, no!" Iris Mary retorted with a good-natured wink. "I am *far* more ferocious!"

The relaxed banter between the two appeared to indicate that perhaps it was permissible to dispense with overmuch stiffness or formality, though Alyce sensed, without being told, that the limits had yet to be learned, especially for those of her race, and especially in light of the warning Iris Rose had just given her.

Nonetheless, by the time both stood in the full attire of their new situation, each with hair now tamed to a single plait down their backs, the future appeared far less bleak than they had come to fear. Sister Iris Rose was humming contentedly as she made a last inspection of each girl's attire, adjusting a cincture here, a fold of skirt there, and Iris Mary was smiling as she brought out two wreaths of dried flowers.

"By rights, these should be made of fresh flowers," she said, handing one to Iris Rose, "but the truth is, we rarely know enough in advance to prepare them—so dried ones have to suffice. Besides, it's winter, so the choices are few. But you'll only wear them for your reception by Reverend Mother, until you're veiled."

"I hope that's only a figure of speech," Marie said. "We don't intend to become nuns, you know."

Iris Mary made a clucking sound, looking faintly amused as she put her wreath on Marie's head. "Certainly not, child. I can imagine the sorts of tales you've heard about life in some convents, but I can assure you that no one is here who does not wish to be here."

"Then, what's this about veils?"

"Actually, they're more like kerchiefs, tied underneath your plait," Iris Rose assured them. "Not terribly attractive, but they're very practical."

"You *will* receive an actual veil," Iris Mary added, turning to fuss with Alyce's wreath, "but it's simply a plain white one such as any well-bred girl might wear, held in place by a rainbow-plaited fillet rather like your cinctures—and you'll only wear that on Sundays and other formal occasions. It's quite pretty. But the *reason* for having you wear a version of our habit is so that you'll blend in better with the vowed community, which is less disruptive to *us*. I promise you that there is no agenda more sinister than that."

"You see, Mares?" Alyce murmured aside to her sister. "I told you it would be all right."

"I suppose," Marie replied, though she still looked not altogether convinced.

To the relief of both of them, their formal presentation to the mother superior was considerably less daunting than they had feared. Accompanied by Sisters Iris Rose and Iris Mary, they made their way out along the cloister walk and through a side door into the chapel—and this, too, was not the dark, oppressive place they had feared.

A sweetly sung hymn of welcome met them even before they passed through the rainbow-arched doorway—the combined voices both of sisters and of students; and though the day had been bleak and wintry for the ride to Arc-en-Ciel, the Chapel of the Rainbow was a place of lightness and peace, purest white where stained glass did not pierce the outer walls, and ablaze with color at east and west, both from glorious rose windows and from scores of candles set behind shades of vari-colored glass around the altar.

Enfolded in light and sound and a hint of floral incense, they followed the two sisters down a stretch of carpet woven to give the impression of walking along a rainbow, passing between the center-facing choir stalls of the students and community. Jessamy came out to meet them as they advanced, conducting them thence to the sanctuary steps, where the three of them paused to reverence the altar beyond.

Before that altar, Mother Iris Judiana rose from a simple stool to receive them, accepting Jessamy's curtsy with a nod and a smile, then opening her arms to embrace her. Alyce and Marie had also dipped in respect as Jessamy made her reverence, and now curtsied more deeply as Jessamy drew back from the mother superior and turned to present them.

"Mother Iris Judiana, I have the honor to present my heart-daughters, the demoiselles Alyce and Marie, children of my dear friend Stevana de Corwyn, the late heiress of Corwyn. Their dear brother will be Duke of Corwyn when he comes of age, and likewise Earl of Lendour upon the death of their father, Keryell of Lendour, who has asked that they be given into your care to learn the gentle arts suitable to their rank."

"I am pleased to receive them, dear Jessamy," said Mother Iris Judiana, smiling as she extended her hands to the two girls. "May they be a credit to this house, and cleave cheerfully to its discipline. Let them now be enrolled under the favor and protection of our Lady of the Rainbow, signifying the same by their signatures in the great book of our house."

With those words, she signaled them to rise, Jessamy leading them before a small table to one side, where lay an open book displaying a mostly empty page. Two much younger girls stood to either side of the table—students, by their dress—holding a rainbow-striped canopy above it. A somewhat older one in novice habit stood behind the table, bearing a quill and inkwell, and curtsied to the pair of them as she held out her implements.

"Darlings, this is my daughter, Sister Iris Jessilde," Jessamy said softly, nodding fondly to the girl holding the quill. "It will be her honor to enroll you under the Rainbow."

"It is for the schooling only," Alyce said in final confirmation of their intent, as Jessilde put the quill in her hand. "We make no vow save to keep the discipline of this school."

The older girl answered with a merry smile beneath her rainbow-edged white veil, amusement crinkling at the corners of eyes as blue as cornflowers, and the two girls holding the canopy giggled good-naturedly.

"Be assured, there is no trickery here," Jessilde murmured. "You are perfectly free to stay or to go—save that the wishes of your father or guardians may require what you would otherwise, of course. But this is not a prison. No one will try to force a religious vocation that does not exist."

The assurance rang of truth—and Alyce had been probing gently to be certain of it—but she still turned briefly to the previous page of the book to confirm what she was signing. A heading on that page declared it to be the first entries for the term begun the previous Michaelmas.

Feeling somewhat foolish, she signed her name with care and handed the quill to Marie, who also seized courage and affixed her name beneath that of her older sister. When they had done, Jessamy moved between them and took a hand from each, leading them back before the mother superior, with the rainbow canopy accompanying them.

There, at a sign from Jessamy, the pair of them knelt at the feet of Mother Iris Judiana, who took a pine sprig from a silver pot offered by another of the girls and sprinkled them with holy water in the sign of the Cross.

"Let these daughters be veiled according to the custom of our house," she said in signal to two more girls, who approached with fine white linen draped over their arms.

The veiling itself was something of an anticlimax. As Jessamy removed the dried floral wreaths from both bowed heads, the girls with the veils performed their offices, bidding Alyce and Marie to hold the front edges of the veils in place while rainbow-plaited fillets were bound across their foreheads, entirely suitable for the lives they were to lead for the next few years. Once veiled, the pair were conducted by Mother Judiana herself to seats in the back row of the students' choir stalls, these to be their assigned places henceforth.

There followed a sparse few words of welcome and of notification regarding the rest of the day's schedule, and then an adjournment to the refectory for a plain but substantial supper. Shortly after that, they were shown to the rooms they would share, each with a roommate. Alyce's was a lively redheaded girl called Cerys; Marie was paired with a younger girl called Iery. To their surprise, the rooms were cozy and warm, if sparse, each with a heavy wool curtain covering its single small window and several rushlights set in wall niches.

"I know it must seem rather modest, compared to what you've been accustomed to," Cerys told her, indicating the whitewashed walls of their room, "but in truth, we don't spend much time here, other than to sleep. We each have a coffer in the common room, for our clothing—except for our night gowns. Those go under our pillows. And you do have an aumbry cupboard there, on your side of the bed, for a few personal items."

Alyce noted the arched cupboard door set into the wall on the left side of the wide bed, the crucifix at its head, and also the tiny fireplace in one corner of the room, radiating a comforting amount of heat. There was also a close stool in another corner of the room, for use during the night.

"We're allowed a fire in the morning and at night," Cerys added, noting her new roommate's scrutiny. "A lay servant cleans out the night ashes and starts the morning fires, and comes back later to lay the night fire, but we have to clean out our own morning ashes after morning prayers and breakfast, and empty our own chamber pot. We usually take turns doing that. Sister Iris Anthony says that it's good experience for well-bred girls to perform such duties for themselves, so that we'll know what's involved when we must manage our own domestic servants."

"That's probably true," Alyce said, somewhat surprised that there had been no trace of resentment in the other girl's tone. She tried the edge of the bed and glanced at her companion. "Cerys, do you like it here? I mean, *really*."

"Oh, I do," Cerys replied. "Mind you, I wouldn't want to stay here forever—I don't think I could ever be a nun!—but my father is only a simple knight. If I expect to marry well, I must be properly prepared to run a noble household."

"I see," Alyce murmured.

For the next little while, until time for evening prayers, Cerys chattered away about life at the school and Alyce mostly just listened, though it did give her a somewhat better idea what to expect. She saw Marie briefly before evening prayers, and met Iery, who was quiet but seemed to have a sense of humor.

"I like her," Marie whispered, as they settled into their stalls for the final service of the night. "Maybe this will be all right after all."

Bed followed evening prayers, and Alyce lay awake far longer than she usually did, close beside Cerys for warmth. When she finally did sleep, she did not dream.

Chapter 9

"Stand ye in the ways, and see, and ask for the old paths, where is the good way, and walk therein."

—JEREMIAH 6:16

THEIR new life at Arc-en-Ciel began in earnest the next morning. Jessamy and Jesiana had stayed the night, and rose for early Mass in the convent's chapel, then broke their fast with Jessilde and the rest of the community before making their good-byes, leaving Alyce and Marie to settle into their new situation as best they could.

By and large, this proved far less difficult than they had feared. The nuns, for the most part, were gentle and kind, and quickly warmed to the lively and talented sisters from Lendour. Acceptance came more slowly from the other girls, but they, too, gradually began to relax and include the newcomers among them. Marie and Iery got on famously, and Cerys proved to be amiable and genuinely kind, and soon included Alyce in her friendship with another girl their age, called Zoë, who would quickly become Alyce's particular friend.

For the rest, Alyce soon decided not worry. If a few of the girls kept their distance—and some of the nuns as well—most of them were no worse than indifferent, and seemed not to mind that two more Deryni were now among them. The way had been paved by Jessilde, who apparently had long since proven her harmlessness to the satisfaction of the community.

Which left the demoiselles de Corwyn to contend with the

reason they had come to Arc-en-Ciel in the first place: to continue their education as young ladies of gentle breeding.

They found the cycle of instruction in the convent school somewhat different from what they had known in their father's hall, where they had studied many of the same subjects as their brother. Though Alyce had always been the stronger student, both were competent in the basic skills of reading, writing, and ciphering, and had a far better background than most of their classmates in history, the classics, and languages.

These accomplishments, while acknowledged as commendable, were considered far less useful than the domestic skills that were the focal point of the curriculum at Arc-en-Ciel: household management, simple physicking, and even surgery, along with the regular regimen of devotion and religious instruction that one might expect in a religious establishment.

And of course, there was the ubiquitous needlework to occupy hands not busy with other tasks: sempstering and fine embroidery, mending, spinning and weaving—all reckoned to be essential skills in the repertoire of all gentlewomen, if only so that they might oversee such work by others when, eventually, they must run their own households. Music, drawing, and dance provided a further soupçon of gentler diversion. The purity of Marie's voice soon singled her out for extra tutelage in choir and musical ensemble. Alyce's fine calligraphic hand raised appreciative eyebrows in the convent's scriptorium.

"Your calligraphy is exceptionally clear, my dear," Sister Iris Althea told her, casting her gimlet glance over a fluent practice page. "Already, your work is more than good enough to serve in any lord's secretariat. If you continue to apply yourself, you could be a true artist."

"Thank you, Sister," Alyce murmured. "I have been fortunate enough to have excellent teachers."

"And they have had a worthy pupil," Sister Iris Althea said graciously. "I wonder if you would be willing to try your hand at some fine copy work for the library? We have several volumes that have become finger-soiled and difficult to read, despite the reminders I give our girls to take care in their handling, and I have been wishing to replace them for some time."

Alyce allowed herself a shy smile, unused to being acknowledged for an adult accomplishment.

"I hope that I may be of assistance, Sister—if you truly think my work is good enough."

"Oh, 'tis more than good enough, child—or, I should say 'Lady Alyce,' for this is not a child's work. As you come to know our library, you will find many manuscripts in regular use that are not nearly so fine." She smiled and gently cupped Alyce's cheek, smiling with genuine warmth. "I shall speak to Mother Judiana about you, dear. It seems that Lady Jessamy has brought us yet another treasure."

The very next day, Alyce was given her own carrel in the scriptorium, close to one of the fireplaces and near to a glazed window, though the winter sun offered little in the way of illumination. Still, there were candles aplenty, as many as she needed, and the space became a favorite personal haven in the days and months ahead. In time, it also became a place to tutor other students of promise, including her friend Zoë Morgan, whose quick wit and sense of humor often brightened her day.

Half a dozen others gradually admitted Alyce to their circles of more particular friends. Marie likewise found a few special friends with whom to share girlish confidences.

As for the rest, those who were indifferent at least were not hostile, and soon allowed the newcomers to settle into quite tolerable anonymity. The two sisters found that the school habit helped a bit, since everyone looked more or less the same, differing largely in height and girth and the color of the braids hanging from beneath each shoulder-length veil or kerchief.

Among the sisters, Alyce found somewhat more ready acceptance. Sister Iris Rose shifted from mere acquaintance to actual friend, as did Iris Mary; and Jessilde MacAthan became a friend as well. And ruling them all, Mother Judiana showed herself unfailingly benevolent, wise, and fair-minded.

The sole note of discord that gradually arose was the antipathy that soon developed between Alyce and the chaplain of whom they had been warned. There were three priests responsible for the community's spiritual well-being—offering daily Mass, hearing confessions, and teaching the odd catechism class or bit of church history in the convent school—

and with two of them, she had no problem. The eldest, called Father Deuel, was a semi-invalid, and could be crotchety when his arthritis was bothering him, but seemed to embody everyone's idea of what the perfect uncle or grandfather should be: genuinely fond of all his charges, and inclined to turn an indulgent eye on all but the most serious transgressions.

The next in seniority, Father Benroy, was equally indulgent, with a fine calligraphic hand and failing eyesight that kept him mostly confined to the very close work of the scriptorium. Over the first few weeks of Alyce's regular presence there, the pair of them developed a cordial working relationship based on mutual respect for one another's artistry, and Benroy soon began to offer her extra tutelage.

The third man had none of the positive qualities of the first two: Father Septimus de Nore, who taught catechism, prepared the girls for Confirmation, and was known to be an extremely punctilious confessor, especially of Deryni. Only a few days after their arrival, Jessilde repeated Sister Iris Rose's warning, and stressed the importance of absolutely avoiding him at confession.

"He abuses his office, if there's any whiff of a Deryni 'taint'—and you and I and Marie are more than merely tainted," Jessilde confided, during the hour of recreation the girls were allowed with the community before evening prayers. "There's nothing to be done about the classes he gives. He'll try to bait you, but you mustn't let yourself be drawn into argument with him. Eventually he'll win, whether he's right or not—and as a priest, he has the authority to make life difficult for us."

"That hardly seems fair," Alyce muttered. "Who does he think he is?"

Jessilde gave her a sidelong glance. "'Fair' has nothing to do with it, Alyce. He's the brother of a bishop—and moreover, a bishop who hates our kind. There's been many a burning in Carthane attributed to Oliver de Nore—and the two brothers are cut from the same cloth. If Father Septimus chooses to enforce the letter of law—and he usually does—he can be extremely difficult."

"*He* couldn't burn anyone—could he?" Alyce asked, shocked.

"Not here—and certainly not without cause that absolutely

couldn't be ignored," Jessilde replied, with a shake of her head. "I'm sure that you would never be so foolish as to give him such cause.

"As for lesser transgressions—well, fortunately, Mother Judiana has enough rank to protect us usually." She cast a fond glance toward one of the fireplaces in the common room, where Judiana sat laughing and smiling with two other sisters and several of the older students. "She's a duke's daughter by birth—and the superior of Arc-en-Ciel always ranks as a baroness in her own right: one of the perquisites of it being a royal convent. We were founded by a Bremagni princess, you know."

Alyce nodded thoughtfully. "I knew that," she said vaguely. "But—is she really the daughter of a duke? I wonder that she'd be allowed to take the veil."

Jessilde laughed gently. "You don't yet know Mother very well. She's a very strong-minded woman, and a very kind and good one. But she comes from a very large family—two brothers and four sisters—so I'm sure her father was happy enough to see her enter the convent. I know he sent her with a handsome dowry. She was the favorite of his daughters, and she found her vocation at a very early age."

Alyce guessed that such a background probably would make Mother Judiana a very formidable opponent, if crossed. Fortunately, she soon learned that this formidable nature was focused on being advocate and defender for those in her charge, whether sister or pupil. Though Father Septimus blustered a great deal, and settled into a pattern of confrontations with Alyce in catechism class, his frustration only mounted as he discovered himself unable to follow through on any of his veiled threats.

"I don't expect that you are even capable of understanding the concept of redemption, Mistress de Corwyn," he muttered so that only Alyce could hear, one afternoon as she tried to slip out of his classroom after a particularly acrimonious class debate on salvation and redemption. "And I don't recall that I have ever seen you at confession. Of course, I would expect a soulless Deryni like yourself to avoid that sacrament whenever possible—and to lie, if you cannot. Your kind are damned anyway."

Alyce held her temper only with the greatest of effort. The

rest of the class had already fled from the classroom, but the priest had moved between her and the doorway to block her escape. Beyond, she could see Zoë and Cerys lingering just outside the open door.

"With all respect, Father, you are, of course, entitled to your opinion," she said quietly. "However, Father Benroy is my confessor, not you, and will vouch for my faithfulness to my religious duties."

"You insolent hussy!" Septimus hissed, stepping closer and glaring down at her. "Pretending piety and innocence, when every word that passes your lips spreads corruption! I *will* check with him, you know."

"You are welcome to check with whomever you like," Alyce said evenly. "But the state of the soul you do not think I have is the affair of my confessor alone—and God, of course. But certainly not you. Good day to you, Father."

With that, she dropped him a curtsy—correct to the letter in technical exactitude but devoid of any genuine respect—and darted past him, seizing the arm of the astonished Zoë to propel her and Cerys on along the corridor. All three of them were shaking by the time they gained the safety of the cloister yard—though at least Father Septimus had not followed them.

"Alyce, you mustn't taunt him!" Cerys whispered, eyes wide. "He's a pompous idiot, and everyone here knows that, but his brother *is* a bishop."

"All true," Alyce agreed, "but he is *not* my confessor! And he can't excommunicate me just because I voiced an opinion differing from his."

"Don't be too certain of that," Zoë murmured.

But the matter seemed to drop there. There were no repercussions during the following week—and Father Septimus was coolly civil enough in class. Still, Alyce told Father Benroy about the incident, and Jessilde—and also Mother Judiana, when Jessilde urged her to go to the convent's superior.

Judiana heard the report in silence, making no pronouncement about the relative appropriateness of the behavior on both sides; but before summer's end, a new chaplain came to Arc-en-Ciel, a merry catechist called Father Malgar de Firenza, and Septimus de Nore found himself transferred to a prestigious parish in Cassan. Nothing was ever said of the circumstances behind this transfer, which had also been a promotion for Father Septimus, but all the community breathed a little easier for his departure.

That summer also brought a surprise visit of old friends from home: Sé Trelawney and Jovett Chandos, knighted the previous Twelfth Night in Rhemuth, who arrived bearing letters and gifts for the demoiselles de Corwyn from their brother and their father. With the two young knights came their old tutor from Castle Cynfyn, Father Paschal Didier.

The arrival of two handsome young men at Arc-en-Ciel set many a heart aflutter, even though the pair were allowed no farther than the guest parlor and chapel. The bearded Father Paschal inspired more thoughtful contemplation, elegant and somewhat exotic in his flowing black robes and the black, flat-topped cap of the R'Kassan clergy, with knotted prayer beads wrapped around one wrist.

The priest's visit came as something of a surprise, albeit a most welcome one. For while his previous remit ostensibly had been the religious and secular education of Corwyn's heirs, it also had included instruction in other disciplines apt to raise eyebrows in his charges' present circumstances—a resumption of which their father now proposed.

"The choice is yours, child, if you would rather I not proceed," Paschal told Alyce, when she and Marie had read the pertinent letter from their father and passed it on to Jessilde, who had brought them to this meeting in the guest parlor. Sir Sé was standing with his back against the door, head bowed; Sir Jovett remained in the corridor outside the room, as further security against interruption.

"I will not deny that there is some small risk in what your father has asked," Paschal went on, "but both he and I believe the risk is acceptable. And Lady Jessilde, I have permission from your mother to include you in the instruction I give to Lady Alyce and Lady Marie, if you wish it."

"I don't understand," Jessilde murmured, her face pale beneath the white of her novice veil as she looked up from the letter. "How is this possible?"

"That one of our blood may validly wear this?" Paschal replied, briefly lifting the plain wooden priest's cross that hung against the breast of his black robes. "Let us merely observe that not all the world is like Gwynedd. I am Bremagni-born, though I was educated at Nur Sayyid and the R'Kassan seminary at Rhanamé. It is true that, even there, our kind must go warily, but perhaps because of the Torenthi royal house, the Eastern Patriarchate of Holy Mother Church has always been . . . 'flexible' regarding holy orders."

"'Flexible?'" Alyce said.

Paschal shrugged and smiled faintly. "One of the privileges—and duties—of the Patriarch of Torenth is to preside at the empowering of Torenthi kings," he said. "This requires certain . . . skills . . . that are nowhere to be found among Gwynedd's clergy.

"The Eastern Hierarchy acknowledges the usefulness of such skills, at least in moderation, but also recognizes the potential for much abuse, should their number come to be dominated by men who can wield such powers. To minimize this danger, Eastern canon law stipulates that human bishops must always constitute a majority within the hierarchy. Thus far, the measure has proven effective."

"A practical resolution of a very real human fear," Jessilde said thoughtfully, nodding agreement.

"Father Paschal, I can tell her about this later," Alyce said impatiently, finally daring to interrupt. "Are we to have a session today? How long can you stay?"

"Patience, child!" Paschal said with a laugh. "We have leave from your father to abide here for several days, and I have already explained to Mother Judiana concerning your father's wish that I brief you regularly about the state of affairs in Corwyn and Lendour. She has agreed. In return, I have offered to celebrate Mass tomorrow morning, to give respite to the chaplains of this house. But we shall need to be both concise and circumspect about your 'briefings,' as you can imagine."

Marie, hitherto largely silent, glanced at Jessilde, concerned. "Is it safe for him to do this in a religious house?" she whispered, wide-eyed.

"So long as we exercise due caution, there should be little danger," Jessilde replied.

"Precisely," Paschal said. "To that end, I have been obliged to somewhat restructure my methods of instruction—and the presence of Sir Sé and his companion should ensure that we are not disturbed without due warning. In the future, should they not be able to accompany me, I shall ask the three of you to keep watch, each in turn, while I work with the other—assuming, of course, that Sister Jessilde wishes to avail herself of my instruction," he added, with a glance at the young religious, who nodded.

"Excellent. In a moment, then, dear Sister, I shall need leave to probe behind your shields, so that I may assess your present level of ability. You will kindly prepare yourself. And Lady Alyce, you will come and sit beside me, please," he added, seating himself near the window and patting the bench beside him. "With your permission I should like to resume your training by imprinting a set of 'lessons' for you to contemplate until my next visit. Then I shall do the same for your sister—and also give you the 'briefing' that Mother Judiana expects you to receive, if not in the manner she expects."

Alyce smiled as she came and sat beside him as instructed, seizing his hand to kiss it in affection and respect.

"Thank you, Father," she whispered. "I have longed for this day."

"I know, little one. And believe me when I tell you that you are a worthy pupil. Relax now and open to me," he instructed, passing his free hand downward before her eyes, which closed as she felt a familiar lethargy wash across her consciousness, product of training triggers set long ago, master to pupil.

"Excellent . . . now deeper . . . Good . . ."

Thus did the Earl of Lendour's household chaplain take up his tutorial duties again, not only with Alyce and Marie de Corwyn but now with Jessilde MacAthan as his pupil as well, in quarterly installments that soon took on a rhythm of regular and welcome visits. Though Sir Sé and Sir Jovett did not always accompany him, as Earl Keryell made increasing use of their services, Paschal brought letters from both young men when he could, and almost always from Ahern. Keryell's letters were less regular, perhaps at the instigation of his new wife, but Alyce and Marie were relived to note that no new Lendour heirs were forthcoming.

Meanwhile, the residents of Notre Dame d'Arc-en-Ciel came to look forward to the visits of the serene and somewhat exotic R'Kassan priest, whose arrival was always much welcomed, for along with the letters he carried for his noble charges, he always brought news and amusing anecdotes from the outside world, and sometimes new manuscripts for the convent library, and dainty sweetmeats for everyone.

The girls, for their part, flourished under the discipline of the convent school, with sufficient solitude to reinforce the inner work that Father Paschal set for them each time he came to visit and also the leisure to pursue the artistic potentials being developed by their convent training. Marie was developing into a lutenist of promise, to accompany her vocal talents; and Alyce's calligraphic skills continued to unfold, to the delight of Sister Iris Althea and Father Benroy. Nor could any find fault with their growing domestic competence, or their adherence to the disciplines of their faith. Both girls were confirmed shortly after Easter of their second year there, when a bishop came up from Rhemuth to administer that sacrament.

On a personal level, as Alyce continued the shift from girlhood to young womanhood, she was also learning important lessons. Though she continued to share a room with Cerys, and the two enjoyed an amiable enough relationship, it was Zoë Morgan with whom she found herself spending most of what leisure time they were given, not only because the two of them often worked together in the scriptorium but because Zoë's father, when he came occasionally to visit his daughter, often brought letters from Jessamy and even from the queen, that must be delivered in person.

These visits, though infrequent, became occasions of welcome diversion, not only for Zoë, but for Alyce, Marie, and Cerys as well. Though the girls had not been long at court before they came to Arc-en-Ciel, Alyce well remembered the tall, sandy-haired knight usually to be found not far from the king's side, and fell gratefully into the fatherly affection he offered to his daughter's friends.

Sir Kenneth Morgan tended to stay for several hours when he came to call, delivering his letters and then regaling his appreciative audience with the latest news from court. In addition, he usually included all of them in the largesse of marchpane sweets and other dainties he sometimes brought as a special treat.

Sometimes, when absent on the king's business, he sent letters to Zoë by royal courier, and always included a few words of fond comment for his daughter's friends. Very occasionally, if he had chanced to see Earl Keryell in the course of his duties, the courier's pouch would also include a letter sealed with the Lendour arms, but both Alyce and Marie understood that their father was much occupied in the king's service, and accepted that he had little time for correspondence. Also, they suspected that letters were actively discouraged by their stepmother.

Drawn into this semblance of substitute family with Zoë's father, then, it was little wonder that Alyce should come to regard his daughter as another sister. Since Zoë already had sisters aplenty, it had not occurred to Alyce that the feeling might be mutual, but their friendship was growing strong, whatever one called it.

Just how strong became apparent one wintry afternoon early in 1084, more than a year after Alyce's arrival at Arc-en-Ciel, as the two of them worked alone in the scriptorium. Earlier, Father Benroy had given them both a tutorial on painted capitals, for Zoë had been turning her focus increasingly to the illumination of the pages Alyce penned. Their assignment had involved a foliated and illuminated *D* for *Dominus,* with a furry creature of their choice peeking from amid intertwined vines. As Zoë surveyed the squirrel she had painted, cleaning one of her brushes on a bit of rag, she glanced across at Alyce's considerably less competent lion nestled amid oak leaves. Their slanted writing desks faced one another against a narrow shelf that held several unlit candles.

"Your lion looks like he could use a good meal," she said good-naturedly.

"Like a fat squirrel, maybe?" Alyce retorted, not looking up as she scraped at a vexing smudge on one of her lion's ears.

"Don't sulk. Your calligraphy is better than mine will ever be," Zoë replied. "D'you think it's about time for some extra light?" she said, glancing over her shoulder at the window behind her. "And I don't know about you, but I could use another log on the fire."

"I'll do it," Alyce said, happy enough to set aside her stylus.

Taking one of the candles over to the fireplace, she lit it from what was left of the fire, then set it on the hearth while she encouraged a renewed blaze with several new sticks of firewood, watching until they had caught. Both she and Zoë wore close-fitting cuffs to keep their sleeves clean, and had put aside their veils while they worked. As Alyce returned to the desk with her lit candle, she gave the other girl's blonde braid a playful bat.

"Hey!" Zoë said, though she was smiling as she said it.

"That's the paw of my lion, chastising you for saying that he looks ill-fed," Alyce said with a grin, as she sat again and leaned forward to light several of the candles between her and Zoë.

"Well, he does," Zoë replied.

"So he'll eat your squirrel, and that will solve the problem," Alyce said. As she set down the candle she had used to light the others, Zoë leaned closer and blew one of the candles out.

"What are you doing?" Alyce murmured, startled.

"Changing the subject," Zoë replied "and making a point."

"What point?"

Zoë made a pointed sweep of the room with her gaze, even leaning far enough to one side for a good look at the closed door, then returned her gaze to Alyce.

"The point is that I know that you didn't need the fire to light a candle," she said very softly. "Alyce, there's no one else here—and you wouldn't have frightened me."

Alyce felt her mouth go dry, and a cold chill clenched at her stomach. She had been extremely circumspect about using her powers since coming to Arc-en-Ciel, other than when working privately with Father Paschal and Marie and Sister Jessilde—and Zoë could know nothing of that. Could it be that she wanted a demonstration?

"Are you asking what I think you're asking?" she whispered.

Zoë nodded—and deliberately blew out another candle, her sea-gray eyes not leaving Alyce's.

"You want to see me do it."

Zoë nodded again.

Rolling her eyes briefly heavenward, Alyce glanced behind her at the closed door, extended her senses to scan the corridor outside—utterly deserted—then turned back to Zoë and passed a hand over the two candles Zoë had blown out. As she did so, both flared back alight.

Zoë flinched back involuntarily and her jaw dropped, but there was only delight writ across her face as her gaze shifted from the candles back to Alyce.

"You really can do it!" she whispered.

Rolling her eyes again, Alyce gave a sigh. "Well, of *course* I can do it. It's one of the first things we learn—that, and this." She lifted one closed hand between them, wrist upward, and conjured handfire in her palm as she opened her fingers, revealed as a faintly glowing sphere of green fire.

"Oh!" Zoë breathed, enchanted anew, and apparently still not frightened.

Shaking her head in amazed disbelief, Alyce quenched the handfire and glanced at the door again, leaning closer to her friend.

"Why did you ask me to do that?" she asked.

Zoë colored slightly and glanced down at her lap. "I—Alyce, I know what you are—and I obviously don't think that what you are is evil, or I wouldn't be saying this to you. I also know that you're very careful not to do anything here that might . . . frighten people.

"I didn't think that what you did was frightening," she went on less certainly, as she dared to look up, "but I think *you* must find it frightening to be so alone, knowing that most people *are* afraid of . . . what you are. I just wanted to say that, if you ever want to talk about it. . . ."

Abruptly she stopped talking and glanced at her hands, clasped tightly in her lap, lips also clamped together, clearly afraid she had said too much. Alyce merely stared at her in astonishment for several seconds, uncertainty warring with the impulse to reach across and take her hand in reassurance.

She had been Truth-Reading Zoë Morgan as the words came tumbling out, and had no doubt that they had come straight from the heart. She had come to trust Zoë more than any other human she had known. But was it enough, merely to trust in the goodwill of another, no matter how well-intentioned, when one's very life could hang in the balance?

"Zoë, what is it you want me to do?" she asked softly.

"I—suppose that I want you to feel that you can talk to me about—about whatever is most important to you, the things that frighten you, the part of your life that you can't discuss safely with anyone else. I want you to tell me about what it's like to be—what you are." Zoë glanced nervously at the door.

"I want to know if it's true that our two peoples once worked together openly, and if it is, I—think I want to learn to do that, too," she finally blurted. "I know that will probably mean—letting you touch my mind, but I—I'm willing to do that, because I love you and trust you like a sister!"

Tears were welling in her eyes by the time she had finished, but when Alyce would have spoken, Zoë held up one hand and shook her head.

"No, don't say anything yet. There's more I need to say. I know that you must talk about these things with your sister and with Sister Jessilde, because she's—what you are. And I think that Father Paschal must be one, too, though I don't know how that's possible, with him being a priest and all.

"But I think that the real reason he comes here so often is not just to bring you letters and presents from home, or to tell you what's happening there, but so that he can continue your training. And Jessilde either helps him, or he's training her, too. If I'm wrong, tell me and I'll be quiet, but that's what I think."

Alyce had listened to this unfolding of logic in disbelief, though she was quite certain that Zoë was absolutely earnest in what she was saying. She was also wondering whether, if Zoë had reached such conclusions, others also might have done so. Caution urged her to simply seize control of the other girl's mind and erase all memory of this exchange, also blurring the logic by which Zoë had arrived at her all-too-perceptive conclusions—and that was what Father Paschal would have advised, she felt certain.

But another part of her rejoiced in her friend's unsolicited and tearful declaration, and was already considering ways in which she might allow what was being asked. To have a friend with whom she could be utterly candid, in *everything* . . .

"Zoë, have you told anyone else about these astonishing suspicions?" she asked softly.

Zoë drew herself up indignantly. "Certainly not!"

"Not even your confessor?"

"Not even him. No one," Zoë said emphatically.

Alyce drew a deep breath and let it out slowly. Whether she obeyed her head or her heart, she would have to set certain controls, to protect both of them; but especially if it be the latter, best it be with permission and cooperation. And she would need both time and privacy to do that properly—luxuries she did not have at the moment, for the bells would soon be ringing for the evening office.

"Zoë, give me your hand," she murmured, laying hers on the shelf between them.

In the other's eyes, she could see uncertainty warring with the trust just declared, but Zoë Morgan did not hesitate to place her hand in Alyce's, even though it was trembling.

"You are so brave!" Alyce whispered, lightly closing her fingers around Zoë's. "I know you said you weren't afraid, and I know you meant it, at the time. But how could you *not* be afraid?—though I promise you, on my immortal soul, that I'll not hurt you."

She cupped her other hand over their joined ones and dared to send a gentle tendril of calm across their link. At the same time, she bypassed Zoë's will to resist and began teasing out the necessary threads for plaiting a quick protection that must suffice until she could do the job right—or until Father Paschal could be persuaded to assist her. Zoë had gone very still, and a little glassy-eyed.

"Zoë, understand that it will take some time to do what really needs to be done," Alyce whispered as she worked, "and we don't have that time right now—not to do it properly. But in the meantime, I need to protect both of us."

"Are you—reading my mind?" Zoë managed to whisper, eyelids fluttering.

"No, I'm not—and I won't, without your permission—but I *am* setting up certain safeguards. For now, I'll simply require that you speak of this to no one. From this moment, you will be physically *unable* to speak of it, other than in my presence and with my permission. In fact, until I tell you otherwise, you'll have only vague recollections regarding what we've just discussed, and what's happening to you now. Later, I'll give you back full memory, but for now, that's what I need. I'd like it to be with your consent."

Zoë gave a slight nod, almost drifting into sleep.

"Good," Alyce said. She gave the captive hand a squeeze and released it, also releasing Zoë to the controls she had just set. "You know, we'd better clean up here, or we'll be late for chapel. Tomorrow we can pick up where we left off."

And by tomorrow, Alyce thought to herself, *maybe I'll have figured out the best way to do what needs to be done. But oh, Zoë, bless you for your faith!*

Zoë blinked and ventured a faintly bewildered smile that

dissolved into a yawn. "Goodness, it's been a long afternoon, hasn't it?" she said. "I can't imagine why I'm so tired. I hope I don't nod off during evening prayers."

"We both could use some fresh air," Alyce agreed.

"YOU are right that I would not have approved," Paschal said the next time he came, after Alyce had sent Zoë for refreshments, and told him what she had done. "But having said that, I must confess to being most impressed at how far you have brought her along." He had been examining one of Zoë's illuminated pages, but Alyce knew he was not referring to the artistry of pen or brush or paint.

"Indeed, your work appears to have been both subtle and effective," Paschal continued, sitting. "Had you not told me, I would not have thought to look at her more closely—which I now must do, as soon as she returns; you know that."

Alyce only nodded, saying nothing.

"I would ask what you were thinking," Paschal went on, "but the answer to that is clear. She is fond of you, and you of her—and I know it will have given you much comfort to find a friend on whom you may rely—and that may well be true, within these walls. But it is a short-sighted measure, Alyce."

"Could you not reserve that judgment until after you have examined her?" Alyce said boldly.

"I could—and I shall," he replied, rising as Zoë re-entered the room with a tray decked with cups, a jug of wine, and a plate of sweet cakes and nuts. "Zoë, dear, put those down and come here, please."

Apparently unconcerned, Zoë did as he requested, coming fearlessly to look at him in question. "Yes, Father?"

"Have you ever seen Lady Alyce conjure handfire?"

The bald question took Zoë totally by surprise, but she only said, "That is forbidden, Father."

"Answer the question!" Paschal snapped, feigning anger, though his flicker of thought to Alyce acknowledged the deft evasion in lieu of an answer.

"No, Father, I have not," Zoë said, looking mystified.

"Say that you have never seen her conjure handfire, or kindle fire from the air," Paschal persisted.

"But, I never have—"

"Say it!" Paschal commanded again.

Looking puzzled rather than alarmed—and it was clear to both Paschal and Alyce that Zoë believed she was telling the truth—Zoë said patiently, "I have never seen Alyce conjure handfire, or kindle fire from the air. Father, why do you keep asking me this?"

"He asks to test both of us," Alyce replied, smiling as she came to put an arm around Zoë's shoulders. "And we've both passed. You may remember and speak freely now."

An odd look came over Zoë's face as her gaze flicked between Alyce and the priest, but when her lips parted to actually speak, Paschal shook his head and came to brush his fingertips lightly across her forehead, exerting control.

"Relax, don't speak," he murmured, letting Alyce help him guide the compliant Zoë into a chair.

He spent some little while probing his subject, testing the safeguards Alyce had set, *tsking,* adjusting, then withdrew, leaving Zoë drifting in trance.

"Very nicely done, my dear," he said quietly to Alyce. "I believe that only one of *us* could bypass what you have done—and that is hardly a danger, I think. I shall be quite interested to observe where all this leads.

"Of course, you must both be careful not to provoke undue attention," he went on, "for if it came to be suspected that you had interfered with her mind, you and she could both be in a good deal of danger; but here in the shelter of the convent, you should have little to fear. You have learned your lessons well—and better than that, you have applied them with both restraint and compassion. She is a true friend, Alyce."

"I know, Father—and thank you," Alyce murmured.

"Thank *you,*" he replied, lightly touching Zoë's hand. "And now, perhaps dear Zoë might pass some of the those sweet cakes to a hungry old priest, for I find myself grown quite peckish with all this talk."

Chapter 10

"Hear counsel, and receive instruction."

—PROVERBS 19:20

MEANWHILE, as Alyce and Marie made lives for themselves at Arc-en-Ciel, life at the court of Rhemuth settled into welcome domesticity. All through the first half of 1083, both Prince Brion and his secret half-brother continued to thrive; and early in July, shortly after their respective birthdays—Brion's second and Krispin's first—the queen was delivered of another prince, Blaine Emanuel.

"Sire, you have another fine son," Jessamy announced happily, emerging from the queen's bedchamber with a squalling, red-faced bundle wrapped in a coverlet of Haldane scarlet. "Methinks this prince will be another bold one, like his brother."

"But they shall be friends," Donal insisted, an arm around his own brother's shoulders as he and Richard came to inspect the newborn infant, followed by a handful of assembled ministers. "Brothers should always be friends."

A covert look passed between Jessamy and the king as he briefly folded back the coverlet, for both knew that the remark had included her Krispin as well as the two trueborn princes.

"The queen seemed not to labor overlong with this one," Donal observed. "Is she well?"

"Aye, well enough, Sire—given that birthing a baby is aptly termed 'labor.' Would you care to return your new son to his mother's arms, and tender your admiration for the fruit of her labors?"

He gave a boyish grin and took the squirming bundle from her arms, leading the parade of courtiers into the queen's bedchamber, where Richeldis lay propped against a pile of snowy pillows in the great state bed, one of her ladies tidying the long braid lying over one shoulder.

"Madam, I am come to bring your son back to you," Donal said, bending to lay the child gently in the curve of her arm, "and I congratulate you on labors well spent. He is beautiful. I thank you."

Richeldis inclined her head with a hint of mischievous smile. "And I thank *you,* Sire," she replied,"though perhaps next time, you might give me a somewhat daintier daughter?"

He laughed aloud at that, echoed by the polite chuckles of the courtiers around him, then bent to kiss her forehead before shooing all of them out of the birthing chamber, himself following. Later that night, following on an informal supper in the upper council chamber, he and a few of his close associates drank the health of both mother and child.

"Gentlemen, I give you the new prince: Blaine Emanuel Richard Cinhil Haldane," he said, after Richard had toasted the queen. "May he have a long and happy life, and may he be a credit to his house."

Seisyll Arilan, included among their company, drank the toast dutifully enough, but his thoughts drifted, as they so often did, to another child of the royal household, and how he might gain proper access to that child. The Camberian Council's inquiries about young Krispin MacAthan cropped up with annoying regularity, and regularly he explained how it was not possible to make close examination of any child of the royal nursery without arousing suspicion.

Besides, he reminded them, even if their worst fears came to be realized and young Krispin proved to be the king's son, the child surely could constitute no threat to their designs for many years, and not without much training that certainly would come to light before it could constitute a real danger. Would they have Seisyll risk his own position of vantage within the royal household on only the possibility that the child was more than met the eye?

"An audacious possibility *has* occurred to me," Oisín Adair said thoughtfully, after yet another such discussion, some months after the birth of the new prince. As all eyes turned toward him in query, he shrugged.

"I travel a great deal, as you know. Last week, my business took me to Ratharkin, to deliver a pair of broodmares to the governor. R'Kassan creams they were—very fine specimens.

"While there," he went on, lifting a restraining hand at Vivienne's scowl of impatience, "I found myself dining at the governor's table. And who should I find seated across from me but Sir Morian du Joux, who once was known as Morian ap Lewys."

"No!" Vivienne said sharply, before Oisín could continue. "If you're thinking to send him to assess the boy, no."

"Well, he *is* the boy's uncle," Khoren said reasonably.

"I don't know," Seisyll said doubtfully. "Vivienne, I know that you've never trusted him, because of his bloodline, but he's been under our direction since the age of nine. It was Sief who kept him from court all these years, and who got Donal to go along with it, by suggesting that a Deryni placed at the Mearan court would be an extremely valuable asset."

"He is still Lewys ap Norfal's son," Vivienne said stubbornly.

"Yes, and he has acted competently as our agent for more than twenty years, and has never put a foot wrong," Michon pointed out. "I had part of his training, Vivienne. Oisín is right; I don't know why it hasn't occurred to us before."

"I regret that it has occurred to us *now*," Vivienne muttered.

"Would Jessamy allow access?" Dominy asked, ignoring the remark. "I know he's her brother, and Krispin is his nephew, but has he even been back to Rhemuth since the boy's birth?"

Seisyll shook his head. "He didn't come to Sief's funeral—not that there was any love lost there, or that he could have heard the news and arrived in time. Besides, he and Jessamy probably haven't seen one another more than half a dozen times since before their father's death; he'd been fostered to court several years before that. After Sief married Jessamy, he did his best to poison the relationship between brother and sister, in hopes that this would keep her from corrupting him."

"Was there actually a danger of that?" Khoren asked.

Oisín gave a snort. "Who knows? If we were talking about

horses, I'd say that blood will tell. But Michon is right. So far as Morian is concerned, he has never, ever put a foot wrong."

Barrett de Laney, who had remained largely silent, jutted his chin in the direction of Oisín.

"What would it take, to get Morian back to Rhemuth to meet his nephew?" he asked.

"The king would have to summon him," Seisyll said promptly. "Or Morian would have to present a convincing reason for a personal visit to Rhemuth, something requiring that he report to the king in person. *Or,*" he added, at Barrett's gesture encouraging further development of this line of thinking, "the governor could be induced to *send* him to the king on some convincing pretext—and Morian does have the governor's ear . . . and the situation in Meara is sufficiently volatile that Iolo Melandry does send regular reports to Rhemuth, and might want an occasional report to carry the weight of Morian's verification that the information he's been gathering is true."

"My thinking, precisely," Barrett said with a faint, tight smile. "Oisín, could you work with that?"

"You mean, could I approach Morian and ask him to manipulate the governor, to get himself sent to Rhemuth?" Oisín replied.

"Exactly that."

Oisín considered briefly, then nodded, grinning. "I can be in Ratharkin within the next week. We shall see what can be arranged."

THERE was no working Portal in the palace at Ratharkin, but one had been established decades earlier at a manor half a day's ride north of the city, formerly held by a Deryni lord but now occupied by a minor baron of the Old Mearan aristocracy. Oisín Adair sold horses regularly to Sir Evan Sullivan, whose daughter had married a Connaiti princeling, and Oisín also had set certain controls in Sir Evan so that he could show up unannounced and obtain use of a horse without anyone remarking on his sudden presence. Accordingly, not a fortnight after his meeting with the Council, Oisín made his way to the Portal at Sir Evan's manor of Arkella, borrowed a horse, and set out for Ratharkin, arriving at midmorning.

The R'Kassan cream that he was riding turned heads as he drew rein in the stable yard, and seemed to conjure most of the stableboys and squires within minutes—and also the attention of the animals Oisín had delivered to Governor Melandry a few weeks before, who whickered and called to the new arrival; R'Kassan creams seemed to prefer the company of other cream horses, and had eyes for no steed of any other color.

The commotion also produced Iolo Melandry himself, who cast an appraising eye over Oisín's mount.

"That almost looks like one of the beasts from Arkella," he said.

"It *is* one of the beasts from Arkella," Oisín replied, to forestall too much speculation. "My own threw a shoe not far from there, and I had to walk there and beg the use of this one. I mayn't stay long, for I've business in Kindaloo on the morrow, but I hoped I might impose briefly for some refreshment. It's a ferocious hot day."

"Then, you must come in and take some wine with me," Iolo said, blissfully unaware that Oisín was encouraging his impulse for hospitality. "And I shall ask Sir Morian to join us. He shares our love of fine horseflesh, as you know."

Oisín did know, and had planted that observation as well. Within minutes, the two of them were sitting beneath a breezy, shaded porch atop the palace walls, sipping chilled wine while Iolo reported on the progress of the horses he had bought from Oisín, and the difficulty of finding good trainers.

Very shortly, Morian ap Lewys du Joux made his appearance, booted and spurred from an earlier ride, and buckling a silver-mounted Kheldouri dirk over a loose-fitting tunic of cool Cassani linen that fell to mid-thigh. In contrast to this relaxed attire, he wore his auburn hair sleeked back severely in a soldier's knot, braided and clouted at the nape of the neck. Though he and Oisín affected only casual pleasure to meet again, a quick communication passed silently between them, such that, as Morian came to take the cup of wine Iolo offered, the merest contact of their hands was sufficient for Morian to trigger the controls long ago set, taking the governor instantly from full awareness into drowsing trance.

When Morian had deepened that trance, instructing his subject to relax and enjoy his wine, he pulled a stool closer to sit beside Oisín as the two of them gazed out over the city.

"I am somewhat surprised to see you here," Morian said to him aside, sipping at his wine.

"No more surprised than I, to be sent," Oisín replied. "I have a somewhat delicate mission for you."

"Indeed."

"You have never met your nephew, I think," Oisín said.

Morian turned to gaze directly at Oisín. His eyes were a startling deep blue, almost violet.

"My sister's child," he said. "And why would I want to do that?"

Offering his open hand, Oisín invited a direct link, smiling faintly as the other instead touched fingertips lightly to his wrist. But the contact was sufficient for the necessary rapport, by which Oisín quickly imparted the Council's speculations regarding the child—and their suspicions regarding the death of Morian's brother-in-law, and the king's probable part in it, and possibly Jessamy's as well.

Morian said nothing as he drew his hand away, also ending the rapport, only taking up his cup again to sip at his wine as he gazed out over the city.

"I haven't seen my sister above a dozen times in the past thirty years," he finally said, not looking at Oisín. "Sief discouraged it—and I understand why. But what you've suggested is—quite astonishing." He glanced into his cup, speculating aloud.

"Poor Sief. We never really got on, but he didn't deserve that. I was got away from my father before I could be 'tainted'—I know what he's said to have done—but Sief never trusted my sister. An odd basis for a marriage, don't you think?"

" 'Better to marry than to burn,' to quote Holy Writ out of context," Oisín said. "In the case of your sister, better to marry her off than to kill her off. At least you didn't face that."

"No." Morian sighed. "Very well, I'll do it. It will take some time to set up an excuse to go to Rhemuth—or to have Iolo send me."

"Understood," Oisín agreed. "I think there is no great urgency, since the boy is not yet two—and it's understood that you'll need to make careful preparations. But we do need to know what we're dealing with."

Morian shook his head, still trying to take in the concept of a nephew who might also be the son of the King of Gwynedd.

"Morian," Oisín said softly, guessing the line of the other's thinking, "it isn't as if we're simply talking about another royal bastard."

"I know that," Morian replied. "And if it was done, it appears to have been done deliberately—and if deliberately, then for a reason. The question is, what reason?"

"We'll worry about that once we discover whether he *is* Donal Haldane's son," Oisín said, tipping back the rest of his wine. "I'd best be off—or shall I stick around, so that you don't have to explain my sudden departure to the governor?"

"No, go ahead. I might as well begin setting up the idea of sending me to Rhemuth, while I already have him in control. And if I'm going to do that, it's easy enough to cover your departure."

"As you will, then," Oisín replied, standing. "Good luck to you."

IN fact, it did not prove feasible to go to Rhemuth that season or even the next, for the rumblings of unrest in Meara were sufficiently troubling that Iolo Melandry preferred to keep his aide close by his side—or else out in the field gathering intelligence, as only a Deryni might do. During those two years, the king sent his brother Richard twice to that troubled province to observe and report back, and sensed that the time was approaching when only his own presence would suffice to restore order.

But he put it off, because unrest of another sort was brewing closer to home, in Carthane to the south, where an itinerant bishop called Oliver de Nore was gaining notoriety for his rigorous enforcement of the Statutes of Ramos—yet another cause for concern to the Camberian Council.

The Statutes of Ramos had been formulated nearly two centuries earlier, in the wake of the Haldane Restoration, and severely limited the participation of Deryni in the life of Gwynedd. Though de Nore had no specific authority to enforce the secular aspects of the Statutes, canon law was a bishop's stock in trade, and sometimes allowed him leeway surely never intended by the formulators of those Statutes. As the decade wore on, de Nore could take credit for the persecution, incarceration, and even execution of scores of men and women, some of them of long-hidden Deryni bloodlines.

Most poignant were the deaths of those discovered while trying to gain access to the priesthood, long forbidden to those of their race; and for such men, the penalty was always death by fire. Their fate, in particular, elicited impassioned anger and debate among the members of the Council, for they were well aware that, until all were once again free to take up priestly vocations, Deryni would never regain a full partnership with the humans among whom they lived.

FORTUNATELY, de Nore and those who constituted ultra-conservative elements within the Church's hierarchy in Carthane did not yet seem inclined to insist that their interpretation of the Laws of Ramos should extend beyond Carthane's borders, much to the relief of the three Deryni then resident at the Convent of Notre Dame d'Arc-en-Ciel. Since the ouster of Bishop de Nore's brother as a chaplain, nearly four years before, royal patronage and the convent's proximity to Rhemuth had kept at bay any further infiltration by would-be zealots. Or perhaps the presence of two important royal wards had buttressed the status of Arc-en-Ciel as a sanctuary for certain select Deryni.

Nonetheless, by late April of 1085, as Alyce de Corwyn helped with preparations for the clothing of a new novice and the profession of final vows by the Deryni daughter of Jessamy MacAthan, initial reports were trickling into Arc-en-Ciel of renewed violence in Carthane, and an outbreak of rioting in Nyford. The day before the ceremonies were to take place, Father Paschal arrived with more detailed news that kept him sequestered with Jessilde and Mother Judiana for several hours, while the community continued to prepare for the next day's celebrations.

Much had changed at Arc-en-Ciel since Paschal's last visit. Much to their delight, Alyce and Zoë now shared a room, though the circumstances by which this had occurred had surprised them both. For Alyce's original roommate, Cerys Devane, had experienced a religious epiphany the previous winter that surprised even herself, and had moved into the postulants' dormitory at Easter to prepare for reception as a novice at the same time Jessilde made her final vows.

"Cerys, are you sure?" Alyce had asked her, remembering the other girl's protestations when they first met, that she could never be a nun.

"No, I'm not at all sure," Cerys had admitted, though her face had glowed with an inner radiance that none could gainsay. "I only know that I've never been happier in my life, and that this seems to be the place God wants me to be."

"But, you were here before, and you're *still* here," Alyce had said reasonably.

"Of course I am," Cerys replied. "But God is *here,*" she touched the flat of her hand to her heart, "and I sense that there's more I'm meant to be doing in His service. I don't yet know what, but isn't that part of what a novitiate is all about?"

Whatever the true reasons for the decision, it had left Alyce without a roommate after Easter—and Zoë's roommate, a rather plain Llanneddi girl called Edwina, had announced her plans to leave early in June to be married out of her father's castle near Concaradine.

So Zoë had asked permission to move in with Alyce, leaving Edwina the privacy of her own room for her last few weeks at Arc-en-Ciel. The arrangement had allowed the new roommates far greater privacy to continue exploring their enhanced relationship, but even so, they preferred not to speak openly of what they were doing.

Father Paschal told me that the king and queen are coming tomorrow, Alyce sent to Zoë, when they had settled into bed and doused the nightlight.

That's nice, Zoë returned sleepily. *I think my father is coming, too. I may not get to see him again before he takes off for Meara in June.*

The exchange was not the same kind of mutual rapport that might have been enjoyed by two Deryni, for it required physical contact, and that Alyce initiate the link—and that Zoë offer no resistance—but the result was useful, nonetheless, especially in an environment where one must be circumspect.

I hope he'll be safe, Alyce sent. *My father and brother are going as well. Meara isn't a place I'd particularly want to go, with all the troubles there.*

Speaking of "safe," Zoë said, *should I be worried about other Deryni who might be there tomorrow?*

I'm not sure, Alyce replied honestly. *But Father Paschal told me that he tried to probe you from across the room, since that's what another Deryni might do—though only if he or she had reason to be suspicious. Still, there will be at least a few here tomorrow: Jessamy and her children, and maybe some of the in-laws from her eldest daughter's family. There could be others as well, that we don't know about. But you passed muster.*

Well, that's a relief, Zoë responded. *But maybe, just to make sure, you ought to shut me down until tomorrow's ceremonies are over.*

That's what Father Paschal suggested, Alyce sent. *You know, you're getting far too good at this.*

We'll credit that to your ability as a teacher, Zoë returned, as she yawned hugely. *I am but a mirror to reflect your own brilliance. Why? Did he think there was any real danger?*

I don't think so, Alyce replied. *But it doesn't hurt to be safe. I'll do it in the morning.*

Maybe we should just go a-Maying instead, Zoë said. *Tomorrow is going to have entirely too much ceremony and far too many important people.*

Go to sleep, Alyce ordered. *Tomorrow, we're both going to need all our wits about us.*

Chapter II

"Thou shalt also be a crown of glory in the hand of the Lord, and a royal diadem in the hand of thy God."

—ISAIAH 62:3

FESTIVITIES the following day were to begin at noon. As expected, Jessamy rode up from Rhemuth to witness her daughter's final vows, bringing along Jessilde's two younger sisters and also young Krispin, just turned three.

As a courtesy to Jessamy, the king and queen also made the journey up from the capital, their presence lending additional solemnity to the occasion, even though it was a private visit. Prince Brion, who was almost four, rode proudly at his father's saddlebow; the toddler Blaine, much to his disappointment, was relegated to a well-padded horse-litter with his mother, who was six months gone with child.

The three-year-old Krispin had expected to share that fate, but to his glee found himself hoisted up before Sir Kenneth Morgan, who had come along as the king's aide, and also to help supervise the three boys—and to visit with his daughter.

The convent chapel was packed even before the royal party's arrival, not only with the families of the two principals in the day's ceremonials but with local folk come to catch a glimpse of the king and queen.

"It's rather like a wedding," Jessilde had told Alyce, Marie, and Zoë early that morning, amid the bustle of last-minute preparations. The previous afternoon, while the nuns saw to the final cleaning of the convent church and made certain that linens were pristine and habits brushed up, the students had woven floral garlands to bedeck the altar rails and pillars in the nave, and now were finishing the final touches. It was Jessilde herself who had made the wreath of multi-colored roses for Cerys.

"These have opened nicely," she said, adjusting one of the pale pink ones. "She'll wear her hair loose on her shoulders like a bride, and her best gown, all of it covered with a very fine, very long white veil."

"Is there a bouquet?" Marie wanted to know. "I can't remember whether they carry flowers or not. I've only seen this happen once before."

"No, *these* will be her flowers," Jessilde replied. "She'll carry a lighted candle instead—*carefully,* lest she set her veil alight!—and her parents will conduct her down the aisle while you and the rest of the choir sing the *Ave Vierge Doreé.*"

"I don't think her parents are entirely happy about her decision," Zoë said. "Her mother looked like she'd been crying when they arrived last night, and her father hardly said a word."

"They had a rich husband all picked out for her," Alyce said. "Of course, he was old enough to be her father—and nearly, to be her grandfather."

"I'm sure they did," Jessilde replied. "She's a beautiful young woman, and she would have made a fitting adornment to any lord's court." She flashed an impish smile. "Of course, God had other plans for her."

Marie screwed up her face in a grimace of dismay. "Somehow, I don't think that being a bride of Christ is quite the same."

"No, it's much better!" Jessilde said happily, "at least for me. And for Cerys." She picked up the finished floral crown. "I'd better go and help her finish dressing."

They had decked the chapel with flowers, bursting from vases to either side of the altar and garlanded all along the altar rails, in addition to the garlands festooned across the ends of the benches set to either side of the rainbow-carpeted center aisle, where the guests would sit. Flowers also bedecked the fronts of the choir stalls, and hung in swags from the canopies over the back row. The altar wore a blanket of roses as a frontal, and had acquired a rainbow canopy of fine tapestry, with threads of gold woven amid its many colors, so that it glistened in the light that poured through the east window, already aglow from the colored glass.

By noon, the church was packed, Marie with the soloists of the choir, Alyce and Zoë amid the other students in their places with the general choristers, the sisters, servers, and clergy waiting ready for the entrance procession. As the last stroke of the Angelus bell faded into stillness, the choirmistress moved before the choir, gathered their attention with a glance, and raised her hands in signal for them to rise.

With the first sweet notes of the *Salve Regina,* sung a cappella in three-part harmony, the two girls given the honor of conducting the king and queen to their seats started forward, with the royal couple and the two young princes walking under the rainbow canopy they carried. Zoë's father and one of the queen's ladies followed behind them as the royal party were led along the rainbow carpet and into the choir, where they were shown to seats of honor on the Gospel side, nearest the altar.

Sir Kenneth caught his daughter's eye and winked as he took a seat next to the king, also sending an amiable nod and a smile to Alyce; the young princes sat dutifully between their parents. In the nave, Jessamy stood before a front bench with her two younger daughters and Krispin, also on the Gospel side—and on the Epistle side were Cerys's brothers and sisters, all dressed in their finest. Their parents waited at the rear of the nave with the daughter soon to be received under the rainbow, for her reception would precede Jessilde's final vows.

Others, too, had particular cause to be present here today. Standing in the row behind Jessamy and her children, Alyce noticed a pretty, dark-haired young woman who looked a lot like Jessamy, who glanced back at the double line of blue-robed sisters now starting down the aisle behind the crucifer and two torch-bearers. By the woman's expression, as she saw Jessilde among them, Alyce decided that the one who looked like Jessamy must be her eldest daughter Sieffany—which suggested that the two men next to her, farther from the aisle, were probably her husband and her father-in-law, both of them Deryni.

It occurred to Alyce that Jessamy had mentioned the father-in-law before, and had said that he came occasionally to court—Michon de Courcy, was it?—and the son was Aurélien. Jessamy had not said it in so many words, but Alyce had been left with the distinct impression that the father was a formidable Deryni, indeed, and to be avoided, if at all possible.

Certain it was that Jessamy did not look pleased to have him standing behind her, and had positioned herself as a buffer between him and her youngest, the boy Krispin, sitting quietly in the aisle position. Surely she did not think that Michon would hurt the boy?

The sisters filed into their stalls and the clergy took their places to begin the Mass, for the two ceremonies would take place within that context, following the Gospel. After the opening prayers, the readings spoke of being called by God, and the symbolism of the rainbow as a sign of His promise, and then a pious account of the apparition by which the Blessed Virgin had made her will known concerning the foundation of what became *l'Ordre de Notre Dame d'Arc-en-Ciel*.

At the conclusion of that reading, as the girls with the rainbow canopy went back up the aisle to fetch Cerys and her parents, a hush settled within the sun-drenched brilliance of the chapel, and then Marie's pure voice lifted in the first verse of an old Bremagni bridal hymn, *Ave Vierge Dorée*. The rest of the choir joined in as two of the youngest girls from the school strewed fragrant rose petals before the bridal party as Cerys's parents led her down the rainbow aisle. Uplifted before her, Cerys bore her candle of profession as if it were the most precious treasure the world could offer.

With all eyes focused there, young Krispin chose that moment to dart from his mother's side and into the choir to join the two princes, eliciting smiles and a few suppressed giggles among the girls of the convent school, a stern glance from the king, and an indulgent hug of the culprit from Queen Richeldis as he settled happily between her and Prince Blaine for a better view of the proceedings.

Murmurs of amusement gave way to sighs of wistful admiration as Cerys passed into the choir, for she had never looked more beautiful, or more content. Her figure-skimming gown of costly damask was the rich lilac hue of hyacinths, shot with gold, her loose hair tumbling down her back like a cascade of flame, and crowned with roses in every color the convent gardens had to offer. A veil of sheerest gossamer fell to her waist in the front and onto her gown's short train in the back.

By contrast, her mother looked like a plump and somewhat gaudy songbird in a gown of several shades of blue and green, with tears brimming in her blue eyes as she and her husband, a shorter and more somberly dressed man of middle years, presented their daughter before Mother Judiana, seated on a cushioned stool at the foot of the altar steps, and returned to sit with their other children.

There followed an exchange of questions and answers between superior and postulant, after which Judiana folded back the front of Cerys's veil and conducted her to the altar, where they set the candle at the feet of the statue of the Virgin, then passed though a side door while the choir sang another hymn.

When they returned to bow before the altar, Mother Judiana with the veil over one arm, the new postulant wore the pale blue habit of the order, much as she had done while a student with the other girls, but now with a snowy wimple close-covering her hair—save for the bright-flame tail of it, now braided and hanging down her back—and the wreath of roses now set atop.

This she removed and lifted up in offering before laying it reverently on the altar. Then she came down off the altar pace and lay prostrate in the midst of the choir, arms outstretched, Judiana covering her from head to toe with the fine veil she had worn and then kneeling beside her, while the community sang a litany of the saints in antiphon, answered by the choir of the school.

When they had finished, Judiana assisted Cerys to rise and led her back to the stool at the foot of the altar steps, sitting as the new novice knelt to offer up her joined hands between Judiana's and made her first profession of chastity, stability, fidelity to monastic life, and obedience. After that, she returned briefly to the altar to sign a copy of the promises she had just made, before kneeling again before the community's superior.

All that remained was the veiling of the new novice, accomplished very simply as two novice members of the community brought the white veil with its rainbow edge and held it taut above her bowed head while Judiana pronounced the formal words of blessing:

"Dearest daughter in Christ, henceforth to be known among us as Sister Iris Cerys, receive this veil in token of your chastity, and as a sign that you are enfolded in our Lady's grace and received within the embrace of the rainbow, a symbol not only of God's promise to have mercy on His people, but of our Lady's reassurance that she shall be our Advocate in the day of final Judgment.

"And though you now shall endeavor to dwell beneath the rainbow, turning your face toward the brightening sun, may the cloud-white of the novice veil remind you that you have yet to achieve the fullness of that rainbow-vision that comes with true knowledge of the Son of God."

She draped the rainbow-edge over the new novice's wimple, arranged the veil's folds on her shoulders, then set her hand on it as she pronounced the words of final blessing, *"In Nomine Patris, et Filii, et Spiritus Sancti, Amen."*

With that, while the choir sang a joyful *Alleluia,* Judiana traced a cross on the new novice's brow, conducted Sister Iris Cerys to the place in choir that henceforth would be hers, and returned to the stool before the altar.

On a visual level, the reception of Jessilde's final vows was far simpler, though it held a greater poignancy for those who understood its greater import. Coming before the community's superior, Jessilde placed her hands between those of Judiana and pledged her lifelong promises, repeating the traditional monastic vows Cerys had just made—and she, like Cerys, went to the altar to sign her agreement to the vows just sworn.

But then, instead of lying prostrate before the altar, she stood close before it and spread her arms in self-offering, leaning forward then to rest her forehead against the snowy altar linens as she sang an exhortation from the Psalms, repeated by the choir:

"Suscipe me, Domine, secundum eloquium tuum, et vivam. . . ." Receive me, O Lord, as Thou hast promised, and I shall live; and disappoint me not in my hope. . . .

This exchange they sang three times, Jessilde beginning on a slightly higher note with each repetition and the choir answering, after which she came to kneel once more before Judiana, bowing her head as the white veil of a novice was removed, shears brought on a silver tray, and the back of her wimple loosened so that Judiana might release the coiled braid of her hair and cut it off, close at the nape.

This time two vowed sisters brought the rainbow-edged blue veil that would replace the white one; but before doing that, Judiana removed the plain blue scapular that Jessilde had worn as a novice and replaced it with one embroidered along the lower edges with rainbow bands. Her words, as she laid the pale blue veil across Jessilde's head, were similar to those she had spoken earlier:

"Dearest daughter in Christ, known among us as Sister Iris Jessilde, receive now the veil of a fully vowed member of this order, the clear, celestial blue of our Lady's mantle, enfolding you in the bright rainbow that signifies God's promise and our Lady's benison. May you dwell ever in the Son-light that creates this Sign, *In Nomine Patris, et Filii, et Spiritus Sancti, Amen.*"

As she had done for Cerys, now she traced a cross on Jessilde's forehead, before placing a gold ring on the marriage finger of her left hand. Jessilde raised that hand above her head, so that all could see the ring, then bent to kiss Judiana's hand before being raised up.

After that, she took back the coiled braid of her hair from the silver salver and laid it on the altar in offering, as Cerys had offered up her flower crown. One day, in one of their sessions with Father Paschal, he had told Alyce and Marie and Jessilde that, in the days before the great persecutions, the men of the all-Deryni Order of Saint Gabriël had worn a similar braid, though of four strands, never cutting their hair once they had made their vows; and if forced by circumstance to cut their braids, had been obliged to dispose of the braid in ritual far more intricate than Jessilde's simple offering.

Alyce thought about that parallel all through the Mass that followed, wondering how many others within these walls were aware of that ancient Deryni custom besides those Father Paschal had told.

MICHON de Courcy knew, though he would have been surprised to learn how many others present were also privy to that knowledge. His purpose in attending Jessilde MacAthan's final profession, while ostensibly to honor this important milestone in the life of his son's sister-in-law, was actually a long awaited opportunity to hopefully gain him access for that closer look at her younger brother; for there had been little doubt in Michon's mind that the boy's mother, Jessamy, would ride up from Rhemuth for the event, and probably would bring all of her younger children—as, indeed, she had done.

Not that she had been pleased to see Michon in the party with her eldest daughter—though, given his familial connection, he was certain that no one else would have thought his presence inappropriate. The king and queen certainly had been cordial enough.

But he suspected that it was Jessamy who, to remove young Krispin from such close proximity to a man who might uncover the truth about him, had instigated the boy's sudden dash forward to sit with the princes—though Krispin's impulsive action was not altogether inappropriate or unexpected, under the circumstances. The young princes *had* occupied the best seats in the house for a close view of the proceedings; and though, by special dispensation, the Mass ran well into the afternoon, the three boys had been quite well behaved, given their young ages.

But though Michon had feared that the change of seating arrangement might stymie any chance of success in the true purpose of his presence, he found his opportunity later that evening when, after supper in the refectory with the rest of the close family and friends invited to stay the night, he chanced to be walking in the cloister garden. After pausing to chat briefly with Sir Kenneth Morgan and his daughter—and Lady Alyce de Corwyn, in whose presence he kept himself carefully shielded—he noticed three dark heads clustered somewhat conspiratorially in a sheltered corner of the garden, one of their owners poking at something on the ground. Wandering closer, he saw that the object of their interest was a very small, very dead bird—a swallow, by the look of it, not yet fully fledged.

"What a pity," he said, as he crouched down casually among them. "What do you suppose happened?"

There in the convent garden, none of the three showed any

sign of wariness, for they had seen Michon in the church, sitting behind Krispin's mother, and knew he was kin to one of the nuns.

"I think he falled out of his nest," said Prince Brion, who was senior of the three both by age and by rank. Under the eaves above them, Michon could see the bulges of several tiny nests plastered close against the rafters.

"But, why didn't he fly?" Blaine said plaintively.

"Because his wings are too small," Brion replied, grasping the tips of both tiny wings and stretching them out to display their juvenile state. "See, they're only little. But I think he was going to be a swallow, like those up there."

He glanced upward at a nest tucked up under the eaves, with several little heads looking down at them with beady little eyes. Nearby, several adult swallows were clinging to precarious toeholds amid the ends of the rafters, heads swiveling to watch them.

"I see more babies up there!" Blaine cried.

At the same time, Brion started to turn the bird over for a closer look at the markings on its throat, but Krispin recoiled, wrinkling up his nose in disgust.

"Ugh, it's got crawly things on it! Leave it alone!"

Brion abandoned the bird at once, wiping both hands against his crimson tunic, and Blaine hastily backed off a step, lower lip a-quiver. He collided with the crouching Michon, who slipped a comforting arm around him and also took the opportunity to do the same to Krispin.

"It's all right, son. That's part of nature's way," he said, reassuring young Blaine and, at the same time, quickly daring a very gentle touch of the other boy's mind—and then a deeper probe, when the first touch seemed not to be noticed. "Do you think we ought to bury him?"

"That's a good idea," Brion said. Already showing signs of leadership, he immediately started to scoop out a suitable hole with his bare hands.

"Maybe he's just sleeping," young Blaine said hopefully, as he watched his brother dig.

"No, I'm afraid he's dead, son," Michon replied.

"But—why did he falled out of the nest?" Blaine insisted. "Why didn't the mama bird or the papa bird help him?"

"I'm sure they wanted to," Michon assured him, redirecting the boy's attention to the adult swallows watching from above. "I'm sure they're very sad. Don't you see them looking down at us? They're watching to make sure we take good care of their baby."

"Oh," said Blaine, apparently satisfied with this explanation.

"Shouldn't we wrap him in something soft then, before we bury him?" Krispin asked, turning to look at Michon. "I can get a handkerchief from Mama. . . ."

"I have another idea," Michon replied, for he did not want the boy to go just yet. "Birds are nature's creatures. Why don't you line his little grave with leaves, or flower petals? That would make him a very soft bed."

"An' it will make him smell better, too!" Brion said, looking up with a pixie grin as he continued to scoop fresh earth. "Blaine, you go get some flowers."

As Blaine raced off to pillage the nearest rosebush, ruthlessly pulling off the heads of several blown blooms, Krispin glanced up again at Michon, still taking comfort from his embrace.

"You know a lot about birds, don't you, sir?" he asked.

"Well, I know a lot about a few things and a little about a lot of things," Michon admitted. "I do know that your particular bird would have grown up to be a very fine swallow. I love watching them wheel in the sun. . . ."

And as Blaine returned and the three boys set about shredding roses and lining the little grave, Michon continued to crouch among them to encourage and advise—and was able to probe undetected into young Krispin's mind, discovering most of what he had come there to learn.

Chapter 12

"Thy men shall fall by the sword, and thy mighty in the war."

—ISAIAH 3:25

"I'VE finally managed a look at Krispin MacAthan," Michon announced to the Camberian Council a few days later, accessing their meeting place from the Portal at Rhemuth Cathedral. "I cannot tell you for certain that he is Donal Haldane's son; but I *can* tell you that I do not believe Sief can have been his father."

After deflecting their startled flurry of questions and demands for clarification, he reached his arms to either side to link hands with Barrett and Vivienne, flanking him left and right, and waited while the others did likewise, drawing them quickly into a deep rapport that enabled them to share what he had learned. When they came out of the trance, his fellow councilors glanced uneasily among themselves, uncertain what it all meant.

"Far more useful, of course, would have been to question Jessamy directly," Michon reminded them. "Krispin himself knows nothing of the man whose name he bears, save what he has been told. And if Donal Haldane *is* his father, I still have no idea how that came to pass."

"In the usual way, one would assume," Oisín murmured, in a droll aside to Seisyll.

"Whatever his paternity," Michon went on, ignoring the remark, "we are fortunate, indeed, that Krispin MacAthan—

or Krispin Haldane, as he probably should be called—exhibits none of the worrying characteristics that made his grandfather so dangerous. Nor does he seem to favor his mother, in that regard. If anything, he somewhat reminds me of Morian—who will need to be told that he need not pursue our previous request," he added, with a glance at Oisín. "All things considered, his Deryni heritage, combined with whatever it is that makes the Haldanes so curiously formidable, seems to have produced a child of quite interesting potential."

Dominy raised an elegant eyebrow. "Pray, define 'interesting,' in this context," she said.

Several of them smiled ruefully at that, and Michon shrugged. "The boy is only three. If we cannot bend him to our purposes, he can always be eliminated later on. But this one bears watching, I think. Actually, the boy is nearly of an age to begin his training as a page—which means that he will be far more accessible in the future. Accordingly, it might be profitable for Seisyll to watch for opportunities to gain his friendship."

"I have been doing that for the past three years," Seisyll replied, "but it is true that he should become more accessible in the future. And it's a relief to know that we need make no immediate decisions."

"There is another decision that will require our attention sooner rather than later," Michon went on. "I saw Keryell's girls while I was at Arc-en-Ciel. They've both become quite the beauties."

"Probably as well, then, that they are locked away in a convent for now," Dominy said mildly. "What are they now? Maybe fifteen or so?"

"Fourteen and fifteen," Barrett replied. "Ripe enough for marriage."

"Yes, well," Seisyll muttered. "The last time I spoke to Keryell about his plans for them, he was quite willing to be guided by our recommendations. And I can guide the king, of course. I have him thinking about several likely candidates who would inject the right Deryni blood into the Corwyn line."

"Those matches aren't nearly as critical as they once might have been," Oisín pointed out. "Rather, we should be thinking about a match for their brother Ahern. He is easing nicely into the promise of his line, and his father has been campaigning him rather heavily the past year or so. When the time comes, he should make quite a formidable Duke of Corwyn."

Vivienne had been nodding as he spoke. "Ah, yes. Surprisingly good bloodlines. I know that no one was pleased when Keryell seized Stevana de Corwyn and married her by force, but the outcome has been most salubrious—and even Keryell himself seems to have come around to the discipline of the Council."

"Perhaps we should send him on a mission to Carthane," Dominy said. "Something must be done about Bishop Oliver de Nore. . . ."

BUT for Donal Haldane, while Carthane and its Deryni persecutions remained a troublesome source of periodic unrest, it was westward that he looked with increasing uneasiness, for Meara remained yet unsettled. His sons were thriving, the harvests plentiful, and with the decade at its mid-point, even Nimur of Torenth seemed to have turned his aspirations away from Gwynedd, campaigning eastward past Arjenol that season. By September of 1085, when Queen Richeldis presented Donal with the dainty daughter she had longed for, christened Xenia, the king could look back on several seasons of peace, though most of the year to date had been bracketed with military readiness.

That spring, acting on rumors of growing unrest in Meara, Donal had appointed his half-brother, Duke Richard, to assume active field command of the Gwyneddan Army. Richard, in turn, had spent the summer organizing the Gwynedd levies and drilling the standing units—and to good purpose, for August had seen a royal birth in Meara: a son, to the Princess Onora, who was daughter of the present Mearan pretender, Prince Judhael.

The birth of a male heir had rekindled Mearan aspirations to independence, even though the marriage of Donal's father with Roisian of Meara was to have settled the Mearan succession after the death of her father without male issue. Prince Judhael was Roisian's nephew, son of the Princess Annalind, who had been Roisian's twin.

But the widow of the last prince, the Dowager Princess

Urracca, had promoted the cause of Annalind, the younger twin, over that of Roisian, whom she deemed a traitor to her land for having married Malcolm Haldane. All three were now long dead—mother and both daughters—but Annalind's son Judhael had begun to attract renewed support among Mearan separatists. During that winter following the birth of Judhael's grandson, his wife—who was Llanneddi, aunt to Queen Richeldis—wrote several times to her niece in Rhemuth, warning that, if a Mearan accommodation could not be reached, their respective husbands were headed for war.

All through that winter and into the spring of 1086, much of the gossip and speculation at the court of Rhemuth was focused on the prospect of rebellion brewing in the west. At midsummer, the king gave his brother Richard a commission as acting viceroy of Meara and sent him to Ratharkin to set up a court of inquiry, with instructions to enlist the full assistance of the Lady Jessamy's brother, Sir Morian du Joux. By this, he meant Deryni assistance.

Serving as the prince's advisors and staff were Lord Seisyll Arilan, Sir Kenneth Morgan, and Keryell Earl of Lendour, who brought along his son Ahern. In addition, the king sent summons of array to two of his earls whose holdings lay near Meara's borders, and who thus had a personal interest in holding the peace in Meara: Jared of Kierney and Caulay of Transha, both of them in their youthful prime and both bringing small but powerful levies to enforce the king's authority, if necessary. Finally, as a sign of his personal authority, the king also sent along a squadron of Haldane lancers.

By Lammastide, Duke Richard had assembled his team in Ratharkin and begun to hear grievances. By Michaelmas, it had become clear that most of the Mearan complaints were groundless or trivial, and that the Mearans were but wasting the court's time.

Matters came to a head late in October, though the aftermath fell just short of all-out war. It was Keryell and Ahern who, on the eve of the Feast of All Saints, just managed to foil an assassination plot that might have claimed Richard, the royal governor, and perhaps several more high-ranking Gwyneddan men—except that Ahern de Corwyn had chanced to detect the rebels' intentions before they could be fully carried out, he being young and, therefore, not fully under their suspicion. Nor was it widely known in Meara that he and his father were Deryni.

The concerted response by the king's men was enough to prevent serious harm to Richard himself, but not enough to save Keryell and several Haldane lancers who were cut down in the fighting. Two of the assassins were also killed outright.

"How could this have happened?" Richard whispered, nursing a badly bruised hand in his chambers that night with Seisyll, Morian, and the two young earls whose levies had provided the military force for a successful defense. Sir Kenneth Morgan, tonight acting as Richard's aide, was pouring wine for all of them, and sported a bloodied bandage across his forehead and a blackened right eye. "Jared, how many others did we lose?"

"Five of your Haldane lancers, two of my own, and one of Caulay's, your Highness," Jared replied, "and we could lose several more from their wounds. Keryell's boy may lose a leg. The knee was shattered."

"Damn!" Shaking his head, Richard let it fall heavily onto his undamaged hand. "Bad enough, to lose his father. And now, if he lives, he'll be a cripple all his days."

"Your Highness, this canna be allowed tae go unpunished," Earl Caulay said, his border brogue thick with emotion, for the man he had lost had been a cousin. "If ye dinna nip it in the bud right now, there'll be another full-scale rebellion within five years, mark my words."

"I agree," Seisyll said. "The plot obviously had been long in the planning, and it very nearly succeeded. It seems clear that they were after you—and that is a direct attack on the king your brother."

"I can't argue with that," Richard said. "How many prisoners have we?"

"Eight," Morian replied promptly. "And we killed another ten."

"Did many escape, do you think?" Richard asked.

Seisyll exchanged a glance with Morian. The two of them had gone among the prisoners a few hours earlier, reading their guilt.

"I doubt it," Seisyll said.

"Most of the prisoners are known trouble-makers," Morian added.

Richard slowly lifted his head. At thirty, he was a seasoned warrior, already with a reputation on and off the field, but in this hour he looked far older.

"I am minded to hang them all, gentlemen," he said, "for only by sharp example may we hope to discourage future treachery of this sort. I do not doubt that Caulay is right: that we shall have to mount another punitive expedition here within the next few years. But stern measures now might postpone it a while longer." He sighed. "I like it not, that I must be the one to send word of our losses to my brother. I had not thought to lose him an earl on this mission, and especially not . . ."

His vague sigh in the direction of Morian made it clear that he was regretting the loss of Keryell's Deryni skills as well as the man himself. The others exchanged grim glances, but when no one else spoke up, Sir Kenneth said gently, "Shall I prepare the execution order, your Highness?"

WORD of what Richard had caused to be done reached Rhemuth on a wet and blustery morning some five days later, though he and his returning troops—and the bodies of the slain—would not arrive for another fortnight. With the news from Ratharkin came lists: those killed or executed in the king's name and those who had died in his service.

Donal received the report, both verbal and written, in the snug withdrawing room behind the screens at the end of the great hall, and immediately called for an aide and a clark. Sir Kenneth Morgan had brought the news, muddy and rain-bedraggled, and shifted uneasily from one booted foot to the other as the king read, wringing rain from a sodden hank of sandy hair pulled back at his nape. Doing his best to stifle a sneeze, he let a squire exchange his dripping cloak for a warm, dry blanket and sat as Donal waved him to a stool set close before the fire, gratefully accepting the cup of mulled wine a page thrust into his fist.

"How bad is it *really,* Kenneth?" the king asked, still scanning the lists.

"Bad enough, Sire," Kenneth replied. "We were very, very lucky that our losses weren't worse."

As Kenneth closed cold-numbed fingers around his cup

and took a long pull at his wine, Donal said, "I see here that you and Keryell may well have saved my brother's life—that you were the heroes of the day. Did you know that Richard said that in this letter?"

Kenneth nearly choked on his wine, looking up in surprise mixed with faint discomfiture. A knight of only minor holdings, about to turn forty, he had been the king's loyal servant for more than half his life—still well fit for field or council table, but hitherto quietly resigned that fame and fortune were unlikely to be his.

"I'll take that as a 'no,'" Donal said, quirking him a faint smile.

"I but did my duty, Sire, as I would have done for you," Kenneth said, when he had stopped coughing.

"Well, you did it very well, and I'll not forget. Now, go get yourself a hot meal and a bed." As Sir Kenneth rose to do the king's bidding, the summoned men entered, the aide saluting with fist to breast and the clark bowing over the writing case clutched to his chest.

"Again, well done," Donal said, as the exhausted man took his leave. "Tiarnán, I have just received ill news from Ratharkin," he went on, beckoning the aide closer. "Who are Earl Keryell's stewards in Lendour and Corwyn, in his absence?"

"In Corwyn, that would be the seneschal of Coroth, my Liege," the aide replied, glancing after Sir Kenneth. "For Lendour, I don't know; I would need to make inquiries. Has something happened to Earl Keryell?"

"Unfortunately, it has." Donal handed Tiarnán the lists he had just received. "There was an assassination attempt. Richard is safe, and he hanged all the perpetrators, but Keryell is slain, and five lancers, along with several others from Kierney and Transha. Keryell's son is gravely wounded. I'll ask you to notify the families of the lancers; their names are there." He nodded toward the lists in Tiernán's hand. "Father Farian will help you with the necessary letters, and I'll need to send some of my own. As for Keryell's daughters, I think that warrants more personal attention." He rose and stepped into the corridor to summon a page.

"Ivone, please ask Lady Jessamy to attend us," he said. "Tell her I shall need her to ride to Arc-en-Ciel at once. And have Sir Jiri Redfearn assemble a suitable escort. It's vile weather to send her out, but this kind of news comes best from another woman—at least the bare bones of it."

As the page scurried off to carry out the king's instructions, Tiarnán quickly scanned down the lists, grim-faced, shaking his head.

"Ill news, indeed, Sire. I recognize several of these names—on both sides. And with Ahern injured and still under-age, it occurs to me that you'll need regencies in Lendour and Corwyn. Do you wish me to summon the appropriate men?"

Donal shook his head. "Not at this time. Just advise the stewards what has happened, and say that I have taken Corwyn and Lendour directly under my protection for the nonce, pending more permanent arrangements. If young Ahern doesn't live, Keryell's daughters are about to become very important heiresses."

THE page who summoned Jessamy to join the king did not know the reason, but his instructions that she was to prepare to ride to Arc-en-Ciel told her that it must concern Alyce and Marie, or possibly Zoë Morgan, whose fathers were presently on assignment in Ratharkin. Everyone at court knew the precarious nature of Duke Richard's mission in Meara, and what other high-ranking lords were in his party.

The king was dictating to Father Farian when she entered the room, now dressed to accommodate the freezing rain outside. Nearby, Sir Tiarnán MacRae was busy with his own pen and parchments. One look at their faces warned her that the news must be bad, indeed.

"You sent for me, Sire?"

He sighed and looked around at her, waving dismissal to the page who had brought her and also casting an absent glance at Tiarnán and the young priest, who now were conferring in low tones.

"I've had ill news from Ratharkin," he said without preamble.

"Yes, Sire," she murmured. "Not of Duke Richard, I trust?"

"No, he is well, thank God, but Keryell Earl of Lendour

has been slain, along with several others, and his son is sorely wounded. His daughters must be informed. I'll not burden you with details that are better saved for *them,* but you should know that young Ahern may yet succumb to his injuries—though he was yet alive when the news left Ratharkin."

"That is, at least, one blessing," she murmured. "Have you word of Sir Kenneth Morgan? His daughter is also at Arc-en-Ciel."

"Tell her that he is well," the king replied. "He brought the news, and I have sent him to bed." He shook his head wearily. "I do not envy you this mission, my lady. Would you rather I sent another?"

"No, Sire," Jessamy said softly. "Better it comes from me than from a stranger."

Donal nodded. "Thank you. I had hoped that would be your answer. I've asked Sir Jiri Redfearn to assemble an escort. He should have horses ready by the time you reach the stable yard."

"Thank you, Sire," Jessamy murmured. "Do you wish us to stay the night at Arc-en-Ciel or to return immediately? The weather—"

"—is beastly, I know," the king said, finishing her sentence. "Let the girls decide—though I see no need for overmuch haste. Kenneth said that the bodies of the slain will not reach Rhemuth for a week or more." He paused a beat, sorrow in his face. "You'd best be on your way."

"Very good, Sire," she whispered, sinking in an obedient curtsy.

AN early dusk was descending as the sister-portress admitted the half-dozen riders drawn up in the driving rain outside the convent gate. Lady Jessamy MacAthan was well known at Arc-en-Ciel, and her instructions were accepted without question as she bade one of the sisters to take Sir Jiri and his men into the outer parlor to warm before the fire.

"Pray, bring them dry blankets and food and drink as well," Jessamy said, letting another sister take her own sodden cloak and exchange it for a dry robe lined with fur. "I come on the king's urgent business, and must speak with Alyce and Marie."

"They are with a visitor, my lady," Sister Iris Agatha informed her. "Their family chaplain. Do you wish me to interrupt them?"

Jessamy looked at the blue-robed sister sharply. "Father Paschal is here?"

The sister nodded. "He is, my lady. They do have permission for him to call on them. Their father gave his leave shortly after they joined us."

"Oh, I'm well aware of *that*," Jessamy assured her. "I'm simply glad to learn that he's here. Unfortunately, I bring ill news concerning Earl Keryell. He's been killed in Ratharkin, and the girls' brother is seriously wounded. I've been sent to fetch them back to Rhemuth. I'm sure Father Paschal will wish to accompany them."

"Indeed, I'm sure he will," Sister Iris Agatha replied, eyes wide with surprise and compassion. "Are we—at war with Meara?"

Jessamy gave a weary shrug. "I would assume not, since the king said nothing of that. I have no details, save that Zoë Morgan's father brought the news—so she, at least, may rest easy. May we go now?"

WHEN, after a discreet knock, Zoë herself opened the door of the writing room adjoining the convent's main library, Jessamy brushed past her with only a perfunctory greeting, leaving Sister Iris Agatha standing outside as she pulled the door shut behind her. Across the room, the Corwyn sisters were rising from seats before the fire, near to a slight, black-robed figure bent over a brown leather satchel.

"Tante Jessamy!" Alyce cried, delighted, though her face fell as she saw the older woman's somber expression, and her sister grabbed her hand, apprehension growing. Now sixteen, Alyce de Corwyn was coming into stunning young womanhood, with creamy skin and dark-lashed eyes the same blue as her fur-lined over-robe. Marie, a year younger, was of rosier complexion, with a bronze braid instead of Alyce's gold, but equally attractive.

"Tante Jessamy, what's wrong?" Alyce asked, when the older woman did not immediately speak. "What can have brought you out in such dreadful weather?"

Saying nothing yet, Jessamy came to slip an arm around the

waists of both girls and hug them close in greeting, gazing past them at the man in R'Kassan clergy robes, who straightened to give her a guarded inclination of his head. Clergy trained at the great R'Kassan seminaries were widely respected for their erudition and soundness of doctrine, but it was not widely known that priests like Paschal sometimes ventured quietly into Gwynedd by special mission, usually as private chaplains and tutors of noble children.

That some of them were Deryni was even less well known. But because their first duty was to their patrons rather than local bishops, and because they tended to keep a low profile, they usually were left alone. Jessamy had met Paschal briefly at Carthanelle, when Keryell of Lendour had given his daughters into the queen's keeping, and she was well aware of who and what he really was.

"Lady Jessamy," Paschal said neutrally, though his eyes showed a hint of wariness at her presence. "I trust you are in good health."

Inclining her head, Jessamy drew the girls with her closer to the fire, and Paschal.

"I am, Father, I thank you," she said, belatedly remembering that she had left Zoë standing anxiously beside the door. "Zoë, come here, child. There's been ill news from Ratharkin. Your father is unharmed, but—"

Marie's hands had flown to her mouth as Jessamy spoke, and she gave a little gasp.

"Is our father dead?" she breathed, her voice quavering with dread.

Wearily Jessamy gave a nod, drawing the younger girl into the circle of her arms and letting Zoë go to Alyce.

"I fear that he is, my dear. I am so very sorry. He fell in the king's service, protecting Duke Richard. I have no further details at this time."

"And what of our brother?" Alyce demanded, clinging to Zoë. "Say that *he* is not dead as well. . . ."

"He was alive when the news was sent," Jessamy allowed, "though I am informed that he was wounded. But we must not give up hope, dear child."

Going suddenly white, Alyce sank down on the stool where she had been sitting, an anxious Zoë sinking beside her as Marie began sobbing in Jessamy's arms.

"Our brother *is* dead, isn't he?" Alyce murmured numbly, starting to shake in Zoë's arms as Father Paschal came to sit on her other side. "He's dead, but you aren't telling us."

At Jessamy's pointed glance toward Zoë, Father Paschal reached across to set his hand on her shoulder, extending controls. As her eyes closed and she slumped against Alyce, Jessamy nodded her thanks and returned her attention to Alyce, all the while stroking Marie's hair.

"Darling, that isn't true," she said truthfully. "I cannot guarantee that he is still alive, but I swear to you that, when the news was sent, he still lived. Read the truth of what I am telling you, Alyce—or Father Paschal can confirm it for you, since I know he has been reading me as we speak. I wish I could give you more certain reassurance, but I cannot, dear heart. You must keep hope alive, and storm heaven with your prayers. They expect that it may take as long as a fortnight for Duke Richard and his party to return to Rhemuth. Meanwhile, the king asks that you return to court."

Jessamy's calm, reasoned statement broke the final barrier holding back Alyce's tears. For the next little while, she leaned against Father Paschal and sobbed her heart out, with Zoë oblivious beside them.

When, finally, the sobbing eased and Alyce raised her head, snuffling and wiping at her eyes with her sleeve, Paschal allowed Zoë to stir, blurring her awareness of the passage of time. As Zoë straightened, she pulled off her veil and handed it to Alyce, who did a more thorough job of wiping her eyes and then blew her nose. Marie, too, had begun to compose herself, and Jessamy pulled off her veil and bade Marie use it mop her face.

"My dears, I am so very sorry," Jessamy murmured. "Would that I could have brought you better news. Shall we ask Zoë to bring you something warm to drink?"

Alyce started to shake her head, still dabbing at her nose, but Jessamy was already urging Zoë to go, and Father Paschal was also indicating that this was a good idea. When Zoë had gone, Marie came to sit beside her sister, laying her head on Alyce's shoulder and snuffling softly. Alyce glanced around listlessly, hugging her arms across her chest, then whispered, "We shall never come back here, shall we, Tante Jessamy?

Now that our father is gone, I fear that the king will see us soon married."

The words transported Jessamy back to the awful night her own father had died, though at least she did not think that Donal would force these girls into a totally detestable match. At least not while their brother yet lived.

"He has said nothing to me on that account," she said truthfully. "And provided your brother recovers—and God grant that he shall!—*he* will have some say in whom you wed. But this is not the time to worry overmuch about that."

Alyce said nothing, only slipping an arm around her sister's waist, spent by her weeping. "I suppose we must go tonight to Rhemuth."

"No, we have the king's leave to delay until tomorrow," Jessamy replied. "And I think you would take comfort in bidding your friends farewell. Perhaps in the morning, before we leave, Father Paschal would offer Mass for your father's soul," she added, with a glance at the priest, who nodded.

"I shall ask Mother Judiana," he said. "I'm certain she will have no objection. And of course I shall accompany you to Rhemuth—and to Cynfyn, after that. My place now must be at Lord Ahern's side—and to comfort his sisters."

Jessamy nodded. "Then, we should see about getting a few things packed, girls. You need not bring much with you—"

"But, what of my books, my manuscripts—?"

"Those can be sent later," Jessamy assured her. "More important just now is to find warmer clothing for both of you, for the ride back to Rhemuth will be cold as well as wet. I did bring some oiled cloaks for you, such as the soldiers wear, well-lined with squirrel, but you will need warm gloves and hats."

"I'm certain those can be found," Alyce said dully. "Oh, Tante Jessamy, what's to become of us?"

"You shall be the toast of the king's court," Father Paschal said with a tiny smile. "And when the time comes, your brother shall find himself inundated with suitors for your hands."

"If he lives," Marie said bleakly.

Chapter 13

"Let your laughter be turned to mourning, and your joy to heaviness."

—JAMES 4:9

THEY rode out of Arc-en-Ciel shortly before midday of the following morning, though whether the falling snow was better than the rain and sleet of the day before, Jessamy could not say. Alyce and Marie rode together, Jessamy beside the priest, with Sir Jiri's household escort divided ahead and behind and Jiri himself bringing up the rear. All of them were well-muffled against the cold and the very sticky snow, and no one said much. As Jessamy had suggested, they carried little with them.

By the time they reached Rhemuth later that afternoon, the light snowfall of the morning had become far more serious, to the point of seriously slowing their progress. Accordingly, all in their party were weary and chilled to the bone by the time they rode into the castle forecourt. As grooms took the horses on into the stable yard, Sir Jiri Redfearn immediately conducted his party through the great hall and into the withdrawing room behind the dais, pausing en route to let them shed their sodden outer cloaks beside one of the great hall fireplaces.

In winter and in the increasingly chilling days of autumn, Donal was wont to use the chamber as his preferred workroom, and today was dictating correspondence to a clark working at a table near the fire, pacing as he spoke. Behind him, several more men were quietly conversing on a bench and several stools closer to the fire. All of them rose as Jessamy and the two girls entered the room, followed by the priest, and Donal lifted a hand in signal for the clark to cease his writing.

"Brother Brendan, we'll finish that later; you may go," he said. "And the rest of you as well—save for Sir Kenneth. Ladies . . . please come and warm yourselves by the fire; you must be frozen. And you as well, Father. Please be welcome. Ivone, warm up that wine for them, and Jiri, please ask the queen to join us."

As Sir Jiri left on his errand, and most of the men before the fire gave way to the newcomers and left, Donal exchanged a measuring glance with Jessamy, who returned a nod of reassurance. He then bent his gaze toward Alyce and Marie, who were sinking uncertainly on the bench to either side of Jessamy, steeling themselves for the further news they did not want to hear. Behind them, the squire was setting out cups for mulled wine, and Sir Kenneth had emerged from shadow, his sandy hair glinting in the firelight as he gave a grim nod to Alyce and Marie.

"Dear Alyce and Marie," the king said gently, moving a stool in front of them and sitting, "I am so sorry to bring you back to Rhemuth with such ill tidings. I hope your journey was not too taxing."

Alyce remembered proprieties well enough to glance toward Father Paschal, still standing a little apart from them.

"It was very cold, Sire, but thank you for your concern. May I present Father Paschal Didier, our father's household chaplain and our tutor of many years. He happened to be visiting Arc-en-Ciel when . . . the news arrived."

Donal spared a sparse nod in acknowledgment of the priest's bow and gestured for him to sit, Kenneth also taking a seat near the king, though farther back.

"I am grateful for your presence, Father—though I would wish that we met under happier circumstances." He sighed and turned his attention back to the two girls. "I fear I have no further news beyond what Kenneth brought yesterday, so I cannot tell you whether your brother yet lives. His injury itself was not life-threatening, but the damage was severe, and infection is always a concern."

"Perhaps we might know more regarding the nature of his

wounds, Sire," Alyce replied, strain making her voice quaver. "Is he fit to travel? Pray, do not spare us, for I have learned much of surgery and physicking at Arc-en-Ciel, and would know what we must expect."

At Donal's glance, Kenneth cleared his throat uneasily and sat forward a little.

"Alyce, your brother and your father very probably saved Duke Richard's life," Kenneth said, not answering her question. "Mearan separatists had plotted to slay the duke and as many as they could of the delegation, but Lord Ahern discovered the plot in time to raise the alarm, so that we were not taken totally by surprise. In the fracas that followed, your father then killed at least four attackers before he finally took a mortal wound."

Marie closed her eyes, biting back tears as Kenneth continued.

"Your brother also acquitted himself well, and aided me in wrestling your father's killer to the floor, holding him helpless until others could take him captive, along with several more of the rebels. Rarely have I seen a lad of his age fight more bravely or with more skill."

"You have avoided speaking of his wound," Alyce pointed out.

Kenneth briefly bowed his head, then looked at her again, not sparing her.

"Unfortunately, the fighting was still in progress, my lady, and your brother took a leg wound that shattered the left knee. The surgeons are hopeful that he will survive, but he may lose the leg."

"Dear God," she breathed.

"Alyce, my brother's own battle-surgeon is caring for him," Donal assured her, as the queen and one of her ladies entered the room and all of them rose. "Ah, there you are, my dear. Our Alyce and Marie are in need of your comfort."

Shaking her head in sympathy, Richeldis came to Alyce and Marie with open arms, sadness written across her pretty face as she enfolded both younger girls in a sisterly embrace.

"Dear Alyce, Marie—I was truly sorry to hear about your father."

"Thank you, Madam," Alyce murmured, as her sister began crying again. "Sire, my brother—is it truly safe to move him, wounded?"

Donal moved aside so that his young wife could take his seat on the stool, for she was again with child.

"I am told that he would not stay at Ratharkin," said the king, "and that he asked for you often in the days immediately after his injury." He smiled grimly. "Master Donnard felt that it was safer to move him than to have him pine for his sisters' loving care."

Alyce had been biting at her lower lip as the tale unfolded, her fear mirrored in her eyes, and she swallowed with difficulty before speaking.

"But—he *is* going to live . . . ?"

"Alyce, I can only tell you that he was alive when I left a week ago," Kenneth said, "and that the surgeons are hopeful that he shall remain so. He is young and strong."

"If it's any consolation," Donal added, "Richard hanged the perpetrators to the man—eight of them—and we have the names of several more who appear to have eluded capture, at least for now. I fear this means that we must expect more trouble in the future, but perhaps the example of those executed will at least postpone another Mearan expedition for a year or so. And your father's sacrifice for Gwynedd will not be forgotten."

Tears were spilling from Alyce's lashes now, but she brushed at them impatiently with the back of one hand, lifting her chin bravely.

"And what is to become of *us,* Sire?" she murmured.

"Alas, that cannot be determined until we know whether your brother will survive," Donal said reluctantly. "He became Earl of Lendour upon the death of your father, of course, though it will be another ten years before he may wield the full authority of that office; but I shall certainly allow him a say in your fate. For now, until he is mended, your place is at his side."

Alyce inclined her head, blinking back more tears.

"Thank you, Sire. And if he does *not* survive?"

Donal glanced at Richeldis and Jessamy, then back at Alyce and Marie, regret in his gaze.

"That would be . . . difficult, on many levels—and believe

me, child, I understand what now concerns you," he said gently. "You both are of an age to marry soon. Perhaps you have even begun to form personal preferences, though I know you are aware that, being who you are, duty may well oblige you to marry other than where your heart might wish."

Alyce nodded, tight-lipped, and Richeldis glanced beseechingly at her husband.

"My lord . . ."

"No, she must know the full extent of how things lie," Donal said, not relenting. "Alyce, your brother has suffered a grave injury in my service, and may not survive. If that should come to pass, I assure you that I should regret that greatly.

"However, if that should occur—or if he should die without a male heir," Donal went on, "the two of you would inherit. It would be complicated, so we shall worry about the details when and if that should become necessary. But whatever else may befall, your eventual husbands will have serious responsibilities, because of who and what you are, so you will appreciate why they must be carefully selected."

"Donal Haldane, you are no help at all!" the queen declared, as Marie wailed and Alyce began sobbing. "You make it all sound so dreadful and official. But girls, you may be certain that, when the time comes, the king will choose you gentle husbands—else he shall not often have his queen in his bed!" she added, with an admonitory glance at Donal.

Donal managed a half-hearted chuckle at that, indulgent of what he knew was an attempt to reassure the frightened girls, and Jessamy drew both of them into the circle of her arms again.

"Shu-shu-shu," she murmured, "we shall not speak further of marriages just now. Your Majesties, methinks these pretty maids have grieving to do, which is best done in private, in Aunt Jessamy's arms. Come, darlings. I shall have an extra bed made up in my own chamber for the night. Nothing need be done in haste. We have time and enough to ponder what the future may bring."

ALYCE awoke the next morning to find herself alone in Jessamy's great bed. Marie was nowhere to be seen. She could hear activity through the partially open doorway into the next room, so she rose and made hasty ablutions, re-braiding her hair and dressing hurriedly in her blue school gown, which was all she had, and poked her head next door to investigate.

Next to the fire, Jessamy and Mistress Anjelica were pulling a tawny gold under-tunic over the head of a child—revealed to be Krispin, as his tousled head emerged from the neck of the garment. Nearby, a somewhat recovered Marie was braiding the hair of Jessamy's youngest daughter, now eight. Both children looked to have grown a handspan since Alyce last had seen them. Krispin grinned at her as his mother turned aside to retrieve a comb from the mantel. Now nearing five, he was turning into a handsome young man.

"Look, Mama!" he said, pointing.

"Well, good morning," Jessamy said, as she and the others turned and saw Alyce. "We were going to let you sleep awhile longer." She grimaced as she tried finger-combing Krispin's tangled hair, and handed the comb to Anjelica.

"Good heavens, Krispin, did you stand on your head while you slept? Jeli, I'm about convinced that this child invites mice to nest in his hair when he goes to bed for the night. God alone knows how he manages to get his hair so tangled, just from sleeping."

Alyce smiled bravely and came to crouch down beside Krispin, who had his boots on, but with the laces dangling. The boy grimaced as Anjelica began working the tangles out of his hair.

"Good morning, Krispin—and Seffira," she said.

Seffira broke away from Marie to come and give Alyce a welcoming hug.

"Cousin Alyce, I'm so sorry. Mummy says your papa has gone to be with my papa. I'll bet that makes you sad."

Marie pressed her lips tightly together and turned away, obviously schooling her own composure, and Alyce felt her throat start to tighten. She spent several seconds returning Seffira's hug before gently propelling the child back to Marie's ministrations.

"It makes me *very* sad, Seffira," she agreed, turning her attention to the lacing of Krispin's boots. "And my brother was hurt, too. That also makes me sad."

"Where did he get hurted?" Krispin wanted to know, yelping as Anjelica worked at a particularly troublesome tangle.

"In Meara," Alyce replied without thinking. "Oh—it was his knee that was hurt," she added, realizing what the boy was really asking. "But it happened while he was helping catch some bad men—and he was very brave."

"What did the bad men do?" Seffira asked.

"Well, some of them had killed our papa. And some of them had tried to kill the king's brother."

"They tried to kill Duke Richard?" Krispin asked, indignant. "He's the bravest knight in the world! When I grow up, I want to be just like him!"

"Well, that's a very fine thing to want," Alyce agreed, as Anjelica finished combing the boy's hair, only just controlling a smile. "Duke Richard is a very brave knight."

"Mummy, I want to wear my page tabard today!" Krispin declared, sliding from his stool to head for a trunk against the outside wall. "Duke Richard likes us to look smart!"

Jessamy captured him before he could get very far, and Anjelica came after him with a fur-lined over-tunic.

"Well, Duke Richard isn't here right now, dear, so let's save the tabard until he gets back," Jessamy said, as she and Anjelica pulled the garment over Krispin's head.

"When will that be?" Krispin demanded.

"In a week or two," Jessamy replied. "That's after we've been to Mass next Sunday, and maybe after we've been to Mass *another* Sunday."

"Oh." Krispin set his hands on his hips and gave an exasperated sigh, then grinned. "That's all right, then. If it got dirty, he wouldn't like that." He looked up engagingly at Anjelica. "We get something to eat now, Jeli?"

"Yes, we get something to eat now, love," Anjelica said, taking the boy's hand. "Seffira, you come as well. Prince Brion will be waiting for both of you."

As she left the room, both children in tow, Jessamy sighed and settled on Krispin's stool, turning her gaze toward Alyce and Marie. "I think Anjelica and I are getting too old for running after little ones," she said. "Mothering is a job for the young. Alyce, it's good to have you back, even under such circumstances. How did you sleep?"

Alyce ventured a bleak smile. "Well enough, all things considered." She shook at a fold of her skirt, mud-spattered along the hem. "Would you look at the state of this gown?"

"There's a brush behind you, dear. And after we've broken our fast, we shall ask among the other ladies and see what can be assembled in the way of essentials." She went to one of the large coffers in the room and lifted the lid to rummage. "Meanwhile, let's see if we can't find something suitable in here. The first thing we'll need will be proper mourning for both of you. The king has ordered a Requiem Mass at noon, for all those slain."

"I hate black," Marie said bleakly, as Jessamy produced an armful of fine black wool from the depths of the coffer and shook it out, testing the length against one, then the other of her charges.

"I'm sure you do," Jessamy murmured, one eyebrow raised, as she pressed the gown into Marie's arms and continued her rummaging. "Unfortunately, the two of you are no longer children. This is the royal court, and all eyes will be upon you in the days to come, and especially once your brother returns to Rhemuth.

"Therefore, both of you *must* wear mourning," she concluded, hauling out another black gown for Alyce. "And with your fair coloring, you'll both look quite stunning—though that is hardly the purpose of the exercise. Now, go and try those, and then go down to the hall for something to eat. This afternoon, we'll have the sempstresses up to take measurements for a few new things. Off with you now."

IN the coming days, while they awaited Ahern's return, along with the body of their father, Alyce noticed a subtle change in the way they seemed to be perceived at court. Whether out of sympathy for their bereavement, or the queen's personal intervention, or simply because they were now older, both the sisters found themselves far more readily accepted than when they last had lived at court, four years before.

Which should not really have surprised them. Because of the nature of appointments to the queen's household, faces came and went, some girls staying only for a season, with many a nubile young lass coming from as far afield as Carthmoor, Marley, and Rhendall in search of suitable husbands—a crusade whose excitement was usually shared by all the younger members of the royal household, often in the form of new wardrobes.

Perhaps because neither of the demoiselles de Corwyn yet entertained aspirations of matrimony for themselves—and had an unmarried brother who was the very eligible future Duke of Corwyn—most of the girls now serving in the queen's household rose eagerly to this latest challenge, bending their efforts to the assembly of suitable gowns. Some of the garments were made afresh, a few gleaned from others' coffers, but the result was a modest wardrobe for each in the allotted time.

Among the instigators of this energy and largesse was a baron's daughter from Cassan, called Elaine MacInnis, some two years younger than they, whose cheerfulness and sense of style had already made her the petted favorite of most of the older women.

"It's a pity that you must wear black for a while," Elaine said to Alyce, as she and Lady Megory, one of the queen's permanent household, adjusted the hem on one of the new gowns taking shape in the hands of the sempstresses. "But we've given you something else for Christmas and Twelfth Night at Cynfyn. It's *almost* black—a very deep green—but it will have rather nice embroidery at the neck. If we get that part done, of course. Lady Jessamy is working the pattern."

Elaine's good nature was contagious, and Alyce soon found herself relaxing a little—which, in turn, seemed to enable others in the royal household to relax as well. This boded well for the future, if the goodwill persisted when they returned from Cynfyn.

In the meantime, she and Marie spent many an hour starting to settle into other aspects of life at Rhemuth: making the closer acquaintance of the children, exploring the castle's corridors, daring occasional forays into the royal library and scriptorium, and praying daily for Ahern's safe return. Later, they would look back on those days as a welcome interlude of ordinary contentment, temporary respite from the renewed sorrow to come.

Chapter 14

"Now therefore let me go up, I pray thee, and bury my father."

—GENESIS 50:5

IT was early December when the bodies of the slain came back to Rhemuth, with the first snows powdering the rooftops and gusting down off the plains north of the city. For those whose loved ones had resided at the capital, that essentially would be an end to it, as their families laid them to rest from the churches where they had worshipped in life. For Keryell, there still remained the final journey home, and for his son and heir, the uncertainty of his own future.

Duke Richard and Seisyll Arilan rode at the head of the cortege, and retired immediately with the king, to give him an update on the situation in Meara. Most of the Haldane lancers had remained in Ratharkin with Earl Jared, in case he needed assistance in the immediate aftermath of what had happened there, but with winter setting in, it was unlikely that any serious trouble would erupt again until the following summer. The Dukes of Cassan and Claibourne had returned to their lands with their troops, and remained on alert, but they, too, would be locked down against any serious campaign until the weather eased late in the spring.

For Alyce and Marie, the reunion with their brother was tearful but joyous. Young Ahern had survived the initial crisis of his wound, despite his insistence on being moved, and thus far had even kept his leg; but he was exhausted and in great pain by the time he arrived in Rhemuth with the baggage train that brought the bodies. To everyone's great relief, the surgeons now predicted that amputation probably could be avoided, but the shattered knee would heal stiff and unbending. That was better, by far, than losing the leg, but he was well aware that his injury probably had put paid to any career as a warrior or, indeed, for any other activity requiring great mobility. Whether he would even ride a horse again remained another question yet to be answered.

Fortunately, Ahern possessed a keen mind and varied interests, as had many an earl and duke before him, and had received a solid grounding in the administrative skills necessary to his rank—and owned the distinction of belonging to the only ducal family in which his Deryni bloodline was at least tolerated. He also possessed a precocious grasp of military strategy that had already brought him to the attention of both the king and Duke Richard—acumen that, once he was fully recovered, might still enable him to make useful contributions as a tactician.

But few could see much trace of that promise in the gaunt, white-faced youth strapped to the horse-litter that Master Donnard led into the castle yard that bleak December day, shivering with fever and with splinted leg aching and rattled from the journey overland from Meara. And though his sisters bore up bravely at the sight of the shrouded bundle that was their father's body, wrapped in the red and white banner of his arms and escorted by Sé Trelawney and Jovett Chandos, it was Ahern for whom they now wept, for he scarcely knew them as they came to shower him with relieved kisses, so racked was he by fever.

Torn between duty to the living and the dead, Alyce delegated Marie and Sé to go with Master Donnard and the king's own physician to see their brother settled into quarters in the castle. Meanwhile, she and Jovett accompanied her father's body to the chapel royal, where Father Paschal and the royal chaplains would keep watch through the night.

But they remained there only long enough for the obligatory prayers proper on receiving a body at the church before retiring to Ahern's bedside. There she and Marie kept tearful company beside him until he slid at last into merciful sleep, eased past pain by the physician's medicines but also helped along, when he slept at last, by Alyce's Deryni touch. The two of them stayed beside him—praying, hoping—until Jessamy finally insisted that they go to bed.

The following day, the king and queen and all the court of Gwynedd attended the Mass offered by Father Paschal for the soul of Keryell Earl of Lendour—in the chapel royal rather than Rhemuth Cathedral or even the basilica within the walls of Rhemuth Castle, for Ahern was insistent that he be allowed to stand upright before his father's coffin, braced on crutches and supported by the two young knights who had brought him from Ratharkin. His sisters stood to either side, gowned and veiled in black, and managed not to shed a tear where anyone could see.

Prince Richard Duke of Carthmoor led the cortege that set out the following morning for the Lendouri capital of Cynfyn, where Earl Keryell would be laid to rest with his ancestors. In addition to an honor guard of Haldane lancers, King Donal had sent along half a dozen of his senior knights to remain in Cynfyn and assist its seneschal in setting up the council that would advise the new Earl Ahern until he came of age, still ten years hence. The late earl's chaplain, Father Paschal, was also in the party, along with the sisters of the new earl, several of the queen's ladies as chaperones, assorted domestic servants, and the two young knights who had accompanied Keryell from Ratharkin.

During the week-long journey across the great plain east of Rhemuth, the two girls took turns keeping Ahern company, one sharing the wagon where he lay with his splinted leg pillowed and stretched before him, the other riding elsewhere in the party. Alyce made a point of varying her position in the cavalcade, riding sometime with the other ladies or Father Paschal and sometimes even at Duke Richard's side, but Marie, more often than not, could be found beside Sir Sé Trelawney.

The weather turned colder as they traveled eastward from Rhemuth, with occasional sleety showers, but at least the snow held off. By following the southern bank of the River Molling, they managed to avoid the worst of the weather already sweeping down from the north. Though the temperature plummeted at night, and their horses crunched through a heavy rime of frost every morning, any serious snowfall held off until they were making their final ascent into the Lendour foothills.

They arrived at Castle Cynfyn but a fortnight before Christmas, under a soft curtain of gently falling snow. Entering the castle bailey through the outer gatehouse arch, the cortege passed upward along a narrow avenue lined with Lendouri archers drawn up as an honor guard to admit the late earl to his capital for the final time. Interspersed among them were many of his retainers from Coroth, come to pay their respects, for Keryell had also been principal regent for Corwyn after the death of his children's mother, Stevana de Corwyn.

Deinol Hartmann, their father's seneschal, was awaiting their arrival on the steps of the hall, along with the wife their father had taken some three years previously. Now twice a widow, the Dowager Countess Rosmerta stood icy and remote in her widow's weeds, at her side a grown daughter from her first marriage, effusive in her greeting of Duke Richard, the king's brother, but according her stepson only the barest of curtsies as Sir Deinol bent to kiss the boy's hand in affirmation of his new status. Alyce and Marie she acknowledged hardly at all.

Keryell Earl of Lendour lay that night before the altar of the church within the castle walls, guarded by his men. The evening meal in his hall that night was a joyless, strained affair, with the bachelor Duke Richard seated in the place of honor at the right hand of the widow, whose attempts to engage his interest were politely turned aside; he and his knights retired as soon as could be reckoned seemly.

Alyce and Marie were not present to see it, for they took a sparser meal in Ahern's room with Sé and Jovett. Later, while Father Paschal sat with Ahern, the two knights accompanied Alyce and Marie on a late-night visit to the church, where they were heartened to see the dozens of folk from round-about come to pay their final respects and offer up a prayer, for Keryell had been much respected in the lands he had ruled.

Father Paschal celebrated the Requiem Mass the next morning, after which Keryell was laid to rest beneath the floor of the castle's private chapel, directly before the altar. Duke Richard lent an extra dignity to the affair by his mere presence, and let it be known how much his brother esteemed the sacrifice made by the late earl—and spoke, as well, of the courage and honor of the new one.

Ahern bore up manfully throughout, allowing himself to be carried to the church in a litter; but from there, for the interment, he hobbled the distance between church and chapel on his crutches, though the effort exhausted him. Keryell's widow made much of her rights and prerogatives, so his daughters were mostly ignored.

That night, when the castle at last settled into sleep, the two sisters retired wearily to the chamber that been Alyce's in childhood, bundling up in fur-lined cloaks as they huddled on a pile of sheepskins spread before the fire. Picking up a stick of kindling, Marie began poking among the embers.

"So," she said. "Our father is dead and buried. And what shall become of us *now?*"

Alyce slowly shook her head. "Who can know? In the short term, I suppose we go back to Rhemuth after Christmas and Twelfth Night."

"I wish we could stay with Ahern," Marie muttered mutinously.

"You know we can't." After a moment, Alyce gave a heavy sigh, clasping her arms around her knees to rest her chin on one forearm.

"This doesn't much change our situation, you know," she said. "Until and unless Ahern has children, preferably sons, we're still only heartbeats away from the succession of a dukedom and an earldom."

"*You're* only heartbeats away," Marie replied. "You're the oldest."

"Yes, but if I die without heirs, *you're* the heir."

Her sister did not look up from her prodding of the fire.

"What if I don't *want* to be the heir?" she muttered.

Alyce smiled bleakly and reached across to clasp her sister's hand.

"Then, pray for our brother's health—and mine," she said.

AHERN mostly slept for the first few days after his father's burial, leaving Duke Richard to begin shaping the council that would assist the new earl as he began taking up the reins of his new rank. Virtually everyone interesting was involved in the process, even Father Paschal, so Alyce and Marie spent the first few days re-exploring their favorite childhood haunts—and avoiding Lady Rosmerta. Which was not difficult, because the widow mainly kept to her own rooms.

But each evening, as the newcomers relaxed into the resuming pace of life at Castle Cynfyn, the sad castle hall slowly began to regain a softer air, as the gentle sounds of lyre and harp and occasional sweet voices were heard increasingly during supper, slowly lifting spirits into the hopefulness of the Advent season. Most of Ahern's council were older, and preferred Duke Richard's company to that of mere adolescents, but Sé and Jovett made certain that the new earl's sisters did not lack for company.

Sometimes, on bright, clear mornings when the sun set the snow all aglitter, the four of them would venture out on brief, brisk rides through the surrounding hills, though always attended by at least half a dozen other knights. As Christmas approached, Alyce began to notice that her sister was often in Sé's company, and almost always managed to ride beside him when they went on their outings.

But the two young knights were not often available in the daytime, and the weather was gradually worsening as Christmas approached. It was on a cold, blustery day that kept everyone inside, a few days before the Christmas Vigil, that Alyce found herself recruited with her sister to decorate the castle chapel for the solemnities of Christmas Eve, for the coming of the Holy Child was still an occasion for rejoicing, even if hearts still were heavy with Keryell's passing.

"I think this needs more holly," Marie said, though with little enthusiasm. "What do you think?"

They were huddled on a bench at the rear of the chapel with a firepot at their feet, surrounded by evergreen boughs and runners of bright ivy and sprigs of red-berried holly. They had already plaited the first half of a garland intended to adorn the altar rail, and Alyce was laying out the framework for the other half.

She glanced at her sister's work and reached for another trailer of ivy.

"It looks all right to me."

Marie gave a sigh and tucked in another sprig of holly anyway.

"I still wish we could stay here with Ahern."

"Don't you mean with Sé?" Alyce replied, arching a delicate eyebrow at her sister.

Marie blushed furiously and ducked her head closer to her work.

"Don't try to deny it," Alyce said. "I've seen the two of you, making eyes at one another."

Marie glanced sidelong at her sister, trying unsuccessfully to control a grin. "Are you going to tease me forever, now that you've guessed?"

"Well, maybe not forever." Alyce smiled. "But don't get your hopes up, Mares. I suspect that the king has someone more lofty in mind for you than a simple knight."

"He is hardly simple!" Marie said indignantly.

"Not in the sense I know you mean," Alyce agreed. "But marriage with him would not advance any of the king's concerns. Unfortunately, that's what our marriages are for."

"What if we ran away?" Marie said.

"And do what? Get married anyway? They'd catch you, Mares. And then they'd annul you, and probably lock you up in a convent somewhere until they married you by force to someone else. And Sé would be disgraced—maybe even found out."

"You're so mean! It isn't fair!"

"'Fair' has nothing to do with it. I'm reminding you of realities."

"*Fah!* for realities," Marie muttered. "I *want* him, Alyce."

"And I want lots of things, dear sister, but merely wanting is not necessarily enough."

The sound of approaching footsteps stayed her from saying more, and she fell silent, glancing up distractedly as someone in a flash of saffron-colored skirts and a cloak of forest green came in and deposited an armload of scarlet ribbons and pine cones at their feet.

"I'm so glad you've used mostly pine and ivy instead of holly," said a low, musical voice. "The pine has a much nicer smell. But I thought you might like to work some color in with it. Besides, I'm avoiding Lady Rosmerta."

Both sisters broke into appreciative grins. In the months following Keryell's remarriage, Vera Howard had been one of several well-born girls fostered to the household of his new countess—much to the indignation, at first, of Marie, who had tearfully suggested that perhaps their father's motives had been more self-serving than altruistic, by installing half a dozen nubile young women in the very accessible context of his new wife's boudoir.

"That sounds like jealousy to me, Mares," Alyce had declared, trying to cajole her sister out of her mood. "I know you're angry with Father, for sending us away; and I know you don't much like the Lady Rosmerta—I don't, either. But by that reasoning, we were living in the queen's household for the convenience of the king—and you know that isn't true!"

Marie had *humphed* at that, and flounced around the room for several minutes, but finally had agreed, albeit grudgingly, that Alyce was probably right. When, a few months later, the two of them had actually met some of their stepmother's fosterlings, in conjunction with a brief visit by their father and stepmother en route to Twelfth Night court in Rhemuth, even Marie had actually liked the other girls.

They especially had liked Vera Howard, the one who had just joined them: a lively, well-spoken lass with honey-brown hair falling straight to her hips and gray-green eyes that recalled the luminance of sunlight on a tranquil sea. Vera's father was Sir Orban Howard, a knight with lands not far from Castle Cynfyn, and her mother and theirs had been close friends.

"I've given up working with holly," Alyce informed the newcomer. "It prickles your fingers to death—though it does have nice color. But the ribbons will be just what's needed. I don't suppose you'd like to give us a hand?"

"Actually, I did come to offer a bit of help," Vera replied, "though not with pine boughs." She quirked them a guileless smile and turned briefly to pull the chapel door closed, then sank down beside Alyce on the bench. As she stretched one hand before them and opened it, a spark of greenish light flared in her palm and quickly took on the shape of a winged gryphon less than a hand-span high.

The apparition turned its head as if to look at both of them; then, as it spread its wings, seemed to fold in on itself before disappearing with a faint *pop* that was more felt than heard.

"Who are you?" Alyce demanded, though instinctively she

kept her query to a whisper, for it was clear that Vera was Deryni like herself. Marie merely stared at the other girl in wonder.

Vera ventured another tentative smile. "Your father told me that I am your sister."

"What?" Marie blurted.

Shaking her head, Vera laid one finger across her lips in an urgent sign for silence, cutting her off in mid-word.

"I promise you, it isn't what you're maybe thinking," she whispered, humor crinkling at the corners of her eyes, "though our sire *was* quite the ladies' man. Actually, you and I are twins," she said to Alyce. "Fortunately, not identical, though I would love to have had hair like yours." She nodded toward Alyce's pale braid. "But if we'd been identical, our parents never would have been able to carry off the deception."

"But—how is that possible?" Alyce whispered, stunned.

Again glancing toward the door, Vera delved into the bodice of her gown and withdrew a folded piece of parchment, well sealed with green wax.

"This is for you," she said, holding it up so that the seal was visible.

The familiar imprint on the seal showed the Corwyn gryphon as an escutcheon of pretense over the arms of Lendour, as Keryell had used them in his capacity as Earl of Lendour and one of Corwyn's regents.

"I see that you recognize the seal," Vera went on. "Before Father left on this last Mearan expedition, he asked me to keep this for you, in case anything ever happened to him. He said I was to make certain you read it in a safe place, where you wouldn't be disturbed, because it can only be read once."

At Alyce's look of bewilderment, Vera shook her head. "Don't ask me more until you've read it—and I trust you've been Truth-Reading me while I'm telling you this. I know you can do that."

As Alyce slowly nodded, Vera turned the packet of parchment to display writing on the side without the wax seals.

"You recognize the hand?" she asked, as Marie crowded closer to see it as well.

Alyce swallowed audibly and nodded.

"All right, here's what you need to do." Vera placed the packet in Alyce's free hand and closed the fingers around it.

"Take this up to the altar rail, as close as possible to Father's grave. That way, if anyone should come in while we're doing this, they'll think you're simply praying. Marie and I will continue making garlands, and if necessary, I'll fend off intruders."

"What if it's Father Paschal?" Marie asked. "He could come through the sacristy."

"It's all right. He knows about this."

"Father Paschal knows about *you?*" Alyce broke in.

"Well, of course. Who do you think trained me?"

"But—he never mentioned—"

"No, and he hasn't told *me* much about *you,*" Vera countered. "That was to protect all of us. Especially in your case, he was somewhat concerned that Father had given Lady Jessamy access to some of your training triggers."

"She's rarely used them," Alyce murmured, stunned. "We've not spent that much time at court."

"Would you necessarily *know* if she'd used them?" Vera replied. "She did come occasionally to Arc-en-Ciel, didn't she?"

"Well, yes—but Jessilde was usually with us then."

"Jessilde—who is Jessamy's daughter. It isn't likely, Alyce, but they could have been working together, to check on you occasionally, if only to see how Paschal's training was progressing. Now does it become clear why Father felt the need to be so careful?"

"But, she would never—"

"Alyce, we *don't know* what she would *never* do," Vera pointed out. "Have you forgotten who her father was?"

"I—hadn't thought about that," Alyce admitted.

"I didn't think you had. And I believe that Paschal has avoided reminding you, for fear of planting an idea in your mind that Jessamy might discover, if she did try to abuse the trust she was given."

Alyce found herself shivering at the idea that Jessamy might have been doing just that, without her knowledge. Marie's eyes were huge with wonder.

"If that's a real concern," Alyce whispered, "what happens when we go back to court? For the next few years, we're going to be there all the time, now that Father is gone."

"Father Paschal intends to modify your triggers before you leave—though I don't think he intends that Lady Jessamy should know. And he certainly doesn't intend that she should know about me. Ahern, of course, doesn't know anything about any of this, except that I've been fostered here for the past three or four years."

After a few seconds to digest what Vera had just revealed, Alyce said dazedly, "I had no idea about any of this. . . ."

"Which was the purpose of the exercise," Vera replied. "But right now, you need to deal with what Father left for you. Before you break the seal, kiss it—and make sure that your tongue touches the wax. That's part of the means by which the spell is activated for you, personally—I knew you were about to ask," she added with a grin.

Despite her mixture of surprise, curiosity, and annoyance that their father had not better prepared her for this, Alyce managed a tentative smile.

"If we really are twins, I suppose there'll be no keeping any of my secrets from you in the future," she said.

Vera grinned. "Father Paschal has always warned me that there are disadvantages as well as advantages to being Deryni." She brushed her hand over Alyce's, closed around the parchment packet.

"Now, there will be two messages inside. I'm told that the visible one is a simple bequest of some items of jewelry—which is all anyone else would see, if they opened it. The other message is for you alone, written between the lines of the first one. When you open the letter, that second message will glow slightly, so you needn't worry about having enough light to read it. Make certain you read it through slowly, because you only get one chance; the writing will disappear after you've read it."

Alyce swallowed down the lump that was rising in her throat.

"I—believe you," she whispered. "It's all just so—so—"

"—unbelievable. Yes, I know." Vera smiled faintly. "It's so audacious, I still hardly know whether to love him or damn him," she confessed. "But I truly believe that he loved *us*—enough to do what he had to do, to give at least one of us the chance to develop our gifts away from public scrutiny, without having to contend with—well, with people knowing what we are." She glanced away briefly before continuing.

"I'd known him all my life, though I didn't know who he

really was until I came here. So far as I or my 'parents' knew, he was simply my godfather, just as he was godfather to many other children of his vassals—though there weren't any others *exactly* like me," she added, with a quick smile at Alyce. "He had me fostered here after he sent the two of you to court and Arc-en-Ciel—which he felt was the safest place he could send you, while he began bringing me into the family picture and started my training—and yes, I do have quite a lot of training now. Fortunately, Lady Rosmerta is not Deryni, and hadn't a clue what he was up to—silly cow!"

Marie gave a nervous snicker. "We *must* be sisters. Alyce and I don't like her either."

"I don't suppose she's all that bad," Vera replied. "You might even spare her a little pity. She knew she wasn't barren, because she has a grown daughter by her first marriage, but Father wouldn't give her any more children. He needed a wife, so that he could bring me into the picture, but he didn't want to complicate the succession. In hindsight, I think he gambled quite a lot on Ahern—an unfortunate wager, as it happens, given his injury—but he may be able to overcome it. And meanwhile, he had us." She cocked her head at the parchment in Alyce's hand. "You must be bursting to read that. Have you done this before?"

Alyce shook her head. She had been numbly Truth-Reading everything Vera said, and had no doubt that everything was true. Truth-Reading was among the rudimentary skills that their father and then Father Paschal had taught her and Marie—and Ahern—during their early years: a particularly useful survival skill for any Deryni, as was the ability to block pain and to induce sleep—skills she had used in easing her brother's discomfort en route here.

The procedure to which Vera was referring was simple enough on the receiving end; it would not have been so simple for their father, in the setting up. But now she was eager to learn what instructions their father had left her.

"I know the theory," she whispered. "I can do it. And you'll keep a lookout?" she added, glancing at the chapel door.

"We shall be the perfect decoys, if anyone should come," Vera said with a grin. "Now, Marie, we still have a lot to do. You might at least *try* to look like you're enjoying plaiting evergreen garlands."

Her ready smile brought a smile to Marie's lips as well, and the other girl re-applied herself to the task as Alyce rose and headed toward the altar. Vera took up a position just inside the door, which she pulled slightly ajar.

Alyce could feel her heart hammering as she padded softly down the chapel's short nave, the parchment packet closed tightly between her cupped hands. Three days before, at her father's interment, the air had been redolent of fine incense and the more cloying perfume of floral tributes. Her stomach stirred a little queasily as she skirted the slab under which Keryell lay, doing her best to recall the incense rather than any faint charnel scent she might imagine in this part of the chapel.

Steadying herself against the altar rail, she genuflected to the Presence signified by the lamp burning above the tabernacle, then eased to her knees, stretching one foot behind her, under her cloak, so that it touched the corner of the grave slab under which her father lay. Then, after mouthing a brief prayer, both for the occupant's soul and her own blessing, she dipped her head briefly to kiss the seal as she had been instructed—and hesitantly swept it with her tongue.

Nothing happened—at least that she could detect—though the taste of honey lingered as she carefully broke the seal. Fragments of brittle wax showered the altar rail as she opened the parchment. Between the penned lines of the promised bequest, written in her father's tight, crabbed hand, she began reading the glowing words, quite distinct in the semidarkness of the silent chapel.

Beloved Daughter, it began. *In receiving this letter, you will already have made the acquaintance of your twin sister. I ask your forgiveness for the deception I have carried out, in keeping you apart thus far, but your mother and I agreed before your birth that this solution, painful as it was for both of us, represented the best hope of allowing at least one of our children to grow up sheltered from the stigma so often attendant upon those of our blood.*

Happy coincidence suggested the means by which this might be accomplished. It happened that, at about the time your mother fell pregnant with you and your sister, she learned that Lady Laurela Howard was also with child. After a few months, we determined that your mother carried twin girls—and conceived a daring plan.

Since your mother and Lady Howard had been friends since

childhood, it was arranged that the two should share their confinements at Cynfyn, for one another's company and so that Laurela might avail herself of the midwife serving my household. Unbeknownst to Laurela or her husband, your mother's second-born was then to be presented as a supposed twin to the child Laurela carried—which is exactly what was done, except that her own child was born still. Thus, what began as a regrettable but necessary deception chanced to have an unexpected and doubly felicitous outcome, easing the sorrow of Laurela's loss as well as our own—to surrender our beloved daughter into the keeping of another, for her safety's sake.

I pray that you can forgive what I have done, and that you may now make the better acquaintance of your twin sister, Veralyn Thamar (de Corwyn) Howard. I have provided for her such training as I could, in the hope that she may share this legacy of our mutual birthright with you.

My devotion to both of you, my darling daughters, and to dear Marie as well.

Your loving father, Keryell

Even as Alyce read the final words, through a blur of tears, the glowing script was fading from the page. The last line alone lingered for a moment longer than the rest, superimposed over the more mundane message penned on the page, before likewise dispersing like wind across water.

Chapter 15

"And ye shall read this book which we have sent unto you."

—BARUCH 1:14

ALYCE shared what she had read with her sisters—Marie first, since they were accustomed to working mind-to-mind. Marie wept with emotion when it was done, then dried her tears—glad ones, this time, unlike those of the previous weeks—and gathered up the finished half of the garland to take it to the altar rail, humming one of the more sprightly antiphons of Advent as she carried it down the center aisle.

"She's quite amazing, isn't she?" Vera murmured to her twin, watching Marie retreat. "And very young."

"She was always Father's pet," Alyce replied, smiling. "And she *is* still just fifteen."

"Yes, I tend to forget that," Vera said wistfully. "Ahern is so mature for his age." She shrugged and jutted her chin toward the letter still in Alyce's hand. "Shall we?"

They returned to the bench where Vera first had found them and settled in amidst the stockpile of pine boughs and ivy, laying the ivy matrix and a few pine boughs across their laps—diversion, in case anyone should enter.

Alyce had feared it would not come easily, for other than with Marie, the greatest part of her previous contact with other Deryni had been with Father Paschal, and then always as pupil with teacher. Some little there had been with Jessilde, as part of training exercises, but always under Paschal's supervision. Interaction with Ahern had been mostly during their childhood, when none of them knew much; their mother had died young, and their father had mostly left their training to Paschal.

Provision also had been made so that Jessamy might tutor her and Marie, but the pair had been too short a time at court for that to happen. In truth, Alyce had always harbored a certain reticence concerning any too-close interaction with Jessamy, godmother though she was—and "Tante" Jessamy, by her own mother's wishes.

She could not explain that reticence. It was not precisely come of any mistrust she felt toward Jessamy herself, but rather, an uneasiness over the apparent ambiguity of a Deryni being openly tolerated at court, in the queen's own household—though perhaps a woman was not deemed to be so great a threat as a man.

Alyce had also heard tell of a brother of Jessamy, called Morian, long assigned to the governor's staff in Meara, who made discreet use of his powers in the service of the king; she had no idea what the Bishop of Meara thought about this bending of secular and canon law. Perhaps it was a prerogative of kings, that *sometimes* it was acceptable that *some* Deryni function openly, despite what bishops said.

Nonetheless, this apparent contradiction regarding Jessamy and her brother had convinced Alyce that it was probably safest not to invite any untoward scrutiny of whatever abilities she herself possessed—and that included scrutiny by Jessamy. The feeling had intensified once she resumed her training with Father Paschal at Arc-en-Ciel. It was nothing he or anyone else had told her; she simply knew.

She also knew, in much the same way, that she need have no such reticence with Vera, who was her sister and her twin, and with whom she had shared their mother's womb. Not that mere willingness or even eagerness to also share their minds was sufficient to enable the easy doing of it—not when most of the focus of Alyce's training thus far had been geared toward keeping others *out* of her mind, or only allowing access to selected parts of it—or, wielding her power as the weapon it was, insinuating her own mind into another's, to impose her will.

No, in this instance there must be a balanced melding of

senses, engaging the powers of mind as tool, not as weapon. Turning more knee-to-knee with her twin, Alyce drew another fortifying breath and laid their father's letter across her open palms between them, blue eyes meeting sea-gray as she invited contact. With the touch of Vera's hands on hers, with their father's words between them, she bade her shields to retract, flinching at the first brush of that other mind.

But Vera knew far more of such matters than she, and had been taught how to ease the process.

"Don't resist," she whispered. "Relax your shields. You're trying too hard." *Don't make it happen . . . let it happen,* she went on, shifting easily into mind-speech. *Good . . . just relax. We can do this. . . .*

Once past that point, as Alyce yielded to her twin's greater skill, their deepening rapport segued into a sharing that was profound. It left both of them blinking back tears of wonder, grinning and even laughing aloud as they embraced, and brought Marie back to the rear of the chapel to see what was so amusing.

"That's all very well for the two of you," she said, flouncing onto a seat beside Alyce in mock resentment and showing them her hands. "I'm all sticky with pine sap—though it does smell rather nice," she added, sniffing at her fingers, "and the two of you have just been gossiping away."

"Not gossiping—communing," Vera murmured. "Oh, it *is* going to be wonderful, having sisters—though we'll have to be very careful."

AT first, they did, indeed, go very carefully, though the friendship suddenly blossoming among the three of them soon became obvious to all.

"I knew the three of you would get on wonderfully," Ahern told Alyce, after Mass on Christmas Eve, as he hobbled painfully beside her on his crutches. "I think she's always been my favorite of Rosmerta's fosterlings. Father always liked her, too."

Carefully shielding the *reason* for Keryell's fondness, Alyce merely said, "She *is* great fun."

"She is," Ahern replied. "I shall hate to see her leave. Unfortunately, Rosmerta will be taking all her household with her, when she goes back to her father. You *did* know that our esteemed step-mama is leaving . . . ?"

"Well, there's nothing for her *here,* now that Father is gone," Alyce replied.

"Yes, well, good riddance," he said, his voice brisk. "But Sir Deinol's wife has agreed to act as my chatelaine for the time-being, since I know that you and Mares can't stay indefinitely."

"You know that we *would* stay, if we could," she assured him.

"No, I know that you must go," he said. "Just promise me that you'll write often, and that you'll come to visit, when you can."

LATER, when she told her sisters of the conversation, they reluctantly agreed that Ahern should not be told of the blood-tie that bound them, at least for the present.

"If he did know, though," Alyce said, "it *would* make it easier in some respects. I think *he* thinks he fancies you, Vera—but we can't have him courting his sister."

Vera rolled her eyes. "Did he tell you that?"

"No, but it's clear that he's fond of you."

"The dear boy. He *is* sweet—but in a few days, that won't be a factor," Vera said. "He's right that I'll be going with Rosmerta. Until my parents say otherwise, I have no choice." She shrugged at their knowing glances. "Well, *they* think they're my parents. Right now, the three of us are the only ones who know the truth of the matter—and Father Paschal, of course."

"Why can't we tell Ahern?" Marie asked.

"Because he's terrible at keeping secrets," Alyce replied. "At least he always was, as a child. Anyway, he doesn't need to know right now. It would be unfair to burden him with such knowledge while he's still recovering his health—and figuring out how to be an earl. Once we've gone back to Rhemuth, he's going to be very alone."

"I'm afraid she's right," Vera said to Marie. "This isn't the time to tell him. Our parents paid too high a price to make sure no one knows what I am. We mustn't do anything to jeopardize that."

"Exactly," Alyce said. "But we *can* do something to get Father's plans for you back on track. I thought to ask the queen about bringing you to court, when we go back to Rhemuth."

"To court?" Vera breathed.

"Why not? You've already been part of an earl's household. Don't think for a moment that this wasn't part of Father's plan for you. I'm sure he intended to arrange an extremely advantageous marriage, so that your eventual children—his grandchildren—would be in positions to improve the lot of our people. And no one would know that any of you are Deryni."

Vera was nodding by the time she finished, and Marie was grinning.

The queen is very kind," Marie said. "And so many handsome young knights at court! Think what a fine marriage you might make!"

"There is that," Vera agreed.

"Then, it's settled," Alyce said. "We'll make inquiries as soon as we return.

THE household of the late Keryell Earl of Lendour kept the feasts of Christmas at Castle Cynfyn, though the observances were muted because of his recent death. Two days after Saint Stephen's Day, to no one's particular regret, his widow announced, from the back of a horse, that she was departing at once for her father's lands near Dhassa.

"Madam, I am certain that my father did not intend that you should be turned out of your home," Ahern said dutifully, standing in the snowy yard with a hand on her horse's bridle, and balancing on one leg and a crutch.

"No, I am resolved," Rosmerta replied. "I have had several weeks to consider, while I waited for my husband's body to come home. But God did not consent to give me children by Lord Keryell, so there is nothing for me here. I wish you well, Ahern, but you do not need my presence. You must make a life of your own."

There was nothing he could say to that, for while his relationship with his stepmother had been civil, at least in his father's presence, there had never been true warmth between them.

"At least permit me to send an escort with you," he said, beginning to weave on his feet.

"I thank your courtesy, but my father has sent men of his own," she replied, nodding toward the half dozen liveried men interspersed among the sumpter animals and the mounts of her household and servants. "I desire to greet the new year with the family of my birth. God grant you health, my lord."

With that, she headed out the castle gate, her daughter at her side and with Vera among her household—hopefully, only for a few weeks or months, until Alyce and Marie could speak to the queen about her.

By Twelfth Night, the customary time for formal transactions of important business in any lord's hall, Ahern was sufficiently improved in health to preside at his first official court as Earl of Lendour—yet unconfirmed in his full authority, because of his youth, but lawfully acknowledged by the presence at his side of Duke Richard, who witnessed the investiture of the new earl's council of advisors and took their fealty in the name of the king his brother. Two days later, Richard bade all farewell and departed for Rhemuth, and life began to settle into some semblance of a pattern of daily life for the new young earl.

Not for several weeks, as Ahern and his seneschal reviewed the inventories of the late earl's possessions, was it discovered that certain valuables had gone missing.

"You don't suppose that Rosmerta could have taken these?" Ahern asked, as he showed the list of missing items to his sisters. "Some of the jewelry was left to you in that letter from Father."

"Then, I expect that Rosmerta's coffers have been considerably enriched by the appropriated items," Alyce replied. "Can aught be done about it?"

Ahern shook his head. "Probably not. Just be glad that she didn't have any sons. If she had, I'd probably be dead—and she'd be working on the two of you."

Marie wrinkled her nose. "I still don't understand why Father married her."

"'Better to marry than to burn,'" Ahern muttered, coloring slightly as Alyce looked at him sharply. "Well, he was a man of—passions," he added, somewhat lamely. "Though, in this case, I think I'd rather he had diddled with serving wenches."

Alyce only rolled her eyes, though she made a mental note to ask their sister to look into the matter further.

Meanwhile, the winter snows swept in, rendering travel difficult, especially for an invalid who must still travel by horse-litter—though, in truth, young Ahern had made no plans to move before the summer, when he would visit his lands in Corwyn. Fortunately, he gained strength almost daily, though his shattered knee continued to give him pain, albeit tempered by the nursing of his sisters.

Early in February, however, Sir Kenneth Morgan arrived with orders recalling the demoiselles de Corwyn to Rhemuth—with his daughter Zoë at his side.

"The queen particularly asks for your presence," Kenneth told them, when the girls' joy at their reunion had subsided enough for him to get a word in edgewise. "Her lying-in will soon be upon her, and she greatly desires that you attend her.

"She also has graciously offered my dear Zoë a place at court, as further incentive to speed your return," he added, slipping a fond arm around his daughter's waist.

"Alyce, I was presented at Twelfth Night court!" Zoë blurted, joy in her sea-gray eyes. "You should have seen my beautiful gown! And I've brought a new gown for each of you as well: presents from the queen and Lady Jessamy. We're done with our school habits! I'm to stay at court with Father, and attend the queen—and try my hand in the king's scriptorium, if I desire it!"

Few developments could have cheered Alyce more—and the queen's request underlined a more serious reason for their return to court, for all were well aware of the dangers of childbed. Still, Alyce turned to her brother in concern.

"Would you prefer that one of us remain with you?" she said. "I know that your knee still pains you."

Ahern had graduated to a walking stick to help him hobble around the castle, and thwacked it lightly against the thigh of his propped-up leg, mustering a brave smile.

"No, the queen needs you more than I do," he said lightly. "*I'm* not the one who's having a baby. Go to her. I'll manage."

* * *

THEY left the following day, riding fast along the road that skirted the River Molling, as it lazed its way westward across the great Gwynedd Plain. They arrived in Rhemuth mid-February, only days before the queen was brought to bed of another Haldane prince. Eased by the ministrations of Jessamy and Alyce, the latter grown considerably more knowledgeable from her studies at Arc-en-Ciel, the queen's labor was hard but short, at least some of her pains blunted by Deryni magic—much to the annoyance of a new royal midwife, who firmly believed that the travails of birth were a woman's just recompense for the sins of Eve.

"You have another son, Sire," Alyce said, emerging from the birthing chamber while Jessamy and Marie cleaned up mother and child. "He is perfect in every way, and his mother is well."

Bursting into a wide grin, Donal gave a relieved sigh. "Thanks be to God!"

Later that evening, when the mother had rested and the babe was rousing from sleep, the girls brought the rest of the royal children to see the new arrival.

"Come and greet your new brother," Alyce said to Princes Brion and Blaine as she shepherded them into their mother's bedchamber.

Zoë was carrying their sister, the Princess Xenia, who squirmed to get down as Jessamy helped the queen to sit more upright and the midwife lifted the child from his cradle to lay him in his mother's arms. The king had already visited the pair, and now was gone to inform his council of the safe delivery of the new prince.

"Isn't he beautiful?" Alyce whispered, as young Brion stood on his tiptoes for a closer look.

"He's just a baby," piped Blaine, sounding a little disappointed.

"Well, he was just born," Brion replied, quite reasonably. "Mama, can I hold him?"

Richeldis laughed gently as the babe nuzzled closer to her breast. "Maybe tomorrow, darling. Right now, he's very hungry, and Mama is very tired."

"But, you been in bed all day, Mama," Blaine pointed out.

"Yes, but your mama has been working very hard," Jessamy explained, smoothing the younger boy's jet-black hair. "Shall I lift you up so you can see him better?"

Nodding solemnly, Blaine held up his arms to be picked up. Brion was already clambering up the side of his mother's bed to see, assisted by Alyce. Xenia, too, was reaching toward the baby and her mother, so Zoë obliged by bringing her closer.

"Ba-bee!" Xenia crowed, reaching out to stroke the infant's blanket.

"What're we gonna name him, Mama?" Brion wanted to know, grinning as a tiny hand closed on his forefinger.

"Well, your father has suggested Nigel," Richeldis replied. "What do you think?"

"Nigel's a good name!" Brion agreed, nodding. "Now I got *two* brothers, named Blaine an' Nigel!"

"And a very pretty sister!" Zoë added, bestowing an audible kiss on the cheek of the squirming Xenia.

THE arrival of the new prince, coupled with having Zoë with them again, helped both Alyce and Marie ease back into life at court, now on a far happier note than the weeks before Christmas, while they waited for their father's body to return. And as spring eased toward summer, preparations for the June wedding of another of the queen's ladies likewise occupied both minds and hands, for the dashing Sir Jared McLain, Earl of Kierney, had claimed the hand of Elaine MacInnis.

"I still cannot believe my good fortune," Elaine confided to Alyce and Marie, soon after their return to Rhemuth. "Apparently our fathers made the arrangements at Christmastime. He asked me on Saint Stephen's Day, and our betrothal took place at Twelfth Night court."

"How I wish we could have seen it!" Marie declared, honestly delighted. "What a couple you shall make—for he is one of the comeliest men at court. Everyone says that he's ever so brave and dashing!"

"More important, he is kind and gentle," Alyce agreed, not

giving voice to a vague misgiving, for Elaine was but fifteen. "But—shall you live in Kierney, Elaine? I fear we shall never see you!"

Elaine shrugged, a tinge of wistfulness crossing her fair features. "It is far away, I know. But his sons must be born on his own lands—and I hope I shall give him many! Besides, when he is duke, he will be called often to court—and I shall come with him, when I can." She gave them a bright, delighted smile. "And both of you shall be married and with families of your own, before you know it."

"Pray God that it will be to as much contentment," Alyce said, with a glance at her friend, whose smile had turned a little wistful.

To the relief of both girls, the king gave no indication that he intended to rush the disposition of their marriage portions, but allowed them to return to their previous pursuits in the queen's household. Alyce focused on the education of the royal children, while continuing to avail herself of the royal library and the scholars who passed through court—and delighted in executing commissions of special documents for the king's chancery, for which Zoë provided illuminated capitals and embellishments.

Marie's pure voice soon brought her to the attention of the royal music master, who groomed her for performances both in the chapel royal and as entertainment in the king's hall; and her skills with loom and embroidery needle were much sought by the artisans who spent their days creating tapestries for the great hall. In addition, the sisters' suggestions to the queen regarding Lady Vera Howard met with royal approval, to the end that Vera soon joined the ranks of the queen's demoiselles.

"Believe me, Lady Rosmerta was *not* happy to receive the queen's summons," she told them privily, the first night after her arrival, as she dug in the recesses of a capacious leather bag. "She will have been even less happy when she discovered that I left with *these*."

She pulled out a wooden box the size of a man's two hands and opened the lid for Alyce's inspection. Inside, wrapped individually in pieces of crumpled linen, were most of the items of jewelry listed in their father's bequest: several rings and brooches, a bracelet, and a necklace of emeralds the size of a man's thumbnail, with blue fire at their hearts.

"Ooooh, Alyce!" Marie breathed, as Alyce lifted out the necklace.

"I remember seeing our mother wear this," Alyce murmured, turning it in the candlelight. "Family tradition has it that it once belonged to the Lady Tayce Furstána, a first cousin of the King of Torenth, whose son became the first Duke of Corwyn."

"Then, it's good that it comes back into the family," Vera said, looking pleased with herself as Marie plucked out a gold bangle set with opals and sapphires. "And doesn't that bracelet appear in that painting of Stevana at Cynfyn?"

Alyce nodded. "Aye, the one at the top of the main stair." She watched her younger sister slide the bangle onto her wrist and turn it appreciatively in the light.

"So much for Rosmerta," Marie said, smiling smugly.

"Not entirely," Alyce replied, taking the bracelet back from her sister. "She'll probably try to claim that Vera stole them. But we'll take them to the queen for safekeeping, and send to Ahern for the letter Father left."

Chapter 16

"Then shall the lame man leap as an hart . . ."

—ISAIAH 35:6

MUCH to their relief, no complaint came from Rosmerta, but Alyce sent to their brother anyway, that a fair copy might be made of the bequest, witnessed by Father Paschal under seal.

The next several months passed quickly, with all the ladies of the royal household happily focused on the upcoming nuptials of Elaine MacInnis and Jared McLain, which took place at the end of June in St. Hilary's-Within-the-Walls, the royal basilica adjoining Rhemuth Castle. As a personal favor for the wedding day, Alyce allowed Elaine to wear the Furstána emeralds. It was an occasion of pageantry and celebration, for Jared McLain was Earl of Kierney and heir to the Duchy of Cassan; but it was a day also tinged with sadness, for the newlyweds soon left for Kierney. The new Countess Elaine would be sadly missed from the queen's household.

That was the summer, in the fifteenth year of King Donal's reign, that Donal Haldane began his great inquest of all the lands in Gwynedd, even more ambitious than the one carried out by his father, King Malcolm, to mark the twenty-fifth anniversary of the great Battle of Killingford.

Then the royal commissioners had sent deputies only into the heartlands of the kingdom: from the Purple March southward across the great Gwynedd Plain as far as Carthmoor and Corwyn, and northward along the Coamer Mountains through Lendour and as far north as Eastmarch. This time, the inquiries would include all of Old Kheldour: the Duchy of Claibourne, the Kheldish Riding, and the Earldoms of Marley and Rhendall. Donal had hopes for including Cassan and Kierney as well, but they lay close to rebellious Meara, so he was not certain that local conditions would permit such activities—but that decision could wait while the rest progressed.

That summer was gentler than some in recent memory, so the commissioners were able to make good progress as the lazy summer days eased into autumn. Likewise, as the months wore on, the demoiselles de Corwyn made plans for their promised visit to their brother in Cynfyn—with some trepidation on Alyce's part, for her sister and Sir Sé had been exchanging letters with alarming frequency since Easter, along with the progress reports that Ahern sent regularly, first from Corwyn and then from Cynfyn once again. Though Vera was obliged to remain behind, having no legitimate reason to accompany them, Alyce enlisted Zoë to come along and help her keep Marie in line regarding Sé.

The news was encouraging, at least where Ahern was concerned. Earlier in the spring, he had made his promised visit to Coroth—by horse-litter and coach, much to his disgust—again accompanied by Duke Richard as he was presented to the council ruling Corwyn until he should reach the statutory age of twenty-five.

From there, after escorting Ahern back to Cynfyn, Richard had returned to Rhemuth, in case his presence should be required in Meara that season—and Ahern had set about recovering as much as he could of his former abilities. It had caused him no little pain as he began to exercise again, for he was constantly testing the limits of his strength and endurance, but he was determined that his injury should be as little an impediment as possible.

He had taken up the bow first, before he could even stand for very long, for he could shoot while perched on a stool, with his stiff leg propped in front of him. Competence with a bow did not require agility of foot, but strong arms and a steady eye.

By midsummer, his accuracy had surpassed even the level it had been before he rode off to Ratharkin the season before. When he could stand longer, he also resumed whacking at a pell with his sword—dull drill, starting over with exercises he had first learned as a small boy, but it served the double purpose of building up his sword arm again and venting his frustration at his limitations.

As the summer wore on, he began to shift his thinking to his strengths instead. He would always find it more comfortable to walk with a stick, and would never recover the agility on foot that he formerly had enjoyed; but he found, to his relief, that riding was not the impossibility he had feared—though he must mount from the right instead of the left, since he could not bend his left knee. In time, he would learn to vault astride, unimpeded by the stiff knee.

His first few times back in the saddle—using a mounting-block, much to his disgust—his thighs had ached for days afterward, and his seat had been atrocious. But lengthening the stirrups improved his stability and his comfort, and gave him the leeway to develop a different style and balance to accommodate the stiff knee.

Soon, as his healing stabilized and his strength returned, he was riding at the quintain again, resuming his drill with sword and lance. Sé and Jovett worked with him daily, and Sir Deinol, his seneschal in Cynfyn, kept him to a disciplined regimen of physical training. Early in the autumn, as campaign season waned, Duke Richard again rode over from Rhemuth, also escorting the young earl's sisters for their promised visit, and, after watching Ahern train for several days, declared his belief that, if Ahern continued his present progress, the accolade of knighthood might not, after all, be beyond his reach in another year's time.

No news could have lifted Ahern's spirits more, or those of his sisters. Hearing Richard's declaration, Ahern resolved to redouble his efforts, taking advantage of Richard's presence to beg his personal tutelage, which Richard gladly gave.

"He *could* do it, couldn't he?" Alyce said to Sé and Jovett, the day before she, Marie, and Zoë were to start back for Rhemuth with Richard and his party. "He could still win the accolade."

Standing along the barrier fence of the tilting yard, the five of them were watching prince and future duke spar from horseback with blunted swords. Both men were laughing, and Ahern let out an exuberant "Aha!" as he scored a stinging hit on Richard's shoulder with the flat of his blade, much to Richard's consternation and delight.

Sé smiled and nodded, watching every move of both men. "There's precedent. Over a century ago, there was a King of Gwynedd who mostly fought on horseback. Javan Haldane was his name. He was born with a clubbed foot, so he had to wear a special boot—which made him not very nimble when it came to swordplay on the ground, but on a horse, there were few who could match him. Mounted, his actual sword and lance work were excellent, and he was a superb bowman.

"Very sadly, none of that could save him, in the end. He was betrayed by his former regents, ambushed in the field. Archers shot his horse out from under him and then cut him down without mercy, along with two of his closest friends. I believe one of them was a distant cousin of yours, Lady Zoë."

"Charlan Kai Morgan," Zoë said, nodding quietly. "My father shares a middle name with him. I remember being taken to his grave when I was a child. He'd been King Javan's squire when he was still prince. He died at Javan's side, trying to defend him."

"Then your father is the latest in a long tradition of loyal Morgan service to the Haldanes, isn't he?" Jovett said admiringly. "Aside from Duke Richard, perhaps, I can't think of anyone I'd rather have at my back in a fight than Sir Kenneth. Well, maybe Sé," he amended, with a teasing glance at the other young knight.

"Well, now that Ahern is making such an amazing comeback, we *will* make a rather formidable trio, won't we?" Sé said easily.

All of them gasped as Ahern evaded a particularly deft maneuver on the part of Duke Richard and wheeled his mount for another pass.

"Would you look at that?" Jovett cried.

"It's all thanks to you and Sé," Alyce said, unable to take her eyes from the field.

"No, it's all thanks to Ahern's determination," Sé countered. "We simply encouraged him to do what only he could do—*and* we bullied him occasionally, in the beginning, when the frustration made him falter. But his recovery has been a result of his own hard work. A lesser man might have sat back with his leg propped up and rested on the laurels of his valor at Ratharkin. But just look at him!"

He gestured toward the field, where Ahern and Richard were engaged in an astonishing display of horsemanship, breathless with the sheer joy of partnership between rider and steed, wheeling their mounts and darting, feinting, neither ever managing to land a blow on the other.

"What more could one ask of any man?" Sé went on. "Especially one who has answered the challenges he has done. And he is still only sixteen. What will he be two years from now? I have little doubt but that Richard will urge the king to grant him the accolade. On that day, you may be certain that Jovett and I shall be present."

THEY stayed but another day in Cynfyn before heading back for Rhemuth, arriving early in October. The children of the royal household all were thriving, especially the newest prince, but the choicest gossip stirring the queen's household was the news that the Lady Elaine, wed in June to the son of the Duke of Cassan, in distant Kierney, was expecting their first child the following May.

"Goodness, they didn't waste any time!" Alyce said, as she and Marie joined Vera in her room for a snack of cakes and ale, to share the news from Cynfyn. Since Zoë was also with them, and had not been told of Vera's true parentage, the three sisters took care to guard their speech.

"Well, Jared will be duke someday, so he needs to secure the succession," Vera said. "The same could be said about your brother. I don't suppose his eye was caught by any of those pretty maids in Coroth?" she added, with a twinkle in her eye.

Alyce shook her head. "Not that I was aware of. He seems to have been far more focused on getting back his health—and he's succeeding marvelously!"

In ever-more-delighted detail, she described Ahern's dexterity on horseback, and his skill on the field with Duke Richard.

"We talked about little else on the way back from Cynfyn," she concluded. "Duke Richard was most impressed by how far he's come."

"It sounds like he'll receive his accolade after all, then," Vera said. "That's wonderful news. Now we just have to find him a lovely girl to be his future duchess. How about you, Zoë? Alyce, wouldn't you and Marie love to have Zoë for a sister?"

"*I* would," Marie said promptly.

Zoë blushed furiously, flattered by the compliment, but Alyce's smile of agreement had a more thoughtful cast to it. In fact, she had noticed Ahern watching Zoë more than once, when he thought no one was looking—and Zoë herself had seemed somewhat taken by the young earl, and certainly dazzled by his horsemanship and sheer determination.

"I would say that such a development is not beyond the realm of possibility," she allowed. "He did seem—attentive."

"Alyce!" Zoë protested, blushing even more.

"I predict nothing . . . ," Alyce said, raising both palms in a protestation of innocence. "I merely comment on what I have noted, when neither of you thought I was watching. And I would be willing to bet that a letter from him will arrive before the month is out."

"Oh, you . . . !"

"No, you!" Alyce countered, as she glanced at Marie and Vera and the three of them pounced on Zoë for a bout of tickling that continued until all four of them were breathless with laughter.

"Oh, stop, stop!" Zoë begged. "You'll have Lady Jessamy in here, wondering what on earth is going on!"

Her caution was enough to deflate their brief digression into childishness, though all of them were grinning as they ranged themselves against the fat pillows piled at the head of the bed and caught their breath.

"How I do love all of you," Alyce murmured, when she had caught her breath enough to speak. "Promise me that we shall always be friends and sisters—regardless of who Zoë marries!"

"We promise," the others said in unison, taking Alyce's hands and joining them, clasped in their own.

"Friends and sisters forever!" Vera added. "No matter what happens."

ONCE returned to Rhemuth, the four friends settled quickly back into the routine of the court, now with

Vera as a welcome part of their circle. Now relieved of some of the tutoring duties that previously had occupied her. Alyce found more of her time freed up to pursue her own interests, returning to her explorations of the royal library and in the scriptorium. And these were interests shared by Zoë.

During their absence in Cynfyn, the first returns had begun to trickle in from the king's commissioners of inquiry, and were being compiled by a battery of scribes and copyists now filling the chancery and several additional chambers in one of the garden wings. As she and Zoë became acquainted with the compilations now starting to take shape, and recognized the scope and importance of such a survey, the two of them began to conceive a fitting acknowledgement of the king's foresight in ordering such an undertaking.

"This really will be an incredibly useful document," Zoë said, when they had pulled out several scrolls from King Malcolm's commission of inquiry and compared selected entries against the current commission's findings.

"It will, indeed," Alyce agreed. She leafed through another packet of parchment scraps bundled together by baronies and townlands. "I wonder if the king might like to have a special, illuminated extract of the collated returns from some small area, perhaps with fine calligraphy and some illumination—nothing too ambitious. If we started right away, we perhaps could have it ready to present to him at Twelfth Night court."

"This is still very early in the process," Zoë replied, holding one of the slips closer to a candle to read its heading. "What area did you have in mind? What area is *complete* enough, at this point?"

"I know it can't be perfect," Alyce said. "Compiling *all* the returns will take several years. I think King Malcolm's inquiry took more than two, and some returns were still missing when they stopped working on it. But I thought we might start with Dhassa. For some reason, that seems to be fairly complete."

"I've heard they're very punctilious in Dhassa," Zoë replied, scanning the cramped lines on an irregular scrap of parchment. "I suspect it comes of keeping track of all those tolls to get into the city, because of the pilgrimage sites. But we could do an illuminated cover page, and fancy capitals for the sections dealing with the actual shrines. Have you ever been to Dhassa?"

"No. But there must be people at court who have."

"We can talk to them, then, and get some descriptions. It would be fun to incorporate some of the local features. But no scrawny lions!"

Alyce grinned. "I promise—but only if you promise not to include any fat squirrels."

"Agreed!"

THEY enlisted the patronage of the queen to assist in their undertaking, and had the thin volume ready for Twelfth Night court. Alyce had compiled the text and copied it out in her best court hand, Zoë had done the illuminations, and Marie and Vera bound it in crimson velvet embellished with silk and gold laid-work on the cover and along the spine. They had wrapped it in white linen tied with a length of creamy yarn, and Alyce hugged it to her breast as the four of them waited at the back of the great hall.

But first came the business of the court: the formal enrollment of new pages, including a proud Prince Brion—Prince Blaine and Krispin looked on jealously; the pledging of new squires, and several knightings, though the girls knew none of the newly dubbed young men.

Late in the day also came Sir Rorik Howell to report the death three days before of his father, Corban Earl of Eastmarch, and to pledge his fealty to the king, thereby obtaining the right to enter into his inheritance.

"We receive this news with much sadness, Sir Rorik," Donal told the muddy, exhausted young man who knelt before him, offering up his father's seal as earl, as a sign that he acknowledged the king's right to confirm the succession. "Nonetheless, we understand that your father was ill for many months, and that release will have been a blessing, for him and for his family."

"God grant that he now rests in peace, Sire," Rorik murmured dutifully—and Alyce could Read that his regret was genuine. "I pray that I may be as wise a guardian of his people."

"They are now *your* people, Rorik Howell Earl of Eastmarch," Donal said, enfolding the young man's joined hands in his and raising him up. "Accordingly, before these witnesses, I hereby receive your pledge of fealty and I confirm you in your lands and honors. Go to bed now, young Rorik, for I know you have ridden solid for three days, and probably will have ruined several good horses in the doing of it. Tomorrow, when you have rested, we shall make more formal acknowledgement of your new status."

A murmur of sympathy and approbation followed the new earl as he bowed and retreated from the hall, followed by a squire who had been directed to see to his needs. There came next an announcement by an emissary of the Earl of Transha that the wife of young Caulay MacArdry was lighter of a son and heir, born the previous October and christened Ardry. The news of the birth somewhat lightened the sober air left in the wake of the sadder news brought by Rorik of Eastmarch, and left the king in mellower mood by the time the formal business of the court had ended. As he and his queen retired to the withdrawing room behind the dais, for a break and light refreshment while the hall was set up for feast to follow, the girls followed at the queen's beckoning.

"Sire, I have conspired with the demoiselles de Corwyn and their friends to produce a special Twelfth Night gift for you," the queen said, as she and king settled into chairs before the fire and the girls hesitated at the door.

"A gift?" the king said, setting aside his crown and running both hands through his thinning hair.

"Aye, my lord. Ladies?"

At the queen's gesture, the four of them came to kneel at the feet of the royal couple, Alyce still clutching their precious manuscript to her breast.

"Sire, you will be aware that Twelfth Night marks the Feast of the Epiphany, when, by tradition, three kings brought gifts to the newborn Child in Bethlehem. This is why we give gifts at this season, in memory of their gifts."

"That is true," the king said patiently, smiling faintly.

"This past year has marked the giving of another great gift: your Majesty's great commission of inquiry, by which the rights of lords and commons throughout this land shall be safeguarded and preserved."

Tremulously she offered up her package in both hands, placing it in his.

"In the spirit of this season, then, the four of us decided to create a modest memento to commemorate the importance of this latest inquiry—an extract of the findings concerning the city and environs of Holy Dhassa—and we have set it forth in a form befitting its importance in the history and preservation of our land, and hopefully pleasing to your Majesty."

She watched as he untied the yarn holding the linen wrappings in place, his eyebrows rising as he turned back the linen and caught his first glimpse of what lay within.

"My lord," said the queen, "Lady Vera and Lady Marie created the binding and its fine embroidery. The illuminations are Mistress Zoë's work, and the scrivening was done by Lady Alyce. The balass rubies and the gold bullion thread for the binding were my own humble contribution. I hope you are pleased," she concluded, as the king opened its cover, greatly touched, and turned the first page slightly toward the queen.

"What a truly remarkable gift," he murmured, as Richeldis ran an appreciative finger along a bit of the binding. "I shall look forward to finding the time to examine it properly. Dear ladies, I thank you. Now, where is my new page?" he added, turning to look for Prince Brion, who was standing proudly behind his father in his page's livery, craning his neck to see.

"Boy, take charge of this, please—and mind your hands are clean! Ladies, I see a squire lurking by the door, waiting to unleash petitioners, but I shall charge my son and heir to guard this well for me." He leaned forward to kiss the hand of each of them, then nodded to the squire as he put his crown back on.

"Let's have the first one, Gerald. "I should like to see everyone that I must, before the feast is served."

AFTER Twelfth Night, the rhythm of life at court settled back into its usual routine. The first months of the new year were marked by heavy storms and freezing cold, leading to a late spring. Perhaps because of the sharp lesson of two years previously, Meara was still quiet, but Iolo Melandry, the royal governor, warned that the peace was precarious, and might not hold.

The peace did hold, all through that season, but word came early in the summer that the newly married Countess Elaine, a bride of less than a year, had died in childbed after delivering a son. The boy's father had christened him Kevin Douglas McLain.

"What a tragedy," said Queen Richeldis, hugging the infant Nigel to her heart when she heard the news.

"Was she even sixteen?" one of the other ladies asked, shocked.

Alyce shook her head sadly. "No."

"Her husband is to blame!" another muttered.

"No, she was unfortunate," the queen replied, for both she and Jessamy had borne their first child younger than Elaine.

"Indeed," Jessamy said quietly. "Sadly, such is often the fate of our sex."

Chapter 17

"So they oppress a man and his house, even a man and his heritage."

—MICAH 2:2

THE peace looked likely to hold in Meara that summer, perhaps partially because Duke Richard made a progress into Kierney and Cassan, to show the royal presence at the courts of Earl Jared and Duke Andrew. In May, he had ridden up to the red walls of Jared's seat at Castel Dearg only hours before the birth of the McLain heir—and had mourned with Jared when pretty Elaine slipped away soon after. He would stay on patrol along their Mearan borders for several months.

The king took advantage of the respite to spend time with his young family—fortunately, as it happened, for trouble flared unexpectedly toward the end of summer: not in Meara, as one might have expected, but in Corwyn, on the opposite side of kingdom.

"Torenthi raiders crossed the river at Fathane and harried as far south as Kiltuin," Sir Sé Trelawney reported, addressing king and council in emergency session on a steamy August evening. "Scores were killed or injured, and Kiltuin town was looted and burned. It—ah—has even been suggested that some of the raiders were princes of the blood, and that rogue magic was employed. Ahern will be investigating those claims," he added, with a speaking glance at Alyce and Marie, who had been asked to sit in on the session. "The bishop is said to be livid."

As his council muttered among themselves, Donal cast another glance over the report Sé had brought from Lord Hambert, the seneschal of Coroth. It was the same that Hambert had sent to Ahern to inform him of the raid, and was stark in its assessment of the situation.

My lord, your father would not have allowed this to go unpunished, Hambert had written. *The raiders destroyed most of the town, looting and burning with abandon, and even violated many of the women. In some cases, women and children were ridden down in the streets. I chanced to be traveling in the region soon after it happened, and was told by the town's headman that those responsible were definitely of Torenth, and had boasted that none could bring them to task for their actions, since the king is an old man and his brother is occupied with affairs in Meara. They also believed that, with Earl Keryell dead, you would not be able to take up Corwyn's defense, being young and unfit. . . .*

"Lord Hambert and the Corwyn regency council have already sent stiff letters of protest to the court of Torenth, deploring the incident," Sir Sé was saying, "and Ahern will be in Kiltuin by now, carrying out further investigation. But this is not the first such border violation, as we all know. One would think that the Torenthi would have learnt their lesson in the Great War."

"'Twas clearly a blatant venture of opportunity," said the Archbishop of Rhemuth, forging directly into the discussion. "They know that the king's attention has been focused on Meara, and that Corwyn is in the hands of regents for its duke, who is a minor and a cripple to boot!"

"More agile a cripple than many a man with all his faculties intact," Sé said pointedly. "And crippled he was in the king's service."

"Let be, Sir Sé," Donal said mildly. "What concerns us at this time is a fitting response in Corwyn—which Lord Ahern and his regents seem to have begun quite nicely. Kenneth, how many ships have we at Desse?"

"I don't know, Sire, though I can have that information for you by morning."

"Fair enough," the king agreed. "Jiri, how quickly can we raise sufficient troops to take a policing force into Corwyn?"

"That depends on how many men you have in mind, Sire—which, in turn depends on what ships are available."

"Let's plan for about forty. We'll ride down to Nyford for ships, if we must."

Jiri Redfearn nodded. "In that case, perhaps a day or two, then."

"Which?" Donal demanded. "One day or two?"

The king's sharp tone elicited a whispered conference.

"Tomorrow?" said Jiri.

Donal nodded. "By noon."

"Yes, Sire."

"See to it, then. Sir Tiarnán, you'll leave at once for Kierney, to find my brother and inform him what's occurred. He may well be in Cassan by now, but it would probably be wise for him to return to Rhemuth. It's late for any serious trouble in Meara this season. Seisyll, I'll ask you and the archbishop to form an interim council of regency with the queen, pending Richard's return." He slapped his hand flat against the table in annoyance. "Damn! I did *not* want to campaign this season. Why couldn't those misbegotten Torenthi stay on their side of the river?"

LATER that night, as the castle bustled with preparations for a departure the following noon, Alyce and Zoë conferred together in low tones while they waited for Marie to come in.

"You *know* she's with Sé," Alyce whispered, slightly scandalized. "Please God she doesn't do anything stupid."

"She loves him," Zoë said simply. "I gather that he loves her, too. He's going off to battle. Sometimes common sense goes out the window."

"Well, it mustn't, if you're the sister of a future duke," Alyce muttered.

A fumbling at the door announced the arrival of said sister, looking flushed and happy, giggling as she closed the door behind her.

"And where have *you* been?" Alyce demanded, though she kept her voice low.

"Well, I might have been in Paradise with Sé, if Lady Jessamy hadn't come along when she did," Marie said pertly, flouncing onto the bed with them.

"Mares, you *didn't!*" Alyce gasped.

"We didn't do what we both wanted to do, but it wasn't for want of—well, wanting to," Marie replied. She hugged her arms across her breasts and sighed.

"Oh, Alyce, it's so unfair! Sometimes I want him so badly, I think I'll die if I can't have him. We were only kissing at first. We'd found a quiet corner out in the cloister walk, well away from prying eyes. But then he started touching me, ever so gently, and I got all quivery inside. It felt . . . *wonderful!* My knees started to go all wobbly, and—"

"Tell me that's when Lady Jessamy came along!" Alyce begged, hanging on her every word.

Laughing aloud, Marie shook her head and threw an arm around both of them.

"No, he started fumbling with the laces on his breeches then, and *that's* when Lady Jessamy came along!"

"No!" Zoë breathed, as Alyce rolled her eyes heavenward.

"Sadly, yes," Marie said. "Had she not come when she did, I'm not sure what might have happened—though I *have* heard it said that there are many ways that a man and a maid may pleasure one another. . . ."

Both her companions smothered groans at that, in a mixture of sympathy and envy, but the telling had exhausted all three of them. Only a little longer did they talk, before Zoë betook herself to her own bed and the sisters settled down to try to sleep.

Next morning saw many a tearful good-bye as the king's expedition assembled in the castle yard, with wives and children and sweethearts gathered to bid them Godspeed. Sir Sé Trelawney, sitting his horse beside the king, restrained himself from too effusive a farewell to the demoiselles de Corwyn or their friend Zoë Morgan, whose father also would ride with the expedition, merely bending to salute each proffered hand with a chaste kiss.

But more than one sharp-eyed lady of the queen's household noted that his lips lingered on the hand of the younger sister of his lord, and several cast calculating glances after Marie as she and Alyce left the yard with Zoë, noting how the three then scurried to a vantage point on one of the west-facing battlements, where they might watch the column's progress southward along the river road.

* * *

THE king's party took ship in Desse, as hoped, sailing uneventfully down the River Eirian and thence around the head of Carthmoor, arriving in Coroth harbor in mid-August.

Young Ahern met them at the door to Coroth Castle's great hall, walking with the aid of a stick, but on his feet to welcome his king. Nor had he been idle in the fortnight since the raid on Kiltuin.

Immediately upon hearing the news, he had directed his Lendour regents to echo the complaint already lodged with the court of Torenth by his regents in Coroth—the decision of a mature and astute young man, and one that had been heartily endorsed by his council. He then had taken horse with Sir Jovett Chandos and some thirty men and ridden directly to Kiltuin, to inspect the damage there and speak with some of the survivors. He had found half a dozen of his Corwyn captains and fifty men there before him, doing their best to ascertain just what had happened.

By the time the king arrived in Coroth, Ahern had assumed decisive leadership with both his councils of regents and had begun orchestrating a diplomatic exchange on which Donal himself could not have improved. In fact, his respective regents had become sufficiently confident of their young lord's judgment that they were beginning to function as advisors rather than regents: a state of affairs not at all to the liking of the Bishop of Corwyn, who pointed out at the first opportunity that Ahern was yet a full eight years from achieving the age at which a Deryni might lawfully exercise the full authority of a ducal title.

In light of Ahern's undoubted ability and loyalty, Donal found himself mostly unconcerned over this technical breach of the law, but he did promise the bishop that he would somewhat rein back his fledgling duke, for he did not want to precipitate an incident with the religious authorities. Shortly after his arrival, Donal met privately with young Ahern for nearly an hour, then invited the Corwyn council to join them.

Not that his reaction was all the bishop could have hoped for. Assuring them that he could find no fault with anything that had been done, the king confessed himself obliged to make it clear that proprieties must be maintained, and that their young lord must not presume to present himself as duke in fact. Later, however, he observed to Lord Hambert that Ahern, at seventeen, seemed easily capable of exercising the full authority of his ducal rank . . . were he not Deryni.

Meanwhile, the flurry of exchanges between Corwyn and Torenth was yielding interesting results. In noting the protestations of outrage on the part of Corwyn, the chancery of Nimur of Torenth, in turn, had acknowledged (in view of the numerous affidavits of witness from Kiltuin) that yes, it appeared that subjects of Torenth might possibly have strayed across the border area adjoining Kiltuin, and perhaps had been guilty of over-exuberance regarding insults offered by the inhabitants of said town.

But it was flatly denied that King Nimur's sons might have been among the culprits; and certainly, no reparations would be forthcoming. The correspondence on this matter was already voluminous.

"It appears that King Nimur means to smother the matter in paperwork," Donal remarked, when he had gone over the exchanges with Ahern and his council. "I don't suppose it's possible that the witnesses might have been mistaken—that it wasn't the Torenthi princes after all?"

"Not unless someone was impersonating them," Lord Hambert said with a snort. "The local priest in Kiltuin is something of an armorist; he knows what he saw. Most of the men wore Torenthi livery—they made no attempt to conceal who they were. But he was quite clear that two of them wore variations on the Torenthi royal arms. He's convinced they were two of Nimur's sons."

"And you trust his judgment?" Donal asked.

"I do, Sire. Furthermore, one of the ravaged women drew out the device worn by the man who defiled her. She got rather a better look at it than she would have wished. The drawing is there on the bottom of the stack."

Nodding, Donal leafed through the sheaf of parchment depositions and cast an eye over the last one in the stack, noting the somewhat shaky sketch of the Furstán hart on a roundel, differenced with a bordure. In a somewhat more confident hand, someone had tricked in the colors: the tawny field, the leaping black hart against a white roundel, the white border denoting cadency, though the king could not recall which particular Furstán owned the bordure charged with five black crowns.

"Well, he certainly appears to have been presenting himself as a Furstán," Donal observed. "That alone should get him dealt with by his own folk—unless, of course, that's exactly what he was."

"He was a Furstán, Sire," Ahern said confidently. "Believe me, I *know* this." The look he gave the king as Donal glanced up at this very positive declaration made it quite clear that the boy had confirmed the information by Deryni means.

"Indeed," the king said softly.

Ahern merely inclined his head slightly, his eyes never leaving Donal's.

"Well, then," Donal said. "We shall have to ensure that King Nimur is not allowed to argue this point. Reparations are required." He pushed back from the table and rose, and the others likewise came to their feet. "Perhaps Lord Hambert would be so good as to assemble a suitable foray party, to ride with my own troops. I am minded to make an incursion of my own into Torenth—to discover more facts, of course. And if my men should find opportunity to seize goods in recompense for what happened at Kiltuin—so much the better. I will, however, require that they conduct themselves in a more seemly fashion than our Torenthi raiders. Is that clear?"

As Lord Hambert made a bow, Ahern merely smiled and said, "Abundantly, Sire. And might I request that I may be permitted to ride at your side?" He tapped his stiff leg with his stick and cocked his head at the king. "I think you will discover that this has not slowed me down."

"That has already been my observation," the king replied. "And I am proud to have you in my service."

AHERN'S service proved itself more than once in the days that followed. His daring strategies, worked out with the king, enabled Gwyneddan raiding parties to harry Torenthi border towns with sufficient regularity that, by early September, King Nimur's ministers were seriously discussing the payment of reparations. Donal had hoped to call Nimur's sons to account, at least tendering an acknowledgement of their offenses and an offer of official apology, but it gradually became clear that, on this point, Nimur remained unbending.

But in all, the course of this late campaign—far different from any prospect in Meara—was going satisfactorily. Periodically Donal sent progress reports back to Rhemuth, both to his queen and council and to Ahern's sisters. Whenever these official missives were dispatched, additional letters went along under Ahern's seal. Though, officially, these came from Ahern, Donal was well aware that the courier's pouch always included at least one letter from Sir Sé Trelawney to Marie de Corwyn. In the course of the sea voyage to Coroth, Donal had become well aware of Sé's affection, from childhood, for the Corwyn sisters, and for Marie in particular, and wondered how long it would take Sé to approach him about asking for her hand.

Which permission he was inclined to grant, since he liked young Sé Trelawney, and suspected that the young man might even be Deryni—though he had never been able to confirm this, for Sé religiously avoided any circumstance in which it might be possible for the king to determine this by casual means.

Donal knew of Sé's longstanding friendship with Ahern, and trusted Se's loyalty because he trusted Ahern's; but actually calling the question might put Sé into danger that was not necessary. Donal, unlike his bishops and clergy, was disinclined to enforce the rigorous exclusion of Deryni that had been the official policy of Gwyneddan law for more than a century—perhaps because he suspected that his own odd powers might be somehow related to those wielded by the Deryni. He had once asked Jessamy about it, but she did not know. She did know of his suspicions about Sé, and saw no harm if it were true.

BUT the letters themselves were gradually building on a resentment that very much generated harm, though none could have predicted it save for one affronted damsel of the royal court, increasingly bitter as the summer waned and letters continued to arrive for the Corwyn sisters. The Lady

Muriella saw how the face of Marie de Corwyn lit with excitement whenever letters arrived from Corwyn, and how she always drew aside for a private moment in the garden to read the ones addressed to her, and how she then added each new missive to the growing stack secreted under her pillow, tied with a grass-green ribbon.

One day, when the sisters were safely away for the afternoon, riding with the young princes in the castle's lower ward, Muriella even dared to slip into the pair's room and lift the pillow, carefully sliding out the most recent of the letters to quickly scan its content. To her surprise, there was nothing overt, but that did not lessen her resentment of the attention Sé was lavishing on the pair, and on Marie in particular.

Her resentment grew and festered as the summer wore on, only intensified by her awareness that her rivals were Deryni. And in the daydreams of many a long, sultry summer afternoon, she found herself idly envisioning all manner of dire fates for the pair.

In truth, she could scarcely imagine that the dashing Sir Sé would truly prefer the pallid good looks of the sisters de Corwyn over her own, more voluptuous dark-haired beauty. She wondered whether they might be using their accursed Deryni magic to ensnare his affection—a scandalous offense, since the church held all use of the dread powers of the Deryni to be anathema.

She didn't know whether a Deryni could be burned for using his or her powers to secure another's affections, but it was immensely satisfying to imagine the pair dragged to stakes in the city square below, shorn of their bright locks and trembling with terror as the executioners bound them with chains amid the piles of faggots stacked high, and brought the fiery brands, thrusting the fire deep into the kindling so that the hungry flames soon rose to devour them.

She had laughed aloud at that very satisfying image, though she had soon dismissed it as highly unlikely to happen, given the queen's affection for the pair. Besides that, it would be most difficult to prove any misconduct on their part without Muriella herself becoming involved—and that might well put Sé off her for good, thereby totally defeating the purpose of the exercise. No, getting rid of the sisters was definitely desirable, but there must be some more subtle way to do it.

It was on a showery afternoon early in September that the idea came to her, as she puttered in the stillroom with a decoction of fragrances derived from roses, lavender, and honeysuckle. Muriella had amassed considerable knowledge of herb lore during her several years at court, not only aromatic and culinary herbs but medicinal ones. Sometimes she assisted Father Denit, the queen's chaplain, in the preparation of simples for use by the royal physician; and on that day, as she and the priest checked the stocks of medicinal herbs, she found her fingers lingering over those substances whose use required extreme caution: substances that could kill.

Shocked at her own audacity, she tried to put such thoughts from her mind, forcing herself not to react, but the notion would not leave her. The next day found her in the royal library, poring over a particular herbal. And gradually, a plan began to take shape, involving a confection of ground almonds, honey, and certain other substances that might be added to the almond paste.

It could be done, she decided. It would be dangerous, if she were found out, but was Sir Sé not worth a little risk? Her disdain for her rivals was well known, so she would need to recruit an unwitting accomplice to her plan, but that, too, could be done. The more she considered, the more possible the prospect seemed. For with Marie out of the way, and perhaps Alyce as well, Muriella was certain that she could win the affection of the dashing Sé Trelawney. . . .

MURIELLA seized her opportunity on a sultry day late in September, when a series of seemingly unrelated events chanced to spiral into disaster. It began as Lord Seisyll Arilan strolled into the castle gardens, having spent the morning in council with the queen and the Archbishop of Rhemuth—always a less than pleasant prospect, because Archbishop William made no secret of his dislike of Deryni.

Accordingly, Seisyll was always extremely careful never to put a foot wrong, in his dealings with the man. He understood that William MacCartney was likely to be the next Archbishop of Valoret, when Michael of Kheldour died; and while he had no particular quarrel with Gwynedd's Primate, he knew he would be greatly relieved to have William MacCartney as far away as possible.

That afternoon, however, Seisyll had aspirations in another direction altogether. For with both the king and Duke Richard away from court for the past several months, Seisyll had been watching for an opportunity to have his own look at Master Krispin MacAthan—or Krispin Haldane, as Seisyll increasingly believed the boy to be. Not since Michon's encounter with the boy in the cloister garden at Arc-en-Ciel had anyone from the Camberian Council been able to conduct even a cursory examination. But on such a lazy, hazy summer afternoon, with formal training sessions suspended and most of the children of the royal household at leisure, who knew what might be possible?

He had chosen his time with care, at an hour when many of the adults and not a few of the children were apt to be drowsing, even napping—and who would suspect otherwise? As Seisyll strolled, he took himself to the vicinity of the castle's apple orchard rather than the more formal gardens that lay adjacent to the royal apartments, for he had heard mention that some of the younger boys, Krispin included, had lately conceived a passion for toy boats, which they were wont to try out in the fishpond that served the castle kitchens.

He pulled an apple from one of the trees and began to eat it as he passed through the orchard, peering beyond to where he believed the pond to be. He saw the squire first: a reliable young man in Haldane scarlet, reclining in the shade of another tree and also partaking of the orchard's fruit as he watched the three younger boys crouched at the water's edge.

The tallest of the boys was definitely a Haldane prince, as the second sable-headed lad might also be, all of them dressed in a motley assortment of well-worn and nearly outgrown summer tunics, sleeves rolled above the elbows and tunic-tails ruched up between bare legs as they waded ankle-deep in the shallows and shepherded the boats. The creamy sail of the red boat was painted with a Haldane lion, proclaiming it to be the property of Prince Brion. Another boy with brown hair was fiddling with the saffron sail of a blue-painted boat—the lad's name was Isan Fitzmartin, Seisyll recalled.

Krispin MacAthan's boat was green, and sported a sail of the dull red-ochre hue common to the Southern Sea. All three boys straightened attentively as Seisyll approached, and the squire sat forward and started to get to his feet, but Seisyll waved him back as he nodded to the boys and came to crouch down companionably at the water's edge.

"Good afternoon, your Highness—and Master Krispin, Isan," Seisyll said amiably. "Those are very fine boats you have there, but do you think Cook will mind that you're frightening his fish?"

"Good afternoon, Lord Arilan," Prince Brion replied, speaking for the three of them. "They *are* fine boats, aren't they? Master Edward, the carpenter, made them for us, and some of the queen's ladies sewed the sails."

His sunny smile clearly was meant to distract Seisyll's interest in the frightened fish, and the impish grins of Krispin and Isan were likewise endearing. As the young prince turned to prod at his craft with a stick, and Isan set his boat back adrift, Seisyll reached out with his mind to gently nudge the red and blue boats out of reach of their owners, as if wafted by a wayward breath of breeze. Krispin's, by contrast, drifted a little closer.

"And very fine work it is, too," Seisyll agreed. "Krispin, may I see that one?"

Nodding solemnly, Krispin plucked his boat out of the water and waded closer to Seisyll to extend it for inspection.

"Ah, yes, indeed," Seisyll said, laying hands on the craft but also overlapping the hands of its owner, holding it, turning it to other angles, but not actually taking it—for by doing so, he was able to make and keep contact, at the same time extending a probe.

"Yes, that's very fine," he said, tilting the boat this way and that. "When I was a boy, I had a boat very like this one. My father made it for me—and one for my brother. We used to race them across a millpond in the village green near Tre-Arilan.

"I believe that was the summer I dreamed of becoming a great sea-farer, for my father had taken us to Orsalia earlier that summer, on one of the great galleys of the Duke of Corwyn's caralighter fleet. As I recall, he made the boats for us while we were on that journey. At the time, I didn't realize that sea voyages can actually be quite tedious. To me, it was sheer excitement."

All three boys had been listening with rapt attention as Seisyll shared this boyhood reminiscence—which was time enough for the master Deryni to note several startling similarities between Krispin's psychic resonances and those of the king.

"Was it very fast, my lord?" Krispin asked eagerly.

"Not very," Seisyll said lightly. "I expect your boat is far faster. In fact, mine was appallingly slow. And it hadn't nearly as nice a sail as yours."

He used the boy's pleasure at this compliment as cover for deftly disengaging his probe, also setting a gentle blur over any memory of the contact. It would not hold up to close scrutiny, but no such scrutiny was likely if no suspicion was raised.

"No, yours is far finer than the one I remember," Seisyll went on. "The sail is particularly fine. May I ask who made it for you?"

"Lady Marie did the stitching, my lord," Krispin replied, beaming as he stood a little straighter. "She's ever so nice. But Mother gave her handkerchief, and Lady Muriella helped me gather the right herbs to dye it. And Lady Zoë painted the lion on Brion's one." He cocked his dark head wistfully. "It must be an awful lot of work to be a girl, my lord."

Chuckling, Seisyll gestured toward the other two boats, now beginning to catch the breeze and move back toward their respective owners. Glancing back in that direction, Krispin smiled sunnily and turned to set his own boat back in the water, giving it a gentle push to send it on its way. As its sail caught a breeze and continued to move, the boy straightened to watch it go. Beyond, a duty squire entered the garden with a travel-stained knight in tow—apparently a messenger carrying dispatches, for he was rummaging in a leather satchel slung over one shoulder.

"Look, a messenger!" Prince Brion cried, pointing.

"Where do you think he's come from?" Krispin said.

"Let's go see!" said Isan.

Instantly the three boys bolted in that direction, leaving the boats abandoned in the fishpond. Smiling, Seisyll bent and willed the boats close enough to retrieve, then set them in a row at the edge before following after. Unless he was greatly mistaken, the just-arrived messenger was one of the knights who served Ahern de Corwyn—which meant that there would be news possibly requiring the attention of the crown council.

DEEPER in the main garden, not far from the royal apartments, the arrival of the messenger was also noted by Marie de Corwyn, as his attending squire led him in the direction of the queen's solar. She had washed her hair earlier that morning, and was combing it dry in the dappled sunshine underneath a rose arbor. She rose expectantly as the messenger drew near, about to pass not far away, and he saw her and raised one gloved hand in greeting.

"Jovett!" she called. "Have you anything for me?"

"That I do," the young man replied, grinning as he held up a folded and sealed square of parchment. "And your brother also sends you his duty and respect."

She blushed prettily and ran to take it from him, standing on tiptoes to kiss his cheek, then ran her fingertips over the seal as he continued on. It was a scenario enacted half a dozen times in the course of the summer, as the king's expedition in Corwyn stretched on, and no one thought it odd.

One discreet observer, in fact, welcomed it, for it provided the opportunity she had been waiting for. A little while later, when the queen had received the messages and assembled the crown council to deal with them, one of her ladies pressed a small package into the hands of a junior maid of honor, with instructions to bring it immediately to the Lady Marie.

"Say that the Corwyn messenger omitted to deliver this when he first arrived," Muriella told the girl. "I believe he said that it comes from her brother."

The girl's name was Brigetta Delacorte. She was a shy young thing, only recently come to court. A child, really. One who Muriella knew could be intimidated into silence, if the need arose.

"You'd best go now," Muriella urged, with a sweet smile.

Chapter 18

"Hast thou children? Instruct them,
and bow down their neck from their youth."
—ECCLESIASTICUS 7:23

MARIE had returned to her arbor seat and was reading Sé's letter when young Brigetta Delacorte found her.

"Lady Marie, look what your brother has sent you," the girl said, offering the package timidly. She was young and petite, only barely come to womanhood, and awed with life at Rhemuth. "I suppose it must have been at the bottom of the messenger's pouch."

Marie looked up in some surprise at the small bundle the girl extended, wrapped in a piece of fine ivory damask and tied with a length of green ribbon. It was about the size of a man's hand—a box, by the feel of it, as she took it from Brigetta and hefted it in speculation.

"What on earth?" she murmured delightedly.

As she set it on her lap and pulled the tails of the bow to untie it, Brigetta stood beside her, watching eagerly as the length of green silk unfurled.

"What do you think he's sent you?" the girl asked, craning to see.

"Well, I won't know until I open it, will I?" Marie replied.

She handed the ribbon to the younger girl, then began unwrapping the box from its swath of damask. Beneath the folds of fabric, the box was revealed as quite a handsome item, polished smooth and lightly stained to a walnut shade. The confectionary scent of honey and almonds and roses drifted upward as she lifted the lid to discover more damask—and under it, half a dozen rose-shaped sweets, each adorned with real rose petals sticky with crystallized honey.

"Ooooh, marchpane!" Brigitta murmured. "Wherever did he get it? I *love* marchpane!"

Laughing, Marie took one herself and extended the box. "Have one, then—but only one. And I'll want to share them with the others."

"Mmmm," Brigetta sighed, as she bit into hers and savored the flavor. "Heavenly!"

"Yes, indeed, very nice," Marie agreed, nibbling at her piece. Across the garden, she could see Prince Brion approaching with young Krispin and Isan; she wondered what had happened to their boats. The crown prince was not fond of marchpane, but she knew Isan fancied it; she wasn't sure about Krispin. As they saw that she had noticed them, they broke into a run to join her. Smiling, she beckoned them closer, holding out the box as they came crowding around.

"What's that, Lady Marie?" Prince Brion demanded.

"Marchpane, which you don't like," Marie replied, offering the box to Isan. "But Isan likes it. And how about you, Krispin?"

Grinning delightedly, Isan plucked out one of the pieces and popped it whole into his mouth, cheeks bulging as he chewed it and pleasure lighting his blue eyes. Krispin, less adventurous than some, eyed the dwindling box of marchpane somewhat dubiously.

"Go ahead and try it," Marie urged. "How else will you know whether you like it or not?"

Thus encouraged, Krispin plucked out one of the pieces and cautiously bit off half of it. But after a few chews, his grin faded to dislike and he spat it out.

"*Fah!* What *is* that? I thought it was made of almonds!"

"It *is*," Brion said. "Ground-up almonds."

"Then, what's this on top?"

"Rose petals with honey," Marie said. "You don't have to eat it if you don't like it. Why don't you give the rest of your piece to Isan, rather than waste it? *He* likes it."

"Here, take it!" Krispin said, depositing the remains of his piece in Isan's somewhat grubby hand.

Hurriedly Isan finished chewing his first piece, swallowed

it, and popped the second piece into his mouth before anyone could change their minds.

"And that's all there'll be, for you lot!" Marie said firmly, replacing the lid on the box and setting it aside as she finished her own piece. "I'll save the last two pieces for people who will appreciate them. This has come all the way from Corwyn."

"From Sir Sé?" Isan asked, a gleam in his eyes.

"Actually, this is from my brother," she informed him. "A messenger just arrived from Corwyn."

Prince Brion grinned ear-to-ear. "But it *could* have come from Sir Sé. He really likes you, doesn't he? Do you think my father will let him marry you?"

Chuckling, Marie gave him a nonchalant shrug. "I don't know, your Highness. I hope so."

"I'll ask him," Brion said, drawing himself up importantly. "I think it would be a good thing. And you like *him,* don't you?"

"Yes, I do," she admitted.

Krispin nodded toward the letter now weighted down by the box of marchpane. "Is that from him?"

"Yes, it is," Marie replied. "And I hadn't finished reading it yet, so perhaps you boys could be about your business. What happened to your boats?"

Brion ducked his head guiltily and gave her a tentative smile from under the ebon shock of his hair. "We left them by the fishpond. Lord Arilan said we were scaring the cook's fish."

"Well, if you were sailing them there, I suspect you *were* scaring the fish," Marie replied. "And if Cook finds them, you know what he'll do."

"He'll stomp 'em flat!" Isan declared, big-eyed with horror.

"We'd better go get them!" Brion said. "C'mon!"

As the three bolted in the direction of the kitchen yards and the fishpond, Marie noted that Brigetta was still standing awkwardly by.

"You'd better go dear. The queen is always famished when she's come from meeting with the council of state," she said to the girl.

Smiling, Marie watched Brigetta as she went on her way. As an afterthought, she took up the ribbon from the wrappings of the marchpane and tied it around her neck, humming happily to herself. Then she took up Sé's letter, helped herself to another piece of marchpane, and settled down to read.

It was not until nearly half an hour had passed that she began to feel a little queasy. At first, she found herself regretting that second piece of marchpane; then she attributed a faint abdominal cramping to the imminent onset of her monthly courses.

She laid Sé's letter aside and rubbed distractedly at her stomach, thinking that it was a little early for cramping. After another minute or so, a much stronger cramp bent her double, and a sudden bout of nausea caused her to vomit unexpectedly—several times.

She felt no better when she had done so. As she tried to stand, her legs gave way beneath her and she sank back onto the arbor seat, overcome by a bout of dizziness as more cramps doubled her over and a burning sensation began to radiate outward from her stomach.

Instinctively she knew that this was no monthly cramping. Could it, indeed, have been Ahern's marchpane?

Or—had the marchpane, indeed, come from Ahern? Brigetta had *said* it did, but—

Dear Lord, Brigetta had eaten one of the sweetmeats, too—and young Isan! Had Krispin eaten one? No, he had tried it and spat his out—and Isan had eaten the remainder of that piece!

She fumbled the lid off the wooden box and stared stupidly at the remaining dainty. As she did so, the sickly sweet scent of almond and honey and roses made her heave again, gasping as she collapsed to her knees, clutching at her middle. And she also seemed to be having trouble catching her breath. She could feel a heaviness in her chest, as if a giant hand were closing around her lungs to suffocate her; yet when she clamped shaking fingers to the pulse-point at her throat, her heart rate was so slow and so weak that she could barely find it.

She thought to look around her then, searching for someone to help her, but there was no one in sight.

IN the queen's chamber, the council meeting being concluded, the queen's ladies were helping their mistress to partially disrobe for an afternoon nap. Alyce was attending her, and also Jessamy, Brigetta, and Zoë. Muriella was tuning a psaltery near an open window.

"Well, ladies, it appears that the king will be able to return shortly," Richeldis said, pulling the pins from her dark hair and shaking it loose before lying back on the day-bed. "Alyce, he sends glowing reports of your brother, who has acquitted himself quite admirably, both in the council chamber and in the field."

Alyce smiled contentedly and settled at the foot of the queen's day-bed to remove her shoes.

"I would be surprised if it were otherwise, Madam," she said. "Zoë and I watched him ride against Duke Richard last autumn, when he was only partially recovered from his injury. He must be far better now. But he has had exceptional teachers, including the king himself."

"True enough," the queen agreed. "Ah, Jessamy, that feels so wonderful!"

Jessamy had begun massaging the queen's temples, and smiled distractedly, though she said nothing, for she had noticed that Brigetta was looking decidedly unwell.

"Brigetta, are you ill, child? You're suddenly looking very pale."

Brigetta had been pouring a cup of chilled wine for the queen, but set it shakily aside and turned away, clutching at mouth and abdomen as she darted toward the garderobe.

"I do beg your pardon," she managed to murmur, just before she was taken with a violent fit of vomiting.

Jessamy went after her immediately, as did Alyce. The queen sat up in some concern. Muriella had stopped her idle plucking at the strings of her psaltery, and stared after the stricken Brigetta in horror.

Together, Alyce and Jessamy tried to comfort Brigetta as she continued to heave, Alyce holding the girl's hair out of the way and Jessamy venturing a probe.

"Child, child, what is it? Was it something you ate?"

"The marchpane! It must be—!" Brigetta managed to gasp out, between gagging fits. "Lord Ahern sent it. S-some of the boys ate it, too—and Marie. Dear God, I can't breathe!"

"Which boys? How much? Where are they?" Jessamy demanded, as Alyce recoiled from the pain washing through the stricken girl.

"She's poisoned!" Alyce blurted. "*They're all poisoned!* But Ahern can't have sent poisoned marchpane!"

"Krispin!" Jessamy cried, for she saw Brigetta's memory of all of them partaking. "And Isan—dear God! They're in the garden!"

"Sweet *Jesu,* no!" the queen cried, trying to lurch to her feet. "Jessamy, do something! Find them!"

Alyce was already dashing toward the door, heart pounding, reaching out with her mind to Marie, calling, a part of her sickly aware that it was already too late. And even as she ran, Jessamy close behind her, she realized who had given the marchpane to Brigetta to deliver: *Muriella!* And suddenly, it all became horrifyingly clear.

She faltered, outrage drawing her back, but her sister's need—and that of the children, the innocent children!—was far greater than her desire for immediate justice.

"It was Muriella!" she said breathlessly over her shoulder to Jessamy as they ran toward the gardens.

"I know," Jessamy gasped, and seized the arm of a guard as they came abreast of him, pausing only long enough to bark out a single command.

"Go to the queen's solar," she ordered, "and arrest Lady Muriella!"

They had seen the location in the garden where Marie had been reading her letter. At the path to the arbor, Alyce split off in that direction, leaving Jessamy to continue on toward the castle's fishpond.

As Alyce approached, she saw the rumpled blur of her sister's peacock-colored gown, stark against the creamy stone of the bench beneath the arbor, and the tumble of her loose hair veiling her face. With a little cry, she ran to Marie's side and swept the hair aside, but the blue eyes were open and empty, the fair face already waxy pale. Sobbing, Alyce gathered her sister to her breast and held her, weeping for her loss—for Marie's loss—for all the tomorrows that now would never be.

But urgency soon drew her from her own grief, to see what help she might render to Jessamy, for she knew, from the brief images she had read from Brigetta, that the tragedy did not stop here. With a little sob, she gently shifted her sister onto clean grass and scrambled to her feet, dashing off the way Jessamy had gone—and found her beside the fishpond in the kitchen yard, weeping as she cradled the lifeless Isan in her arms. Young Prince Brion was hugging a very frightened and wide-eyed Krispin, who at least did not appear to be too affected other than being very shocked. Jessamy's cries had brought several kitchen servants into the doorway to investigate the source of the distress.

"Alyce—oh, thank God!" Jessamy sobbed, looking up. "Take Krispin inside at once and make him vomit! Give him the whites of half a dozen eggs, and then a great deal of water with plenty of salt in it."

"But I didn't eat any! I spat it out!" Krispin insisted, as Brion began dragging him toward the kitchen and Alyce hesitated uncertainly.

"Is Isan—?"

"Yes, he's dead!" Jessamy cried. "And God knows what I shall tell his mother. He had nearly twice as much as the others. Dear *God,* how did we not see this coming?"

Suddenly very weary, Alyce started to sink down numbly beside Jessamy, but the older woman seized her roughly by the shoulder and gave her a shake.

"Don't you dare!" she whispered vehemently. "Go and tend to Krispin. There's nothing to be done here. Save your passion for the living!"

Half-dazed with shock, Alyce straightened and followed after Brion and Krispin, pushing past the servants in the doorway. In the bustling kitchen beyond, preparations were underway for the evening meal.

Forcing herself to focus, Alyce herded the two boys ahead of her until she spotted a basket of eggs. She seized a large cup as she changed course in that direction, nodding toward the nearest pair of kitchen maids.

"You," she said to the younger one, "fetch us some fresh water—at once! And you," she said to the second, "separate the whites from half a dozen of those eggs and put them in this cup. Brion, bring Krispin over here!"

"But I didn't eat any of the marchpane!" Krispin protested.

"We must make sure," Alyce replied. "Hurry!" she added aside to the white-faced servant, who was breaking eggs and tipping the yolks back and forth between the two halves of each, letting the whites drain into the cup Alyce held. "My sister is dead. By now, so is Lady Brigetta. And Isan."

The boys' faces drained of color, and anger flashed in young Brion's gray eyes.

"Who did this terrible thing?" the crown prince demanded.

"I don't know," Alyce replied. "I think it was Lady Muriella."

"But, why?" Krispin wanted to know, tears spilling down his cheeks.

"I don't know." Alyce took the cup, now half-filled with egg-whites, and put it into his hands. "Now, drink this—all of it!"

"No. It's slimy. It'll make me puke."

"That's the whole point. Drink it!"

At the same time, Prince Brion gave his shoulder a shake and repeated, "Drink it, Krispin."

The younger boy braced himself and drank, forcing himself to gag down the contents of the cup in three large swallows. When he had finished, Alyce refilled the cup from an ewer the younger servant had brought, added a generous measure of salt and stirred it with a finger, and ordered the boy to drain that, too—and then a second cup. As he labored to finish the second draught, making a face, she pulled an empty basin closer, nodding for Brion to hold it under Krispin's chin.

"Revolting, wasn't it?" Alyce murmured, cupping the back of Krispin's head with her hand. "Believe me, I do understand. Now open your mouth."

Too startled to resist, Krispin obeyed, only to have Alyce poke two fingers down his throat, at the same time pressing his head over the empty basin.

The result was immediate and spectacular. When Krispin had finished retching, Brion dutifully holding the basin and looking scared, one of the kitchen maids brought him a clean towel, another offering one to Alyce.

"Will he be all right, my lady?" the girl asked.

"I think so," Alyce replied numbly. "It doesn't appear that he actually got a dose of the poison, but I couldn't risk not doing everything I know to do. It was in some marchpane, but he said he spat out what he tried."

One of the women was inspecting the contents of the

basin while Brion helped Krispin wipe his mouth and Alyce washed her hands in another basin a young kitchen maid had brought.

"Marchpane, y'say?" the woman said, shaking her head. "Well, I don't see no trace of that, my lady. I doubt he'd had anything since this morning."

"For which, God be praised!" Alyce murmured, drying her hands.

Welcome relief flooded through her like a physical wave, and she leaned heavily on the vast kitchen table. But this momentary respite quickly gave way to recollection of less favorable outcomes: images of her sister lying dead in the garden, and the innocent Brigetta stricken in the queen's chamber—and Isan, who had eaten more of the tainted marchpane than any of the others, likewise dead. A sob welled up in her throat, but she mastered it and laid her arms around the shoulders of Krispin and the prince.

"That was well done, gentlemen," she murmured, hugging both of them close. "You were very brave."

"What about Isan?" Brion asked hesitantly. "Is he really . . . ?"

"I'm afraid he is, your Highness," she replied.

"I want to see him!" Krispin said boldly.

"There is nothing you can do for him now," she said. "But your lady mother will be frantic to know that *you* are safe!"

Chapter 19

"Wrath is cruel, and anger is outrageous,
but who is able to stand before envy?"
—PROVERBS 27:4

THE prince's mother was, indeed, frantic, but not alone for worry over her son. Watching white-faced and silent as men from the castle guard wrapped the body of the unfortunate Brigetta in a cloak to carry it from the room, the queen jumped to her feet as Alyce came in with Prince Brion and Krispin. In the room beyond, Jessamy was trying to comfort Lady Megory Fitzmartin, the mother of Isan, who was holding her dead son in her arms and keening, rocking him back and forth. Lord Seisyll Arilan stood just inside the door, apparently enlisted to carry the dead boy back to his mother.

Seisyll turned as Alyce entered with the two boys, and the queen tearfully held out her arms to her son. Brion ran to her, burying his face against her waist, starting to cry at last as his mother shed more tears of sheer relief.

Krispin held back at first, then pressed past Seisyll into the room beyond and stared at the dead Isan as his mother silently embraced him. Meanwhile, in the queen's chamber, her other ladies were staring at Alyce, Vera and Zoë among them, their eyes begging her to say that none of this was real. All had been weeping.

"Majesty, I don't think Prince Brion has taken any harm," Alyce managed to murmur, not looking at Vera or Zoë. "Krispin seems fine as well. Is Lady Brigetta—"

The queen bit at her lip and looked away, holding her eldest more tightly. "Dear child, there was nothing we could do. And your sister—?"

Alyce shook her head, lowering her gaze and choking back tears. Beyond the queen, Zoë gave a sob and Vera went even paler than she had been, but dared not show the true extent of her grief.

"Dear God . . . ," the queen murmured.

Alyce drew a deep breath. "What has happened to Lady Muriella?"

"I don't know," the queen said dazedly. "She ran from the room, heading toward the main keep, and I heard guards running in that direction a while later. . . .

"But, do not tarry here, dear Alyce. Go to your sister, by all means. I am so sorry! Oh, that *spiteful* Muriella! Why did she do it?"

Alyce only shook her head and fled—but not to her sister, who could not be helped in this world, but to see what had become of Muriella.

The castle was in an uproar, with armed and angry soldiers moving everywhere, purpose in their looks and strides. When Alyce could make no immediate sense of what was happening, she caught the sleeve of a passing sergeant who usually had kind words for her.

"Master Crawford, please—can you tell me whether they have found the Lady Muriella?" she asked.

"No time now, m'lady," he grunted, shrugging off her touch and hurrying on. "She's run up the north tower, she has."

He was gone at that, ducking into a turnpike stair to clatter after others also headed upward. Heart pounding, Alyce followed, gathering up her skirts to climb as fast as she could, stubbing her toe on one of the stone steps and nearly sent sprawling.

She heard shouting as she ascended, and a woman shrieking, and—just before she reached the final doorway onto the walkway along the battlement—a renewed chorus of shouted demands by heated male voices, punctuated by a woman's anguished scream that faded and then was cut short by the distant, hollow thump of something striking the ground far below.

"Christ, I didn't think she'd jump!" one of the men was

saying, peering over the parapet as Alyce pushed her way among them.

"Well, she *has* saved herself from hanging or worse," said another, cooler voice.

Steeling herself, Alyce forced herself to peer between two of the merlons studding the crenellated wall, down at the crumpled heap of clothing and broken bones now sprawled in the courtyard below, where a pool of blood was rapidly bleeding outward from Muriella's dark head. Gagging, she turned away, one hand pressed to her lips and eyes screwed tightly closed, grateful for the hands that drew her back from the parapet.

"Lady Alyce, you needn't look at this," someone said, not unkindly.

"She killed my sister, and Lady Brigetta," Alyce managed to whisper, before gathering up her skirts to flee back down the turnpike stair. "And she killed a little boy. . . ."

By the time she got down to the courtyard, a crowd had gathered: soldiers and courtiers and servants and a stranger in priest's robes, who had just finished anointing the body. Seeing him, Alyce pushed her way through the crowd and stood there, numbly staring down at the dead woman, until the priest glanced up at her.

"Child, there is nothing you can do," he said, closing his vial of holy oil.

"And there is nothing *you* can do, either, Father," she replied in a low voice. "Do you know how many lives she has taken today, besides her own?"

The priest's face tightened, but he said nothing, only shaking his head.

"She poisoned three people, Father," Alyce went on, outrage in the very softness of her tone. "She murdered two innocent women and an innocent child—and very nearly killed another child. It could as easily have been one of the royal princes! And you would absolve her of *that*?"

A uneasy murmur rippled among the onlookers, and the priest slowly stood, looking her up and down.

"Are you not one of the heiresses of Corwyn, a Deryni?" he said coldly.

"What difference does that make to the three she killed?" Alyce snapped. "Does it make them any less dead?"

A soldier leaned closer to the priest to whisper in his ear, and the priest's face went very still.

"The deaths are regrettable, of course—as is hers," the priest said. "But it is up to God to judge her—not me. And it is not the place of a Deryni to instruct me in my duties."

Alyce only shook her head and turned away, closing her eyes to the sight of him and the dead Muriella. She could hear the muttering following her as she made her way out of the crowd. When she found her way back to the garden arbor where she had left her sister, the body was gone, but as she glanced around in dismay, one of the gardeners approached her awkwardly, cap in hands.

"Monks came to take her away, my lady," he murmured. "Brother Ruslan said to tell you that she would lie in the chapel royal tonight. I'm very sorry. She was very kind, even to a mere gardener."

She stared at him blankly for several seconds, then gave him a grateful nod. His name was Ned, she recalled, and he had always had a gentle word for both her and Marie.

"Thank you, Ned," she whispered.

In a daze, she made her way to the chapel royal, where two black-robed monks were setting up a bier in the aisle before the altar. But of any bodies, there was no sign.

Forlorn, not knowing what else to do, she knelt at the rear of the chapel and said a prayer for her sister's soul—and for Isan, and for Brigetta, and even for the wretched Muriella—then rose and went forward to where the brothers worked.

"Could you tell me where the bodies have been taken?" she asked.

The older man looked up pityingly and gave her a neutral nod.

"You'll be asking after the women?" he said.

She inclined her head in return.

"We're told that some of the sisters from Saint Hilary's are looking after them," he informed her. "But they'll lie here tonight. Except for the one who took her own life, of course."

"What about the boy?" Alyce asked dully.

"There was a boy as well?" the younger brother asked, shocked.

Mutely Alyce nodded.

"Dear *Jesu,*" the elder brother whispered, as both crossed themselves.

"In all fairness," she forced herself to say, "I do not think the boy was meant to die—or the second woman. Or the one who planned the deed—God forgive her, for I cannot. I can only imagine that it was conceived in unreasoning jealousy, and went disastrously wrong. The poison was meant for my sister alone, but four now lie dead as a result of this day's work." She shook her head. "I'll leave you to your duties," she murmured, as she turned and fled.

Grief urged her to look further for her sister, but reason reminded her of other duties to the living. Lady Megory had lost a son, and the young princes had lost a comrade. She returned to the queen's solar to find Richeldis and her ladies helping the bereaved mother wash and prepare her son's body for burial.

Comforted by Zoë and Vera, Alyce wept with them and watched as they tenderly laid young Isan Fitzmartin in the queen's own bed, where the ladies would keep watch beside him during the night. A little while later, now accompanied by Zoë and Vera, she withdrew again to find the body of her dead sister.

THEY found both Marie and Brigetta now lying in the chapel royal, where the sisters from Saint Hilary's-Within-the-Walls had lovingly prepared the two for burial, laying them out upon a bier strewn with rose petals. Each had been dressed in her finest gown, crowned with a floral wreath and veiled from head to toe with fine white linen, like brides arrayed for their bridegrooms. Alyce was reminded of the veil Cerys Devane had worn for her novice profession at Arc-en-Ciel; but Marie had never sought such a life.

A lock of Marie's bronzy hair had tumbled loose from under her veil and down the side of the bier, and Alyce gave a sob as she saw it and came to touch it with a trembling hand. At the sound, one of the sisters spreading fresh linens on the altar turned a sympathetic face toward the newcomers. She was hardly older than they, and looked to have been weeping.

But before she could speak, her older companion inclined her head toward Alyce.

"A terrible sadness," she said quietly. "But they are with God now."

Gently Alyce reached out to lay one trembling hand on the bulge of Marie's folded hands beneath the veil covering her, her vision blurred by tears.

"Dear God, I had thought I had no tears left to weep," she whispered, crumpling to her knees to rest her forehead against the edge of the bier.

After a moment, blinking back tears of her own, Vera sank down beside her, one arm around the shoulders of her twin, and Zoë knelt on Alyce's other side.

"Could you please leave us for a moment?" Zoë said softly to the two sisters.

In unison, the pair inclined their heads and padded silently from the chapel, settling to wait outside until the visitors should finish paying their respects.

NOT far from the entrance to that chapel, Seisyll Arilan watched for a long moment, then turned to make his way toward the stables.

The day's events, of a certainty, required a report to the Camberian Council, not only to share his impressions regarding young Krispin MacAthan—which easily could have waited until the next regularly scheduled meeting—but now to report the untimely and quite senseless death of Marie de Corwyn. The death of a Deryni heiress of her importance would require the Council to considerably reshuffle their careful strategies regarding desirable marriage alliances. But before he went to tell them, he intended to have a look at the body of the accused poisoner.

Because the wretched Muriella had taken her own life, she lay not in the chapel royal or even in one of the side chapels of Saint Hilary's-Within-the-Walls but in the castle's stables, in one of the loose boxes usually reserved for foaling, laid out on boards across a pair of trestles. Two of the queen's maids had washed away the blood and dressed her in a clean white shift, wrapping her shattered head in linen bandages, so that she looked like a nun.

Now one of the maids was sewing the dead girl into her burial shroud while the other tucked bunches of sweet herbs amid the folds of fabric. A wreath of rosemary lay beside the basket of herbs. Both of the maids looked up guiltily as Seisyll appeared at the stall door, and they dropped him nervous curtsies.

"Is that the girl who fell to her death? Muriella, I believe?" Seisyll asked, jutting his chin toward the corpse.

The girl sewing up the shroud gave him a fearful nod.

"Aye, m'lord—poor lady. She'll get nae better wedding wreath," she added, nodding toward the circlet of rosemary. "But she didna' mean to do it."

"She didn't mean to do it," Seisyll repeated, raising a quizzical eyebrow. "What—she didn't mean to kill herself, or she didn't mean to kill all those people?"

His rapid-fire questions silenced the speaker, but the other girl boldly lifted her chin to him.

"She didna' mean to kill *anyone,* m'lord! 'Specially not the boy." The other girl was now nodding emphatic agreement. "But she was fair green wi' jealousy!"

"Jealousy of whom?" Seisyll demanded.

"Why, the Lady Marie," came the prompt reply. "Everybody knew that—'cept Marie an' her sister, o' course. Marie was fair smitten wi' Sir Sé Trelawney, an' too besotted to notice that Muriella fancied him, too."

"Indeed?" Seisyll murmured. "So she did mean to kill her rival, at least. And when that went all wrong, she killed herself?"

Both girls nodded wordlessly, wide-eyed.

"Poor, stupid, cowardly child," Seisyll muttered under his breath.

"Will she—burn in hell, m'lord?" one of the girls asked tremulously.

"Probably," Seisyll retorted, then softened at the look of horror on the two faces. "But perhaps not, if we say prayers for her soul." He reached over the door to the loose box and lifted the latch. "Why don't we say a prayer for her now?" he said, coming inside to slip between the two, a hand on each shoulder pressing them both to their knees.

At the same time, he extended his powers and took control of both of them, kneeling between them then to reach deeper memories from each. If anyone came upon them, it would appear to be only what he had claimed: the three of them kneeling in prayer for the deceased—and that was all the girls would remember.

A superficial dip into both young minds gained him little information beyond what they had already told him. And even the more rigorous process of taking a death-reading from the unfortunate Muriella failed to reveal much more.

The poisoned marchpane had indeed been intended for Marie alone—or possibly her sister as well, for Muriella had liked Deryni no better than she liked any rival for the affections of Sir Sé Trelawney. But she certainly had never thought that anyone else would sample the marchpane: not young Isan or the other maid of honor, and certainly not Krispin or Prince Brion. Seisyll shuddered at the thought of how close the crown prince had come to death—spared by the simple happenstance that he did not care for the sweet confection.

Nor had Ahern de Corwyn had any part in the plan, though he supposedly had sent the marchpane. Muriella had invoked his name in order to allay any suspicion on the part of Marie, never thinking beyond the initial stages of her plan—for surely, even if the Delacorte girl had lived, and held her tongue, it still would have emerged that Ahern knew nothing of marchpane. And it had been blind fear of the hangman's rope that had impelled Muriella to throw herself from the castle wall, when she knew herself discovered and her oh-so-clever plan gone horribly wrong.

"Stupid, *stupid* little girl!" Seisyll whispered under his breath, as he came out of trance, having set his instructions in the minds of the two maids.

Leaving them on their knees to pray a while longer, he rose and gazed down at Muriella for a long moment, gently shaking his head, then wearily picked up the wreath of rosemary from atop the basket and put it on her bandaged head.

Though the church taught that suicide was a mortal sin, Seisyll had never been able to accept that teaching as an absolute. Muriella had been frightened and desperate enough to take her own life rather than face up to the consequences of her actions—which had certainly been horrendous—but he thought that if she burned in hell, it would not be because she had loved and then had feared. And even the murder of three innocents besides herself could be forgiven, in time, if the murderer truly repented.

But that was for Muriella to sort out with her God. For himself, Seisyll could only breathe a final prayer for her soul, with an appeal to the Blessed Mother to take this foolish child into her loving care and eventually restore her to grace.

Pityingly, he brushed his fingertips across the dead girl's cheek in farewell, then bent to press a holy kiss to her brow before turning to go.

Chapter 20

"May choirs of angels receive thee . . ."

—INTROIT FOR THE FUNERAL LITURGY

THE following week would pass in a numb blur of grief for Alyce de Corwyn, for she now must bury her sister, as she had buried her father but two years before. As she had done after her father's death, she traveled back to her ancestral lands—not to Cynfyn, for Marie had been little a part of that, but to Coroth, the Corwyn capital, where this latest scion of the line of Corwyn's dukes would lie with her ancestors.

In this season of the year, still languishing in the heat of the summer just ending, the cortege wound its way southward only as far as Desse, following the royal road that ran along the east bank of the River Eirian. Thence the party transferred to the relative comfort of one of the king's galleys for the voyage into the great Southern Sea and thence around the horn of Mooryn, heading eastward then until at last they sighted the twin lighthouses guarding Coroth Harbor.

The news, of course, had reached Corwyn's capital well in advance of the funeral party, sent by fast courier the very day of the tragedy. The king had been out hawking on the moors the day it arrived, with Lord Hambert, the Seneschal of Coroth, and the Tralian ambassador, attended by Sir Jiri Redfearn, Sir Kenneth Morgan, and Sir Sé Trelawney, along with a handful of knights. It was a bright day in early October, and the expedition was to have been the last such junket before Donal's planned departure for Rhemuth in a few days' time.

Ahern had begged off, declaring himself possessed of a mild indisposition.

Donal had braced himself for bad news when he saw the look on the messenger's face, as the rider in Haldane livery reined in his lathered horse and sprang to the ground. The man himself had known little of the tragedy beyond the stark fact that several had died in Rhemuth as a result of poison hidden in a parcel of sweetmeats, but Seisyll Arilan's terse missive held a fuller story.

The poison appears to have been meant for the Lady Marie, Seisyll had written, in a letter folded around another, smaller square of folded parchment, *but she shared the treat with Lady Brigetta Delacorte and some of the children—none of the princes, for which, God be praised, but young Isan Fitzmartin is dead. Ostensibly, the sweets came from Lord Ahern, in the diplomatic pouch from Corwyn, along with the enclosed letter from Sir Sé Trelawney.*

Donal's eyes darted to the folded square he had removed from inside Seisyll's letter, then skimmed on down the page.

Young Krispin MacAthan tasted one of the sweetmeats but did not like it, and spat it out, Seisyll declared. *He came to no harm. Not so, young Isan, who ate the rest of Krispin's share, in addition to his own. He perished, along with Lady Marie and Lady Brigetta. The poisoner, Lady Muriella, threw herself from one of the parapets when she saw what she had done.*

The king's relief that Krispin had survived was tempered by regret at the names of the dead—the sad waste of it. And but for the grace of God, any of his true-born sons might have perished as well.

Very sadly, it now fell to him to inform young Ahern de Corwyn of the death of his twin sister. Donal could not, for the life of him, remember what the Lady Brigetta Delacorte looked like, or even the jealous and spiteful Muriella, but Marie de Corwyn, besides being a valuable heiress, had been a delight to eye and ear, a notable adornment to the court of Gwynedd. Furthermore, the loss of her marriage as coinage of political expediency was greatly to be regretted. Sadly, no one would ever know what might have become of young Isan—an engaging and promising boy, now gone as if he had never lived.

"Ill news, Sire?" Sir Kenneth asked quietly.

Slowly Donal nodded, not speaking as he opened the second folded piece of parchment, addressed on the outside to the Lady Marie de Corwyn. He recognized the handwriting, for Sir Sé Trelawney had been serving as secretary for much of the recent correspondence with the court of Torenth. The content of the letter had largely to do with the minutiae of life at the Corwyn court—nothing at all improper or intimate—but he could guess how it would have thrilled the fair Marie to receive it.

"Sir Sé," he called, lifting his gaze and the hand with the letter toward that young man, tending the hawks a little ways away.

Sé gave the hawks into the care of a nearby squire and came at once, curiosity in his eyes.

"Sire?"

"Yours, I think," the king replied, handing him the letter. "May I take it that you know nothing about a parcel of marchpane sent to the Lady Marie in the last diplomatic pouch to Rhemuth, ostensibly from her brother?"

Sé shook his head distractedly, his face blanching as he glanced at the letter and recognized his own handwriting.

"Sire, on my honor—nothing untoward—"

"I do not question your honor," the king said quietly, briefly lowering his eyes. "And I know you are innocent of anything besides the letter you wrote." Reluctantly he then handed Sé the letter from Seisyll Arilan. "I'm very sorry, son."

Only a faint breeze stirred, there on the moorland—that and the soft whuffling of the horses nearby, and the screech of a hawk—as Sé read what Arilan had written, his embarrassment turning abruptly to stunned disbelief.

"No!" The word escaped his lips before he could stop it, his breath catching in his throat as he raced through a second reading of the letter in hope of finding some reprieve that he had missed. Tears were welling in the blue eyes as he then looked up at the king, every line of his body begging for it not to be true.

"It can't be. It isn't possible."

Sadly Donal shook his head. "I cannot think Lord Seisyll would make up such a thing, lad. I was aware of your affection for Marie—though obviously, neither of us was aware that the Lady Muriella had fixed her heart on *you*." He sadly shook his head. "And how badly wrong it went. Not only did she eliminate her rival, but two more innocents as well—and then took her own life."

Sé screwed his eyes tightly closed, battling for control. "Had I been there," he whispered, "and known her to do this deed, *I* would have taken her life. Dear God, I was mustering my courage to ask you for Marie's hand—little though I am worthy of her. We had hoped we might be married!"

"Sé, Sé—dear boy," Donal murmured. Having lost his first wife and many a friend, over the years—and nearly having lost Krispin—he had an inkling what Sé must be feeling.

"We'd best go back to Castle Coroth," he said aside to Sir Kenneth. "Young Ahern must be told, and I've no stomach for any more hunting today."

WITH almost military precision, Sir Kenneth called in the others of their party and organized the return to Coroth. They found Ahern de Corwyn up on the castle's highest parapet, leaning on his stick and gazing out to sea toward the west, where any approaching ship from Rhemuth would first appear. Gaining this vantage point could not have been easy, for stairs were still a major challenge for Ahern's stiff knee. But when the king saw Ahern's face, he knew that the messenger must have given him at least the gist of the message he carried, before heading out to the moors to find the king.

"Ahern?" the king said quietly.

The young man turned his face toward the voice, his profile still and drawn against the lowering twilight.

"I heard," he replied. "My sister Marie is dead."

The starkness of his tone had a finality about it that sent a chill up Donal's spine.

"It's because she was Deryni," Ahern went on, in an even softer voice. "Oh, I know Muriella was jealous. Both Marie and Alyce had mentioned her in letters, over the past year or so. She fancied Sé, I gather. But I can't imagine that she would have acted, if she'd thought she was only competing with another ordinary woman. And Marie was *not* ordinary."

"No, she wasn't," the king replied.

Ahern heaved a heavy sigh and turned his face back to the

sea. "I'd like to be alone now, if you don't mind. I expect it will be a few days before the ship arrives with her body."

"Ahern, I—"

"You needn't worry that I'll do myself harm," the young man said firmly. "Please, Sire. Go."

TWO days later, just at dusk, a royal galley under bellied sable sails glided into Coroth Harbor between the twin lighthouses known as Gog and Magog, each with a signal beacon already lit for the night. Amidships, beneath a striped canopy of gold and Haldane scarlet, Alyce de Corwyn stood with a protective hand atop her sister's white-draped coffin, gowned in unrelieved black and with a black veil wrapped closely about her head, covering her bright hair. Zoë Morgan and Sir Jovett Chandos flanked her, and the ship's crew stood to attention along the rails to either side, interspersed with the men of the royal honor guard sent along from Rhemuth at the command of the queen, black crepe tied to each man's sword-arm, bared heads bowed in respect.

The long-drawn question of a lookout's horn floated across the light chop with the clang of the harbor-buoys as the galley skirted between the two sea jetties of tumbled granite blocks, answered by a deeper horn-blast from the shore. The sounds had always welcomed Alyce home in the past; now they cried out the sadness that accompanied the ship like a cloak.

Her brother and the king were waiting on the quay with Sé Trewlawney and a contingent of Corwyn archers drawn up as an honor escort, each holding a torch aloft. Ahern's council and all the knights who had come with the king's party stood among them, solemn and silent, as were the townspeople gathered behind them, for Corwyn's people had come to admire and respect their future duke and his sisters.

Deftly the steersman brought the galley close to the quay, where he turned the craft into the wind and the crew scrambled aloft to furl the sable sail. At the same time, men waiting ashore threw lines across to those on deck, so that the vessel could be warped alongside the quay.

The king came aboard at once, not waiting for a gangplank

to be set in place, leaving young Ahern to stand with Sé and the other royal officers. Alyce accepted the king's condolences in silence, then moved to the rail and, as soon as the ship was made secure, went ashore and into the arms of her brother.

"I am *so* glad to see you!" Ahern whispered, as they clung to one another. "I think I sensed that she was gone. The night it must have happened, she was in my dream. Actually, I dreamed about both of you. But when the messenger arrived, a few days later, I know what the news was that he brought."

She drew back a little and sadly shook her head—but without tears, for she had spent herself of tears days before.

"You cannot imagine how awful it was," she said quietly. "And it might have been far worse. As it was, two more died with our sister—three, if you count Muriella. Poor, stupid cow!" She drew a breath. "How is Sé bearing up?"

Ahern shook his head. "Not well. He was in love with her. They hoped to be married, if the king agreed. And I think it might have been allowed, if—"

He broke off, biting at his lip, and Alyce hugged him closer. After a few minutes, Sé and four of the archers from his honor guard came aboard to bring the coffin off the ship, Jovett joining them, bearing it on their shoulders as they fell into place in the funeral cortege that would take Marie to Coroth Cathedral. There she would lie in state through the following day, so that Coroth's citizens might pay their respects.

Though the ship's escort joined that of the king, marching solemnly in the foot procession that now started toward the cathedral to a muffled drumbeat, Alyce accompanied the king and her brother in the vast, boxy carriage that had brought them down from the castle. Alyce sat next to Ahern, hand clasped tightly to his; Donal was seated opposite. The leather side-curtains were rolled up and secured, so that the occupants could be seen, but the crowd gathered along the Via Maris was there for the coffin, not the carriage that followed it, quiet and respectful, men doffing their caps and women dropping little curtsies as the cortege passed, a few crossing themselves. Zoë rode behind with the maid who had accompanied them, in a pony cart led by her father.

They rattled along in taut silence for several minutes, the thud of the drums somewhat blurred by the clangor of iron-bound carriage wheels on cobbles, until the king finally said,

"I would have given your sister to Sir Sé, you know." He gave an apologetic shrug at their looks of surprise. "Yes, he'd made it clear that they were fond of one another. And after word came of her death, he came to me and confessed everything. And yes, I know what he is," he added, as both of them became suddenly guarded. "I'd guessed, before, but he confirmed it."

He glanced out the window briefly, then returned his attention to the two of them.

"If I'd been what the bishops would have me be, as a king, that could have been an end to him, of course—but I'm not. Some would even condemn the fact that the three of us are sitting here, having this conversation. Some would say that I or my ancestors should have routed out the seed of Corwyn years ago, root and stock, that I should have given the duchy to a human line.

"But we Haldanes have always sensed the usefulness of having a Deryni House in Corwyn, as a buffer with Torenth. It isn't something I'd expect the bishops to understand—they certainly don't approve—but they don't rule Gwynedd; I do. And it's been my choice, and that of my predecessors, to keep a Deryni line on the ducal throne in Corwyn—and to shelter certain other Deryni at my court. I very much regret that my sheltering of your sister was not sufficient to keep her safe. But human jealousy is something that can't easily be predicted."

"What—will happen to Sé, Sire?" Alyce asked pleating together folds of her skirt.

Donal cocked his head at her. "Do you fancy him?"

She looked up sharply. "You mean—to marry him?" she asked in a small voice.

"I told you I would have given him your sister. I shall do the same for you, if you wish it."

She swallowed with difficulty, then gave a small shake of her head.

"Then, is there someone else you fancy?"

"No, Sire. But Sé is like another brother to me. I could not *marry* him—unless, of course, you desired it."

"Dear Alyce." The king glanced at her brother. "Your sister knows her duty, Ahern. But this is not, perhaps, the time to speak of marriages. One day soon, I shall ask both of you to marry as I direct. But I think we first must bury your dear sister."

Very shortly, the carriage rattled to a halt before the cathedral's great west portal. When a footman had opened the carriage door and set steps in place before it, the occupants alighted, the king holding back briefly to admire the six black horses hitched to the carriage, while brother and sister followed their sister's coffin up the cathedral steps.

It was Father Paschal who met them just inside, Coroth's bishop having found excuse to be away from the capital for the week, rather than preside at the funeral obsequies of a Deryni. But the cathedral chapter had not scrupled to receive the body of this latest daughter of Corwyn. They waited now, lined up across the top step, before the great doors, each bearing a thick funeral taper of fine beeswax in his two hands. When Paschal had censed and aspersed the coffin at the great west door, the monks led it inside, softly chanting an introit borrowed from the priest's Eastern heritage, intoned over a continuous "ison" or drone:

"Chori angelorum te suscipiat . . . In paradisum deducant te angeli . . . Memento mei, Domini, cum veneris in regnum tuum. . . ."

"May choirs of angels receive thee . . . May the angels accompany thee to paradise . . . Remember me, O Lord, when You come into Your kingdom. . . ."

The haunting orison drifted on the stillness as Marie de Corwyn was borne down a center aisle strewn with the flower petals that should have led her to her marriage bed. Young girls crowned with flowers accompanied the white-draped coffin to its resting place before the altar, each carrying a single red rose.

The catafalque waiting to receive her was likewise strewn with flower petals, and the girls sweetly laid their flowers atop the coffin when it had been set in place. After that, all those in the funeral party knelt for prayers led by Father Paschal.

THEY laid Marie de Corwyn to rest two days later, in the crypt of the cathedral where her ancestors had worshipped and married and where many of them had been buried. Her tomb would lie between those of two other Corwyn women who had predeceased her: their mother, Stevana de Corwyn, and *her* mother, the incomparable Grania.

Afterward, as mourners filed back up the steps to the nave, preparing to disperse, Alyce saw Sé hanging back from the others, and felt the brush of his mind as he gazed at her, willing her to look in his direction.

Disengaging from the company of her brother and the king, she went back to her sister's sarcophagus and knelt beside it, ostensibly to pray. Sé lingered until all the others had gone, then came to kneel beside her, laying one hand on the alabaster lid of the sarcophagus. There had been little opportunity for private conversation until now.

"I wish I had known that the king looked kindly on the prospect of our marriage . . . ," he said softly.

Alyce gently shook her head. "That would not have saved her," she whispered.

"Probably not." Sliding his forearm onto the lid, Sé bent to touch his lips to the cool stone, then straightened again, not looking at her.

"Did she suffer?" he asked.

Alyce started to shake her head in automatic denial, then drew a resolute breath. Lying to another Deryni was fruitless, even if intended to give comfort.

"The poison . . . would have affected her breathing," she murmured truthfully. "Little Isan and Brigetta as well. I—don't know what *they* might have suffered."

"Dear God . . . ," he whispered, his eyes bright with tears as he lowered his forehead onto his arm.

"Sé, what will you do?" she asked, after a few seconds.

He raised his head, wiping across his eyes with the back of his hand, not really seeing her.

"I'm not yet certain," he said dully. "I had begun to plan for a future that no longer exists. Now that she is gone . . ."

He shook his head, swallowing hard.

"Alyce, I may leave Gwynedd," he went on. "I don't know that I care to live anymore where our people are so despised."

"But—it was jealousy that killed her, not our blood," Alyce protested.

"Is that really true?" he asked. "I'm not certain. If Marie hadn't been Deryni, do you think Muriella would have dared to do what she did? Hatred was certainly a factor."

"Perhaps. She certainly wasn't fond of me or Marie." After a short pause, she said, "Are you aware that the king offered to give you my hand, in place of Marie's?"

He nodded bleakly. "I sensed that he might. But I don't think that's what either of us wants, is it, dearest sister?"

As he slid his hand over hers, she shrugged and smiled faintly. "Probably not—though he's said that he intends both me and Ahern to marry soon. Nor can I quarrel with his reasoning. Ahern must marry and produce an heir, and I—" She shook her head in resignation.

"Until the future Duke of Corwyn *has* produced his heir, I am a valuable inducement for the loyalty of some ambitious courtier. I wonder that he even offered me the choice to marry you. But if I cannot marry for love—and I wish there *were* someone I pined for—at least let my marriage serve the interests of the king."

Sé smiled bitterly. "You have been bred *too* well to your duty, Alyce. Fortunate the man who wins your hand."

She gave him a wan reflection of his own smile, then looked away again.

"Sé, what *will* you do?"

"Well, I do intend to go away for a while." He turned his gaze back to Marie's sarcophagus. "I thought to seek counsel of my father, back at Jenadûr."

"But—what about Ahern? He *needs* you."

"Only in a general sense," Sé replied. "He'll have Jovett—and there are at least a dozen other good men, both here and in Lendour, who are eager to help him become the man he is meant to be. I think that his handling of this business up in Kiltuin may well have turned the tide in his favor, to win him his knighthood despite his knee.

"As for needs—I, too, have needs, Alyce." *As does our race,* he added, in a tight-focused burst of mindspeech.

Both intrigued and caught off balance by this abrupt change of direction, she laid her hand over his and invited a melding of their minds, but he shook his head.

"I mayn't speak of it yet," he murmured.

She nodded, then turned her gaze back to her sister's tomb.

"This touches on your threat to leave Gwynedd," she said quietly. "If you did leave, where would you go?"

"That has yet to be determined," he allowed. "I have taken

counsel of Father Paschal, who suggests that a few years' training at Djellarda would be useful; there is an inner curriculum. I might even investigate the knights at *Incus Domini.*"

"The *Anvilers?*" Alyce looked up with a start.

"Well, some believe they may have been inheritors of at least a little of the old knowledge, from the days before the Restoration," Sé admitted. "Some of the Knights of Saint Michael ended up there, you know. And maybe even some Healers. Of course, that was generations ago."

The very prospect was intriguing. Alyce, too, had stumbled across vague references to such connections, and could readily understand how the allure of possible rediscovery might appeal to the finely honed mind of Sé Trelawney. But to pursue that quest would, indeed, take him far away.

"I shall never see you again, shall I?" she whispered.

"It isn't my intention to stay away forever," he said gently, lifting her hand to press it briefly to his lips. "On the other hand, I honestly cannot say what God might have planned for me. After you have left, I shall, indeed, go to my father for a few weeks at Jenadûr—Ahern knows this. In the spring, I may ride east.

"But I shall write when I can; and I promise you that, come what may, you shall see me at Ahern's side, when he is called to his knighthood, whenever that may be. Beyond that . . . I just don't know."

Chapter 21

"Whose hatred is covered by deceit,

his wickedness shall be shewed before the whole congregation."

—PROVERBS 26:26

ANOTHER week the king's party remained in Coroth. By mid-October, with Nimur of Torenth having offered a token payment of reparation to Kiltuin town—solely as a gesture of goodwill toward its inhabitants, though he swore that his kin had had no part in what had happened there—Donal of Gwynedd was able to withdraw his troops and return to Rhemuth, leaving Ahern and his council of state in Corwyn to oversee a return to normal relations along that portion of the Torenth border.

Alyce and Zoë returned as well, though they found the rhythm of life at court much changed. Marie's absence was keenly felt in the royal household—and Isan's as well, for his mother rarely smiled in those next months. Prince Brion and the other boys missed their playmate for a while, but Duke Richard's return had ensured that the normal cycle of study and practice at arms resumed. By early November, the castle's squires, pages, and would-be pages had begun to practice for their service at Twelfth Night court, which would soon be upon them.

For the king, it was a time to assess both the events of the summer and the likely events of the coming year, for the chill winds of autumn whispered increasingly of the growing disquiet in Meara. The intelligence Richard had gathered during his summer progress north of Meara only confirmed it; and

Jared Earl of Kierney, who had traveled back to Rhemuth with the duke the month before, was able to offer further insights and speculations.

The Mearan prince born three summers before was reported to be thriving, and rumors suggested that his mother, the Princess Onora, might be once again with child. Iolo Melandry, the royal governor in Ratharkin, declared himself convinced that serious rebellion was brewing, and Jessamy's brother Morian had uncovered several serious instances of sedition.

The warning signs could not be ignored. Late in November, once the snows had rendered any serious military threat unlikely, the king began quietly summoning certain of his key vassals and commanders from the north and west to attend him in Rhemuth, soliciting their recommendations, beginning to hammer out plans for a probable campaign in the spring.

Among those summoned to the king's counsels was Ahern de Corwyn, fresh from his successes of the previous summer. After but a few days of watching him interact with the other commanders, Donal of Gwynedd began sounding out his brother about the possible reactions to knighting Ahern at the upcoming Twelfth Night court.

"So, what do you think?" the king asked, after reeling off his reasons. "Are there apt to be objections?"

"None that will be voiced," Richard replied. "Other than from churchmen, perhaps, because of what he is. In any other candidate, the knee would have put him out of the running—it *is* a handicap, when he's afoot. But you'll find few better in the council chamber, as we've seen this week; and I've sparred with him often enough to know that he swings a mean sword. Even with his bum knee, put him on a horse and he can ride circles around me—and even around you, when you were in your prime."

Donal chuckled, well aware that he was quite past that prime, but gratified that there were others willing and able to deal with the more physically demanding aspects of rulership—and not really minding that that part of his life was now behind him.

"I'll take that as a compliment to *him,* rather than a snide comment by a younger brother on my advancing age," Donal said. "But you're right—all that bashing and thrashing *is* for younger men. Fortunately, young Ahern is well qualified for both—and for the more subtle disciplines of the council table and strategy board. If that business at Kiltuin had to happen, I'm glad it happened the way it did, because it gave me an opportunity to watch him at work. In time, he could even be the equal of Damian Cathcart, or Jeppe Lascelles at Killingford."

"Christ, I remember meeting General Jeppe when he was a very old man," Richard murmured. "If you're comparing Ahern to him, we've a real treat to look forward to, by the time he reaches his prime. I'd definitely go ahead and knight him, Donal—and I'd also confirm him in his Lendour title."

"Really? The bishops wouldn't like that," Donal reminded him.

"Of course they wouldn't like it. He's Deryni, and they're bishops, and by the letter of the law, no Deryni may come into the full authority of high rank until he reaches the age of twenty-five. Not fourteen, and not even eighteen, but twenty-five. Those are stupid laws, Donal, and you should change them."

"I've thought about it," Donal conceded. "And one day, I might just do it. But in the meantime, I do have to keep at least a reasonable peace with my bishops. Did I tell you that the Bishop of Corwyn wouldn't even celebrate the Requiem for Ahern's sister? The family chaplain did it.

"Fortunately, the bishops aren't going to excommunicate me or him for confirming him to an earl's coronet before he turns eighteen. We're only talking about a few months, after all; and given his past services to my crown, there's no question but that he's prepared to put his life and his talents on the line again, in my service."

"It's the talents that the bishops don't like," Richard pointed out. "And they'd happily take his life."

"Well, not until I've had his service in Meara again," Donal declared. "And meanwhile, come Twelfth Night court, I intend to knight him *and* confirm him as Earl of Lendour. We'll save the ducal recognition until they've gotten used to a Deryni earl."

ALYCE de Corwyn was one of the few with advance knowledge of the king's plans regarding her brother—

necessary, since it was she who had the privilege of girding him with his white belt. Sir Jovett Chandos buckled on the golden spurs, and it was Sir Sé Trelawney, arrived only minutes before the ceremony, who presented him with his sword, black-clad and silent as he knelt to watch the king's Haldane blade flash above the head of his childhood friend, the flat of it touching right shoulder, left shoulder, and head.

Ahern himself was not able to kneel as the three other young men did, who were dubbed that afternoon, but the king had made a point of reiterating the high points of the new knight's exemplary service, both the summer previous and three years before, and personally assisted him to rise from the faldstool moved into place before he was called forward.

And while the Archbishop of Rhemuth cast cold glances at the king, both then and later, when Ahern was called forward to be formally invested as Earl of Lendour, the king again spoke of Ahern's sterling service hitherto, and kissed him on both cheeks before placing the coronet upon his brow and the gold signet on his finger, emblematic of his new legal status.

When Ahern reiterated the fealty he had sworn at his knighting, now pledging further leal fidelity as earl, several dozen knights of Lendour and of Corwyn knelt at his back, affirming their support and loyalty as well. Though Gwynedd's clergy might have their doubts about this setting aside of the law, Ahern's record spoke for itself among Donal's other knights. If any disagreed, no one spoke out.

As for Sir Sé Trelawney, present as promised, he appeared much changed in the months since Alyce last had seen him. His long black robe, fastened at the shoulder, had a vaguely eastern look to it, unrelieved by any color save the white slash of his own knight's belt. In truth, he looked as much the monk as warrior now, a close-clipped beard exaggerating the leaner lines of a form that now was almost ascetic in its sparseness.

Afterward, he had words of congratulation for Ahern, and a kiss on the cheek each for Alyce and Zoë, but he did not stay long after court, quietly riding off into the snow whence he had come, while the hall cleared to set up for the feast.

I think he may have made profession with the Anvilers, Alyce whispered mind to mind to Vera, who was seated across from her and sharing a trencher with an exceedingly attentive Earl Jared McLain. *I had hoped he might stay longer.*

Vera, offering Jared a morsel of succulent pheasant lavished with plum sauce, spared her sister a sympathetic glance.

I'm sorry, she sent. *I know you were fond of him.*

Turning her attention back to the revelry in the hall, Alyce forced a resigned smile as she lowered her head slightly to listen to a comment from Sir Jovett, seated on her other side.

Her brother, meanwhile, seemed to be quite enjoying the company of Zoë Morgan. He had put aside his coronet, but his gold signet flashed in the light of candle and torch as they fed one another tidbits. Sometimes his lips nibbled near her fingertips, or his hand lingered near hers, occasionally caressing the back of a hand, brushing a wrist. Later in the evening, Alyce saw the two of them standing in a shadowed recess of one of the window embrasures, Ahern with one hand set on her waist and she with her face upturned to receive his chaste kiss, fingertips brushing at his chest.

"For someone who made little of our suggestion that she might really become our sister," Alyce said to Vera much later, in the room the three of them now shared, "it did look like the two of them were getting along rather well."

Vera laughed and wrapped a shawl more closely around her shoulders, settling down beside Alyce on the sheepskin rug before the fire.

"It did, indeed. I noticed them well after dinner, sitting in one of the window embrasures, just holding hands and looking into one another's eyes. I—uh—don't think they noticed me."

"I don't think they noticed much of anyone besides one another." Alyce picked up an ivory-backed brush and began brushing her hair, gazing into the fire.

"Oh, Vera," she said after a moment. "Six months ago, it was Zoë and I who were waiting for Marie to come in. I hope Zoë will be luckier in love."

"So do I," Vera replied. "I think Ahern is quite smitten. And I think Zoë would make him quite a wonderful duchess. Here, give me that and I'll brush." She took up the brush that Alyce surrendered and fell to, saying, after a moment, "What would you think of having *two* duchesses in the family?"

Alyce turned to stare at her twin, eyes wide. "Jared McLain?" she breathed. "Truly?"

"Well, it's early on, as yet," Vera said, smiling somewhat self-consciously, "but he does need a wife—and a mother for that baby boy of his. One would think he invented babies. At first, he spoke of little else—until he started asking about *my* family. Apparently, the daughter of a Lendouri knight would be well regarded in Kierney—and Cassan."

Alyce found herself containing a grin. "Well, Keryell *was* a Lendouri knight, among other things," she said. "And he would have approved of such a match for you, I feel certain." She cocked her head to one side. "Could you find contentment as Jared's countess, and eventually his duchess?"

"I think I could," Vera said softly. "He's *very* sweet and gentle—and he isn't at all as grand as I'd feared."

Giggling together, they sat there, gossiping and brushing one another's hair, for the best part of an hour before Zoë came tiptoeing in, quite flustered to discover that they were still awake.

"I'm not even going to ask," Alyce said, laughing, as Zoë dropped onto the sheepskins between them and reached for one of the cups of mulled wine set on the hearth. "We both saw you with Ahern earlier this evening."

"Well, I *might* have been with someone else," Zoë said slyly, gulping down some of the wine. "But I wasn't," she added with a grin.

She set down the cup and hugged her arms across her chest, closing her eyes in happy remembrance.

"We talked about Cynfyn, and Castle Coroth, and he asked me if I liked them. He told me about growing up with you and Marie—and Vera, I'd forgotten that you lived at Cynfyn for a while as well, after Alyce and Marie came to Arc-en-Ciel. He showed me the signet that the king gave him today, and asked if I'd like to try it on."

"Now, *that* sounds *serious,*" Vera said, grinning. "He's only just got it, and already he's letting pretty girls try it on."

"Well, he will need a bride," Alyce said reasonably, "and the king told us in Coroth that he intends to marry off both of us soon. He thinks a great deal of your father, Zoë. That might make you quite an acceptable wife for a future duke."

"Do you really think so?" Zoë asked, wide-eyed.

"More unlikely things have happened," Alyce replied. "Remember when Marie and I asked whether you were campaigning to be our sister?"

"But, that was just in fun. I never dreamed—"

"Well, you may well dream tonight," Vera said, grinning as she poked Zoë in the ribs. "Alyce, you'll have to speak to that brother of yours, and make sure his intentions are honorable, where our dear Zoë is concerned. Dare we tell her about *my* prospect?"

As Zoë looked at her in question, Alyce slipped her arm around the other girl's shoulders and smiled.

"Zoë darling, it appears entirely possible that both of you may be duchesses someday."

NEITHER of the prospective dukes lingered long in Rhemuth. By mid-January, both had returned to their own lands to hold themselves in readiness for a war all hoped would not be necessary. Their prospective brides pined through the rest of the winter and into spring, though Alyce did her best to divert their energies into the activities of the court and the royal children.

Such diversion served her own purposes as well, as she released her wistful affection for Sé Trelawney to the reality of what she had seen of him during his brief visit in January. Friends they had been during their childhood, and friends they remained; but now Sé had turned to dreams of his own, and a new life with the mysterious and ascetic Knights of the Anvil. That life did not include her, and never could.

TO no one's surprise, insurrection flared again in Meara in that spring of 1089, obliging Donal to mount the threatened personal expedition into that rebellious land. By April, the king had begun to assemble the local levies that would go with him to Meara; the Kierney levies would meet him there, on the plains before Ratharkin.

Though proclaimed Prince of Meara at birth, by right of his Mearan mother, Donal Haldane had actually visited Meara only half a dozen times in his life, and two of those previous ventures onto Mearan soil had been under arms, to put down rebellions. The present insurrection was again centered around Donal's first cousin Judhael, eldest son of his mother's sister Annalind, neither of whom had ever accepted the succession intended by Donal's mother or, indeed, his grandfather. More than a decade had passed since a Haldane king last had ridden into Meara under arms, and the present contretemps came of having stopped short of finishing the task he then had set out to do.

This time his brother Richard rode at his side: a mature and formidable general to whom he gladly had relinquished active command of the Gwyneddan expeditionary force, a generation younger than Donal. For his personal safeguarding, the king had retained a crack bodyguard of fast-mounted Lendouri cavalry captained by Ahern Earl of Lendour, giving him the flexibility to go when and where he sensed he was needed, to assess conditions for himself. Among them, though not part of their number, was Sir Kenneth Morgan, now restored to his function as the king's aide, rarely far from his side since returning from the last expedition into Meara, three years before.

Their advance into that turbulent land was swift and focused, bringing them quickly into the heartland of the rebellious province. Half a day's ride from Ratharkin, the provincial capital, forward scouts made contact with the first wary outriders from the city, where rebels had ousted the royal governor and occupied part of the city. To the king's dismay, initial reports regarding rebel numbers suggested that Judhael of Meara had mustered far more support than initially had been supposed. The prospect gave pause to all previous assumptions that this would be any ordinary quashing of a minor dissident insurrection.

That night, as the king and his army encamped between Ratharkin and loyal Trurill, Donal called his commanders to his tent for a council of war.

"I want to know how it's possible that Judhael can keep alive such support, after so long," the king said, glancing across the grim faces faintly illuminated in the torchlight. "We've had nearly sixty years of wrangling about Meara. Have I truly given these people cause to resent me that much?"

Andrew McLain, senior among Gwynedd's dukes, shook his grizzled head, infinitely patient. His son Jared was already scouring the hills south of Ratharkin, seeking intelligence regarding local opposition.

"Not at all, Sire," Andrew said. "This is a regrettable legacy of your father's generation, and Jolyon of Meara, and the

Great War. Your parents' marriage was intended to resolve the succession of the principality. It was your grandmother who simply would not accept the loss of Mearan sovereignty."

Richard snorted. "Meara was hardly sovereign, even then, Andrew. It's been a vassal state for more than two hundred years."

"A vassal state, yes," said Ursic of Claibourne. "But still with its own prince, its own court. A royal governor is hardly the same, no matter how well liked he may be—and Iolo Melandry, while loyal and competent, has hardly been well-liked in Meara, as you know."

Duke Andrew grimaced and shook his head. "They wouldn't have liked *any* royal governor. You know that, Ursic. These stiff-necked Mearans only understand force."

Donal's sharp glance forestalled any further digression into what was agreed by all present. He was well aware that most of the troubles with Meara during his lifetime could be laid at the feet of the maternal grandmother he had never known. Widowed in the Great War, and beloved of the Mearan people, the Princess Urracca had disowned Donal's mother when, seeking an end to the slaughter, her daughter Roisian had fled to Gwynedd and wed Gwynedd's king. Annalind, she declared, was Meara's true heiress; and by that reckoning, many Mearans regarded Annalind's son Judhael as Meara's true prince. It was Judhael who had sparked the present insurrection, as he had the previous one.

"It won't end, you know," Ursic said. "Not until you've killed off the rest of the line."

Several of the others nodded in vehement agreement, a few murmuring to one another, but Donal set his jaw defiantly, raking them all with his gray Haldane gaze.

"Ursic, these are my own people, my mother's blood kin. I have no wish to slay them."

"But slay them you must, Sire—if not now, then at some time in the future," Ursic replied. "For Mearans will never let go of what they regard as theirs. They are a people of honor and passion, with a vehement hatred for what they regard as betrayal of loyalty. And in their eyes, that was the crime of your mother—that she should abandon her lands and people and give herself in marriage to an enemy of Meara."

"We were *never* enemies of Meara!" Donal snapped, slapping the flat of his hand against the map table. "And my mother was trying to avert the very kind of bloodshed that seems inevitable on the morrow—for I *will* have what is mine!"

"That may exact a heavy price, Sire," Duke Andrew said.

"Then so be it!" Donal retorted, lurching to his feet. "Leave us—all of you!" His ringed hand stabbed emphatically at the tent flap, where Ahern stood guard with Sir Jovett Chandos. "Except for Richard and Morian—and Ahern. You stay. And someone have that scout sent in, who saw the Mearan array at Ratharkin."

In a shuffle of booted feet and creaking harness, the others filed out, leaving Richard, Morian, and Ahern to settle on camp stools as the king motioned them closer and sank into his own chair.

"Well, what is to be done?" he murmured, searching all three attentive faces.

Richard glanced furtively at the two Deryni, then at the carpet beneath his feet, faint apprehension in his expression. At thirty-three, he was just coming into his prime: lean and fit, his shock of sable hair only beginning to silver at the temples, and visible mainly in his close-trimmed beard and mustache.

"It appears you have already decided what is to be done," Richard said quietly, looking up at his brother.

"And you don't approve."

Glancing again at the two Deryni, Richard gave a shrug.

"That isn't for me to say. I'm not the king."

"No. You aren't."

Footsteps and the clink and creak of harness approached outside the tent flap, just before one of the king's bodyguards pulled back the heavy canvas to admit a nondescript-looking scout in dusty tan riding leathers.

"You sent for me, Sire?"

"I did. Sit here, please." Donal hooked a stool closer with a booted toe and indicated it with his chin. "It's Josquin Gramercy, isn't it? Ahern, bring him that writing desk and light, if you will."

Ahern complied without comment, moving the small campaign chest before the stool and setting out parchment, pen, and ink, then bringing a lit candlestick, which he set to the left. Morian had risen to make room, and moved behind the scout as he settled on the stool, one hand casually coming to rest on the man's shoulder. The man started to look up, then seemed to deflate slightly, chin sinking to his chest and eyes closing. Ahern, unaccustomed to seeing a Deryni work so openly, raised one eyebrow.

"Josquin, the king wishes you to sketch out as much as you can remember of the rebel defenses," Morian said in a low voice. "While you are doing that, you will see nothing else and you will hear nothing until I touch you on the shoulder again. Do you understand?"

"Aye, sir," came the whispered reply.

"Good man."

As Morian's hand left his shoulder, the man immediately opened his eyes, took up a quill and carefully inked it, then began sketching out a rough map of the area around Ratharkin, his concentration evidenced by his tongue contortions as he traced each line and letter. After watching him a moment, Donal glanced at Richard and gave a nod.

At once, Duke Richard drew the ebon-hilted dagger from his belt and casually passed its blade close beside the scout's eyes, then let its point sink to lightly touch the man's cheek beneath one eye. Eliciting no reaction, he sighed and resheathed the weapon with a purposeful snick of metal sliding on metal. At no time had the entranced Josquin indicated in any way that he was aware of the test.

"I still find it amazing when he does that," the king said aside to Ahern, as Morian smiled faintly and merely folded his arms, overseeing the scout's work from behind.

Richard gave a snort that was at once skeptical and resigned, casting a furtive glance at Morian as he crouched down beside his brother. "I somehow doubt that yon Josquin would find it so amazing, if he knew. Appalled, perhaps. Donal, does it never give you even the smallest pang of conscience, that you're obliging innocent souls to be party to practices forbidden by the church?"

Donal gave a droll shrug.

"Does the church need to know? Surely, extraordinary measures are justified, to protect the crown I swore to defend."

"Still . . ."

They were watching the map take shape under Josquin's pen when a guard called from beyond the tent flap and then admitted another man to the royal tent, firmly escorted by Sir Kenneth Morgan. This one was a nervous, bandy-legged little individual of middle years, swathed in the upland tweeds widely worn by the local inhabitants. As he caught sight of the king, he snatched off a shapeless tweed cap to reveal a balding pate and twin braids falling to either side of his neck.

"Sire, this is Nidian ap Pedr," Kenneth said, keeping his hand on the man's elbow. "He says he has ridden from Ratharkin, and he claims to have important information for you. He's unarmed."

"Indeed?"

With a glance at his three companions, Donal shifted his camp stool a little to one side of where Josquin was working and gestured for Kenneth to release the newcomer.

"Very well, Nidian ap Pedr, what is it you wish to tell me?" he said.

Biting at his lower lip, cap clamped close to his breast, Nidian dropped to his knees before the king, too frightened to meet his gaze.

"Have mercy, Sire!" he blurted. "I beg you, do not punish Ratharkin for the sins of only a few. I swear to you that we are loyal there! It is the Lord Judhael who makes war against you, and would deny you what is yours. He has men before the city gates, and more who have occupied the fortifications of the gatehouse and keep, against the wishes of Ratharkin's loyal folk. I am come to offer you the assistance of those who keep their oaths."

"Indeed. And how did Judhael manage to gain such a foothold?" Donal asked.

Nidian ventured a quick, desperate glance at the king, then ducked his head again, cheeks flaming.

"In truth, Sire, the Lord Judhael acted before his true intentions became known to us. He has brought men down out of the mountains to the west and raised the standard of rebellion, claiming to be our true prince—and we were content that he should make such claim in local things, so long as he did you proper service as your vassal. But he has seized your Majesty's governor, and I—fear they may have hanged him."

"They've *hanged* Iolo Melandry?" Richard said disbelievingly.

Donal, meanwhile, had seized the wretched Nidian by the

neck of his tunic and jerked him closer, cold anger flaring in the gray eyes. As the man cringed under this sudden onslaught of Haldane anger, hands fluttering weakly upward in a futile warding-off gesture, Donal cast a sharp glance at Morian for confirmation that the man was telling the truth, though he knew from his own abilities that it was so. The Deryni lord inclined his head minutely, but also flicked a meaningful glance in the direction of the altogether too attentive Sir Kenneth Morgan, still waiting near the tent flap.

"The Devil take him!" Donal murmured, enough recalled to the need for caution that he released the hapless Nidian with an apologetic smoothing of the rumpled tunic. "This goes beyond what may be forgiven, even of kin. I should have hacked off the last of that rotten branch the last time I ventured into this stubborn land." He rose and, unable to engage in the restless pacing that usually helped him defuse anger or frustration, glanced back at the bearer of this unwelcome news. "Who else rides with that traitorous dog?" he demanded.

"I—I do not know their names, Sire," Nidian whispered. "But many high-born lords answered his summons to Ratharkin, beneath many a noble banner."

"Hardly noble, if they fly against their rightful king," Kenneth dared to mutter.

The words recalled the king to caution, for even the trusted Sir Kenneth should not be allowed to witness what Donal now had in mind.

"Well, I *will* know who they are," he said softly. "Kenneth, please wait outside, and let no one disturb us for the next little while. I feel certain that Master Nidian can tell us more."

The Mearan looked briefly alarmed as Sir Kenneth dutifully withdrew, but he was given no time to speculate on his likely fate. As the tent flap fell into place, Morian was already moving forward to drop a heavy hand to the back of Nidian's neck, steadying with the other hand as his subject collapsed back on his hunkers, head lolling forward.

"Ah, yes," Morian said after a few seconds, the look of trance glazing the blue-violet eyes. "Master Nidian is, indeed, deficient in the matter of names, but he has an excellent eye for faces and those traitor banners. Judhael himself, of course . . . the Earl of Somerdale and his brother . . . Sir Robard Kincaid and his eldest son . . . Basil of Castleroo . . . Blaise of Trurill . . . Sir

Michael MacDonald . . . and curiously enough, both Judhael's daughters. . . ."

"Both?" Donal said, surprised. "I had heard that the younger one is with child."

"So she is," Morian agreed, seeing what the other three could not. "Far gone with child. I wonder that they would risk her in such an enterprise. But I cannot imagine what other pregnant woman it might be, desperate enough to ride with the royal party."

"It is said that she and her husband dote on one another," Richard offered.

"So I have heard," Donal replied. "That would account for young MacDonald's presence. Seek out such other details as may be useful," he said to Morian. "How is it that he means to assist us?"

After another long moment, Morian smiled and lifted his head, returning his focus to the king.

"It appears that our Master Nidian can deliver what he promises, Sire."

"Show me," Donal said softly.

With a nod, Morian glanced aside at Josquin, who was putting the finishing touches to his map, at Ahern, then gestured toward the remains of their meal, stacked nearby on a silver tray.

"If Sir Ahern would be so good as to clear the supper things off that tray, we'll see what can be done," he said. Keeping one hand on the kneeling and entranced Nidian, he reached across to touch the scout Josquin lightly on the shoulder. "Have you finished, Master Josquin?"

The scout looked up with a start and smiled faintly, setting aside his quill.

"I have, my lord. Will it serve?"

"I'm sure it will serve very well," the king said, rising to delve into a pouch at his waist. "Here's a silver penny for your trouble, Master Josquin—and my thanks for a job well done." He pressed the coin into the scout's hand and clapped him on the shoulder. "Now, go and get a meal and some sleep. I shall need you on the morrow."

As the scout withdrew, grinning sheepishly at this tangible sign of the royal favor, Donal glanced to where Ahern was clearing the supper tray, then moved the campaign chest closer and sat again on his camp stool, picking up the new map. Morian, meanwhile, had hauled the entranced Nidian to his feet and guided him to the stool just vacated by the scout, pulling another stool near and sitting knee-to-knee with him. At his gesture, Ahern set the silver tray across both their laps and moved back to stand behind Morian.

"You will be familiar with the basic principles of scrying," Morian said to Ahern, at the same time directing Richard to stand before the tent flap. "This will be a demonstration of a military application, for gathering intelligence."

He nodded to the king, who leaned back to snare a flagon of wine from a camp table behind him. As he unstoppered it to pour some onto the tray, the reflected torchlight made of the silver tray a blood-dark mirror.

"Nidian, I want you to imagine that you're looking *through* the wine and the tray," Morian said very softly, setting both the other man's hands on the edge of the tray and holding them there with his own. "Imagine that you can see your feet through the tray. Don't try to focus; just relax and drift, let it happen. I give you my word that you'll come to no harm."

The Mearan's eyelids flickered, but his gaze did not waver from the shallow wash of wine. Cautiously Ahern set his hand on Morian's shoulder, trying the most tentative of contacts, so that he could better monitor what the more experienced Deryni did—and deepened the contact as Morian allowed it.

"Now recall what you've just told us, Master Nidian, and what you saw," Morian urged softly. "Don't speak. Simply allow your memories to flow, and try to focus on every detail you can remember."

A faint sigh escaped the man's lips, and his head sank a little lower as the tension eased into expectant silence. After a few seconds, as Donal and Ahern watched and Richard craned his neck to see past their subject, a faint miasma seemed to rise from the surface of the wine, clouding the flat expanse of burgundy with a silvery sheen reflected from beneath, resolving then into misty images of stone ramparts, bartizans with conical roofs, portcullises barring sturdy gates, and defenders massed along the battlements of distant Ratharkin.

The colors of old Meara fluttered above the walls of the ancient city, rather than the scarlet and gold standard of Donal's royal governor. And camped before the walls of the city were the Mearan levies—far more than anyone had thought Judhael could assemble.

At Donal's gesture, Richard came softly closer and the two brothers studied what was shown, noting the troop deployments and encampments, estimating numbers. After a silent interval, Richard withdrew to one side to make notations on the map. When it became clear that no more was to come, Donal tipped the contents of the tray onto grass at one edge of the tent while Morian adjusted Nidian's memory of what had just occurred.

"What will he remember of this?" Richard murmured, as Donal wiped off the tray with a cloth.

"Only that he was asked to report again on what he saw, and that he did so, while notes were taken. That *is* what happened," Donal added, cocking an eyebrow at his brother.

"As you say . . . " Richard murmured.

When they had given Nidian back into the custody of Sir Kenneth, still waiting outside, the king recalled his officers and spent another half hour advising them of a revised strategy for the coming day before settling down for a few hours' sleep.

Chapter 22

"The Lord hath set at nought all my mighty men in the midst of me."

—LAMENTATIONS 1:15

THEY rose before dawn, to prepare for a battle Donal hoped they would not have to fight. After hearing Mass with his officers in the open air before his tent, the king broke his fast while Kenneth armed him and he gave final instructions to his brother. Morian listened silently, already armed and ready, the roundels and martlet on his green surcoat gleaming in the early morning light. He did not ride with the king when the royal party mounted up to make their way to Ratharkin, departing in another direction with a squadron of Claibourne cavalry and orders of his own. Dukes Andrew and Ursic likewise had their orders.

An hour later, the king was drawing rein before the gates of Ratharkin beneath his royal standard, his brother at his side. Ahern and his Lendouri cavalry rode behind him, and a herald rode well before him under a white flag of truce, to carry his terms to the city.

The Mearan answer was an arrow through the herald's heart, defying all conventions of honorable warfare and unleashing the cold relentlessness of Haldane justice: justice which Donal Haldane had the means to deliver. That the rebels were betrayed from within the city they had thought to hold was fitting judgment of their folly as, an hour later, the king's loyal subjects in Ratharkin infiltrated the rebel-held gatehouse and threw open the city gates to their royal deliverers, as Nidian ap Pedr had promised.

The next two hours saw heavy fighting in the streets of Ratharkin, quickly focusing on the rebel-held fortress of the city's inner citadel. Casualties were heavy on the Mearan side and light among the royalist troops. Judhael of Meara soon abandoned his position, seeing the futility of continued resistance in the face of Ratharkin's betrayal. As the vanquished prince fled deeper into Meara, Duke Andrew and his Cassani cavalry in pursuit, some of the junior Mearan royals made a dash southward toward the mountains of Cloome. Donal sent Richard after them, himself remaining in Ratharkin with Duke Ursic and an occupation force to restore order. It was in the great hall of the recaptured inner citadel that they found the body of Iolo Melandry, the city's royal governor, hoisted to the full height of one of the main hammer-beams.

"Damn them all," Donal said softly, as he gazed up at the bloated body and blackened face of the saintly little man he had called friend, who had upheld Haldane rights in Meara for more than a decade. "*Damn* them!" Running a trembling hand over his eyes, he turned to the men at his side, trying to put the image of Iolo's face out of his memory.

"Kenneth, get him down from there," he murmured. "*Gently*. Dear God, that man deserved a better end than this!"

The king lingered in Ratharkin for another week, for a new royal governor must be designated, at least for the interim, and a sharp lesson must be delivered to the Mearans, even though Ratharkin, in the end, had remained mostly loyal to their king. Calling a council of the great lords who had accompanied him on the Mearan campaign, Donal heard their recommendations and assessments of the situation, told them what he would have *liked* to do to the Mearans, then allowed his righteous anger to be tempered by the practicalities of those who would have to keep the peace once he departed.

"Very sadly, I am now short one royal governor, gentlemen," he told them. "At least for the interim, it will have to be one of you. Do I hear any volunteers?"

The men around him exchanged glances. Such an appointment was an honor and an opportunity for advancement, a chance to prove one's worth to the Crown, but it was also a virtual exile; and all were well aware of the fate of the last royal governor of Meara, lying in his coffin in the nearby chapel.

"I know what I'm asking," Donal said, when no one spoke up. "And I don't expect the post to be permanent. We all know that a Mearan is best suited for the position. But I don't know that I have any Mearans I can trust right now. And none of us can go back to Rhemuth until I have someone in place here."

Ursic Duke of Claibourne glanced around the table, then cleared his throat. "If I might make a recommendation, Sire," he said tentatively.

All eyes turned in his direction, for the advice of a duke always carried heavy weight. Donal merely smiled and gave a wave of his hand.

"All right, out with it, Ursic. Who's to be the lucky man?"

"Well, he is, perhaps, a bit young for such responsibility," Ursic allowed, "but he has been well tutored at his father's knee. And that father would not be far away, if he needed assistance from time to time. Until a permanent royal governor can be appointed, of course."

By now, all eyes had turned toward the man obviously fitting Ursic's description: Duke Andrew's son, Jared Earl of Kierney. Though but five-and-twenty, Jared McLain was also a battle-seasoned soldier and a man exceedingly well schooled in the duties he would eventually take on when he succeeded his father as Duke of Cassan—which lands did, indeed, border on rebellious Meara. Said Duke of Cassan had raised one eyebrow at this nomination of his son for such an important appointment, nodding faintly. The prospective appointee looked thunderstruck.

"Well, what do you say, Sir Jared?" the king asked. "Are you willing to take it on?"

Jared's astonishment shifted from shock through consternation into pleased satisfaction. "I am, Sire—if you're sure I'm ready for it. I know that I am young."

Donal snorted and gave the younger man a grim smile. "Old enough to be husband, father, and widower as well as warrior. It occurred to me that you might value some worthwhile work to take your mind from your loss."

Jared glanced at his folded hands on the table before him.

"So long as it does not leave my young son fatherless as well as motherless, Sire."

"Well, we shall certainly endeavor to make certain that does not happen," the king said. "And when I have relieved you of this burden by appointment of a permanent governor, we must see about finding you a new bride. Meanwhile, I trust that you will not be aggrieved to be parted awhile from your infant son?"

Jared fought back an impulse for a grin, and Andrew covered a smile with his hand.

"Sire, I *have* considered taking a new bride," Jared allowed. "But even were I to remarry tomorrow, I would be hard-pressed to quickly reclaim my son from my mother and his doting aunties."

"'Tis true," his father agreed. "My wife and my sisters would be inconsolable, were young Kevin to leave my household just yet. And indeed, since he is my only grandson at present, I confess that I should be less than happy myself."

Sir Kenneth Morgan had snickered at the mention of doting aunties, and shrugged as the king looked at him in question, still smiling.

"'Tis all true, Sire," he said. "One of those doting aunties is my dear mother. At least if the worst were to befall, young Kevin McLain would never lack for kinfolk."

"Then it appears that a tour of service from Jared in Meara would not place undue stress on your domestic arrangements," Donal said to the McLains, father and son.

"Aye, Sire. So long as he fares better than Meara's last royal governor," Andrew replied gravely. "He is my only son, and I shall not get another."

"With one like Jared, you shall not *need* another," the king replied. "And accordingly, I shall be pleased to make him my governor in Meara, at least until next spring."

In one thing only would the king not be moved—and that was the manner in which he chose to pay tribute to his late former governor. Taking counsel of his lords who knew Meara better than he, he agreed to exact no retribution against the citizens of Ratharkin for the killing of Iolo Melandry, knowing that to be the crime of Judhael and his rebels. But on the day appointed for installing Jared Earl of Kierney as Ratharkin's new interim governor, the king summoned all those holding Mearan offices of any description to attend him in the great hall of the citadel and there renew their oaths of loyalty upon Iolo's body, laid upon a bier in the center of the hall and draped to the waist with the king's own Haldane standard.

Only then, after each man had bowed to the body and kissed its slippered toe in homage, were they allowed to approach the new governor and press their foreheads to his hand, in token of their obedience to him and the crown he would henceforth represent. Morian being still in the field, as was Duke Richard, Ahern Earl of Lendour was requested to stand with the king at the side of the hall and gauge whether his subjects were earnest in their acknowledgement of Meara's new governor—for while Ahern was still new in the more subtle applications of his powers, such as Morian regularly employed, he could certainly Truth-Read.

But neither Ahern nor the king could detect any duplicity among the men who came forward to swear; and no one refused to comply. Still, it was with a heavy heart that the king prepared to return to Rhemuth, the immediate crisis having been resolved.

MEANWHILE, they must wait for Richard and Morian, for the resolution of that part of the tale had yet to be learned. It was late in May, on the afternoon before they were to depart, that both Richard and Morian returned. The king had been walking on the ramparts of the inner citadel with Duke Ursic, Ahern, and Sir Kenneth Morgan, having spent the morning going over administrative matters with Jared and the local sheriff, one Wilce Melandry, nephew of the slain Iolo.

It was Ahern who first spotted the banners at the head of the column clattering into the yard below, and touched the king's arm to direct his attention there. Foremost among the banners was that of the king's brother, with his three golden demi-lions replacing the Haldane lion on the scarlet field, though there could be no doubt that Richard Duke of Carthmoor was entirely a Haldane.

"Ah, here's Richard," Donal murmured, and immediately headed down to the yard.

But Richard's news was mixed, and he had brought back none of the important Mearan prisoners for which Donal had hoped.

"We never even got a glimpse of Judhael," Richard muttered, as he and Morian walked with the king into the day-room Donal had appropriated during his stay in Ratharkin. "Morian caught up with Francis Delaney and a few of the others, who'd been escorting Judhael's daughters, but they were odd men out in what turned out to be a suicide stand, so that the women could get away. The only good news on that front—and it sounds calloused, saying this—is that Onora apparently went into labor along the way, and died giving birth, or soon after."

"What of the child?" Donal demanded, waving both of them to chairs.

"Probably dead," Morian replied. "It was a girl, but my informant didn't think it would survive."

"Well, *there's* a blessing, at least," the king muttered. "One less Mearan 'princess' I'll have to contend with. I don't suppose you saw any bodies."

"Not of any Mearan princesses," Morian replied. "I was riding separate from Duke Richard, as you know, and we were the ones to catch up with the rear guard they left behind to create a diversion. We killed most of them outright, gave the coup to the wounded, and questioned the rest before executing them. There were two of note: the Earl of Somerdale's brother and a Sir Robard Kincaid—kin, I believe, to your late aunt's husband. At the time, we thought we might catch up with the others, so we didn't try to bring along any prisoners. They were small fish, in any case."

"No, you did as I would have done," Donal murmured. "I take it that Somerdale had been with them?"

"Aye, and Michael MacDonald, the Princess Onora's husband. They took her body with them, and Princess Caitrin had the babe."

Donal sighed and shook his head, genuinely distressed. "It's bad business, Morian—not that there was any help for it. And no sign of any of the others?" he asked, returning his attention to Richard.

"None. They might have evaporated into thin air, for all we saw of them, once we'd left the area around Ratharkin.

Those mountains to the south are among the most rugged in this part of the country, as you know. And Judhael knows them; we don't."

"No, I'm not faulting you," Donal said. He sat back with a sigh and ran his hands through his hair. "God, I'm getting too old for this—and killing women and children has always been bad business."

"It was their own folly that killed them, Donal—you know that," Richard said.

"I know; they chose to rebel. At least Onora did. But not the babe."

"The sad fortunes of war," Richard said.

"Aye, the fortunes of war," Donal agreed. "And they stink!"

GIVEN the new news Richard and Morian had brought, the king determined to remain in Ratharkin somewhat longer than he had first intended—though, as spring gave way to summer of 1089, Donal of Gwynedd had good reason to be hopeful about the future. While his Mearan campaign had fallen short of the complete success he had sought, several of the principal trouble-makers being still at large, he had dealt expeditiously with the most immediately troublesome of the Mearan dissidents and left a promising lieutenant to take on the duties of interim royal governor, with at least the short-term prospect of enforcing a lasting peace on that rebellious land.

It was well into June by the time the king at last judged it safe to depart for Rhemuth, with the levies of Andrew of Cassan and Ursic of Claibourne ordered to linger in the Ratharkin area before withdrawing for the winter. The king and his party departed at a leisurely pace, for the weather was fine, and more tangible evidence of the royal presence could do no harm in the wake of the Mearan troubles.

But three days out of the Mearan capital, the morning after what everyone had judged quite a respectable meal at a manor near Old Cùilteine, Ahern of Lendour took ill.

At first he tried to dismiss the dull discomfort in his belly as mere reaction to something in the previous night's fare that had not agreed with him, gamely mounting up with the others and falling in beside Sir Kenneth Morgan as they pressed on toward Rhemuth. But within a few hours, the cramping had worsened, obliging him to rein to the side of the road and slide from the saddle for a bout of vomiting.

He had hoped that would ease him, but it did not. Someone muttered about the possibility of poisoning, but the battle-surgeon who probed at his belly shook his head, grim-visaged as he gauged the patient's rapid pulse rate and felt for fever in the stricken man's armpits.

"What is it?" Donal asked quietly, when the battle-surgeon had completed his examination, leaving Sir Kenneth and Jovett Chandos to contend with another bout of Ahern's gasping dry-heaves.

"Not good, Sire," the man admitted, glancing also at Duke Richard, who was listening anxiously. "He should not travel. Is there a house of religion nearby, where the brothers or sisters might tend him?"

"There's an abbey a few miles hence," Richard replied.

"Then I suggest that someone be sent to fetch a wagon. I fear that he could not bear the pain, to ride the distance ahorse."

"Is the danger mortal?" the king asked.

"I fear that it may be, Sire," came the reluctant reply. "We must make him as comfortable as may be, and pray that God may spare his life."

"But—can nothing be done?"

Richard laid his hand on his brother's sleeve, shaking his head. "Only to entreat heaven for a miracle," he said. "Having kept his leg on this same road, however, I fear he may not merit a second miracle, in this life. I have seen these signs before."

They sent a rider ahead to the abbey at once, Richard taking the returning army on to make the next night's camp in the abbey's vicinity. Donal and Sir Kenneth Morgan stayed at the stricken man's side, along with the battle-surgeon, Sir Jovett, and a dozen of Ahern's Lendouri cavalry for protection. The wagon arrived at midafternoon, with two gray-clad sisters riding amid a pile of featherbeds, ready to receive their patient.

Ahern's condition, meanwhile, had continued to deteriorate, his fever now accompanied by chills. The sister who examined him before they loaded him into the wagon looked no more hopeful than the battle-surgeon had been, and *tsked* to her companion as the stricken man was lifted up and settled, groaning.

"Such a handsome young man," she murmured regretfully, shaking her head.

"Is there no hope?" the king asked her, suddenly convinced of the seriousness of the situation.

"There is always *hope,* Sire," the sister replied. "But you must prepare yourself, as must he. . . ."

THEY reached the Abbey of Saint Bridget's just at dusk, where the sisters ensconced Ahern in their infirmary and did what they could to ease his pain. When the king and his officers had taken a hasty supper for which few had appetite, they conferred outside the stricken man's door.

"I regret to inform you, Sire, that he is not likely to survive," the battle-surgeon told them, after conferring with the abbey's sister-chirurgeon. "He has a sister, I believe? She should be told."

"And brought here to be with him," Sir Kenneth blurted, greatly disturbed. "They are Deryni; she may be able to do something."

"And your daughter had hopes of a future with him as well, did she not?" Donal said quietly, for the word had gotten out, in the course of the campaign, that Ahern was much taken with Sir Kenneth Morgan's daughter and, on the night after their victory at Ratharkin, had asked him for her hand—and been granted it.

For answer, Kenneth only closed his eyes, jaw clenching as he gave a jerky nod.

"Go, Kenneth," Donal whispered, clasping the other man's shoulder. "Bring back both of them."

Chapter 23

"And he died, and was buried in one of the sepulchres of his fathers."

—II CHRONICLES 35:24

Two days later, on a sunny morning late in June, Sir Kenneth Morgan urged his lathered steed up the final approach to Rhemuth Castle's gatehouse and clattered into the yard. Summoned by a page, the castellan left in charge in the king's absence came out to meet him as he trudged wearily up the great hall steps.

"Is it ill news from Meara?" the man demanded. "Shall I summon the council?"

"Nay, there's naught amiss with Meara," Sir Kenneth assured him. "The king is on his way back, unharmed, and Jared of Kierney acts as governor in Ratharkin. Where shall I find my daughter, and Lady Alyce de Corwyn?"

On learning that the latter was likely to be in the castle gardens with some of the children, he headed there first, following the page who scampered on ahead of him. Unshaven and stinking from two days in the saddle, he slicked at his hair and tried to make himself more presentable as they passed through a side door of the hall and along a cloistered walkway toward the wider spaces of the parkland beyond. In truth, however, with the news he brought, Kenneth guessed that the finely bred Alyce de Corwyn would take little notice of the bearer of that news.

Indeed, she did not notice him at all at first, lounging in the shade of a fruited pear tree and deeply absorbed in a book, the

Princess Xenia and a large black-and-white cat sprawled with abandon amid Alyce's skirts—a splash of vibrant lavender against the green of the lawn.

Farther beyond, at the edge of the duck pond, a squawking of waterfowl marked the location of two more maids of honor crouched down beside young Prince Nigel, turned two the previous February, pointing out the line of newly hatched cygnets strung behind a pair of swans gliding toward them on the water. Behind the three, various ducks, several aggressive geese, and a pair of peafowl were squabbling for scraps of bread that the boy had cast along the water's edge.

Kenneth's precipitous approach sent alarm among the assorted poultry flocked around Prince Nigel. As the peacock suddenly fanned its tail feathers and emitted a raucous screech that sounded like a child crying for help, young Nigel burst into tears and both Alyce and Xenia looked up—and saw Sir Kenneth Morgan approaching fast, a red-faced page running to keep up. Sir Kenneth looked positively grim, dust-streaked and still lightly armed for travel, and Alyce scrambled to her feet at once, dislodging princess and cat and sending the latter scurrying for safety into the sheltering branches of the pear tree.

"Sir Kenneth, what is it?" she cried. "Is it Ahern?"

"Alyce, I am so sorry," he said, reeling as she flung herself into his arms, searching his eyes for some sign of hope. "He was uninjured in the campaign, but he's taken ill. The king bids me bring you to his side. He lies at an abbey near Cùilteine. He bade me bring Zoë as well. Ahern had asked for her hand when the campaign was finished, and I—had given it," he finished, faltering at his own last words.

"He isn't going to die, is he?" Alyce demanded, desperate for details, but not daring to probe for them—not Sir Kenneth, who was the father of her dearest friend.

"Dear child, I don't know," he murmured, embracing her awkwardly, a detached part of him desperately aware of his disheveled state, concerned that she was ruining her lovely gown.

Alyce left Princess Xenia in the care of the two girls with Prince Nigel. On the way to the queen's chambers to find Zoë, Kenneth told her what he could of her brother's illness, not sparing her any details, for he had too much respect for her not to be honest, even were she not Deryni.

"I have occasionally seen men recover from this, but the outlook is not good. It is an inflammation of the gut, which often ruptures—and then the belly fills with corruption, and the victim dies."

"How long?" she asked breathlessly, as they raced back along a cloister corridor.

"God willing, he will recover. But if not . . . another week or two, perhaps—no more."

"Sweet *Jesu,* no . . ."

THEY had crossed almost the width of the formal part of the gardens as they spoke, and were approaching a set of double doors opening onto the gardens from the queen's summer apartments. Within, in the sunny morning room, the queen lay half-reclining on a damask-draped day-bed, her dark hair caught in a loose plait over one shoulder of her loose-fitting gown and a cool compress held against her forehead. She was bearing again, this new pregnancy discovered shortly before the king's departure for Meara, and she was still much afflicted with morning sickness, as she had been for all but one of her previous pregnancies.

Jessamy sat attentively beside her, hands busy with a drop spindle as she and the queen chatted. Behind them, in a sunnier window, Zoë and Vera and several others were stitching on an embroidery frame, and the ladies Miranda and Tiphane were practicing a new lute duet, albeit somewhat badly, the former making grimaces of distaste whenever the latter plucked a false note, which was often.

The pair stopped playing as the page bowed and entered to state their business, and the other ladies stopped stitching. Zoë rose apprehensively as she saw the expression on her father's face. Alyce held back a little as Sir Kenneth ventured into the room apologetically and bowed to the queen.

"Sir Kenneth, what is it?" Richeldis asked, laying aside her compress and sitting up. "What has happened?"

"I beg you to pardon me, your Majesty," he said. "The king is well, but Earl Ahern is taken seriously ill." Zoë gasped, one hand flying to her lips. "His Majesty bids Lady Alyce to come at once, to care for her brother, and asks for you as well, dear Zoë." He held out his hand to her. "Ahern had asked for your hand, daughter, and pending your consent, I had given it to him."

She flew to him, weeping in his arms while the rest plied him with questions, few of which he could answer. Vera came to Alyce and clutched her hand, offering her silent support.

"My news is two days old. I wish I could tell you more," Kenneth said, as horrified speculation shifted to the practicalities of immediate travel. "I have arranged for horses along the way back. Travel as lightly as you can, but we may be gone for several weeks."

They were on the road again before an hour had passed, dressed in stout travel attire, now accompanied by an escort of four fresh lancers for the protection of the women. Later, both Alyce and Zoë would remember that ride only as a blur of pounding hooves and aching backs and legs, quick meals snatched at intervals along the way, less frequent stops to try to catch a few hours' rest.

For the latter, at least, Alyce could offer assistance of a sort, by means of fatigue-banishing techniques she had learned years before from Father Paschal. For herself and Zoë, this posed no dilemma, for Zoë was well-accustomed to her touch. In the case of Kenneth, though he was already exhausted from his ride to fetch them, she was reticent to offer it; but Kenneth surprised her by asking whether she could do it.

"It doesn't frighten me," he told her candidly. "On those campaigns in Meara, I've often watched Sir Morian work, and occasionally, he's even lent a hand when some of us were dead on our feet and needed to stay alert. It was quite an extraordinary experience, and I don't know why the bishops keep insisting that this sort of thing is wrong."

"Well, they do," she said, half-disbelieving his trust. "Lie down and let me see what I can do."

She took care to go no deeper than she must, for her experience had been largely confined to herself and Zoë, Vera, and of course, Father Paschal. But Kenneth was a good subject, and woke much refreshed an hour later, when they must mount up again.

For herself, her attempts at rest were less successful, for her worry for her brother deepened with every mile they traveled; and though she tried several times to touch his mind, she could not, at such distance and unassisted. She wished Vera was with her, but since their true relationship was still not known, that had not been possible, just as it had not been when she had laid dear Marie to rest.

They passed through the returning army half a day before reaching the abbey, and picked up a fresh escort and fresher horses. Duke Richard had brought the army forward, and reported that Ahern had still been alive when they left him at the Abbey of Saint Bridget's. The king and several dozen of his men had remained behind with the stricken Ahern, to await the arrival of Alyce and Zoë.

Even with the use of Alyce's fatigue-banishing spells, all three of them were exhausted by the time they reached the abbey where Ahern lay. Seeing him huddled in his sickbed, his bedclothes damp with his sweat, did little to lift their spirits.

"Alyce, thank God!" he gasped, as the sisters admitted her and Zoë to his sickroom. "And darling Zoë . . . Alyce, I pray you, help me. . . ."

But there was only so much she could do, even when she had sent the sisters from the room and stationed Sir Kenneth outside the door to keep intruders at bay while she employed her powers as best she could. Zoë held his hand, and bathed his fevered brow, but there was little else she could do.

The king's battle-surgeon now held out little hope. Curled on his side, with his good knee drawn up to his chest, Ahern periodically was racked by rigours, now burning with fever, grown far worse in the four days since Kenneth had left to fetch her. When Alyce tried to examine his belly, it was taut and hard, and extremely tender. Her powers told her only that something was very wrong.

"I fear the bowel has ruptured," the surgeon told her, after she came out of his room. "We have tried to keep him quiet, and have given him nothing by mouth save a little water, but his agony has been intense. And his breath—the *foetor oris.*" He shook his head. "It is only a matter of time."

She cried a little then, weeping wearily against Sir Kenneth's chest, then dried her tears and went back into her brother's room. After putting him to sleep—and breathing a silent prayer that a miracle might yet come to pass—she gave her grim report to the king, then fell gratefully into the bed the sisters provided and slept through the night, Zoë curled dismally beside her.

Ahern was no better the next morning, though at least his night had been peaceful. In truth, he was now slipping in and out of coma, and his features had begun to take on a waxen, transparent quality. A priest had been summoned to administer the last rites, and was waiting outside the room with the king and Duke Richard. Sir Jovett was changing a compress on his forehead, in an ongoing attempt to ease his fever.

"I don't want to die here, Alyce," he told her, rousing at about midday as she and Zoë held his hands and Kenneth tried to comfort both of them. "And I wanted to marry Zoë. I still do!" he declared, turning his burning gaze first on her and then on her father, then lifting her hand to his lips.

"Zoë Morgan, will you consent to do me the very great honor of giving me your hand in marriage?" he murmured.

"I will," she breathed, tears streaming down her cheeks. "I will!"

"Then, someone, fetch that priest," he rasped. "And there should be other witnesses. Is the king about? And Jovett—call Jovett, my faithful friend. . . ."

Kenneth had already gone to fetch the priest, waiting outside with the king and Duke Richard, and returned immediately with all three of them, Jovett following behind.

"But, my lord," the priest was protesting, "he should receive Unction first. He may not have much time."

"Time enough to marry this fair lass," the king replied, grasping the priest's sleeve and propelling him to the bedside. "Do it, Father!"

Trembling, the priest put on his stole and joined their right hands, leading them through a much abbreviated form of the wedding vows.

"Ego conjugo vos in matrimonium: In Nomine Patris, et Filii, et Spiritus Sancti, Amen," he concluded, when they had taken one another for better and for worse, for richer and for poorer, in sickness and in health, until death did them part, and Ahern had given her his name and the gold ring engraved with the arms of Lendour—not yet impaled with the Corwyn arms, as had one day been his expectation, but token, nonetheless, of his intentions.

Only then did he allow the priest to anoint him for his final journey, and give him viaticum to speed him on his way. When he slipped again into coma a little while later, Alyce sealed him from pain and gently kissed his forehead in farewell, then left him in the care of his bride of but an hour, herding everyone else out of the room.

It was but another hour later when Zoë appeared at the door, eyes downcast, and stood aside to let them look beyond to where he now lay at peace.

LATER that morning, after Ahern's friends had paid their respects, the priest who had married him, shriven him, and given him the Last Rites of his faith sang him a Requiem there in the abbey, his soul uplifted by the angel-voices of the sisters who had cared for him in his final days.

Few mourned more profoundly than his king, who knelt beside Ahern's grieving sister and his bride of only hours with his face buried in his hands, pondering what would become of the gaping hole left by the dead man's untimely passing. In his all too short life, Ahern de Corwyn had taken on the mantle of his noble inheritance with passion and courage, overcoming adversities that might have seduced a lesser man into accepting the life of a wealthy and privileged cripple.

Only recently had the first stirrings of a born military genius begun to blossom—along with a quiet self-confidence regarding his Deryni gifts. Both had been of inestimable value in the campaign just past—and both had been lost with his death. Ahern had been but eighteen.

In sum, had he lived, he would have become a formidable Duke of Corwyn, in time. Instead, the mantle of that noble heritage now fell upon his sister Alyce—or rather, her eventual son.

Ensuring that she took a suitable father for that son now became yet another burden that Donal Haldane must bear, for Alyce de Corwyn shared the same blood and heritage as the dead man, and likely with similar potential. Any son of Alyce must be mentored by a father of unimpeachable integrity, with the ability to guide up the boy in the way he should go—a pair of safe hands in which to entrust the power that came with eventually taking the reins of ducal authority in Corwyn.

No such considerations yet stirred the mind of the potential mother of such a duke. For Alyce, the losing of her beloved brother represented a shock not unlike what she had experienced after the death of their father, three years before, and the loss of their sister, not a year past.

Once again, Zoë Morgan knelt at her side, but this time not merely as bosom companion but as sister, briefly bound to Ahern in law and spirit, but fated never to consummate that union. If Alyce now wept, she wept for Zoë as much as for Ahern—and for herself. Her brother's death changed many things. Some things, however, remained sadly and always the same.

The cheerless journey back to Rhemuth with Ahern's body was eased somewhat by Zoë's presence, sharing her grief. Again, the robes of mourning must be pulled from coffers, and again a Requiem was sung for a departed earl of Lendour in the chapel royal, before sending his body home for burial. Though Duke of Corwyn by birth, Ahern de Corwyn had never ruled in his ducal lands, so the decision was taken to inter him at Cynfyn with his father and other scions of the Lendour line.

Much of the next few weeks seemed like a repeat of the obsequies for Keryell three years before, though with an even larger turn-out. Ahern had won the hearts of all his Lendouri subjects during the months of his convalescence and the mastery of his injury's aftermath, and his people had been well proud when the king consented not only to knight him ahead of custom but to confirm him in his Lendour title, also departing from what the law ordinarily allowed.

Corwyn, too, paid him homage in death, in far greater numbers than they had for his father, for Ahern would have been their duke in fact, had he lived; Keryell had never been aught but caretaker, where Corwyn was concerned.

His young widow they took to their hearts as well, with wistful regret that she now would never carry on his line. The knights who would have been his support and mainstay as he took up his duties—Deinol Hartmann, Jovett Chandos, and even Sé Trelawney come from his unknown duties in far R'Kassi—rallied to the support of his sister, promising to keep safe in trust the lands that now would pass through her line instead of Ahern's.

Both Alyce and Zoë were exhausted by the time they arrived back in Rhemuth, though their return at least was marked by happier anticipation as the time approached for the queen's latest lying-in. In addition, the king had appointed a permanent governor for Ratharkin, a baron from the Purple March called Lucien Talbot, which had relieved Earl Jared to return to Rhemuth and make his formal declaration to Vera to become his wife. Very shortly after, Vera had journeyed to her family home near Cynfyn, there to make preparations for a wedding in Kierney the following spring. Letters were awaiting Alyce and Zoë, telling of the wedding plans and inviting their participation in the happy event.

That news, and the birth of a healthy daughter to the queen, early in September, did much to raise the spirits of the court. The baby's christening a few weeks later, as Silke Anne, was cause for rejoicing: renewal of life in the midst of death. Gradually the pain of Ahern's passing began to fade, and gradually, both Alyce and Zoë began to smile again.

It was early November when what began as a day's pleasant diversion set off a chain of events fated to have far-reaching results. The weather, too, had changed, not many days before, and a light powdering of snow lay on the ground: the first of the season. The king was preparing to lead a hunting expedition out into the forests north of the city, and had invited the queen and her ladies to accompany him. It would be her first such outing since the birth of Princess Silke. Richeldis, a fine rider, had been delighted to agree.

Accordingly, certain of her ladies were asked to ride with the royal party, Alyce and Zoë among them. It was an activity usually declined by the older ladies of the court, but the younger ones always relished a day in the field, surrounded by handsome men and handsome horses and with far less scrutiny than was possible within the castle walls.

On this particular day, the king's party included his handsome and unmarried brother Richard, nearly a dozen of Duke Richard's most promising squires, some to be knighted at the Twelfth Night to come, and many of the members of the king's council—perhaps twenty in all, along with as many huntsmen and men-at-arms. Sir Kenneth Morgan rode at the king's side: steady and reliable, attractive enough, but more of an age with Richard's generation than that of the king's other aides and the squires.

The day was sparkling, the sunshine bright and brisk, the horses frisky. They had a good ride for the first two hours, and good luck against the stag. One of the senior squires in the party brought down an eight-point buck, and the falconers totted up a good day's bag in pigeon and rabbit.

The ambush had been planned by someone with disturbing foreknowledge of the king's movements. Fortunately, the archers who carried out the attack were far less efficient. The first arrow only grazed the back of the king's hand, ruining a perfectly good pair of hawking gloves and his good humor; the second took Sir Kenneth Morgan solidly through the back of his thigh, pinning him to his saddle and sending his mount into a fit of bucking affront at this wound to its back. Before a third could be loosed, the king's men had their master on the ground and protected by a layer of knights and squires, and more of them were surging into the trees to isolate and overwhelm the attackers.

Chapter 24

"He shall flee from the iron weapon,

and the bow of steel shall strike him through."

—JOB 20:24

ALYCE would recall the next few minutes as a confusion of screaming and fighting and fear. Riding with Zoë at the queen's side, she heard the king's exclamation and Sir Kenneth's startled cry as his mount began bucking, and saw the riders nearest the king bear him to the ground for safety, others spurring toward the trees, and the source of the attack. At the same time, other men grabbed the queen's reins and drew her away from the confusion, one of the squires kneeing Alyce's mount aside to follow them.

It was all over very quickly. As the king's men dragged several belligerent men from the trees, somewhat the worse for wear, others helped the king to his feet while more men swarmed around Sir Kenneth's plunging horse and wrenched its neck downward, one throwing a cloak over its head to hoodwink it and, hopefully, calm it while others went to the aid of the wounded man.

"Careful! His leg is pinned to the saddle!" one man warned, as Kenneth cried out and groped at the grasping hands when someone started to help him down. "Somebody, make this damned horse stop dancing!"

"The barb's gone right through the saddle," another man said, sliding a hand under the pinned leg. "I think it's into the horse's back as well."

"Well, make him stand still, or we'll have to put him down. Someone loose that girth! Easy!"

The horse was still snorting and prancing, trying to buck, to rear, but its handlers mostly kept it with all four feet on the ground. Kenneth was gasping with pain, for every jigging movement of the animal tore at the shaft through his leg. Boldly Alyce broke away from the queen's party, a horrified Zoë following, and rode to where the drama was being played out, jumping down to join the rescuers.

"Let me help," she murmured, pulling off her riding gloves as she pushed her way through to the horse's head and reached for it.

"Stay clear, m'lady, or you'll get kicked!" one of the men warned, as she skittered back from a flailing hoof. Another was drawing his dagger, obviously intending the *coup de grâce* to still the animal's plunging.

"Let me touch him," she said, shouldering past the man's blade, already focusing her powers as she slipped her hands under the muffling cloak. "I'm Deryni. I can calm him."

A few of them backed off a little at this reminder of what she was, but the horse subsided immediately under the touch of her hand and mind, still whuffling and snorting but with all four legs now firmly planted, head dropping obediently.

"Easy, boy . . . That's it. Good boy. . . . Now, brace the saddle and pull it off with him," she ordered, slipping one hand along the horse's neck to grasp Kenneth's nearest wrist, flesh to flesh. "Give it good support, and try not to hurt him too much. Sir Kenneth, look at me!"

He did, concentrating through his pain—and found himself captured by her eyes, caught by a sensation of falling into them, even as the men began lifting him and the saddle clear of the horse. The movement still hurt him—and he cried out as they carefully lowered him to the ground—but she moved with him, still grasping his wrist, wary of the horse as it was led out of the way, snorting.

Two men continued to support the heavy saddle as two more examined the angle of the arrow jutting from Kenneth's leg. Zoë had crowded in behind Alyce, craning to see her father's condition. As Alyce scrambled to his head, laying both her hands along the sides of his face and taking him into unconsciousness, one of the men carefully wrapped both hands around the feathered end of the shaft, obviously intending to attempt withdrawing it.

"Don't try to pull it," one of the other men warned. "The barb's gone all the way through."

"Just break off the fletching," another man said. "It's going to be easier on him if the shaft is pulled on through, once it's free of the saddle."

"Wait," said another man, working with one hand squeezed flat between saddle and pinned flesh. "I've nearly got it loose . . . there!"

At his nod, men lifted the saddle clear, those closest bending for a closer look at the arrow transfixing Kenneth's thigh. A knot of observers had gathered to give suggestions for separating man and saddle, and now eased forward warily as Alyce, too, shifted her attention to the damage done. Zoë dropped to her knees at her father's head, casting anxious glances between him, Alyce, and the wound.

The tip of the arrowhead, a wicked-looking barbed affair made for bringing down large game—or men—was just protruding from the back of Kenneth's thigh, and would surely do additional damage as it exited, whichever way it was removed. Alyce knew he would also bleed a great deal, though at least the arrow had passed through deep muscle, well away from the great vessel whose severance meant almost instant death.

"I wouldn't break off the arrow just yet," she said, moving one hand to stay the man about to do so. "It may be better to cut the arrowhead off cleanly, back at the castle, and then back the arrow out of the wound, with plenty of shaft for a handgrip. He's going to bleed a great deal."

"Do as she says," came the voice of the king, suddenly among the onlookers. "I won't lose him because we rushed things here in the field. Can he ride?" he asked, crouching down between Alyce and Zoë.

"Not really, Sire. He'd be far safer and more comfortable in a litter or a wagon, if one can be arranged."

"See to it," Donal ordered two of his men. "And go gently, Rannulf. He took that arrow for me."

THEY were several hours getting Kenneth home, carrying him in a litter until they could commandeer a wagon and bed him down in that. They padded out the wagon bed with hay and wadded cloaks to keep the injured leg supported, and Alyce settled down beside him to keep careful watch over his condition. The king had ridden on ahead with the prisoners, and another party had taken the queen and the rest of her ladies back to the castle by the most direct route, though a junior maid had been left behind for propriety's sake, riding just ahead of the wagon with Jiri Redfearn. Zoë rode anxiously alongside the wagon, and half a dozen of his knights behind.

After a while, Alyce allowed Kenneth to regain consciousness, blurring as much as she dared of his pain. She could feel the eyes of the king's men upon her as she sat there—judging, assessing, many of them disapproving—for she had been obliged to use her powers far more openly than was her usual wont; but it was not in her nature to let any living thing suffer, if she was able to do something about it. Sir Kenneth Morgan was the father of her dearest friend, a kind and gentle man, and had always treated her with the utmost courtesy and even affection, though he knew full well what she was.

"I must be dead," he murmured, after a long interval of jouncing along in comparative silence, accompanied by only the rumble of the wheels, the jingle of harness, and the occasional low-voiced converse of their escort.

She looked at him sharply.

"Are you in pain?"

He gave her a faint, strained smile and a slight shake of his head.

"No worse than before, dear girl. But since I am in the keeping of an angel, I can only suppose that I have passed to the next world."

She raised an eyebrow and gave him a genteel snort, along with a faint smile of her own.

"I doubt these gentlemen would agree, my lord." She gave a slight jut of her chin in the direction of the men accompanying them. "Most would judge me anything *but* an angel. But I am glad that your discomfort is not too great."

He raised his head slightly to glance down at his leg, lightly touching the shaft of the arrow with his fingertips, then lay back with a grimace and a sigh, casting a reassuring glance at his daughter, riding along beside them.

"Is the arrowhead embedded?" he asked, returning his gaze to Alyce. "Will it have to be cut out?"

She shook her head slightly. "I think not, my lord—or, only a little, perhaps. It mostly went through—though I fear that your saddle is ruined. And your horse is in a very ill temper—though he is only slightly injured."

He chuckled bleakly at that, smiling faintly as he looked back at her. His eyes were the same shade of sandy steel-gray as his hair, though with a hint of sea-blue in their depths. Though his face was weathered and tanned, bespeaking much service in the field, she sensed that the crinkles at the corners of his eyes came mostly of good humor.

"He isn't a very good horse anyway," Kenneth confided. "I'd meant to ride another today, but the vile beast cast a shoe and there was no time to have it reset." He glanced away with a snort. "Not that *that* horse is much better. When the shoe came off, the nails ripped an almighty chunk out of the edge of his hoof. I suspect he'll be lame for weeks. And I reckon it could be months before a smith will be able to keep a shoe on that foot. But I don't suppose that I shall be riding again very soon anyway. . . ."

He was talking, she knew, to take his mind from his injury. In fact, Sir Kenneth owned excellent mounts, some of them given him by the king. All the horses had been fractious before they rode out that morning, for the weather had turned very cold in the past few days, and a hard frost had been on the cobbles. She had seen Sir Kenneth's first horse cast its shoe in the stable yard as they were mounting up to leave, jinking and kicking out at any other animal that got too near—and somehow managing to catch the edge of the shoe with its own hoof, so that it very nearly fell.

Alyce smiled and nodded knowingly. "I was aware of the incident, my lord. The queen was convinced you were both going down. They should spread more straw on the cobbles when it's frosty."

"A *sensible* horse wouldn't act up like that on slick cobbles," Kenneth retorted. "But he *is* fast—at least when he isn't trying to kill himself and me."

He fell silent at that, tensing as he shifted in the hay, trying to find a more comfortable position. Alyce checked his wound, but he did not seem to be bleeding—though he would, when the arrow was drawn. When he grimaced and closed his eyes, obviously concentrating on trying to ease his pain, she considered nudging him back into sleep; but there were too many eyes upon them.

They rattled into the forecourt of Rhemuth Castle just as the shadows were lengthening. The king's physician and Duke Richard's battle-surgeon were waiting as they carried Sir Kenneth through the hall and into one of the ground-level guest rooms that opened off the royal gardens. The queen joined them very shortly, and directed Alyce to assist the physicians as they dealt with the wound, she and Zoë holding basins and towels as the surgeon eased the arrow through far enough to cut off the arrowhead and then drew out the shaft.

Though Kenneth uttered not a sound as this was done, and bled less than they had feared, his face went gradually more and more taut and pale, until Richeldis nodded minutely to Alyce to intervene. The patient had been given a draught of strong spirits before they began, and now Alyce gave him more, at the same time brushing his mind with hers as she lifted his head to put the cup to his lips, nudging him gently into sleep.

If the surgeon noticed how quickly the draught worked, he said nothing, only bending to his work of cleaning and bandaging the wound, backing off then to wash his hands as the queen laid a hand on the sleeping man's forehead.

"The test will be whether a fever develops," she said, shifting then to help Alyce and Zoë pull the blankets up to cover him. "It appears we should have given him more drink, and sooner. It would have spared him some discomfort. We'll let him sleep now," she said to the room at large. "Alyce, I know you and Zoë will wish to sit with him and keep him comfortable. I'll send someone to relieve you in a few hours."

The guarded look that passed between her and Alyce made it clear what she meant, having experienced the ease of Deryni powers during childbirth and other times of discomfort—though usually from Jessamy. The church did not approve, of course, but it was a perquisite of royalty to ignore certain of the laws that governed ordinary folk, though discretion was always essential, even for a queen.

Still, the wife of the king and the mother of future kings could be forgiven certain lapses, so long as they did not occur too often or too flagrantly; and none could dispute that Sir Kenneth Morgan was the king's good servant, and had taken an arrow meant for his sovereign. Alyce saw the hardening of Father Denit's expression as he watched from the doorway, and guessed that he suspected what had just transpired, but she did not think he would countermand the queen's order, under the circumstances, though he might well mention his displeasure to the king—or to the archbishop. He gave them a stiff nod in lieu of a bow before turning on his heel to leave the room.

"I'll send Jessamy to you a little later. Be careful," the queen whispered to Alyce, briefly hugging her and Zoë around the shoulders before herself departing, along with the physician.

THE care they had taken in dealing with Sir Kenneth's injury soon reaped dividends, for he never developed the fever the queen had feared, and his wound healed cleanly. After a few days, he was allowed to sit with his leg propped up before the fire in his room, where he received daily visitors: Sir Jiri, with a favorite cardounet board and playing pieces, and sometimes ladies sent by the queen to sing for him while they strummed at lute and psaltery and crwth.

He also read a great deal, and was read to, sometimes by his daughter, but more often by Alyce. With the latter, it was usually histories borrowed from the king's library—and sometimes, correspondence sent by the king for his review. But occasionally, she found copies of popular ballads and poetry lying on the cabinet beside his chair. He colored when he saw that she had noticed.

In truth, the convalescent was finding himself most agreeably distracted by the gentle attentions of the queen's ladies, and entertaining such thoughts as had not crossed his mind since the death of his wife, several years before.

Oh, there had been the occasional flirtation with tavern maids and farmers' daughters when he was in the field, and gentle dalliance with certain ladies of his sisters' households when he went home to the ancestral estates of Morganhall to visit his younger daughters, who were being raised by their aunts. But largely, he had thrown himself into his military career, with increasing service to the king himself, growing mostly resigned to the likelihood that he would live out his life as a widower. He was but a simple knight, albeit a trusted servant of the king. What could he offer a woman?—he, whose meager income from the Morgan estates must go to support the children of his youth.

Yet now he was surprised to find himself thinking decidedly domestic thoughts, little though there was any practicality to such thinking. He had not the wherewithal to support a wife and possibly a second family. Even so, the idea began to surface more and more often during those weeks of convalescence, daily in the company of the beautiful and accomplished ladies of the queen's household, and of one young lady, in particular.

Alyce de Corwyn . . . heiress to one of the richest duchies in all the Eleven Kingdoms. She was so far above him as to be the embodiment of a fantasy he could hardly even conceive, at least in this life. When first they had met at Arc-en-Ciel, he had esteemed her as his daughter's friend, almost as another daughter of his own. Now, as their association shifted into adult friendship, he decided that he had not been far off the mark when he had compared her to an angel, during that long, pain-filled journey back to the castle after his injury.

Of course, she *was* Deryni. He had no idea what that might mean in practical terms, but he knew that it put her all but outside the pale where the Church was concerned. Being who she was, she had the protection of the Crown for so long as she walked a narrow path of propriety and care, keeping her powers securely leashed and curbed—she could not help what she was. But were she to stray from what the Church regarded as acceptable for those of her race, even the king's favor might not be enough to save her. Oddly, he had never felt threatened by close proximity to her—or if he had, it was because she was so beautiful, and so beyond his reach.

Further time spent in her company during the weeks of his convalescence only underlined both his longing and the uselessness of it—but still, he continued to catch her image invading his thoughts in many an unguarded moment, and gradually his dreams as well. Once he was back on his feet, walking with a stick at first, he would find himself gazing after her as he took a turn in the royal gardens of a sunny morning, while she and his daughter and the other ladies played with the younger royal children.

He threw himself into his work with a vengeance, spending many a gray morning or afternoon in the king's chancery, reviewing diplomatic correspondence, and attending meetings of the royal council when called by the king. Often he and the king worked long into the night on drafts of documents that needed to be prepared, taking a private supper in the king's apartments while they worked.

It was on one such stormy evening early in December that the queen intruded to inquire about certain arrangements for Christmas court, now in its serious planning stages. Attending her that evening was Alyce de Corwyn.

"My lord, you simply must do something about your sons," the queen announced, before she and Alyce were even properly through the door. "Brion and Blaine are pestering me to distraction about those ponies."

"I told you that I was considering the matter," the king began.

"Well, it simply won't do to keep putting it off," the queen replied. "You aren't the one who has to listen to them, day in and day out—"

"Perhaps we should continue this discussion in private," he said under his breath, as he set a hand firmly under the queen's elbow and escorted her into the next room, closing the door behind them.

After a few seconds, Kenneth exchanged bemused glances with Alyce and he remembered his manners enough to gesture toward the chair at the other end of the table where he and Donal had been working. As had begun to happen increasingly of late, he found himself reacting to her presence like some green adolescent. Each time he saw her, he found her more intriguing, and was struck by her beauty of soul as well as form.

"I do beg your pardon," he said. "Please, sit down. The king is in one of his stubborn moods this evening, so their meeting may take some time. May I offer you some refreshment?"

He nodded toward the flask of wine toward the center of the table, but she shook her head as she sat.

"I thank you, no," she said. "Zoë and I supped with the queen and the royal children earlier. It was hardly fancy fare, but her tastes are simple when she is not required to preside at the king's table."

He nodded agreement and took his seat, several places down from her.

"They are all well, then?" he asked, after a slightly awkward pause, suddenly at a loss for words.

"Aye, they are," she replied. "Except that Prince Brion does long for a R'Kassan barb at year-end. It is all he talks about lately. That was the source of the queen's comments, when we entered."

Kenneth gave a snort, unbending a little. "He is not yet nine. The king will never allow it."

"I *have* tried to prepare him for disappointment in that regard," she replied, smiling. "He rides well, but I fear that a R'Kassan would be quite unsuitable. On the other hand," she added, "I believe that the queen has been making inquiries about Llanneddi mountain ponies for both the older princes."

"Ah, I know them well," Kenneth agreed, warming to the subject of horses, which were one of his own passions. "I rode many a Llanner when I was a boy. Most of them stand only about twelve hands at the withers, but they look a lot like miniature R'Kassans—though with a mountain pony's more sensible temperament. They'd be perfect for the princes, at this point in their training."

"Aye, that's what the queen thought," Alyce replied. "She told me she'd grown up riding them—and her brother still maintains quite a fine herd. . . ."

They continued to discuss horses—a safe topic, Kenneth felt—for most of an hour, until finally the king and queen emerged from their meeting, both of them smiling. The queen, in fact, looked slightly flushed, her hair somewhat less tidy than when she and the king had withdrawn. Both Kenneth and Alyce rose as the royal pair entered.

"That's settled, then," the queen was saying, as she clung to her husband's arm. "You won't forget, now?"

"Of course I won't forget," the king replied. "Now, off with you—both of you," he added, with a nod toward Alyce. "Sir Kenneth and I must finish this document."

The queen arched an eyebrow at him and kissed the air in his direction, smiling, then headed for the door, Alyce hurrying to keep up. When they had gone, Donal sat back down at his place, grinning as he topped up his cup of wine.

"I do love being married, and to that woman," he confided, lifting his cup to Kenneth and then taking a sip. "Kenneth, have you never thought to remarry? You're still a young man."

Kenneth reached for his own cup to cover his discomfiture, wondering whether his interest in Alyce was that obvious.

"Hardly young, Sire. I am three-and-forty, and I have two daughters to support besides Zoë—and I assure you that I am exceedingly grateful of her place here at court. My sisters are raising the younger ones, so I need not worry for their daily care, but they all must be dowered. Hardly room there, I think, for a new wife and children."

"Humph. Then it seems I must find you a rich heiress," Donal said lightly. "You've certainly earned some more tangible mark of my favor than a mere thank-you. How many times is it, now, that you have saved me or one of my family?"

"I was only doing my duty, Sire, as your liegeman," Kenneth protested.

Donal gave a snort. "More than *that,* I think." He cocked his head at the younger man, considering. "I don't suppose you might fancy that lovely filly who was just here with the queen? We heard you talking about horses."

Kenneth felt himself flushing, momentarily at a loss for words. Did the king think he had been campaigning for this all along?

"I would—never aspire that high, Sire. The gift of Lady Alyce's marriage is a powerful bargaining tool. You must use it to bind some great lord's loyalty. You already have my loyalty—and my life, if needs be."

"Yes, I'm aware of that," the king replied, his gaze going distant as he mulled the possibility. "That's why the notion suddenly makes a great deal of sense. For such a marriage would also bind the loyalty of your sons—one of whom would be the next Duke of Corwyn."

Kenneth could feel his pulse pounding in his temples, hardly able to comprehend what he was hearing—and tried not to let himself even begin to hope that it might come to pass.

"Allow me to consider this further," the king said then, standing in his place as Kenneth also got hastily to his feet. "We'll finish this tomorrow. Meanwhile, think on the possibility—that is, if the idea appeals to you."

"It does, Sire—how could I not be honored that you would even think it? But I—I am old enough to be the lady's father. She may not wish—"

"Nonsense. She shall marry where I say she shall. She knows her duty." The king picked up his wine cup and took a deep quaff. "Go now. I must give this further thought. We shall speak again on the matter."

Chapter 25

"A wise man shall promote himself to honor with his words, and he that hath understanding will please great men."

—ECCLESIASTICUS 20:27

NOTHING more was said for many days. It was well into Advent before Sir Kenneth Morgan again found himself in a setting that permitted private conversation with the king.

He and Tiarnán MacRae had spent several hours that morning with the king and Seisyll Arilan, reviewing a sheaf of commissions delivered earlier from the royal chancery, all requiring the royal assent and seal. The snug withdrawing room was the perfect refuge from the weather outside, with a goodly fire on the grate and tapestries hung on the walls to keep the damp at bay: a favorite place for the king to work in wintertime. The scent of cinnamon, cloves, and lemons spiced the air, wafting upward from a pot of mulled wine warming near the fire.

"Thank you, Seisyll, Tiernán. I think that will be all for now," the king said, leaning back in his chair to stretch. "Kenneth can help me deal with the rest of these. How is your leg this morning?" he added to Kenneth, as the others withdrew. "It's a dreadful day outside. Does the cold make your wound ache?"

Kenneth busied himself gathering up the documents, trying his best to be casual as he jogged them into a tidier stack and placed them in front of the king for signature. He had tried not to think too much about what they had discussed the last time they spoke privily—and especially, had tried not to get his hopes up.

"Thank you for asking, Sire. I'm mostly mended, I think. I rode for an hour yesterday, though I *am* feeling the effects today. But I attribute that more to a month out of the saddle than to the actual injury. In all, I am content."

"And I am happy to hear it." Donal scrawled his signature to a commission, glanced at the next, then pushed the remaining pile back to Kenneth. "There must be an easier way to deal with these. If you'll lay them out in a line, on that table over there, I'll move along behind you and sign them. They're the new year appointments, for Twelfth Night court. I approved them weeks ago."

Kenneth did as he was directed, then fetched a wax jack and lit it from one of the candles set on the table where they were working, for the documents must next be sealed. As Donal moved back to the first document, removing his signet ring, Kenneth brought the wax, tipping a little of it at the foot of the first decree.

"Thank you," the king murmured, setting seal to the wax and then moving along the line with Kenneth. "I've done some further thinking on that matter we discussed earlier."

He imprinted his seal again. Kenneth had stiffened, the wax jack in his hands, and turned his gaze cautiously on the king.

"Sire?"

"I am minded to give you the hand of Lady Alyce de Corwyn." He looked up as Kenneth froze. "That *is* what we were discussing, was it not?"

Kenneth found himself going scarlet, and only belatedly moved on to the next document, fumbling slightly as he drizzled the next dollop of wax.

"Sire, I—I had not dared to hope. I am—most grateful, but this still does not address the question of whether the lady will have me."

"If I say she'll have you, she'll have you," the king retorted. "It will be up to you to make the match work. You're a good man, Kenneth, and I should very much like to have your sons serve my sons. If they were also half Deryni, that would please me even more."

"Half Deryni," Kenneth repeated dazedly. "I confess that I had almost forgotten that."

"That the Lady Alyce is Deryni?" The king snorted. "I think that means far more to churchmen than to sensible folk like you and me. It doesn't frighten you, does it?"

"No, of course not," Kenneth replied hastily.

"She'd be an adornment for your arm," the king pointed out. "And her son will be Duke of Corwyn. *Your* son would be Duke of Corwyn, and you would be his principal regent—which means that you would enjoy all the benefits of being duke yourself, other than the title. Alas, I can't give you *that*, but your descendants would have it."

Kenneth found himself grinning ear-to-ear, hardly able to take it all in. "That isn't what attracted me, Sire."

"No, of course it isn't. But it doesn't hurt if one's prospective bride is rich."

"True enough."

"Good. Then, it's settled. I'll have the necessary documents drawn up. The betrothal can be announced at Twelfth Night court."

ALYCE learned of the king's decision several days later, just before Christmas. Quite unexpectedly, Zoë had been sent to Morganhall to spend Christmas with her younger sisters and aunts, so Alyce let herself be caught up in the preparations of the queen's household for the Christmas and Twelfth Night festivities to come.

The Llanneddi mountain ponies for the elder princes had arrived the week before—and one for Krispin as well—so Duke Richard had organized an equestrian display for the squires and pages under his tutelage, inviting the queen and her ladies to observe an impromptu competition.

Alyce was sitting with the queen, watching the young princes tilt at rings on their new ponies, when the king came to sit beside her. Somehow, the queen's other ladies had found things to do that took them out of the royal enclosure.

"A pity it's so cold," Donal said, not taking his eyes from where Prince Brion was preparing to take another run at the rings. "Other than that, are you enjoying the afternoon?"

"I am, Sire," Alyce replied. "The princes are riding very well today."

"So they are," Donal replied. "We have their mother partially to thank for that." He paused to lift the queen's hand to his lips in salute. "It was she who insisted that only Llanneddi ponies would do."

Alyce smiled. "For their size, Sire, they are the finest mounts one could wish—better, even, than R'Kassans, to my way of thinking, if only they grew somewhat larger. I had one when I was young. I adored her."

"There is another who would be adored by you," the king murmured, smiling as he took her hand in his and kissed it. "Oh, not I—or, only in the sense that I adore all the beautiful ladies in my queen's household."

Alyce looked at him sharply, then at the queen, whose expression declared her exceedingly pleased with herself.

"Alyce, dear, he is trying to tell you that he has chosen you a husband," she said. "And in that bumbling way of males, he is trying to be mysterious about it."

Suddenly she glanced out to the field, where Prince Brion was now galloping down the tilting lane, taking one—two—three rings in a row. Both his parents had risen to their feet as he passed, but sadly, he hit the fourth ring a glancing blow and missed taking it.

"Oh, well done, son!" Richeldis cried, waving her kerchief and bouncing up and down on her feet. "Donal, he has *never* done that well before! Wasn't it a brilliant run?"

The king sat back down, tugging at her to sit as well, but he was smiling.

"He did well," the king admitted. "Did you not think so, Lady Alyce?"

Alyce, who had also come to her feet, likewise sank back to her seat beside the king, still reeling from the queen's announcement. Surely they could not be referring to Prince Brion.

"You have chosen me a husband, Sire?" she managed to murmur.

"I have. He was riding earlier. In fact, you commented on his horsemanship, and his skill with the lance."

Numbly Alyce made herself review the last few hours, but no one came immediately to mind. If the man had been riding at the tilt earlier, it was not likely that he was one of the much older men at court—for which she was grateful—but who?

"Alyce," the queen murmured, leaning across the king conspiratorially, "he's referring to Sir Kenneth Morgan. Did you not remark that he rode prettily? And I know that the two of you got on well, while he was convalescing."

Alyce sat back in her chair, somewhat stunned. Though she had much enjoyed his company, it had never occurred to her to think of him as a potential husband.

"You needn't look so surprised," the king said. "I owe Kenneth Morgan my life, more than once—and I must be certain that Corwyn is in safe hands. When I am gone, I will lie easier in my grave, knowing that his sons—and yours—will follow on the ducal throne."

"Oh, pish!" the queen said, with some feeling. "That isn't what a young maid wants to hear about her future husband. Besides, that's years away. Have a care for the child's feelings. It's she who must marry him, after all."

"Hmmm, so she must. But I'm sure he'll make you a fine husband, my dear. You've seen him ride today—and you know that he can carry on an intelligent conversation. What more could a woman want?"

THAT night, lying sleepless in her bed, Alyce reflected that, though her own wishes had little to do with her eventual fate, she was, in fact, quite content with the king's choice for her—especially when she considered how differently it might have gone. Though he might, indeed, be more than twice her age, Sir Kenneth was kind, intelligent, better read than most—and the difference in their ages would become increasingly less apparent as the years passed. Furthermore, unlike many of the gentlemen of the court, he could converse on a wide variety of subjects besides battles and coursers and hounds.

But he did not converse with her of anything the next day, or even the next—though she watched for an opportunity to speak with him. In truth, the king seemed to have taken a perverse pleasure in sending him off on obscure errands, as the feasts of Christmas approached. Indeed, just before Christmas itself, he disappeared altogether for several days.

She wondered whether he might have gone to Morganhall, to visit Zoë and his other daughters and sisters. She wondered whether Zoë yet knew—darling Zoë, who briefly had been her sister and now, it appeared, was to be her stepdaughter as well. Though she longed to write and tell her friend, she had refrained, knowing it was Kenneth's place to tell his daughter first. Neither could she write to Vera, not until the betrothal was announced.

Christmas Eve came and went, with no word, and Christmas itself. Nor was Kenneth present on Saint Stephen's Day morning, when the king and his family usually made a public appearance, processing down to the cathedral in their festive attire.

After Mass, if the weather was not too bad, it was the king's custom to hold informal audience on the cathedral steps, where citizens of Rhemuth might approach with petitions. To one side, the queen and her children always distributed largesse to the poor: clothing, and parcels of food, and a silver penny to each mother who approached with a babe in arms.

That Stephen's Day morning, Alyce was among the ladies attending the queen, helping distribute the gifts to the poor. The day was bright and sunny, if very cold. It was toward noon, when the largesse had nearly been exhausted and the servants were beginning to pack up to leave, that she glanced down into the square, at the bottom of the cathedral steps, and noticed Sir Kenneth and Zoë sitting on a fine pair of red-bay R'Kassan barbs.

She straightened to look more closely. Kenneth was wearing a sumptuous cloak of fine black wool lined with sable, the edges gold-embroidered with a double bordure of flory-counterflory, and had a velvet cap well pulled down on his sandy hair. He was fiddling with the ends of his reins, but Zoë was looking right at her, and lifted a gloved hand to wave furiously when she saw she had caught Alyce's eye.

Alyce waved back, and started down the stairs toward them, but it was Kenneth who dismounted and hurried up the stairs to meet her, offering her a tentative smile as he doffed his cap and inclined his head in greeting.

"Good morrow, my lady," he murmured. "Alleluia, the Son is born."

"He is born indeed, alleluia," Alyce replied, with the ritual response.

"My apologies for being absent without word," Kenneth said quickly. "I had urgent business with my daughters." He glanced around them, then gestured awkwardly toward the cathedral door. "May we speak inside?"

She inclined her head nervously and preceded him up the steps and through the postern door, her heart pounding in her breast. She had known this moment must come. Faced with it now, she was not certain how she felt.

Not speaking, Kenneth led her through the narthex and into the nave, glancing around and then guiding her toward a side chapel that appeared to be unoccupied. When they had entered, he pulled shut the barred gate of wrought iron, not looking at her, then went to the rack of votive lights before the statue of a saint. Cocking her head, Alyce realized that it was Saint Albadore, a patron of lost things. As she drifted closer to the little altar to join him, she saw that he was lighting one of the candles stuck into a pan of fine sand.

"Have you lost something, Sir Kenneth?" she asked softly.

"I have," he admitted. He lifted his wax spill from the lighted candle to blow it out. "I have lost my heart to one of the queen's ladies." He carefully set the spill back into a pot of them, still not looking at her. "Fortunately, she is also one of the king's wards. And to my utter amazement, he has given me leave to ask for her hand in marriage."

"To ask?" she repeated neutrally, though unaccountably, her heart had begun to flutter in her breast. "And suppose that she were not to agree?"

He looked at her then, unreadable emotion flickering across his calm, earnest face, and lowered his eyes. "A less honest man would say that it did not matter," he said softly, "for she would be bound to accept the king's wishes in this regard, and to marry where he chooses."

"And what would *you* say, Sir Kenneth?" she said very quietly. "For I know that you are an honest man."

He turned his face toward the statue of Saint Albadore, biting at his lower lip.

"I would say that I hope she *would* agree. I would say that I have come to regard her with great tenderness and respect, and that I would cherish her all the remaining days of my life." He turned his gaze to her longingly. "I would say that I know I am old enough to be her father, and that I have little to recommend myself so far as fame or fortune are concerned. Nor am I the dashing young swain she might have dreamed of. But if she were to accept my suit, she would find me a kind and loving father to our eventual children, and she would never want for loyalty or compassion."

She had been Reading him as he spoke, and knew that he believed what he was telling her. She had prepared herself for this moment since her conversation with the king, for she knew that he desired this match. She had not expected to be so touched by Sir Kenneth's words.

"These are all commendable virtues in any man," she said. "Indeed, I should think that any woman courted by such a man would regard herself as extremely fortunate."

"Would she?" he murmured, hope lighting his sea-gray eyes. "Would *you?*"

She ventured him a tiny, nervous smile.

"Sir Kenneth, we are both aware of the king's wishes in this matter—and you know full well that, if he has decided to give you my hand, then I am obliged to abide by his decision." Seeing him start to turn away, she reached out to take one of his hands in hers, clasping it between her two.

"Having said that, however, I want you to know that, though I have dreaded this moment since the day my father died—knowing that my marriage would be arranged to best suit the needs of the Crown—I find that, now that it is here, I am both relieved and content that it should be you, asking for my hand."

"Truly?" he managed to whisper.

She gave him a demure glance from under lowered lashes, along with a dimpled smile. "Truly. I must confess that, in my worst nightmares, I feared the king might give me to some horrible, elderly curmudgeon residing in the wilds of Meara or the Connait. But you are hardly such a man."

Still disbelieving, he dared to take both her hands in his, searching her blue eyes with his grayer ones as a faint smile began to lift the corners of his mouth.

"You did not find me a difficult patient, while I was recovering from my wound?" he asked.

"No more difficult than anyone in discomfort, and impatient to be healed and off about his life. In truth, our hours together were a welcome diversion from my usual duties in the schoolroom, dealing constantly with children under the age of ten—and I greatly enjoyed the opportunity to delve deeper into the king's library, in my quest to keep your mind occupied while your body healed.

"Or—no, that is only partially true," she amended. "It was not my pleasure alone, for I do believe you were as eager as I to browse in the old accounts. I came to admire and respect your mind in those weeks of your convalescence. To be courted by you now—and to have the king bless your aspiration—is a development I could not have dared to hope for."

"You truly do not mind that I am so much older than you?" he asked.

She laughed gently, shaking her head. "Truly I do not, my lord—though it *has* crossed my mind that your daughters may find it passing strange, to be acquiring a stepmother who is hardly older than they. I assume that will have been the reason for your recent absence, to inform them."

He allowed himself an easy smile. "Zoë is delighted, as you must have gathered from her greeting outside. Geill and Alazais are unperturbed—and look forward to meeting you in due course. They are fifteen and thirteen," he added, "and quite certain that they are very grown up, indeed."

He flushed slightly in embarrassment and ducked his head briefly, then bent to kiss the back of her hand before he released it. "We'd best join the others, before they begin to talk."

"Do you think they will not talk anyway, when they learn that we are to wed?" she said teasingly. "Oh, they will, my lord—and hardly kindly, some of them. It is one thing for a Deryni heiress to reside quietly in the king's household, under his protection, and even to make discreet use of her powers in the king's service. It is quite another for her to take a husband, and to bear others of her kind. There are some who will resent this match."

Kenneth allowed himself a faint smile. "If they resent it, it will also be because they envy me," he said. "You must wed *someone*, Alyce. Mayhap, if you marry me, there will be less resentment against our eventual sons."

"Or daughters," Alyce murmured, thinking of Zoë and the sisters she had not yet met. "You could sire more daughters."

A flicker of pain came briefly over Kenneth's face. "I have fathered sons," he said quietly. "Sadly, none of them survived. Zoë's mother . . . was not strong."

"I'm sorry," Alyce whispered, Reading his pain as she lightly touched his hand. "I shall try to do a better job. Sons are important to me as well—and to the king. He *will* expect us to produce a proper heir for Corwyn, you know."

He smiled faintly and covered her hand with his, lifting it to press it tenderly to his lips. "Dear, gentle Alyce, you are a brave young woman, to take me on."

She laughed gently and shook her head. "No, *you* are brave, my lord, to take on a Deryni wife. Whatever else may befall, I think it very unlikely that we shall ever find life together boring."

He, too, laughed at that, still half disbelieving his good fortune, and the two of them made their way back out to the cathedral steps, where the royal party were mounting up, preparing to depart. Zoë had dismounted during their absence, and came flying up the steps to throw herself into Alyce's arms with a glad cry.

"Can it really be true?" she whispered.

Laughing, Alyce returned her embrace, as Sir Kenneth looked on indulgently.

"More true than either of us could have dreamed," she replied. "And right glad am I of it. Will you mind that we shall be mother and daughter as well as sisters?"

Laughing, Zoë shook her head. "You shall always be my sister, darling Alyce. And I shall be happy and honored to own you as my stepmother as well. Papa, we are truly blest," she added, shifting her embrace to her father. "I hope you may be even half as happy as you have made me."

"Well, with that for a recommendation, we can hardly go wrong, can we?" Kenneth replied, bestowing a kiss on the cheek first of Zoë and then Alyce.

Chapter 26

"For I was my father's son,

tender and only beloved in the sight of my mother."

—PROVERBS 4:3

IT had been a foregone conclusion that the betrothal of Sir Kenneth Morgan and Lady Alyce de Corwyn at that Twelfth Night court of 1090 would meet with less than universal approval—not because of any failing on Sir Kenneth's part, but because his affianced bride was Deryni. But no one could have predicted the terrible unfolding of other hatreds, as the day progressed.

The day began with the usual sequence of ceremonials customarily conducted at Twelfth Night court: knightings, squirings, and the enrollment of new pages for training in the royal household. Five new knights received the accolade, from diverse parts of the kingdom, and seven senior pages were promoted to squire.

Krispin MacAthan was among four new pages enrolled that day, finally allowed to exchange the play-tabard he had worn in aspiration for the full page's livery such as Prince Brion had donned the previous year. Both the young prince and the boy's mother had made much of young Krispin, to the notable disapproval of a delegation from Carthane. However, this was hardly surprising, since it was widely known that Jessamy and her son were Deryni, and Carthane was the principal venue in which Bishop Oliver de Nore continued to pursue his campaign of harassment against Deryni who stepped at all out of line.

As the king placed the scarlet page's tabard over Krispin's head, he was aware of the minor flurry of disgruntlement generated by this public distinction accorded a Deryni, but he also noted its source: several men in the party of a portly baron called Deldour, who had long been known for his antipathy toward Deryni. The man had been a minor irritant for years down in Carthane, his name periodically linked with the odd incident of Deryni persecution—but nothing serious. He was mostly a complainer and a boor.

His plaint this year, when the time came for presenting petitions for the king's justice, had to do with grazing rights along the Eirian, far from the troubles in Nyford. While he *was* known to be friends with Oliver de Nore, one of the itinerant bishops active in the ongoing persecution of Deryni—and had even taken Bishop Oliver's younger brother into his service as a chaplain—Deldour himself was considered to be a mere irritant rather than any particular threat. The presence of the bishop's brother hinted at potentials for more serious unpleasantness—and Zoë noted him, and recognized him as Alyce's old nemesis from Arc-en-Ciel, Father Septimus de Nore—but she was not about to intrude on the betrothal of her father and her dearest friend by bringing up past unpleasantness.

Lord Deldour's ire had only increased at the feast that followed court, when the king summoned Sir Kenneth Morgan and Lady Alyce de Corwyn to the high table and there joined their hands, lauding Kenneth's faithfulness and valor and, in token of his esteem, declaring his intention that the two should wed. A royal chaplain had been holding himself in readiness, and came at the king's beckoning to seal the betrothal with the blessing of the Church, to much astonished murmuring among the assembled lords and ladies and a renewed wave of mutterings within Lord Deldour's party.

For the most part, however, Sir Kenneth Morgan's change in fortune was lauded as just recompense for faithful services rendered, and brought him many a heartfelt expression of congratulation from friends and colleagues. The king observed this reaction with no little relief as the active feasting gave way to divers entertainments: minstrels and dancing, a troupe of jugglers and a fire-eater, and even a masque prettily played by some of the ladies of the queen's household and several of the older squires, recounting the courtship of Malcolm and Roisian.

Jared Earl of Kierney played the part of King Malcolm, wearing a tinsel crown that looked a good deal like the real state crown that Donal had worn earlier at his official court, with crosses and leaves intertwined; and his own betrothed, Lady Vera Howard, briefly returned to court for Twelfth Night, played the role of Roisian of Meara with sweetness and verve. When "King Malcolm" finally swept his princess into his arms and kissed her heartily, in front of Sir Jovett Chandos dressed as an archbishop in a tall miter, all the audience applauded wildly, shouting and hooting with delight, for the widower Jared and the lovely and spritely Vera were to be married in early May, and the match was popular.

Alyce and Kenneth watched from seats that had been vacated for them at the high table, at the king's right hand, Zoë sitting happily to her father's other side. Dancing followed the masque, interspersed with more boisterous minstrelsy, and the freely flowing wine slowly shifted the atmosphere from decorous to earthy, as couples sought out the shadows of hall and cloister garden. No doubt reminded of the Twelfth Night previous, Zoë grew more wistful as the night wore, and made no objection when her father quietly opined that perhaps it was time to retire.

When the three of them reached the door to the room that she and Alyce shared, she accepted her father's gentle kiss and then disappeared inside. Alyce would have followed her, but Kenneth caught her hand.

"Stay a moment," he murmured, drawing her back from the door. "She will be missing your brother, and probably would like to weep a while in privacy."

Saying nothing, for she knew Kenneth was right, Alyce only nodded and let herself be led into the recess of the next closed doorway, her hand still in his. She, too, was missing her brother, and all the promise lost with his passing—and the night had made her far more aware of the weight that had passed to her own shoulders, with his death. When her own tears started to flow, Kenneth drew her into the circle of his arms and gently pressed her to his chest, simply holding her while she wept, one hand caressing the tumble of her hair.

She began to reclaim her composure after a few minutes, lifting her head to knuckle at her tears with the back of one hand, a little embarrassed by her lapse.

"I'm sorry," she whispered, daring to look at him. "I suppose I needed a good weep as much as Zoë."

"You are surely entitled to weep," he murmured.

He caught her left hand and pressed it his lips, tasting the salt of her tears. As he lifted his eyes to hers, she felt his thumb caressing the ring he had given her only hours earlier, at their betrothal—and the subtle tightening of the arm that still surrounded her, almost a spasm, as if marking some momentous shift in their relationship.

"Alyce," he dared to whisper, so softly that she almost could not hear him, "I should very much like to kiss you."

Her heart had begun thumping in her breast, and her eyes anxiously searched his as she managed a faint nod. Releasing her hand, he brushed reverent fingertips along the curve of her cheek, then gently tilted her chin upward to receive his chaste kiss.

At least it began that way, though that first kiss soon gave way to another that was not chaste at all. The touch of his lips seemed to ignite a delicious tingling from head to toe, and her arms slid up around his neck, pulling him closer. A tiny moan escaped her as his lips nuzzled briefly down one side of her neck and then back to her mouth, his embrace hardening.

She could feel her body answering as he kissed her again, far more thoroughly this time. When, finally, he drew back with a shudder, turning his face slightly away from her, she was trembling and breathless, weak-kneed, and only reluctantly let her hands slip back onto his chest as he dared to meet her gaze again.

"I—think, perhaps, you should go to your room now," he said quietly. "For if you stay here much longer, dear Alyce, I—cannot guarantee that you shall go later with your virtue intact."

She had dared to Truth-Read him as he spoke, and suddenly realized by what little margin he had pulled himself back from taking full advantage of her inexperience. And while her trembling body still declared its willingness—nay, its eagerness—to resume the delicious dalliance of the past few minutes, this was hardly the time nor the place. Sufficient, for now, to know that their eventual union would be no mere coupling out of dynastic duty, but something far more. Just what, she was not certain, but for now, both of them would have to be content to wait to discover it.

"You're right, of course," she whispered, stepping a little back from him, though her one hand lingered on his sleeve before surrendering the touch of him. "I should see if Zoë is all right."

Smiling tremulously, she kissed the fingertips of her right hand, then touched them to his lips as she murmured, "Good night, dear Kenneth."

With that, she made her way quickly back to the door of her own room and went inside, closing and barring it after her.

VERY early the next morning, shortly after first light, a furious pounding on the door brought both Alyce and Zoë bolt-upright in their bed.

"What on earth?" Zoë murmured.

Alyce was already tumbling from the bed and padding toward the door, pulling back the bolt, wrenching the door wide enough to reveal a very frightened-looking squire—one of those promoted from page the day before.

"Lady Alyce, you're to come to the stable yard at once," he blurted. "The king commands it."

"The king? Whatever for?" Zoë asked, coming up behind Alyce.

"There's been an accident, miss," the boy replied.

"What kind of accident?" Alyce wanted to know.

"Just come, my lady, please!" The boy looked scared and desperate. "I'm not to give you any further details."

"Why ever not—?" Zoë began.

"We'd best get dressed," Alyce cut in, starting to close the door and then looking at the boy again. "It's Trevor, isn't it?"

"Yes, my lady." The boy immediately calmed at this remembrance of his name. "You'd best wrap up warm, my lady. It's bitter cold out there. And poor Krispin—"

He broke off, frightened-looking, biting at his lip, and Alyce exchanged a glance with Zoë before closing the door.

"What do you suppose happened?" Zoë whispered, as she and Alyce hastily pulled on warm woolen gowns over their nightdresses, then set about donning stockings and sturdy boots.

"I don't know," said Alyce. "But Trevor was in a dreadful state."

They finished dressing, pulled on warm cloaks and caps and gloves, and raced down to the stable yard right behind Trevor. But to their surprise, he led them on toward the secondary yard, where about a dozen men were clustered around the well-head next to a large watering trough. The king and his brother were watching Sir Tiarnán MacRae and Sir Kenneth help a very young page out of the well itself, where a rope disappeared over the edge.

When the boy had cleared the edge, to be bundled in a warm cloak by Richard, two burly stablemen started to haul on the rope, obviously raising something heavier than a mere bucket of water. The king's physician and Duke Richard's battle-surgeon, Master Donnard, were there as well. All of them looked dreadful.

Pushing down a queasy sensation in the pit of her stomach, Alyce made her way to the side of Sir Jiri Redfearn, Zoë close behind her.

"Jiri, what's happened?" she murmured.

Jiri shook his head, never taking his eyes from the well-head. "Bad business, my lady. Apparently, one of the pages fell down the well and drowned."

"Dear God, which one?" Zoë murmured.

"I'm afraid it's Lady Jessamy's lad, milady," Jiri said. "We've been looking for him most of the night."

"But—how could he fall down the well?" Alyce asked. "Surely it's too narrow."

Jiri shrugged. "We wondered that, too. He went in head-first. They had to send another boy down to tie a rope around his ankles. Only way to get him out."

As he said that, two booted feet appeared over the edge of the well-head—a child's feet—and a flash of crimson page's livery, just before the men closed in around him to block any further view by the two young women.

"Stay here!" Jiri ordered, turning briefly to face them and pointing emphatically at the ground, before heading toward the well at a brisk trot.

Alyce and Zoë could not hear what the men were saying,

but the king himself came to wrap his cloak around the little body as it emerged fully from the well, letting Richard and Kenneth help lay the boy on the ground. The two physicians moved in quickly, but only crouched briefly before reluctantly withdrawing, shaking their heads. Master Donnard looked particularly stunned. After a moment, the king himself came over to where the two young women waited, his face white and drawn. His glance at Zoë allowed for no appeal.

"Leave us, please. I would have a word in private with Lady Alyce."

When Zoë had withdrawn, wandering closer to where two young pages were anxiously craning their necks to see more of the fate of their young friend, the king turned back to Alyce, though not without a backward look over his shoulder in the direction of the well.

"Dear Alyce, I must ask a very great favor of you," he said in a very low voice. "There's been murder done here during the night, and I *will* know who is responsible."

"It was Krispin?" she murmured, stunned. "He was *murdered?*"

Donal closed his eyes briefly and nodded. "Aye, and worse than just murder. And it is I who must tell his mother. And because she *is* his mother, I cannot ask her to do what I now must ask of you."

"What would you have of me, Sire?" she whispered.

"If Morian were here, I would ask him, but—" Donal made a gesture of dismissal of the thought with one hand and returned his stunned gaze to her face, almost as if he had not heard her. "Alyce, I do not know the extent of your training, but I am hoping it will be enough to do what needs to be done. Do you know of a procedure called a death-reading?"

Cautiously she gave a nod.

"And have you had training in its use?"

She allowed herself a slight, ironic smile. "I know the theory, Sire. But I had little opportunity to apply it, at the convent. However, I am willing to do what I can."

He sighed and gave a nod. "I shall have the area cleared, then, so that you may work undisturbed—for I am given to understand that much can sometimes be learned from the place where the crime took place. And I would not expose you to any more notoriety than is necessary, by asking you to work before witnesses who, quite probably, would see such magery as a demonstration of demonic powers. Sir Kenneth, I believe, is somewhat accustomed to seeing you work, from having had you tend his injury last autumn?"

"Yes, Sire."

Donal allowed himself a snort of something approaching relief. "That is well, since you are to be wed. I shall ask him to attend you. Will you need other assistance?"

"His daughter and I are very close, Sire," Alyce ventured. "If I have the assistance of those two, and the yard is cleared, I shall do my best to discover what I may." She could not ask for Vera, for to do so might reveal her secret.

"Excellent. I *will* have the identity of his killers, Alyce," the king warned, fixing her with his gaze. "They used him most cruelly before they threw him down that well. Do you understand what I am saying?"

Speechless, she gave him a nod, trying to keep at bay the image that had flashed into her mind's eye.

"Good. I would know whether it was that or the drowning that killed him. In either case, such men do not deserve to live!"

She bowed her head in acceptance of his instructions. "I shall learn as much as possible, Sire."

Donal sighed and touched her hand with his. "Thank you. It is well—or, as well as it can be, given what has happened. I go now to tell Lady Jessamy. When you are finished here, you might come to her, for I think she shall need the healing sleep that comes best from one of your kind."

"Yes, Sire."

FIVE minutes later, the yard had been cleared and the two stable-arch doors closed, with men standing outside to prevent intrusion. On so bitter a winter day, it was not likely that many would seek the lower gardens or the tilting yard beyond. Kenneth had brought a low bench from the stable and set it close beside the shrouded form of the dead boy. There Alyce sank down, Zoë beside her, Kenneth kneeling on the opposite side.

"This will not be pleasant," Kenneth warned.

"That's why I am here," she said softly. "Let me see him."

At her nod, Kenneth drew back the cloak from the boy's head. The sable hair had streamed away from his face as they pulled him from the water, and lay matted and stiffening with frost at the top of his head, bits of straw spiking it here and there. The gray eyes were open and staring, the fair skin marred by several raw-looking scuffs, probably incurred as he fell down the well. Any bleeding had been washed away by a night in the water.

"Show me the rest," Alyce whispered.

Biting at his lip, Kenneth flipped the rest of the cloak back off the boy's crimson-clad body, which lay in an icy puddle still leaching outward from the water-logged page's livery of which he had been so proud. Again, there were bits of straw stuck to his clothing and freezing in the puddle, and ice was beginning to glitter on his clothing. His scarlet britches were bunched around his knees. Though they had folded his arms across his chest after pulling him from the well, the hands were badly scuffed and raw, some of the nails broken, and several of the fingers jutted at odd angles, as did one wrist.

"Dear God, he did fight them," Alyce breathed.

"Aye, but what could a child his age do against grown men?" Kenneth murmured, his voice catching. "And to use him thus—"

Choking off a sob, he drew the cloak back over the boy's body, leaving only the head exposed.

"Get on with it, then," he said roughly. "Find out who has done this to him!"

She slid to her knees beside Krispin's head, stripping off her gloves and handing them to Zoë, then laid her hands on the boy's head, feeling in his hair for skull injuries, opening his mouth to look at his teeth. One of the bottom ones was missing, but she thought the gap might have marked a shed milk tooth rather than one lost during his ordeal. He had several lacerations that might have occurred in the fall down the well, and one depressed fracture, but given the probable sequence of his assault, she thought it unlikely that the blow had killed him before he could drown.

Hoping for a clue to *that,* at least, she slipped her hands under the cloak and inside his shirt, probing with her powers to check the lungs—yes, filled with fluid, so he *had* still been alive when he went into the water. But if God had been merciful, the boy had been unconscious by then, or soon after. She hoped it had been quick.

"All right, that's the easy part," she murmured, shifting her hands back to his head.

Without further remark, she took several deep breaths and closed her eyes, shifting into trance and extending her mind into what remained of that of Krispin MacAthan. To her surprise, his shields had been fairly well developed for one so young. But in death, little remained of what protection those shields had given him. Slipping past them easily, she began casting for recent memories that she knew, focusing on the glittering festivities of the Twelfth Night court, and Krispin's personal highlight of receiving his official livery as one of the king's pages.

He had been so proud—had been looking forward to this day for several years, and especially since Prince Brion had assumed the royal livery the year before. He had served at table early in the feast, bringing towels and basins of warm water to the worthies at the high table when they first sat down: the traditional first table-service of any new page, offering hospitality to a guest. He had served the queen and then his own mother, both of whom accepted his service with grave attention.

He had enjoyed the feast then, sampling the dainties brought by the older boys and stuffing himself with his favorite things. A little later, he had slipped out to the stables to visit his new Llanneddi pony—the gift of his mother, Alyce, and Zoë, so that the lad would have a mount as good as those of his princely companions.

That had been the beginning of a fatal sequence of events. He had been picking out the pony's feet, bracing each dainty hoof against his lap while he used a hoof pick to rake out muck from the frog.

Excessive zeal seemed, in turn, to have loosened the shoe on the off hind hoof, but he had promised the pony that they would see the farrier in the morning, and even made up a song about clip-clopping across the stable yard to have it fixed. When the two strangers appeared on the other side of the stall door, drawn by his singing and his chatter, they had seemed friendly enough, and had even offered to come into the stall to take a closer look at the delinquent shoe.

Though she tried not to tense, Alyce braced herself for

what she knew must surely be coming next, what she did not wish to know, for the critical moments were surely approaching. And unlike the few death-readings she had performed in the past, usually on bodies come to the convent several days after death—too late to really winkle out much detail—this death was very recent. Furthermore, overnight immersion in the cold water had greatly retarded the entire dispersal process. There was plenty of detail—far more than anyone should have to endure, and especially a child so young.

The two men had come into the stall and closed the gate. Once inside, under cover of admiring the pony and *tsking* over the loose shoe, the pair had overwhelmed the boy before he even was aware he was in danger, one of them clamping a heavy hand over mouth and nose, stifling any chance of drawing breath to cry out as the men roughly bore him down into the straw and began fumbling at his breeches.

Unable to breathe, the boy's resistance quickly had spun into darkness—from which he was shortly roused by the pain, as his assailants took turns using him as a stallion serviced a mare—the only blurred reference his stunned awareness could summon for what they were doing to him.

He had fought them—oh, how he had fought!—flailing with his heels, squirming, biting—anything to escape, to hurt them, to try to make them stop. He had even, through his fog of pain, somehow known that he must try to summon his special powers to defend himself—but he was yet too young, and too unskilled, and could not concentrate, for the pain. And every time he thought he might be about to break free, they had cut off his breathing again, or cuffed him into senselessness.

How long it had lasted, Alyce had no firm sense. But when the pain eventually stopped, there had been another dressed all in black, who had pulled the other men away at first, and turned the boy over in the straw—and recoiled at the sight of his bruised and tear-stained face.

But his supposed benefactor had turned out to be no benefactor at all, and hissed at the other two about "damned Deryni brat!" and "What were you thinking?" just before a powerful hand locked around his throat and squeezed him into darkness once again.

One last time Krispin MacAthan had managed to fight his way back to consciousness, only to find himself being lifted onto the edge of a low wall made of stone—no, the opening of a *well,* he realized with horror, as they stuffed his arms and head into the opening. He had started to struggle again, trying to cry out, but a heavy blow to the side of his head had cut off the beginning of his cry for help.

The last thing he knew, he was flailing for his life as he skidded down the well-shaft, desperately trying to slow his descent with hands, with fingernails, with booted feet that could find no purchase against the slimy stone. The shock of hitting the cold water far below momentarily restored his clear-headedness, but it was too late. His reflex gasp only sucked water into his lungs; and trapped head-down by the narrowness of the well-shaft, unable to twist upright, his only chance of survival ebbed with his fading consciousness.

That final darkness had Alyce gasping, too, as she surfaced from trance, coughing to clear the memory of the cold death that had flooded into Krispin's lungs. As she roused, Zoë threw her arms around her, holding her close, and Kenneth leaned across the boy's body to grasp her wrist.

"Breathe, Alyce!" he ordered. "You're all right. Just breathe."

She did, forcing herself to take a few deep, steadying breaths, then shakily looked up at the two of them, father and daughter.

"There were three of them," she managed to whisper, forcing order and distance on what she had seen and felt. "Two were men-at-arms, I think. They had him first. But it seems to have been the third man's idea to throw him down the well. And no, he wasn't yet dead, at that point. He drowned."

"Could you identify the men?" Kenneth asked.

"If I had suspects to question, I could certainly tell whether they were lying. There was something about the third man. . . ."

Casting back for his image, she closed her eyes to bring it into focus—and opened them with a start as she realized that she knew him.

"Dear God, it was Septimus de Nore!"

"Lord Deldour's priest? Are you sure?" Kenneth asked.

She nodded. "Absolutely. He was one of the chaplains at Arc-en-Ciel, when I first went there. I had several run-ins with him. You remember him, Zoë."

Zoë nodded. "He was terrible. And he hated Deryni."

"And who was he with yesterday?" Alyce persisted. "Lord Deldour, who also hates Deryni." New images came into focus in her stunned mind. "That's what the badges were on the other men's tunics. They were Deldour's men." She swept her gaze numbly toward the stable. "Have they already left?"

"I would be very surprised if they'd stayed around," Kenneth said, getting to his feet. "You're sure about this, Alyce?" he asked, looking down at her. "Deldour is a powerful man, and the priest's brother is a bishop."

"I know who and what they are," Alyce said coldly. "And yes, I'm sure."

Chapter 27

"Blame not before thou hast examined the truth;
understand first, and then rebuke."
—ECCLESIASTICUS 11:7

KENNETH'S quick inquiries in the main stable yard confirmed that, yes, Lord Deldour's party had left the night before, said to be headed south out along the Carthane road. While a cavalry troop made ready to ride, Kenneth told Duke Richard what had been discovered. Delegating Kenneth to take the news to the king, Richard himself mounted up and took out the troop designated to apprehend and return Lord Deldour and those in his company, especially the priest Septimus de Nore.

Once they had gone, Kenneth pressed Alyce for a fuller account of what she had learned, then passed that information on to the king, sparing her that. Meanwhile, women from the queen's household tenderly received the body of the murdered Krispin MacAthan, helping his mother wash away the dirt and blood and dressing him in fresh page's livery before laying him out, at her request, in her own bed, where the women would keep watch and say prayers for his soul.

Later that night, numbed by her loss, Jessamy asked Alyce to join her in her deathwatch, sitting rigid beside her son's body, wordlessly stroking his hand as tears rolled down her cheeks. Though she asked, as a mother must, regarding what had been discovered in her son's death-reading, Alyce declined to add to Jessamy's grief by going into overmuch detail, only assuring her that the perpetrators would be brought to justice.

The king was not in evidence that night, being closeted with his council regarding what should be done when the miscreants were brought in. Whatever Donal's own feelings in the matter, any public display of his grief was carefully tempered to only that expected of one who has seen brutality done to any child. Of his true kinship with the murdered boy, he dared speak to no one, not even Jessamy, in her present state.

Richard and his men did not return that night, but they rode into the yard at Rhemuth Castle the following morning, the eighth of January, with an irate Lord Deldour, Father Septimus de Nore, and Deldour's six men-at-arms under heavy guard. Richard had given Deldour no specifics of the reason for the summons back to Rhemuth, mentioning only that the king had recalled certain business that he wished to discuss with the Carthane lord. Deldour was livid, but Richard had refused to be moved. None of the Carthane party looked happy as they drew rein in the yard and dismounted.

They were even less happy when they found themselves disarmed, Lord Deldour as well—not restrained, but escorted forthwith to the king's withdrawing room behind the dais in the great hall. Deldour complained all the way, protesting his innocence of any wrong-doing, but he fell suddenly silent as he was admitted to the royal presence.

Two chairs of state had been set before the fireplace for the king and queen, who both were dressed in funereal black, both wearing crowns. The two courtiers standing behind them likewise wore black, as well as the young woman standing beside the queen. Ranged along both side walls of the room were archers—eight of them, black crepe banding their upper arms and with arrows nocked to their short recurve bows—each choosing a target as Richard closed the door behind them and stood with his back against it, one hand on the hilt of his sword.

"What on earth is the meaning of this?" Deldour asked, most of his former belligerence evaporating as the gravity of the situation became apparent.

"I, in turn, might ask the same question," the king replied.

"A child was murdered here two nights past. Brutally. Obscenely. By two of your men. And that man condoned and finished the job." His finger stabbed at Septimus de Nore.

"I don't know what you're talking about!" Septimus blustered.

"Do not further disgrace your cloth by a lie," Donal said calmly. "The only remaining question is, which of the six behind you brutalized the boy?"

"This is preposterous!" Deldour blurted. "What on earth would make you concoct such charges?"

"Ask *him* if the charges are false," Donal replied, pointing randomly at one of the men-at-arms. "Did you participate in the rape and murder of one of my pages?"

The man went white, looking wildly at the other men as he fell to his knees, lifting his joined hands to the king in trembling entreaty.

"Sire, I swear I know nothing of this!" he blurted. "I swear to you, on my mother's life—"

"I do not want your mother's life!" the king snapped. "But I *will* have the lives of the men who did this. How about *you?*" He stabbed his finger at another white-faced man. "Did you do it?"

The man melted to his knees, speechless with terror.

"Speak up, man. One word is sufficient: yes or no."

"N-no, Sire," the man whispered.

"And you?" The royal glare shifted to the man directly behind the nay-sayer.

"I am innocent, Sire," the man said defiantly. "What kind of man would murder a child?"

"Two of the men in this room," Donal replied, his eyes narrowing. "But let us see how many of them we have uncovered thus far. Lady Alyce?"

As he turned his head in her direction, Alyce moved softly behind the chairs of state to stand at the king's right hand. With her fair hair covered by a close-wrapped veil like the queen's, the men in custody had paid her scant attention until now. But she saw recognition lighting in their eyes as she moved, remembering her from her Twelfth Night betrothal, and naked fear and even loathing flickered among them.

"The second man is lying, Sire," she said quietly. "And his

accomplice will be one of the three you have not yet put to the question."

The guilty man gave a sob, cringing back on his hunkers and covering his face with his hands. Consternation stirred immediately among the others, stilled only when the bowmen raised their weapons and half-drew in warning. Lord Deldour was staring at the guilty man as if he suddenly had sprouted horns, even shying back from the two men who had been cleared, as they scuttled sideways on their knees, distancing themselves from their wretched comrade.

Septimus de Nore had gone even paler in his black cassock, though he had stood his ground thus far. As the king swept his gaze over the remaining suspects, the three of them sank raggedly to their knees, white faces averted, cringing both from fear of the king's wrath and the even more dangerous scrutiny of the woman whose blood they now remembered.

"Ask him again, Sire," Alyce said softly, indicating the guilty man with a jut of her chin.

"No, *you* ask him this time," the king replied, his voice hard and cold. "Be very specific, and use whatever persuasion you deem necessary."

She looked at him sharply, for she did not think it wise to be blatant about her powers in front of hostile witnesses. But even as she balked at the prospect, a way around it occurred to her.

"Very well, Sire," she murmured, returning her gaze to the guilty man.

He cringed anew, beginning to whimper, but she only continued to look at him until he glanced up again—and found himself snared in her eyes.

"What is your name?" she asked quietly.

"A-Alvin de Marco," he managed to whisper.

"Thank you." She inclined her head to him, aware that all eyes were now upon her. "Alvin de Marco, you have nothing to fear from me, for it is merely my gift to know when a man tells the truth—and when he lies. It is the wrath of the king you should fear, in answer for your crime—and God's judgement, at that final reckoning, if you do not repent of your sins and purge yourself of your guilt."

"Do not *you* presume to lecture *him* about anything to do

with God!" Septimus blurted, livid with anger. "What has a Deryni to do with God? What worth is a Deryni's word? How *dare* you?"

She glanced at him mildly, staying the king's intervention with a slightly raised palm. "I am no longer your student, that you may lecture me, Father. It is not I who am on trial here."

"This is no trial!" Septimus retorted. "You have no proof that any of us had a hand in whatever happened here!"

"You know full well what happened here," the king cut in, "and *I* will decide what is sufficient proof. Proceed, my lady."

Inclining her head, Alyce returned her attention to the cowering Alvin de Marco.

"Alvin, did you assault the boy?"

Sniveling now, trembling, the man gave a nod of his head.

"Say it, Alvin: yes or no."

"Y-yes," the wretched man managed to croak.

"And another man also did the same?"

Again, "Yes."

"Please point him out to us, Alvin."

Trembling, the accused turned on his knees to find his accomplice, but the guilty man had already betrayed himself by the pool of urine spreading outward from his cringing form.

"You miserable worm!" the king said softly, ice in each condemning word. "You have the bollocks to bugger a little boy, but not to admit your guilt like a man. Well, we'll at least see if we can't find a punishment to fit the crime. Captain?"

The officer of the archers stepped forward smartly and bowed.

"Sire?"

"Take those two to the guardhouse and fetch them a priest—not *that* one, because he's disgraced his office, but I'll not deny any man the chance to make peace with God before he dies. It's more than they gave the boy. But when that's done, I want them taken to the stable yard where the crime was committed and strung up—and geld them first. As for *this* miserable excuse for a man," he concluded, glaring at Septimus, "I have an altogether more fitting disposition in mind for *him*."

SEISYLL Arilan had been one of the courtiers attending the king that gray day in January, and was able to report the fate of Septimus de Nore when he met with the Camberian Council a few days later.

"I must give Donal Haldane credit," he said, when he had outlined the basic events of the past week for those unable to be present at a previous emergency meeting. "It was Old Testament justice—there were some rumblings about some aspects of the proceedings—but I think most would agree that the end result did fit the circumstances."

The execution of Lord Deldour's two men had, indeed, been met with general approval, as the word got out. Assaults against children were never condoned or even tolerated, whether the child was human or Deryni. Many years before, disgruntlement about a child predator had lit the first sparks that led to the Haldane Restoration of 917.

The fate of Father Septimus de Nore had sparked rather different reactions, not because he was innocent of murder—because he was not—but because he was a priest, and the brother of a bishop. Grandly claiming benefit of clergy, and making much of his family connection, he had demanded to be bound over to ecclesiastical justice, preferably his brother's, by which he might have anticipated being locked away to a life of penitence and self-mortification—or even gone free with a mild reprimand, since his victim had been Deryni.

But the king had exercised his own notion of justice in the matter of the killing of Krispin MacAthan, and had dealt Septimus de Nore a sentence commensurate with what he had done to his innocent victim. He might be innocent of rapine, but his had been the hands that had tipped Krispin down the well to drown.

First stripping him of his clerical attire—and of undergarments and boots as well—they had flogged him thirty lashes, in token of his betrayal of a child's trust of his office. He then had been shoved head-first down that self-same well into which he had dropped young Krispin—with a rope bound round his ankles and extending back up the well-shaft, to facilitate eventual retrieval of his body.

Because he was larger and stronger than Krispin had been, he had managed to delay the inevitable for close to half an hour, slipping incrementally closer to oblivion; but he had not been able to stop it or reverse it. When, the following morning, his body was pulled from the well, as had been done with Krispin's, the flesh of hands, elbows, and knees was lacerated nearly to the bone—but none had pitied him.

"And good riddance!" Vivienne had said fiercely, when Seisyll finished his account. She and Dominy both had wept when they heard of Krispin's brutal slaying, and the fate of his killers bothered them not at all.

"Aye, but it is having repercussions beyond what I think Donal probably expected," Seisyll replied. "Septimus was the brother of Bishop Oliver de Nore, who is pressing the Archbishop of Rhemuth to excommunicate the king."

"He won't do that—will he?" Dominy said.

"Unknown," Michon answered. "Ultimately, Archbishop William must take his direction from Valoret—and Michael of Kheldour *tends* toward moderation. But neither archbishop has made more than token gestures to curb de Nore's excesses in Carthane. The death of one more Deryni boy, weighed against the dozens who have burned in the Nyford area, counts for very little in the grand scheme of things."

"On the other hand," Khoren observed, "these other Deryni were not possible kin to the king—though Krispin's death does render that question academic now."

"Do you still believe he was the king's son?" Oisín asked Seisyll.

"Most probably," Seisyll replied. "Not that there was any overt sign of it at the boy's funeral. I watched Donal closely, for any indication that his affection for the boy might have gone beyond that of any other page in his service, but he was cool as ice."

"How is Jessamy holding up?" Dominy asked.

Seisyll shook his head, sighing. "She was devastated, as one might expect—and definitely showing her age. She has buried children before, of course—and a husband—and Krispin was laid to rest near them, down in the crypts beneath the cathedral. Very sadly, I think she shall bear no more children, even should she marry again, so Krispin was her last hope of a son. I pity her grief."

"This is all distressing news, to be sure," Barrett said after a moment. "However, I am somewhat heartened by your report of Alyce de Corwyn through all of this sad unfolding. Her handling of the interrogation of the suspects was masterful—avoiding as much as she could of any outward show of her abilities."

Seisyll inclined his head. "True enough. She seemed to sense the importance of caution in the presence of Lord Deldour—for she will have known that, whatever passed in that room, and whatever became of Father Septimus, word would find its way back to Bishop Oliver."

"She has good sense," Khoren agreed. "Fortunately, Truth-Reading is perhaps the least threatening of all our talents, since it does not involve any direct interference with the person being read."

Seisyll gave a nod of agreement. "Aye, it was exceedingly well done. I would love to know what training has given her such wisdom. But since she already knew of de Nore's part in the affair, mere Truth-Reading was sufficient in the case of the guilty pair—and by inducing the one to inform on the other, our Alyce cleverly avoided having to compel answers from any of them.

"And once the first man was discovered in his lie," Michon agreed, "it was he who exposed his fellow—mostly out of fear for what more she might do, if answers were not forthcoming. That is both our strength and our vulnerability among humans—that they *don't know* what we can actually do."

A few of them chuckled at that, for it was perfectly true.

"What has been the reaction?" Barrett asked. "Nothing has yet reached Nur Sayyid."

Seisyll shrugged. "Bishop Oliver is said to be livid over the outcome, as one might expect, but that is largely a question of the authority of the Church, aside from his personal pique at having lost a brother; Septimus *was* a murderer, after all, and had betrayed his office.

"Few question the fate of the two sodomites. Among the common folk—those who know of it—I have talked to no one who argues with the king's disposition of the case. Though some might have stopped short of the gelding, all seem to agree that the punishment did fit the crime—especially since the two did acquiesce to the victim's death."

"Then, it appears we must wait to see what further develops on that front," Oisín said. "I am very glad I do not live down in Carthane." He slapped his palm against the ivory table, shaking his head. "*Why* did they do it?"

"Not for the obvious reasons," Barrett said evenly. "It will not have been a matter of lust. Resentment might be a better guess—even hatred. Young Krispin had been invested as a page that day. Most at court no longer remark that his mother is Deryni, but it is known; and some would resent that he was being brought up with the royal children. He was an intimate of the king's sons—and their *corruptor,* by the reckoning of some, simply by association, by the sheer fact of being what he was."

"Was that sufficient motive to kill him?" Dominy asked.

"It all would have played a part," Michon agreed. "And opportunity also would have been a factor, especially with drink having been taken."

"Then, what about Alyce de Corwyn?" Khoren asked. "She is far more prominent than Jessamy, especially since the death of her brother."

"But she is marrying a human," Vivienne pointed out. "By giving her to Kenneth Morgan, the king has chosen to dilute the blood of the only Deryni ducal line in the land. That would reassure some; it disturbs me. Especially with Corwyn being the principal barrier between Gwynedd and Torenth."

"This is a cause for concern," Michon agreed. "But short of killing off Kenneth Morgan and having one of our kind abduct Alyce and marry her by force, the way her father did with Stevana de Corwyn, there is no way to change what has now been set in motion. Pray, rather, that Alyce de Corwyn quickly bears male heirs—for Kenneth Morgan is a good and honorable man, and will instill the same qualities in his sons. And while you are praying, think how much worse it could be if Alyce bears no heirs at all."

"Feh! A half-breed on the ducal throne in Corwyn!" Vivienne muttered.

"Patience, Vivienne!" Barrett said with a gentle laugh. "Alyce de Corwyn is not yet even wed!"

Chapter 28

"He shall direct his counsel and knowledge,

and in his secrets shall he meditate."

—ECCLESIASTICUS 39:7

DONAL Haldane had not heard the last regarding his disposition of Krispin MacAthan's murderers. The execution of Lord Deldour's two guardsmen was largely accepted as just, under the circumstances, and soon forgotten; however, the killing of Septimus de Nore quickly became a *cause célèbre,* especially among Gwynedd's clergy. Septimus *had* been a priest and the brother of a bishop, and denying him due benefit of clergy was an affront that Gwynedd's hierarchy was not willing to overlook, even for a king.

"They've been waiting for several hours now, Sire," Sir Tiarnán MacRae told the king, in the selfsame withdrawing room where the infamous interrogation had taken place two weeks earlier. Sir Kenneth Morgan and Seisyll Arilan had been closeted with the king all morning, discussing the latest letter of protest.

"I suppose I must see them," the king said with a sigh.

"Aye, Sire, I fear you must," Seisyll replied. "Bishop de Nore is threatening an excommunication, if you do not humble yourself before the Church and repent of your action. For him, it is a personal affront, for you killed his brother; but for the Church, it is a matter of having overstepped your authority, trying a matter that, by canon law, belonged before an ecclesiastical court."

The king had been listening with growing impatience as

Seisyll told him what he did not wish to hear—which was only Seisyll's appointed function, after all—and rose explosively to begin pacing.

"Seisyll, the man murdered one of my pages! *A child!* And why? Apparently, to cover up the crimes of two more men. And why did *they* do what *they* did? Who knows? A passion of the moment? A drunken indulgence? Or was it a lashing out at someone they knew to be Deryni, and therefore to be hated?—and moreover, one too young to defend himself!"

"Whatever their motive, Sire, you uncovered their guilt by employing the assistance of another hated Deryni," Seisyll said calmly. "I think *that* will have stuck in de Nore's craw almost as much as the fact that you executed his brother."

"No one complains when I use Morian's services, in the field," the king muttered.

"No, but Morian is far away in Meara, and that is war," Seisyll replied. "Here in Rhemuth, two weeks ago, you also flouted the authority of the Church. *That* is what will get you excommunicated, if you tread not carefully."

"Do you expect me to apologize? Well, I won't. Nothing can excuse what that foul priest did. *Nothing!* And I think that even King Solomon would have been hard-pressed to render a more fitting judgment."

"Nonetheless, the Church *will* uphold its right to deal with its own," Seisyll replied. "Don't say that I did not warn you, Sire."

"Yes, yes, I've been warned," the king grumbled as he moved to a chair of state facing the doorway. "Come and stand behind me—you and Kenneth, both. We might as well see what this latest delegation has to say."

At his nod, Sir Tiarnán opened the door and gestured into the corridor beyond, whence three clerics shortly appeared. Tiarnán himself stepped outside and closed the door.

Though all three men wore the plain black cassocks of working priests, two of the three sported the purple skullcaps of bishops, with pectoral crosses on their breasts and amethysts on their fingers. The senior of them was well known to the king and his advisors: Desmond MacCartney, auxiliary bishop to William Archbishop of Rhemuth—and William's brother. The other bishop was more recently come to the purple, though Donal had heard that young Patrick

Corrigan was slated for rapid rise in the hierarchy. The third man seemed to be but a priest, though Donal had never seen him before.

The king half-rose as the three men approached, but made shrift to sit again before Bishop Desmond could extend his ring to be kissed. The two bishops exchanged glances, looking far from pleased.

"Thank you for seeing us, Sire," Bishop Desmond said, lifting his head purposefully. "I believe you are acquainted with Bishop Patrick Corrigan—and this is Father Rodder Gillespie, from the Diocese of Nyford."

Corrigan and Gillespie gave the king sparse bows, which Donal acknowledged with a nod.

"I understand that you have some business with me, Fathers?" he said neutrally.

"Yes," Bishop Desmond said simply. "By now, I trust that your Majesty will have read the missive that was delivered earlier today."

"I have."

"And—have you anything to say about it?" Bishop Desmond seemed somewhat taken aback by the brevity of the king's reply.

"Yes," said the king, not backing down before the bishop's gaze. "I do not repent me of my actions concerning the murderous priest Septimus de Nore. His guilt was clear, and his sentence fully justified."

"That is your final statement on the matter?" Desmond said, more a declaration than a question.

"It is."

"Then, I am commanded to deliver this decree of excommunication to your Majesty," Desmond went on, holding out his hand for the document that Father Rodder placed in it, "promulgated in due form by Bishop Oliver de Nore, and to be executed by him with due ceremony—unless, of course, your Majesty would care to reconsider," he added, pausing in the process of offering the decree to the king.

The king's smile was dangerous, the gray eyes cold.

"Bishop de Nore's writ does not run in Rhemuth, my lord, and I do not recognize his authority to impose excommunication on me."

"Do you not?" Desmond replied softly. Tapping the document gently against his chin, he glanced at the two men standing behind the king, then handed it back to Gillespie.

"Fine. Then perhaps you will recognize the authority of your own archbishop. Sire, I shall report your defiance to my Lord William. And if *his* excommunication fails to move you to repentance, perhaps the threat of interdict will make it clear what his Grace expects of a loyal son of the Church. Good day to you, Sire."

With that, he and his companions gave the king curt bows, then turned and withdrew from the chamber, with nary a backward glance. When Tiarnán had closed the door behind them, Donal rose and drew his two companions back to the fire.

"Interesting," he said. "Do you think they'll carry through with their threat?"

"Very sadly, I do, Sire," Seisyll murmured. "Nothing can reverse the death of Septimus de Nore, of course, but you *will* be forced to make peace with the Church, for the sake of all your kingdom. Your provocation was great, but the bishops are correct, in that it was not your place to discipline one of their own."

"But, *would* they have disciplined him?" Kenneth asked.

"Quite so," the king agreed. "And the answer is, no, they would not. My way was best."

"Perhaps," Seisyll said. "But there will be a price to pay for your way."

"Should I have bound him over to whatever 'justice' the Church might have chosen to impose?" the king asked.

Seisyll smiled faintly. "I did not say that, Sire. But there *will* be a price to pay."

THE price, in the short term, was indeed the excommunication that Bishop Desmond had threatened—and surprisingly, excommunication as well for Alyce, whose Deryni powers had assisted in ferreting out the guilt of Septimus and his two fellow-offenders.

"You've done nothing wrong," Kenneth assured her. "You used your God-given gifts to uncover the truth—and truth always comes of God. Septimus deserved to die. It was he who turned his back on God—and reaped his just recompense. This will pass."

"But it does not 'just pass,'" she murmured, clinging to his embrace. "In the eyes of the Church, I am now set apart from God, even more than my blood already had set me apart. No priest may offer me the sacraments." She looked up at him. "We may not even be married, until this ban is lifted."

Anger stirred in his sea-gray eyes. "The Church is not God, Alyce. And not all who serve the Church also serve Him. What of your family chaplain, Father Paschal? Could he not be summoned, and would he not perform the rite?"

"Aye, he would," she admitted, brightening, for she had not yet considered that possibility. "Out of courtesy, he would normally defer to the direction of any lawful bishop, but he is not obliged to do so. They will like it not at all, though, if he should act in defiance of their authority."

"And *I* shall like it not, if our marriage is too long delayed, gentle Alyce." The touch of his lips on hers, at first a token gesture to reassure, began to tease at promises of deeper passions, stirred increasingly in the weeks since their betrothal. And when he briefly let himself drink deeper of her kiss, pressing her body close to his, she knew that she could not long bear to keep him from her bed.

"I could send for Father Paschal," she whispered, as she caught her breath. "He stayed in Cynfyn after Ahern's burial, to assist in expanding the king's regency there, but I know he would come, if I asked."

"Then do it," he urged, and turned her hand to press it to his lips, feeling her delicious shudder as his tongue teased briefly against her palm.

MEANWHILE, the king refused to be moved on the matter of his quarrel with the Church—and at the beginning of Lent, his excommunication was widened to include interdict for the entire archdiocese of Rhemuth. For more than a month he held firm in his resolve, but finally he sent word to the archbishop, requesting his presence at the castle.

"Sire, you cannot allow this to continue indefinitely,"

Archbishop William told him, on the day after what would have been Palm Sunday, had the city not been still under interdict. "You have forced me to close the doors of every church in Rhemuth, and to cut off your people from the solace of the sacraments—and this during Lent, when we should be remembering the passion of our Lord, and recalling His sacrifice for us. Can you not unbend to make this far lesser sacrifice?"

"I cannot regret what I did," Donal said stubbornly. "Septimus de Nore was a disgrace to his calling, a murderer. He deserved to die for what he did."

"Perhaps he did," Archbishop William conceded. "That is not the real issue. Canon law reserves the judgment of delinquent priests to the justice of the Church. The king cannot be seen to flout that law."

"I was unconvinced that justice would be done."

"So you took the law into your own hands," William retorted. "And how is that different from any lynch mob that might flout secular law?"

"His brother would have set aside the law!" Donal said emphatically.

"Perhaps. But we shall never know now, shall we?"

Donal looked away, biting back an angry retort.

"Donal, we must end this impasse," the archbishop murmured. "What would it hurt, to make some small concession? You achieved your aim. Septimus paid with his life. Conceding your error will not undo the justice you saw fit to impose. But you *must not* require your people to suffer further, because of your stubbornness."

After a long moment, the king turned his face slightly toward the archbishop.

"What would you require of me, to make a reconciliation with the Church?"

"Do you repent of your deeds?"

"Of the execution of Septimus de Nore—no. But I regret that I was obliged to bypass the authority of the Church, in my pursuit of justice."

A long silence fell between them as the archbishop considered. Then:

"I am willing to accept that statement as an act of contrition," he said. "However, I would require a more public act of penance."

"How public, and what sort of penance?" the king countered, warning in his eyes.

The archbishop again considered, not flinching from the king's gaze.

"For penance—thirty lashes, as you ordered given to Father de Nore," he finally said, holding up a hand to stay the king's protest. "I would allow the use of a simple leather scourge of four unknotted thongs, rather than the weighted strands customarily used in the flogging of a criminal. But you shall accept this purging in the presence of the full cathedral chapter, assembled within the privacy of the chapter house at the cathedral."

"And you will lift the interdict, and the excommunication?"

"I will," the archbishop replied. "I shall personally receive you back into the bosom of Mother Church and grant you absolution, at which time you will receive Holy Communion, as a sign of your reconciliation. Do you agree?"

Donal closed his eyes for a long moment, then nodded.

"When can it be done?" he whispered.

"A preparation of three days' fasting should be sufficient," the archbishop allowed. "Bread and water only. I suggest you spend it in seclusion. You may have two men to accompany you for the purgation. I should warn you that I shall allow Oliver de Nore to be present with my monks."

"Do not press me too hard, Archbishop!" Donal warned.

"The affront was against his brother," the archbishop replied coolly. "He has a right to be present. But he shall not lay hand on the whip. My monks shall see to that."

Donal let out an explosive breath, then gave a nod.

"Agreed.

"Then, three days hence," Archbishop William said. "And have I your word that you shall abide by these conditions, I shall lift the interdict immediately upon my return to the cathedral."

"You have it," the king replied. "This should be Holy Week. I would not subject my people to any further deprivation."

"A commendable sentiment, Sire. Then, I shall expect your presence on Thursday evening—after Mass and the stripping of the altars, I think. Perhaps an hour after that, when those keeping vigil have mostly gone. That should ensure the privacy you require. We shall await you in the chapter house."

"As you say, Archbishop."

THE king told no one of the accommodation he had reached with the archbishop, though by morning, with the interdict lifted, it could be surmised that some arrangement had been agreed. He canceled all public appearances for the next three days and kept to his private chambers, seeing no one. Limited to bread and water by the terms of his fast, he found his perceptions sharpening at first, and spent a great deal of time considering, as fully as possible, the many interlocking ramifications of the past several months since Twelfth Night.

Most wide-reaching, of course, was the rift he had created between Church and state, by his defiance of canon law—though that was about to be rectified. More personally troubling was the act that had started the unfortunate chain of events. With Krispin dead, not only had he lost a son, but the intended protector for his firstborn.

It was a deplorable state of affairs, and had haunted him increasingly as the weeks passed, for he was growing no younger. The aftermath of Krispin's murder had underlined how precarious was the safety of anyone possessing powers unlike the rest of humankind; pretty Alyce de Corwyn was still excommunicate, and Jessamy had become a pitied recluse, still mourning the death of her son. With the right preparation, young Brion would have powers not unlike those of a Deryni—and might also fall victim to those who hated such things, if he had not protection and guidance.

For that, the king decided he must provide another protector. And as he contemplated this need, a possible plan began to take shape in his mind.

IT was Holy Thursday, the night the king was to present himself at the cathedral, that the Lady Jessamy MacAthan also made her way there, first to attend the Maundy Mass, with its washing of the feet. But then, as the stripping of the altars began, with the solemn processions of the Reserved Sacrament to the altar of repose, she slipped down into the crypt to pray beside her son's tomb.

She had found herself visiting the graves of her children with increasing regularity in the past months, for she had begun to sense that she would not be long in joining them. She now believed a canker to be festering in her womb, and guessed that the affliction very likely would be mortal. At times, when she lay awake in the night with the dull pain gnawing at her innards, she even wondered whether God was punishing her for bearing this, the last of her children, and the only boy among them. Even more, she worried that the boy's father had not been her husband.

"Dear, dear Krispin," she murmured, lifting her head to run a caressing hand across the top of the marble lid, now carved with his name and the years of his brief life. She had brought spring wildflowers to adorn the tomb for Easter, as she had done for her other children buried here, and she shook her head in sad resignation as she inhaled deeply of the flowers' clean fragrance.

"I thought I might find you here," came a low voice from the doorway behind her.

She had not heard his distant footsteps, over the murmur of chanting voices in the cathedral above, but she knew his presence, and only half turned her head toward him, resenting his intrusion.

"Good evening, Sire. I am surprised that you would come here at this hour."

"*You* did."

He came and knelt beside her, bowing his head briefly in prayer and then crossing himself before turning to sit on the kneeler beside her, facing the only exit from the chamber.

"I miss him, too, Jessamy," he said after a moment.

She sank down to also sit, hunkering down in the lining of her cloak, for it was chill in the royal crypt.

"All the same, was it wise for you to come here, being excommunicate?" she asked.

"I, too, have children buried here," he replied. "And shortly, I go to make my peace with the Church. Besides, I left two good men standing guard upstairs. No one may enter save by going past them. And your maid is keeping vigil before the altar of repose—and will do so until I rouse her, or you do."

"Then, you came here specifically to see me," she ventured.

"In part. And to avail myself of the witness of only the dead."

"Then, you chose well, for I shall soon be among them," she said.

"What?" He kept his voice low, but his surprise was unmistakable.

"I have a canker in my womb. I doubt I shall see the autumn."

His silence was like a wall between them.

"I am very sorry to hear that," he finally said softly.

She shrugged. "I am sorry to have to say it. I had hoped for many more years. Sadly, I am not to be granted that." She shrugged again and sighed.

"But that is not why you came down here to seek me out. Nor, I think, was it to visit my son—*our* son."

"No." He turned his face slightly away from her, scuffing at the grit under his boot. "I go later to meet with the archbishop and his monks, to purge myself of my guilt in executing our son's killer—not the man's death, but the going outside canon law to do it. I have been fasting for three days. It is true that fasting sharpens the mind."

"I have long told you that," she murmured, smiling faintly as she leaned her head against the side of her son's tomb.

He inclined his head in agreement, but went on with his previous train of thought.

"I have been thinking about the loss of our son, and how Brion now shall have no protector. One of the men with me tonight is Sir Kenneth Morgan, who is to marry Alyce de Corwyn—who is Deryni. It occurs to me that a de Corwyn son might make an acceptable replacement for . . . the one who was lost."

"How casually you set him aside," she said bitterly. "But then, you did not hold his lifeless body in your arms. You did not see the injuries done it. You did not clutch at the wrenching in your heart when they laid him in this tomb, or feel a part of your soul die as the lid slid into place."

She had felt him tense beside her as she spoke, each new observation like a physical blow, but he only said, "No. I did not.

"But never believe that I did not love him, in my way," he went on, after a few seconds. "What I *could* do, I did—and my purgation later tonight will be the cost of it. But there is nothing that you or I can do to change what was and is. He is gone. I have other sons who must be protected. As a king, I must put that above all other considerations."

"Yes, I am well aware of what you have been willing to do, to protect those sons," she said dully.

"Then, you will understand why I am minded to place that protection into the hands of the next Duke of Corwyn, who will be half Deryni."

She gave a mirthless chuckle and lightly shook her head. "Better half Deryni than no Deryni at all," she said. "But even if Alyce were to wed your precious Kenneth tomorrow, I doubt that I shall ever see any child of that union." She paused a beat. "Or—is it that you do not mean it to be Sir Kenneth's child?"

When he said nothing, she shifted position to stare at him more directly. "Donal?"

"It is the obvious solution to my present dilemma."

"That assumes that she would agree to such an arrangement," Jessamy said incredulously.

"*You* did."

She snorted. "I was a respectable matron with many children already, and a husband I merely tolerated."

"She shall have a husband," Donal said mildly.

"And then you would ask her to bear *your* child? I think not."

"You do not think that I would ask her?" the king countered.

"I do not think she would agree to it," Jessamy said. "And if you took her against her will, all would know of the child's bastardy. Besides, her first son must be the next Duke of Corwyn—and you may not have time to breed a second."

"Her first son shall be duke *regardless* of his father—and I had not thought to take her against her will," Donal said carefully. "I had not thought to let her be aware of it at all. You could help me do that."

"*I—?*"

He gave a careful nod. "Did you not tell me, years ago, that her father Keryell had set certain controls upon her and her sister before sending them to court, and had given those controls into your keeping?"

She turned her face away, troubled by what she was hearing.

"Those controls were set so that I might assist in their training, and to ensure that they exercised due caution regarding what they are. By rights, I should have released her by now."

"But you have *not* released her, have you?"

"No."

"Then, it appears that you can, indeed, help me in what I desire."

A heavy silence fell between them, stirred only by the sound of their breathing for a long moment, as Jessamy weighed her answer. In the cathedral above, the sounds of public devotion were gradually fading away, the last worshippers departing for the night.

"You are asking me to deceive her," she finally said, "to use the trust her father placed in me as a tool for your purposes."

"I am asking you to serve the future of my line," he replied. "Of a time, you believed that to be a worthy cause. Worthy enough to bear me a son in secret, to be the protector and boon companion of Gwynedd's next king."

"A son who now is dead," she said bleakly. "And you would attempt this experiment again?"

"Yes."

She rose, turning to rest both hands on the lid of Krispin's sarcophagus.

"I will not have her reputation sullied. She must be safely married first."

"Of course."

"And she must never know what you do to her. She must believe that any child is her husband's."

"I would treasure such a child as well, for Sir Kenneth Morgan is a good and faithful servant of the Crown, as well as a friend. And there is time for many children of *his* loins. My time is limited."

"Not so limited as mine," she retorted. "Still, I will do as you ask. But you are not to have her maidenhead. At least grant her husband *that* grace!"

With obvious reluctance, he inclined his head.

"There is still the matter of her excommunication," he said. "Once my own is lifted, I shall be free to see to hers. Meanwhile, I believe that she has summoned her family chaplain from Cynfyn, who will perform the marriage regardless. I would hope for a wedding in May or June. And after that . . ."

Jessamy slowly nodded. "I will need to make certain preparations," she said. "I have made little use of the triggers set by her father; those must be assessed, to be certain they shall serve our needs."

"Could not the same purpose be served by a flask of good wine, suitably embellished?" Donal said lightly.

"Once, perhaps. But the getting of a child may take several attempts—though I shall enlist one of the laundresses to begin making note of her monthly courses. From that, I shall be able to ascertain the spans when she is likely to be fertile. And once she is married, you, in turn, must be certain to keep her husband from her during those days, until the time is propitious for your own endeavors."

He gave a nod, closing his eyes briefly against the sight of her, remembering the getting of that son who was lost, and praying that the getting of another would be as expeditious.

"Thank you," he whispered. Silence had settled in the cathedral above as he reached up to take her hand, pressed it to his lips.

"I must go now," he murmured, reluctantly getting to his feet. "I fear that I have an appointment with an archbishop. Be sure that, for the sake of our sweet Krispin, I shall offer up my penance gladly."

MUCH later that night, when the king was safely returned to his bed, his stripes dressed, and Kenneth left to keep watch outside his door, Seisyll Arilan reported to the Camberian Council on what had transpired.

"He had not truly prepared us for what was to happen," Seisyll said, "though we knew that the meeting had something to do with the reconciliation in progress between king and Church. He had gone down into the royal crypts beforehand—to pray, he said, though we had earlier seen Lady Jesamy enter there as well. One may surmise that perhaps he told her of the price he was about to pay for having avenged her son.

"He looked shaken when he came out—though perhaps that

was the effect of three days' fasting. We went next to the chapter house, where the monks had been gathering for the past half hour. The archbishop was there, waiting before the sedilla, and so was Bishop de Nore, the brother of the priest who was executed.

"Before entering the room; the king removed his cloak, his sword, his boots, his over-robe, and gave them into our care, then lay himself prostrate before the two bishops, with the monks ranged around the edges of the room. I could not hear what was said between them, but after a little while, the king came onto his knees and put off his shirt before lying down again, this time with his arms outstretched in a cross."

Seisyll shook his head and let out a sigh, still much affected by what he had seen.

"They flogged him then: thirty strokes, as he had meted out to Septimus de Nore, five strokes each from six different monks. Thank God it was not the flagellum, as was used on de Nore. The weals glistened with royal blood—and it is red, not blue or purple, as some would have it—but he uttered not a sound.

"When it was done, he took back his shirt, kissed the hand of each of the six monks who had flogged him, then knelt before Archbishop William to receive absolution and Holy Communion. He spoke not at all as we rode with him back to the castle. Lady Alyce came to bathe his stripes and anoint them with soothing salves. I do not think he spoke with her, either, though it was clear how he had incurred them.

"I left him sleeping peacefully—on his stomach, to be sure. I think there will be no scarring, but he will not soon forget this night, or the cost of his momentary defiance. At least he is restored to grace."

The others were shaking their heads by the time he finished.

"This is bad business, with the bishops," Barrett said. "I like it not, that the king yielded to their pressure."

"He had little choice," Khoren retorted. "Your bishops in Gwynedd are not like ours in Andelon. Headstrong they are, and blind in the matter of anything Deryni. There will be more trouble, mark my words."

Chapter 29

"Marry thy daughter, and so shalt thou have performed a weighty matter; but give her to a man of understanding."

—ECCLESIASTICUS 7:25

HEADSTRONG the bishops of Gwynedd might be, but there was at least one man prepared to beard them in their den—though in the subtle way only possible for a Deryni. Despite a flurry of letters from Alyce de Corwyn, none finally reached Father Paschal Didier until mid-April. It was early May before he was able to present himself in Rhemuth.

"This should never have happened," he told her, when she had given her rendition of the events of the Twelfth Night previous. "You have done nothing wrong. It cannot be considered a sin to discern the truth—and the truth, in this instance, enabled true evil-doers to be brought to light."

"Nonetheless, I am excommunicate," she replied. "Nor have I been able to ascertain what would satisfy the archbishop. And until the ban is lifted, I am barred from reception of the sacraments. Including marriage."

"Quite so," Paschal said. "And I am of the distinct impression that you favor the prospect of marriage with Sir Kenneth Morgan, and may even be eager for it." He smiled and shrugged at her look of surprise. "A good confessor can sense a change of heart, dear child. I have known since your childhood that the dynastic expectations of your eventual marriage were a cause of concern to you. But Sir Kenneth is not what you feared, is he?"

She shook her head. "Not at all. He is a good man, Father," she said shyly, "tender and kind. To have come to care for him is nothing that I ever could have anticipated, but it . . . happened. And to know that marriage with him would also serve the king's needs is both happy coincidence and an answer to my prayers. With the king's blessing, I would marry him even without the Church's blessing—but I should rather have both. It was Sir Kenneth who suggested that I approach *you* about blessing our union, since he knows of the affection that has bound you to my house for many years. But I cannot ask you to intervene if it would leave you in the ill graces of the archbishop."

"I *have* been obliged to tread a narrow line with your Gwynedd clergy," he admitted, "but in this, it may be possible to . . . adjust the archbishop's attitude."

She looked at him sharply. "You don't mean to tamper with his mind? His absolution must be honest, else it is nothing worth."

"Since the 'sin' to be absolved was no sin at all, it little matters whether the absolution is honest," Paschal replied. "But you need not fear. I shall appeal to a reasoning he cannot resist. Perhaps you would be so good as to ask Sir Kenneth to accompany us to the cathedral tomorrow morning. I feel certain that he will wish to be at the side of his betrothed when she humbles herself before the archbishop and offers her contrition, so that she may be married before God."

"Father, I am *not* contrite over what I did!" she reminded him.

"No, but as a good daughter of the Church, you will tell the archbishop that you wish to purge yourself of any guilt over having done what the king required of you, in confirming the truth of statements made by those involved with the murder of an innocent child.

"The archbishop, in turn, will assign you a period of penitential contemplation at—say—the convent of Notre Dame d'Arc-en-Ciel, which shall also serve as a retreat in preparation for your marriage from that house. This will also remove your marriage from the glare of possibly negative reaction if it were to occur here at court. Does that—satisfy the scruples of your conscience?"

She was grinning by the time he finished, and threw her arms around him in an exuberant hug.

"Father, I do love you! But, will the archbishop truly agree?"

"He will," he assured her. "Your offense was not great—and would have occasioned little comment, had it not been Bishop de Nore's brother involved; Sir Morian does what you did on a regular basis, though that is in Meara. And it would not surprise me if the Lady Jessamy has done it for the king, on more than one occasion.

"Nonetheless, because a bishop's brother *was* involved, and because the bishops must save face, you must be seen to show contrition and make amends for your part in it, victim though you were of the king's expediency—for which *he* has already been forgiven. My part in the affair must be subtle—to . . . *persuade* the archbishop that this is a just resolution—but on a one-time basis, it will be safe enough. Just mind that you do not affront him again, if at all possible."

"It was never my intention to affront him at all," she replied.

"Then, we are agreed," he said, smiling.

THE meeting with the archbishop took place not the next day, but the day following, due to his previous engagements. But other than that, all went according to plan. Gowned and veiled in penitential black, Alyce de Corwyn presented herself before Archbishop William in the company of her childhood confessor and her betrothed, kneeling to beg his forgiveness and praying to be received back into the ranks of the faithful, that she might be free to marry according to the wishes of the king.

The archbishop listened dutifully enough—somewhat stiff at first, in the presence of a priest unknown to him and not under his jurisdiction—but he was won over when Paschal casually drew him aside to clarify a point of Alyce's statement . . . and found himself unaccountably moved to pity.

"It does seem that the king placed you in a somewhat untenable position, obliged to use your powers in his service," the archbishop allowed, when he and Paschal returned to where Alyce and Kenneth still knelt, and Paschal again knelt beside her. "And Father Paschal assures me that your betrothed is an honorable and God-fearing man, who will do his utmost to see that you stray not again into the dangerous proclivities to which your race is prone. Sir Kenneth, do you pledge to do so, that your wife-to-be come not before me again in mortal peril of her soul?"

Alyce could sense the resentment coursing through Kenneth's body as he knelt beside her, but he humbly bowed his head.

"I do pledge it, Excellency."

"Then, I absolve you of your sins, Alyce de Corwyn," the archbishop made the sign of the cross above her bowed head, "and I lift the excommunication imposed in another place, receiving you back into the company of the faithful. For penance, I direct you to present yourself forthwith at the convent of Notre Dame d'Arc-en-Ciel, where I believe you were once a student, and there to make a month's retreat preparatory to your marriage from that place. Father Paschal, I give you license to perform the blessing of such marriage—and hope never again to see any of the three of you before me in any matter of disobedience to Holy Mother Church. Do I make myself clear?"

"You do, your Excellency—and thank you," Paschal replied, bending to kiss the archbishop's ring—and slightly blurring all that had just transpired.

"Thank you, Excellency," Alyce and Kenneth murmured together, also bowing low.

THE resolution greatly relieved the king, when he heard of it, though he was less than pleased to learn that Alyce was to go immediately to Arc-en-Ciel, there to prepare for her wedding.

"I have promised that I shall not touch her before her husband has her," he told Jessamy peevishly, that night before Alyce was to leave, "but I cannot afford to delay overlong. Nor can you."

"My preparations are under way," she replied, "but my strength is not what it once was. I have taken opportunity to examine her old training triggers, and they are intact. I shall give you access closer to your need for them. For now, however, she will be safe enough at Arc-en-Ciel—from Kenneth and from you. When she returns, a married woman, we shall need a few more months to refine the timing of the deed. And you might begin amassing a set of errands for her husband, to keep him from her during the times she is most likely to conceive."

Donal shook his head in both disbelief and resignation.

"How casually I make plans to cuckold my friend," he murmured. "But it must be done." He looked away briefly. "You will attend the wedding? The queen and I shall be present—and it will be I who give away the bride."

"You will not truly have *given* her until all of this is over, Sire," she said, "but at least your participation sets a seal on their marriage, in the eyes of the court. Think carefully whether you really intend to do this thing—for once it is set in motion, you know the deception you will have to maintain thereafter."

"It is, indeed, my intention," he murmured. "For the sake of my son, and out of loving memory of the one who was lost, I must do it."

"Then, God help us both."

ALYCE'S return to Arc-en-Ciel was more an occasion of joy than of penitential gloom. Zoë went with her, to help her prepare for her upcoming nuptials, and Paschal took up residence with the other chaplains for the duration, to be available for the pastoral counseling that accompanied the ostensible reason for Alyce's presence there again. Her only sadness was that she would be missing Vera's wedding, which was to occur while she was on retreat.

Mother Judiana received both girls with open arms, installing them in the room they had shared before, and the other sisters and the students eagerly fell to work on the stitchery for a bridal trousseau. Though Alyce did spend time with Father Paschal every day, in obedience to the archbishop's instruction that this was to be a time of penitence regarding her Deryni nature, the priest geared these sessions more toward the meditations proper to a more traditional pre-nuptial retreat, though without the presence of the groom.

In light of what she had been obliged to do in the wake of Krispin's murder, Paschal also gave her regular sessions of advanced training in the more subtle use of her powers. After one such session, when she had emerged from trance, he looked at her oddly, as if considering whether to share some facet of what had just occurred.

"Are you aware that the old triggers your father set are still in place?" he asked.

"Of course," she replied. "Don't you use them regularly, in our sessions?"

"I do." He paused, again considering. "Lady Jessamy was given access to those triggers as well," he said then. "Has she used them much?"

She shook her head. "Very rarely. I suppose Father's original intention was that she might be able to augment our training. That would have been before he decided to have you come to us regularly."

"That's very interesting," he murmured. "When would you say was the last time she used the triggers?"

"Oh, ages ago. Probably after Father was killed—or it might have been when I brought Ahern's body back through Rhemuth, on my way to take him home to Cynfyn. I was exhausted, and she made me sleep."

"Nothing more recently?"

"No. Why are you asking?"

"Because she appears to have been poking around in the last week or so before you came here," Paschal said baldly. "Have you any idea why she might have done that?"

"None at all . . . no."

"I did not think you did," Paschal replied. "And *that* is very curious—and disturbing."

"But—why would she do such a thing?"

"I don't know. And it is possible there may be some benign explanation—though, by rights, she should have released the triggers years ago, when I resumed responsibility for your training. Were it not for the hidden trace of her most recent contact, I would have attributed the omission to oversight. . . ."

"Paschal, you're frightening me . . . ," she began, eyes wide.

"No need, child," he assured her, patting her hand. "I've taken care of it. I've left the triggers partially engaged, so that you'll give the external responses she expects, if she should try this again; but I've also given you discretion, to override any commands she might try to set. Unless you choose to let her know, she shouldn't realize that anything has changed. I don't know what game she may be playing—but I do know that I want *you* to be the winner, if she insists upon including you in that game, without your knowledge and very possibly against your will."

Alyce gave a shiver, shaking her head.

"It makes no sense. What possible motive could she have?"

"I wish I knew," Paschal replied. "But, put it from your mind for now. You will soon be a bride, and much in your life will change. For one thing, you shall be in your husband's keeping—not Jessamy's, not mine, or even the king's or queen's. You are coming well into your inheritance, dear Alyce, and I am very proud of you."

She came back to his embrace again, basking in the warmth of his affection and praise, and did resolve to put it from her mind.

THE wedding day of Alyce de Corwyn and Sir Kenneth Morgan dawned clear and sunny. Alyce stirred and stretched in the bed she had shared so long with Zoë, opening her eyes to see Zoë gazing at her from the other pillow and smiling.

"What?" Alyce murmured.

Zoë giggled and also stretched. "Just think. In a few hours, you're going to be my mother."

Alyce shook her head, also giggling. "Mother to your sisters, maybe—in time. To me, you shall always be my sister."

"Oh, Alyce, you *are* like a sister to me—far more than my sisters of blood. Promise that you won't forget me, when you're a proper married lady."

"Did you forget *me,* when *you* became a proper married lady?" Alyce said lightly.

"Well, I never was *really* a proper married lady," Zoë said with a touch of wistfulness. "Sometimes I dream about Ahern, and what it might have been like—*you* know."

"No, I *don't* know!" Alyce replied. "At least not yet." She sat up in bed to take Zoë's hand. "Oh, Zoë, just think. A day from now, I shall no longer be a maid—and I shan't even be able to tell you what it was like, because he's your *father,* for goodness' sake!"

"Well, it wouldn't be right, would it?" Zoë said matter-of-factly. "On the other hand . . ." She looked at Alyce slyly. "I'll bet he's a very good lover. He's ever so kind and gentle. Though not so gentle, I'm sure, that he will not give you pleasure! I mean—oh, dear. This *is* going to be complicated, isn't it?"

Alyce laughed aloud at that and tumbled out of bed, rummaging for a robe.

"Get up, you! You must help me make myself beautiful for your father. This is my wedding day!"

THE nuptial Mass was to begin at noon, following on the last stroke of the Angelus. By eleven, the convent chapel was prepared, bedecked with flowers and flooded with summer sunlight. The few invited guests had begun to arrive.

The king and queen had come the night before, taking over part of the guest quarters with the three young princes and Princess Xenia, who was bouncing with the excitement of being allowed to serve as Alyce's flower girl. Also in the royal party were Lady Jessamy and her two daughters still at home, Jesiana and Seffira, along with the king's two principal aides besides Kenneth: Sir Tiarnán MacRae and Sir Jiri Redfearn. Duke Richard was on assignment in the field, and sent his regrets, but Sir Seisyll Arilan had deputed in his place.

From farther afield came the seneschals of both Corwyn and Lendour, along with several knights each, come to witness the nuptials of this daughter of both houses and to express their glad support for the man who now would become a principal regent for both honors. They had met him often in the past, and knew that Ahern had liked and respected him. Sir Jovett Chandos was among them—and Sir Sé Trelawney, once again come from wherever his personal quest now had taken him. The newly wed Earl of Kierney and his bride arrived, and Vera left his side for a time to spend a few moments with her secret sister.

The sisters and students of Arc-en-Ciel had all lent their efforts to the creation of the gown Alyce donned that morning:

a sweep of nubby green silk embroidered with golden gryphons the size of a man's hand, with Kenneth Morgan's gold double-tressure bordure set along the hem. She wore the Furstána emeralds at her throat—and on one wrist, the gold bangle of opals and sapphires that had been her mother's. A bridal wreath of roses in a myriad of hues adorned the tumble of golden hair cascading to her waist, like the one that Cerys Devane had worn to her novice profession; and the now fully professed Sister Iris Cerys was one of the those who held the poles of the rainbow canopy under which the bride would walk down the aisle; Iris Jessilde was the other.

The chapel and players were prepared. The guests, such as there were, had been seated at the westerly ends of the choir stalls, the royal party on the Gospel side—king and queen and royal children, along with members of the king's staff—and Kenneth's sisters and younger daughters with the Corwyn and Lendour men on the Epistle side. The scent of summer flowers floated on the still air, dust motes sparkling in the sunlight that streamed through the great rose windows, east and west.

As the last stroke of the Angelus faded, Father Paschal led Sir Kenneth and Sir Jiri Redfearn from the sacristy to the front of the chapel. The convent's three chaplains were also vested and ready, ranged behind them. When all were in place, Mother Iris Judiana bowed to the four priests, then made her way down the aisle to greet the bride, who was waiting under the rainbow canopy.

At Judiana's approach, Alyce sank to her knees to receive a blessing. Then, as the king helped her to her feet, coming beneath the canopy with her, the sisters and students of the convent choir began the *Ave Vierge Dorée*—and truly, as the pair of them began their walk down the aisle to where Sir Kenneth Morgan waited, she *was* the "golden virgin" of the anthem.

Later, the details of that next hour blurred together in a series of somewhat disjointed images of ceremony. Preceded by the Princess Xenia, who paused every three steps to gravely fling a handful of rose petals into the air, and by Prince Brion in his pages' livery, bearing a cushion on which lay the coronets both of Corwyn and Lendour, Alyce made her way down the aisle on the king's arm, the canopy accompanying them, pausing at the steps into the choir to reverence the altar. Zoë followed behind, as witness and attendant.

Up into the choir then, where the king and Mother Judiana led her out from under the canopy, now no longer sheltered under the Lady's rainbow mantle but given into the keeping of the man in whose hand the king now set hers, kissing her cheek and then stepping back to take his place beside his queen.

Readings, then, speaking of the duty of husbands and wives to one another and to God—and the joy recounted in the Song of Songs:

"Surge, propera, amica mea, Columba mea, formosa mea, et veni. . . ."

My beloved spake, and said unto me, Rise up, my love, my fair one, and come away, for lo, the winter is past, the rain is over and gone. . . .

Next, the vows, kneeling before Father Paschal as he bade them exchange promises, a ring, a kiss. And then the coronets, brought on their velvet cushion by Prince Brion, which cushion she took and extended to her new husband, that he might lay hands upon the two in token of the responsibilities he now assumed as a regent of Corwyn and Lendour.

The remainder of the Mass then—heavenly bread upon the tongue and the sacred cup shared each to each. And after that, the laying of her floral crown at the feet of the statue of the Virgin, bows to king and queen, and the recessional, following the double line of blue-robed students back up the aisle and into the chapel forecourt, where the girls showered them with flower petals as they emerged into the sunlight.

After, there was a festive wedding supper, and good wishes from the wedding guests: Zoë's enthusiastic embrace for both of them, the shy kisses of Kenneth's other two daughters, the awkward embraces of his sisters; the more heartfelt kisses of the three young princes and little Princess Xenia, who kept gathering up the rose petals from the chapel floor so she could shower the couple again; a promise of the king's ongoing protection and favor; Sé's promise that he would always be there, if needed. Vera's grin as she whispered a word or two about what awaited Alyce in the marriage bed.

After supper, the bridal couple were conducted to the principal guest apartment, occupied the night before by the king and queen but now vacated, with their imminent departure to return to the city. When the queen and Jessamy had dressed

Alyce for bed, and Father Paschal had blessed the bed and her in it, everyone withdrew save for Kenneth, left standing against the door, simply gazing at her. In the garden beneath the window, the sweet voices of the students sang a gentle bridal blessing from distant Bremagne, that soon faded into stillness with the sound of departing feet on gravel.

He came to her then, in the twilit summer night, shedding his outer robe to slip into the bed beside her. He lay there on his side for a long moment, simply gazing at her, head propped on one elbow, before lifting a reverent hand to brush along her cheek, across her lips, down the curve of her neck to the ribbons at the throat of her night shirt, briefly caressing the sweet swell of her breast.

"Dear God, you are beautiful, in body and in soul!" he whispered, his eyes never leaving hers. "I asked you once before whether you were an angel, for surely I stand before the gates of Paradise."

As she shivered slightly at his touch, he gently tugged at one of the ribbons until its bow parted, rolling closer then to nuzzle kisses on the creamy skin thus exposed.

"Actually, I've just lied to you," he admitted, raising an eyebrow at her astonished *O* of indignation. "I am not standing *anywhere;* I am lying here beside a beautiful woman who is my wife at last—though a part of me *is* upstanding."

The playful downward flick of his glance to the region of his groin elicited a giggle and a maidenly blush on the part of his bride, after which he resumed his reverent exploration of her neck, loosing another tie, slipping a gentle hand into the open neck of her gown as his mouth sought hers and began to draw her with him into Paradise.

SEVERAL times they had their pleasure of one another that night, and again shortly after dawn, before slipping back into languid dozing for another several hours. Around noon, shortly after the Angelus, they surfaced for a meal, brought to their room by a smiling Sister Iris Cerys, who bobbed in blushing curtsy over the tray she presented as Kenneth opened the door.

Later in the afternoon, the newlyweds emerged to stroll hand-in-hand in the convent garden, beginning talk of plans and dreams. Toward suppertime, others began to appear in the garden. Though most of the wedding guests had left, either the night before or first thing that morning, Zoë and Jiri Redfearn remained, along with Jovett Chandos. The five of them supped together that evening with Father Paschal and Mother Judiana, and spoke guardedly of the state of affairs concerning the bishops.

Alyce, who knew better than any of them just how far the bishop's wrath could extend—and with how little cause—kept largely silent, and lay shivering in Kenneth's arms later that night, until he kissed away her tears and turned her thoughts to more pleasant contemplations.

BUT their idyll of married bliss was not to last. The very next morning, not long after first light, Sir Jiri came knocking on their door with missives from the king recalling them all to Rhemuth.

"The king says there's been trouble up near Sostra. The county of that name belongs to Torenth, of course," Kenneth said, still skimming the king's letter, "but the town of Sostra is Corwyn's, as you know."

Both were aware that Duke Richard had been patrolling along the Torenthi border since mid-May, hoping his presence would discourage a repeat of the incursions into Corwyn two years before.

"It appears I'm to take up some of my regenting duties somewhat sooner than we expected," he went on. "Deinol Hartmann has asked for Jovett as well. We should leave as soon as possible."

They were gone within the hour, Jiri and Jovett in addition to Alyce, Kenneth, and Zoë, clattering into the yard at Rhemuth just past noon.

"Dreadfully sorry to drag you away from your bride, Kenneth," the king said, before briefing the three who would leave shortly for Sostra.

As he drew them toward the maps spread on the table in the summer council chamber, already starting to review details of the reports he had received from Richard, Seisyll Arilan watched silently from the other side of the room, and wondered why the king had lied.

* * *

WHATEVER the reason, Kenneth was away off-and-on for most of the summer and into the autumn, with periodic visits home to deliver dispatches and be reunited with his bride, but never for more than a few days, and never long enough to get her with child.

Jessamy, meanwhile, continued her observations regarding Alyce, recalling her own preparations for the conception of Krispin, and gradually narrowed down a series of optimal target dates.

But Jessamy's health was fast failing. Alyce and the royal physicians nursed her, but there was little they could do besides ease her pain. By October, she was all but bedridden, and early in November asked for Seisyll Arilan.

"I'm told you wished to see me," he said quietly, pulling a stool closer to her bed, at her gesture. Her maid had withdrawn, and they were quite alone.

"I am dying, Seisyll," she murmured. "It may not be today, or even next week, but it will be sooner rather than later."

"I had heard that," he replied. "I am very sorry."

"So am I." She turned her face to gaze at the canopy above the bed.

"Seisyll, we have not always agreed—you and I. I understand, though I do not accept, the reasons that others felt obliged to dictate the course of my life. I have never understood why there was so much antipathy toward my father, but I accept that perhaps there are things I was not meant to understand."

When he said nothing, only lowering his eyes, she went on.

"But you must believe me when I tell you that I have tried to act only in ways that would honor my blood and the love I have come to bear for the House of Haldane."

She paused to cough, and Seisyll watched her in compassion.

"I wish to speak to you of Krispin," she whispered, when she had caught her breath. "He is gone now, so the telling of his tale cannot hurt him, but because of . . . other things that are in progress, you have a need to know. Take my hand, Seisyll."

As he did so, she closed her eyes and pulled back her shields, inviting rapport . . . and gave him the full reckoning of Krispin's begetting, the death of Sief, the deceptions thereafter . . . and now, the plans in train for Alyce de Corwyn, to repeat the king's mission, that another Deryni heir of his body should be conceived to become the protector of Gwynedd's future kings. . . .

"SUDDENLY, so much makes sense," Seisyll told the Camberian Council a few nights later, after leaving Jessamy in a coma from which she was not likely to emerge. "Much we had surmised, but we had imputed malice where there was none. Krispin MacAthan *was,* in fact, Krispin Haldane—and Sief's death was unfortunate, but Donal did not set out to kill him. Had Sief not guessed the truth of the boy's paternity—we all know how jealous he was—all might have proceeded according to plan."

"That still does not answer the question of how the king happened to come by his rather extraordinary ability," Michon said. "Nor does it explain why Donal seems never to have exercised that power since killing Sief."

"No, and Jessamy declined to enlighten me on either point," Seisyll replied. "I was grateful enough that she chose to share what she did—and on her deathbed, in all likelihood."

"Could you not have slipped past her shields, in her weakened condition?" Vivienne muttered.

"Dear Vivienne, there are some scruples that even I will not set aside," Seisyll replied. "The source of the king's power is not nearly so important as the fact that he has it—and that he desires to get another child who will share those powers."

"What?" Barrett gasped, as the others merely gaped at Seisyll in astonishment.

"Whether we like it or not," Seisyll went on, "the notion of a Deryni protector for the Haldane princes was a good one. The matter of Haldane paternity for such a protector is a separate issue, and disturbs us mostly because we did not think of it, I suspect—and because that Haldane bloodline is an unknown quantity, proven dangerous because of what Donal Haldane was able to do to one of us. Sief would not have been an easy conquest."

"Definitely true," Oisín said with a grimace.

"That said, you should know that the king intends to repeat the experiment."

"Well, certainly not with Jessamy," Barrett said mildly.

"Sadly, no," Seisyll agreed. "But the stage is already set for a replanting of Haldane seed."

"In what field?" Oisín muttered.

"Alyce de Corwyn!" Michon declared.

"She is the only appropriate Deryni to whom he has access," Seisyll replied. "None of Jessamy's daughters would do, for various reasons."

"That would certainly explain why her husband has been kept so often abroad since their wedding," Oisín said. "Will the king have had her yet?"

"Not yet, so far as I can tell," Seisyll replied. "I have the impression that he is proceeding with great caution, since the deed must be carried out without the lady's knowledge or consent: an additional factor that will be different from his coupling with Jessamy.

"That makes it likely that he may dare to try it only once, lest her suspicions be aroused—or Sir Kenneth's. Hence, the timing will be critical. And regarding Kenneth—if anything, the king is closer to him than he was to Sief. It will be a betrayal—but one that the king is willing to accept, in the service of a greater cause. And hopefully, Kenneth will never know."

"Sief also was meant not to know," Dominy pointed out.

"But Kenneth is human, and can be controlled," Michon said. "Deceiving Alyce will be far more difficult a matter, even with the triggers Jessamy has given over to the king."

Khoren Vastouni slowly shook his head. "One must admire the audacity of the Haldanes," he said. "Can aught be done to facilitate this mating? For I would be interested, indeed, to see a child of Alyce de Corwyn and Donal Haldane."

"Once more, I fear we must sit back and merely observe," Seisyll replied. "With luck, we shall know soon enough."

BUT it would not come as soon as any of them had hoped, for Jessamy never emerged from her coma, and died shortly before Christmas. Knowledge that she was dying had put a damper on the king's plans in November, and the funeral aftermath and preparations for Twelfth Night and its attendant courts made a December liaison infeasible. It was not until late January that Donal Haldane felt ready to make his move—if ever he was to do it.

The night he finally chose, based on Jessamy's calculations and observations of the laundress she had employed, was one long in careful planning. It was a stormy night toward the end of January, with wind howling among the chimneys and snow piling high in the castle yard. Kenneth had returned two days earlier from a mission down to Desse, exhausted from his ride, and Donal had made certain that Alyce was kept late in the royal nursery that night, tending a feverish child—courtesy of a posset concocted to produce precisely that condition.

The king kept Kenneth very late the next night as well, plying him with drink and a carefully planted suggestion to ensure that he passed out immediately upon reaching his bed, with no inclination to even touch his wife.

On the third night, his hour come at last, the king had also made his preparations, this time with a sedative in the wine he had had served at a supper shared by the pair at his own table, along with the queen. The ensuing drowsiness of both queen and aide had ensured an early night. Both now slept in their respective beds. Alyce had set her cup aside after only a sip or two, but now slept as well, curled in the curve of her husband's body.

Donal watched the pair for nearly an hour through a spyhole in the paneling of their apartment—the one he had chosen especially, after their marriage—stretching forth his powers to confirm the depth of their sleep, until finally he summoned sufficient resolve to proceed.

He had prepared carefully, clothing himself, over his nightshirt, in a long dressing gown of goodly wool, lined with fur, for he had not known how long he might need to lurk in the passageway behind the paneling. Soft boots were on his feet, and a fur-lined cap on his head.

Senses finely attuned, he touched the stud that would let the hidden panel slide back soundlessly, slipping inside and closing it behind him. Softly he walked to Kenneth's side of the bed and lightly touched his temple, profoundly deepening his sleep. Jessamy had taught him how to do that, too. He then moved around to the other side, undoing the front of his robe as he went. Pulse racing, he was already aroused, from the simple daring of the deed he contemplated, but he knew he must first make certain she would not stir while he had his way with her.

Pulling back her side of the coverlet with one hand, he reached his hand to touch her as he had touched her husband, reaching for the controls set by her father so many years before and adjusted by Jessamy for the specific purpose of this night's work. Alyce gave a low moan, but did not stir as he gently shifted her onto her back. But when he started to turn back her nightdress, her eyes opened to gaze at him in shock.

"Sire?" she breathed.

Panic overtook him, and he seized her wrist and reached for the controls again, at the same time trying to pull his robe around him, a part of him unable to comprehend why Jessamy's trigger had not worked. His mind surged across the physical link thus formed, but very solid shields flared between them, and he could not get past.

Anger made his own powers stir more potently, coiling in that secret place behind his eyes, but she only scrambled to a sitting position, her wrist still clasped in his hand, her own powers like an impenetrable wall between them as she laid her other hand on the wrist of her sleeping husband—tried and failed to rouse him.

"How have you done this to him, and what did you intend to do to me?" she demanded.

Once again he tried to take her mind, again clashing against those adamantine shields, feeling the killing power start to stir, as it had with Sief, all those years ago—but abruptly he backed down, releasing her wrist as if it were a bar of red-hot iron. Killing her was the *last* thing he wished to do, even if it meant that there would now be no magical protector for his sons.

"God, forgive me, Alyce!" he breathed.

Burying his face in his hands, he slid to the floor beside the bed, elbows braced against its edge, and wept—for the dead Krispin, for Jessamy, also in her grave, and for the child who now would never be. She watched him in silence for several long moments, again checking the sleeping Kenneth, then shifted to lift his head into her lap, rocking him against her breast as he sobbed on and on—and gradually confessed all.

By the time he had mostly spent his tears, she had wept as well, and scrubbed her sleeve across her eyes as he lifted his head, reluctant to meet her gaze. She said nothing as he hauled himself back up off his knees and gingerly sat on the edge of the bed.

"You must think me a terrible man," he said uncertainly. "And if you did, I would not blame you."

Slowly she shook her head, pitying him.

"No, not terrible," she replied. "But I think I now understand more of what a heavy weight it is to wear a crown. What pain you must have borne, when Krispin died—and to be forced to bear it in secret, unable to express your true loss. . . ."

He nodded bleakly, his anguish etched on his weathered face.

"Jessamy was obliged to bear it all—and all her sacrifice was for naught, in the end." He hung his head. "I don't know why I thought I might repeat the same exercise. I suppose I wanted to re-create Krispin. But of course, that would never have happened, even had I succeeded in what I set out to do tonight. I did consider simply asking you openly—but there was Kenneth, who is my friend—or, who *was* my friend, I suppose, once he learns what has happened here tonight."

"But nothing happened here, Sire," she said softly.

"It *would* have happened, if I'd had my way—much to my shame."

"But it did not." She glanced across at Kenneth, still oblivious. "And it *could* not," she added in a whisper.

He looked at her in question. "I don't understand."

"You should wake Kenneth now, Sire," she said, ignoring his comment. "Or—no, give his controls to me, and *I* shall wake him. And before I do, I shall give him the gist of what has happened—and of your need."

He started to get up, but she stayed him with a hand on his wrist, only nodding toward Kenneth. Bracing himself, the king rose enough to wrap his robe more closely around himself, then settled back again on her side of the bed, stretching then to set his hand on Kenneth's forehead, as Alyce did the same.

The touch of her mind was gentle now, taking the controls he gave, and he bowed his head as he withdrew, in awe of her grace, leaving it to her to do what she felt needful.

After a moment, Alyce, too, withdrew her hand, and

Donal dared to look back at both of them. He saw the tenderness as she bent to press a gentle kiss to her husband's brow, tensed as the other man's eyelids flickered and then the sea-gray eyes opened.

Their gaze was cool at first, appraising, measuring. But then he sat up wordlessly to take his wife in his arms and hold her to his breast, the while not taking his eyes from the king's.

After a moment, as Alyce straightened and turned within the circle of his arm, to lean against his chest and also meet the king's eyes, Kenneth gave a cautious sigh.

"I grieve with you, Sire, for your loss," he said quietly. "You have had to live with your grief in silence, since that awful morning when we found the boy in the well. And I understand what you meant to do, and why."

"Can you forgive me?" Donal managed to ask.

"Yes," Kenneth said. "And I can do more than that—because you are my king, and I and mine are in your service, and in your homage—and in your love, I hope."

"I don't understand," Donal whispered.

Kenneth gave a quiet smile and pulled Alyce momentarily closer to him, gently kissing the lips she turned to his.

"Alyce is already with child, Sire," he murmured. "At least she tells me she is. Apparently, Deryni can sense these things long before another might guess."

"But—how . . . ?"

"Quite frankly, it was probably akin to the way your Krispin was conceived," Kenneth allowed, raising a droll eyebrow. "You gave me little opportunity for more leisurely coupling with my wife, in these past few months. It will have happened last month, when I was carrying dispatches back and forth between here and Coroth. I think I was home for all of an hour that week—and well aware that new dispatches were being readied for my immediate return to the road.

"But one makes do when one must," he said, bending to kiss her again. "And the timing, apparently, was fortuitous."

"This child is truly meant to be, Sire," Alyce murmured. "And I believe it will be a son. If you wish it, he can be *your* son, in every way save of your blood, raised to be a loyal companion and protector to Prince Brion, with the powers of a Deryni to aid him."

"What are you saying?" Donal whispered.

"She's saying that we shall give him to you, Sire," Kenneth said. "Not physically, but in the sense of loyalty and power and utter devotion to your House. If you will have him."

Epilogue

"Before I formed thee in the belly I knew thee,

and before thou camest forth out of the womb I sanctified thee. . . ."

—JEREMIAH 1:5

IN due course, Alyce's pregnancy became obvious to all with eyes to see. The queen, too, was found to be again with child; and the relationship of the two women shifted subtly as Alyce joined her in the role of wife and mother-to-be. Both prospective fathers doted on their pregnant wives, and each paid due deference to the other's spouse. It was a time of tranquility and expectation.

"He actually did it!" said Oisín Adair, in a reaction mixed of amazement and admiration, when Seisyll had reported the dual pregnancies to the Camberian Council. "And not just Alyce, but the queen as well!"

"Well, hopefully not both at once," Vivienne said primly, though she was doing her best not to smirk. "Still, it has been a remarkable achievement. Who would have thought the old man had it in him anymore?"

Seisyll shook his head, smiling. "Never underestimate Donal Haldane," he said. "In his long and colorful life, he has accomplished a great deal that no one would have expected."

"When will she give birth?" Khoren asked.

"Early in the autumn, by all the signs," Seisyll replied. "And the queen at about the same time."

"Just bear in mind that Alyce's child could be a girl," Dominy reminded them.

"That would only matter for the Corwyn succession," Seisyll replied. "If Donal's purpose was to beget a future protector for his sons—a Deryni protector—a woman could serve as well as a man, provided she had the proper training. We could ensure that she had that training. *I* could ensure it; or another could be recruited."

"True enough," Michon agreed.

"Then, it appears we have only to wait until the autumn, to see what fruit is borne from the king's new experiment," Barrett said.

THAT summer was a welcome season of peace, allowing Kenneth the leisure to finally settle into contented domesticity with his new wife. Aside from the three present that January night in their apartments, none knew of the incident. Zoë Morgan spent nearly every waking hour in the company of Alyce and the queen, marveling at these new pregnancies and delighting in the prospect of a new half-sibling.

Toward midsummer, Alyce was able to confirm that her child would be a boy. The king, too, was told, and was present outside the birthing room late in September, when Alyce de Corwyn, wife of Sir Kenneth Morgan, was brought to bed of a hale and healthy son, with wisps of white-blond hair and light eyes already full of infant wisdom. Zoë had attended the birth, assisting the royal midwife and lending the mother her strength, and helped clean up babe and mother before admitting her father to behold his son.

Kenneth entered very tentatively, craning his neck for a glimpse of the babe as he approached his wife's bed. Alyce's face, as she looked up at him over the downy head cupped at her breast, proclaimed joy and contentment along with the weariness of the birthing—and love for the man who sat tentatively on the edge of the bed and bent to kiss her forehead.

"Are you well, dearest heart?" he whispered.

She smiled and lifted her lips to his. "I am well," she replied. "And we have a son, indeed."

As she glanced down adoringly at the child in her arms, briefly pulling aside his blankets to display his perfect form, Kenneth let his eyes drink in the wonder of the babe, bent to kiss the golden fluff at the top of his head.

"May I hold him?" he murmured.

"Of course."

He was cradling his son, murmuring sweet nothings as he sat close beside the mother, when Zoë admitted the king to the chamber and quietly withdrew. Both parents looked up as the king approached, and Kenneth gathered his son in his arms as he stood, beckoning the king closer with his eyes. Donal Haldane's gaze did not leave Kenneth's as he came to stand toe-to-toe with the man who held what had been so earnestly desired.

"Sire," Kenneth said steadily, "eight months ago, in this room, we made you a solemn pledge. You need not fear that we will fail to honor it. We give you a future protector for your sons."

And with those simple words, he laid the child in the king's arms.

"Your Majesty, I am honored to present my son, Alaric Anthony Morgan."

SIX weeks later, in the chapel royal at Rhemuth Castle, the child was officially christened with that name—the Anthony for Kenneth's grandfather, Kai Anthony, who had fought at the side of Malcolm Haldane at Killingford. Also christened on that day was the newest Haldane prince, born a week after young Alaric and given a string of royal names to live up to: Jathan Joachim Richard Urien.

But both boys received illustrious godparents on that day. Duke Richard and Sir Tiarnán MacRae were among those standing for young Prince Jathan; young Alaric had his half-sister Zoë, the visibly pregnant Lady Vera Howard McLain, now Countess of Kierney, Sir Jovett Chandos, in from Cynfyn, and Sir Sé Trelawney. It was not until later that afternoon, while taking refreshments in the great hall, that Lord Seisyll Arilan finally got an opportunity to hold the newly baptized Alaric in his arms—and made a discovery that was to cause great consternation, when he reported back to his colleagues of the Camberian Council.

For, whatever else he was, Alaric Anthony Morgan was *not* the son of Donal Haldane. What he might become, only time would tell.

APPENDIX I

Index of Characters

AHERN JERNIAN DE CORWYN; LORD—son and heir of Keryell Earl of Lendour and Stevana de Corwyn; twin to Marie de Corwyn.

ALARIC ANTHONY MORGAN—infant son of Alyce de Corwyn Morgan and Sir Kenneth Kai Morgan.

ALAZAIS MORGAN—youngest daughter of Sir Kenneth Morgan.

*ALBADORE, SAINT—a patron saint of lost things.

ALEXANDER DARBY, FATHER—violently anti-Deryni priest and former physician in Carthane.

ALINOR CARDIEL, LADY—second wife of Mikhail Prince of Andelon, sister of Thomas.

ALVIN DE MARCO—a guard in the retinue of Lord Deldour.

ALYCE JAVANA DE CORWYN, LADY—elder daughter of Keryell Earl of Lendour and Stevana de Corwyn.

ANDREW MCLAIN, DUKE—Duke of Cassan, father of Jared.

ANGELUS, FATHER—a chaplain to Queen Richeldis.

ANJELICA—maid to Lady Jessamy.

ANNALIND, PRINCESS—a princess of Meara, younger twin of Roisian.

ARDRY MACARDRY—infant son of Caulay Earl of Transha.

*ATUN, PRINCE—late Prince of Andelon, father of Mikhail and Khoren.

AURÉLIEN DE COURCY—son of Michon and husband of Sieffany MacAthan.

BARRETT DE LANEY—blind member of the Camberian Council; brother of Dominy de Laney.

BASIL OF CASTLEROO—a Mearan rebel.

BENJAMIN—servant in the employ of Seisyll Arilan.

BENROY, FATHER—weak-sighted scrivener and chaplain at Arc-en-Ciel.

BLAINE EMANUEL RICHARD CINHIL HALDANE, PRINCE—second son of Donal King of Gwynedd.

BLAISE OF TRURILL—a Mearan rebel.

BRENDAN, BROTHER—a clark at Rhemuth

BRIGETTA DELACORTE, LADY—a junior lady-in-waiting to Queen Richeldis.

BRION DONAL CINHIL URIEN HALDANE, PRINCE—first-born son and heir of King Donal.

BRONNA, LADY—a nurse to the royal children.

CAITRIN OF MEARAN, PRINCESS—daughter of Judhael of Meara, sister of Princess Onora.

*CASSIANUS DE LANEY—deceased older brother of Dominy and Barrett.

CERYS DEVANE—a student at Arc-en-Ciel, Alyce's original roommate, who later takes the veil as Sister Iris Cerys.

*CHARLAN MORGAN, SIR—former squire to Javan Haldane, treacherously killed with him; distant cousin of Sir Kenneth Morgan.

CLARICE, LADY—a lady-in-waiting to Queen Richeldis.

*COLMAN, KING—deceased King of Howicce and Llannedd, father of Queen Richeldis.

*CORBAN HOWELL, SIR—deceased Earl of Eastmarch.

CRAWFORD, MASTER—a guard at Rhemuth Castle.

*CYNFYN OF LENDOUR—deceased son of Keryell Earl of Lendour by his first marriage.

*DAMIAN CATHCART—a general/tactician of the past.

DEINOL HARTMANN, SIR—seneschal at Castle Cynfyn.

DELDOUR, LORD—a lord of Carthane, and one of the ringleaders of an anti-Deryni lay group centered on the ministry of Bishop Oliver de Nore; Father Septimus becomes his chaplain.

DENIT, FATHER—queen's chaplain in 1088.

DESMOND MACCARTNEY, BISHOP—Auxiliary Bishop of Rhemuth, brother of William.

DOMINY DE LANEY—sister of Barrett, member of the Camberian Council.

DONAL BLAINE AIDAN CINHIL HALDANE, KING—King of Gwynedd, Prince of Meara, and Lord of the Purple March.

DONNARD, MASTER—Duke Richard's battle-surgeon in 1086.

*DULCHESSE, QUEEN—childless first queen of Donal Haldane.

EDWARD—a carpenter at Rhemuth Castle.

EDWINA—Zoë's original roommate at Arc-en-Ciel, from Llannedd.

ELAINE MACINNIS, LADY—daughter of Manfred MacInnis and Signe Calder of Sheele; first wife of Jared Earl of Kierney, and mother of Kevin McLain.

EVAN SULLIVAN, SIR—human buyer of horses at manor of Arkella, north of Ratharkin. (Kindaloo is farther along.)

FARIAN, FATHER—a young clark at Rhemuth.

*FERROL HOWARD, SIR—slain 1025 at Killingford with King Urien and buried in crypt beneath Rhemuth Cathedral.

FRANCIS DELANEY—a Mearan rebel.

GEILL MORGAN—middle daughter of Sir Kenneth Morgan.

GERALD—a squire in the service of King Donal.

*GRANIA DE CORWYN, LADY—mother of Stevana and grandmother of Alyce, Marie, Ahern, and Vera.

GWENAËL, QUEEN—Queen of Llannedd and mother of Queen Richeldis.

HAMBERT HAMILTON, SIR—seneschal of Coroth.

IERY—Marie's roommate at Arc-en-Ciel.

ILLANN, KING—King of Howicce and, after the death of Queen Gwenaël, King of Llannedd; brother of Queen Richeldis.

IOLO MELANDRY, SIR—royal governor of Ratharkin, hanged by rebels.

IRIS ALTHEA, SISTER—mistress of scriptorium at Arc-en-Ciel.

IRIS ANTHONY, SISTER—professed nun at Arc-en-Ciel.

IRIS JESSILDE, SISTER—second daughter of Jessamy MacAthan, a novice at Arc-en-Ciel.

IRIS JUDIANA, MOTHER—Superior at Arc-en-Ciel; daughter of a Bremagni duke, educated at Rhanamé.

IRIS MARY, SISTER—a professed nun at Arc-en-Ciel.

IRIS ROSE, SISTER—a novice at Arc-en-Ciel.

ISAN FITZMARTIN—a page in the household of King Donal, son of Lady Megory Fitzmartin.

IVONE—a squire to King Donal in 1086.

JARED MCLAIN, EARL OF KIERNEY—only son of Andrew Duke of Cassan.

*JEPPE LASCELLES—one of the Gwynedd generals at Killingford.

JESIANA MACATHAN—a daughter of Jessamy and Sief MacAthan.

JESSAMY FERCH LEWYS MACATHAN—daughter of Lewys ap Norfal and Lady Ilde; wife of Sief MacAthan. Mother of four living daughters and Krispin MacAthan.

JESSILDE MACATHAN—see Iris Jessilde, sister.

JIRI REDFEARN, SIR—an aide to King Donal.

JODOTHA—a legendary Deryni of the seventh century.

*JOLYON OF MEARA, PRINCE—last sovereign Prince of Meara, husband of Urracca, father of Roisian and Annalind.

JOSQUIN GRAMERCY—a scout in the service of King Donal.

JOVETT CHANDOS, SIR—former squire in the service of Keryell Earl of Lendour, childhood friend of Alyce and Marie de Corwyn, secretly Deryni; knighted with Sé Trelawney at Twelfth Night court, 1082.

JUDHAEL, PRINCE—soi-distant Prince of Meara, first cousin to King Donal, son of Annalind, Princess of Meara.

KENNETH KAI MORGAN, SIR—an aide to King Donal; father of Zoë and two more daughters.

KEVIN DOUGLAS MCLAIN—infant son of Jared Earl of Kierney and Elaine MacInnis.

KHOREN VASTOUNI, PRINCE—member of the Camberian Council.

KRISPIN SIEF MACATHAN—son of Jessamy by King Donal, secretly sired to be a Deryni protector for the royal princes.

LAURELA HOWARD—"mother" of Vera (de Corwyn) Howard.

LEWYS AP NORFAL—infamous Deryni who defied the Camberian Council; father of Jessamy and Morian.

LUCIEN TALBOT, BARON—a baron of the Purple March, permanent royal governor of Ratharkin replacing the murdered Iolo Melandry.

MALGAR DE FIRENZA, FATHER—new chaplain and music master at Arc-en-Ciel after Septimus de Nore.

MARIE STEPHANIA DE CORWYN—younger daughter of Keryell Earl of Lendour and Stevana de Corwyn; twin to Ahern de Corwyn.

MEGORY FITZMARTIN—a principal lady-in-waiting to Queen Richeldis.

MICHAEL OF KHELDOUR, ARCHBISHOP—Archbishop of Valoret and Primate of All Gwynedd.

MICHAEL MACDONALD, SIR—husband of Princess Onora of Meara.

MICHENDRA VASTOUNI, PRINCESS—younger daughter of Prince Mikhail of Andelon.

MICHON DE COURCY, LORD—member of the Camberian Council.

MIKHAIL VASTOUNI, PRINCE—sovereign Prince of Andelon and nephew of Prince Khoren.

MIRANDA, LADY—a lady-in-waiting to Queen Richeldis.

MORIAN DU JOUX (AP LEWYS), SIR—brother of Jessamy, and Deryni.

MUNGO, FATHER—a chaplain in the royal household.

MURIELLA, LADY—a lady-in-waiting to Queen Richeldis.

NED—a gardener at Rhemuth Castle.

NIDIAN AP PEDR—a citizen of Ratharkin.

NIGEL CLUIM GWYDION RHYS HALDANE, PRINCE—son of King Donal and Queen Richeldis.

NIMUR FURSTÁN—King of Torenth.

*NORFAL—a Deryni master.

OISÍN ADAIR—a horse breeder, member of the Camberian Council.

OLIVER DE NORE, BISHOP—itinerant bishop in Carthane, elder brother of Septimus.

ONORA, PRINCESS—daughter of Judhael of Meara, granddaughter of Annalind of Meara.

ORBAN HOWARD, SIR—"father" of Vera (de Corwyn) Howard.

ORIN—great Deryni adept and mystic of the seventh century.

PASCHAL DIDIER, FATHER—Deryni priest from Bremagne, chaplain to Keryell Earl of Lendour and tutor to Alyce and Ahern (and Vera Howard). Trained at Nur Sayyid and the R'Kassan seminary at Rhanamé.

PATRICK CORRIGAN, BISHOP—newly consecrated itinerant bishop.

RANNULF, SIR—along on the hunt at Martinmas.

RICHARD BEARAND RHUPERT CINHIL HALDANE, PRINCE—unmarried half-brother of King Donal, Duke of Carthmoor.

RICHELDIS, QUEEN—second wife of King Donal and mother of his children, a princess of Howicce and Llannedd.

ROBARD KINCAID, SIR—a Mearan rebel.

RODDER GILLESPIE, FATHER—a priest of the Diocese of Nyford.

*ROISIAN, QUEEN—heiress of Meara, eldest daughter of Jolyon of Meara and Urracca; twin of Annalind; wife of Malcolm Haldane and Queen of Gwynedd.

RORIK HOWELL, SIR—new Earl of Eastmarch, son of the late Corban Howell.

ROSMERTA, LADY—third wife of Keryell Earl of Lendour.

RUSLAN, BROTHER—a monk serving at the chapel royal of Rhemuth Castle.

SEFFIRA MACATHAN, LADY—a daughter of Jessamy and Sief MacAthan.

SEISYLL ARILAN, LORD—member of King Donal's council of state and also the Camberian Council.

SEPTIMUS DE NORE, FATHER—brother of Bishop Oliver de Nore, briefly a chaplain at Arc-en-Ciel.

SÉ TRELAWNEY, SIR—former squire in the service of Keryell Earl of Lendour, childhood friend of Alyce, Marie, and Ahern, secretly Deryni; knighted at Twelfth Night Court 1082.

SIEF MACATHAN, JUNIOR—firstborn son of Jessamy and Sief, dead at one week of age.

SIEF MACATHAN, LORD—member of King Donal's council of state and also the Camberian Council.

SIEFFANY MACATHAN DE COURCY—eldest daughter of Jessamy and Sief MacAthan, wife of Aurélien de Courcy.

SÍLE, QUEEN—second wife to King Malcolm Haldane, mother of Richard.

SILKE ANNE ELIZABETH ROISIAN HALDANE, PRINCESS—second daughter of Donal King of Gwynedd and Queen Richeldis.

SOBBON VON HORTHY, PRINCE—sovereign Prince of Thalia and Hort of Orsal.

SOFIANA VASTOUNI, PRINCESS—elder daughter of Prince Mikhail of Andelon and Princess Ysabeau.

STASHA, PRINCESS—wife of Prince Khoren Vastouni of Andelon.

*STEVANA DE CORWYN, LADY—deceased heiress of Corwyn, granddaughter of Stiofan Duke of Corwyn; second wife of Keryell Earl of Lendour, mother of Alyce, Vera, Ahern, and Marie.

*STIOFAN DE CORWYN, DUKE—great grandfather of Alyce de Corwyn.

*TAYCE FURSTÁNA, LADY—first cousin of Festil I King of Gwynedd, wife of Lord Richard du Joux; their son was Dominic du Joux, first Duke of Corwyn.

THOMAS CARDIEL—younger brother of Alinor.

TIARNÁN MACRAE, SIR—an aide to King Donal.

TIPHANE, LADY—a lady-in-waiting to Queen Richeldis.

TREVOR UDAUT—a squire in 1090, just raised from page at that Twelfth Night.

URIEN, KING—Haldane monarch who died at Killingford.

*URRACCA, PRINCESS—consort of the last sovereign Prince

of Meara, mother of twin sisters Roisian and Annalind and also of Magrette.

URSIC, DUKE—Duke of Claibourne.

VERA LAURELA (DE CORWYN) HOWARD—younger twin sister of Alyce, but raised by and believed to be the daughter of Lord Orban Howard and Lady Laurela.

VIVIENNE DE JORDANET, LADY—member of the Camberian Council.

WILCE MELANDRY, SIR—nephew of Iolo, sheriff of Ratharkin.

WILLIAM MACCARTNEY, ARCHBISHOP—Archbishop of Rhemuth.

XENIA NUALA JARONI SWYNBETH, PRINCESS—first daughter and third child of Donal King of Gwynedd and Richeldis.

*YSABEAU, PRINCESS—late wife of Prince Mikhail of Andelon, mother of Sofiana and Michendra.

ZOË BRONWYN MORGAN—a student at Arc-en-Ciel, eldest daughter of Sir Kenneth Morgan.

*denotes a character is already deceased when first mentioned.

APPENDIX II

Index of Places

ARC-EN-CIEL, CONVENT OF NOTRE DAME D'—royal convent and school just outside Rhemuth.

ARDEVALA—a holding of Michon de Courcy.

ARKELLA—manor of Sir Evan Sullivan, north of Ratharkin; location of a Portal.

ARX FIDEI SEMINARY—one of the principal seminaries in Gwynedd, north of Rhemuth.

BELDOUR—capital city of Torenth.

BREMAGNE—kingdom across the Southern Sea from Gwynedd.

CAERIESSE—legendary land that sank beneath the sea.

CARTHANELLE—royal manor north of Nyford, summer seat of the Dukes of Carthmoor.

CARTHMOOR—holding of Prince Richard Duke of Carthmoor.

CASSAN—duchy in northwest Gwynedd.

CASTEL DEARG—Jared McLain's seat in Kierney.

CASTLE CYNFYN—seat of the Earl of Lendour, in the town of Cynfyn.

CASTLE RUNDEL—an hour's ride from Culdi.

COAMER MOUNTAINS—mountain range marking part of the border between Gwynedd and Torenth.

CONCARADINE—free port on the River Eirian.

COROTH—capital of Corwyn.

CORWYN—ancient duchy in southeast Gwynedd, seat of the Deryni dukes of Corwyn.

CÙILTEINE—marcher town in the southwest of Gwynedd.

CYNFYN—capital of Lendour, and Keryell's seat.

DESSE—northernmost navigable point on the River Eirian, several hours' ride south of Rhemuth.

DHASSA—free holy city in the Lendour Mountains.

DJELLARDA—capital of the princely state of Andelon.

EASTMARCH—county in northeast Gwynedd.

FESSY—village in Bremagne, site of an apparition seen near an ancient holy well, where the Ordre de Notre Dame d'Arc-en-Ciel began.

GWYNEDD—principal kingdom of the Eleven Kingdoms, seat of the Haldane kings.

HOWICCE—kingdom linked with the Kingdom of Llannedd, southwest of Gwynedd.

JÁCA—sovereign principality, one of the Forcinn States.

JENADÛR—Sé Trelawney's family seat.

KHELDISH RIDING—portion of the old Principality of Kheldour.

KHELDOUR—ancient principality in northern Gwynedd.

KIERNEY—earldom in northwest of Gwynedd, a secondary holding of the Dukes of Cassan.

KILLINGFORD—site of a decisive battle in the great Gwynedd-Torenth War of 1025.

KILTUIN—small river-port town in Corwyn, north of Coroth.

KINDALOO—a village north of Ratharkin and Arkella, in Meara.

LENDOUR—earldom north of Corwyn.

LLANNEDD—Kingdom linked with the Kingdom of Howicce, southwest of Gwynedd.

MARLEY—earldom in northeast Gwynedd.

MEARA—formerly independent principality west of Gwynedd, now a province of Gwynedd.

MORGANHALL—Sir Kenneth Morgan's estate.

NUR HALLAJ—sovereign principality adjacent to the Forcinn States.

NUR SAYYID—great university in R'Kassi.

NYFORD—capital of Carthmoor; ancient market town and port.

ORSALIA—ancient name of part of Trailia, whence derives the title "Hort of Orsal."

PURPLE MARCH, THE—area north and west of Rhemuth, adjoining Kierney.

PWYLLHELI—capital of Llannedd.

RATHARKIN—provincial capital of Meara.

REMIGNY—capital of Bremagne.

RHANAMÉ—great seminary in R'Kassi.

RHEMUTH—capital of Gwynedd.

RHENDALL—county in northeast Gwynedd.

RHONDEVALA—where Michon's son Aurelien and Jessamy's eldest daughter live.

R'KASSI—kingdom to the south of the Forcinn States, famous for its horses.

ST. BRIDGET'S ABBEY—convent near Cùilteine.

ST. HILARY'S WITHIN-THE-WALLS—royal basilica adjoining the royal palace in Rhemuth.

SOSTRA—a Corwyn town adjacent to the Torenthi county of the same name.

TORENTH—principal kingdom east of Gwynedd.

TRALIA—more recent name of the sovereign principality ruled by the Hort of Orsal.

TRANSHA—small border county in northwest Gwynedd.

TRE-ARILAN—ancestral home of the Arilan family.

TRURILL—barony between Gwynedd and Meara.

VALORET—former capital of Gwynedd; seat of the Archbishop of Valoret, Primate of All Gwynedd.